For T, J, K, and S & M
I love you because you're you.

British Library Cataloguing In Publication Data
A Record of this Publication is available
from the British Library

ISBN 1846852501
978-1-84685-250-3

First Published June 2006 by

Exposure Publishing, an imprint of Diggory Press,
Three Rivers, Minions, Liskeard, Cornwall, PL14 5LE, UK
WWW.DIGGORYPRESS.COM

PRINTED IN THE USA ON ACID FREE PAPER

Acknowledgements

Many thanks to Dr. Morton Lieberman for prompt replies and healing, unremarkable grains of salt among a sea of apples and zebras, bananas and peaches, Eden and Hell...

And, as in all things, thanks and remembrance to the Providence for passion, provision, and patience.

She needed a fuck like nobody's business.

Not your roll of the mill, roll in the hay garden variety kind of fuck, no, nada, nay; make no mistake; a long, hard, fast, slow, unfinished in fact just getting started kind of fuck that skips foreplay, fun fluff that's just as good the fifth as any first time around, and gets right down to business bursting forth; fury and giddiness all rolled into one.

The kind of fuck that takes you to fainting, plays like friends then fights while you fuck, leaving you ready to fast for more. A fuck that flips, dips then dives deep then more into the mysterious damp forest where Eve rules but Dick is king—unless a sexy southern Butch prowls near.

The kind of fuck that waves you on home only to pull back like flames courting moths fanning their wings in preparation of the coming of the Christ 'oh to fuck, fuck, fuck so hard, so fast, so slow, so close there's no room for faking; drilling, dancing, reviving, killing me softly to peace.

The Party

It was the days of wine and roses

Tulips, daffodils, and Moses and I don't mean

Malone.

The days of endless storms

And a wanton, wayward arm, oops, leg that ran

Amuck...

The days of wine and weed and cruises to Belize on a winsome, summer breeze
that breathes new life

n'to my Soul.

The days of milk and honey and tales

A little funny or

Not.

The days of wine and pills, and

Wet, prophetic bills that bore

the

Future...

Trans U

The Harvard of the South was named for its benefactor, Cornelius "Cornie" Vanderbilt, a poor but enterprising attention deficit disordered tyke who dropped out of school at age eleven and ran off to work on ships on Staten Island. Five years later, using a Ben Franklin loan obtained from that which birthed him from the womb, he bought his own dinghy, within eight owned the largest boat business on the Hudson, and soon after christened himself the Commodore.

Later that year the Commodore got bored and decided to explore the steamboat business. Not because he needed the money but because, in his own words, *"I have been insane on the subject of moneymaking all my life.[1]"* Little more need be said except he undercut the competition by better than three hundred percent and in the process became a wealthy, albeit still bored, man.

So he launched a line of luxury yachts that sailed from New York to France.
Inventing the cruise ship industry finally earned him his due for he knew he had finally arrived when the gates of the elite Staten Island social circles swung wide and welcomed their new son in.

"Why," he proposed as they sat down to supper, "Waste money on forks when the future is in rail?"

Before grace could be said he was unceremoniously kicked out sans his own cheap boots, which he took off, along with equally smelly socks, at the dinner table.

Not to be outdone, the Commodore picked himself up, brushed himself off and bought the New York and Harlem Railroad right out from under their snobby noses and in short order became the sole owner of an empire. Never one to follow the crowd he snubbed winning friends and influencing people the old fashioned way for the simplest of reasons—he hated spending money even more than he loved making it.

Aging less than gracefully on Staten Island and still unaccepted by polite society, the cheap, lonely, irascible Commodore received an extended visit from a young, uncommonly hairy yet surprisingly

---

[1] Cornelius Vanderbilt quoted in the New York Daily Tribune, March 23, 1878.

handsome southern gentleman. Little more need be said except the rich old bastard took a particular fancy to his new furry friend who did what many, to include God, swore only death could—separate the crude sailor from a single penny. This money, one million dollars of it, was used to found Vanderbilt University.

When the doors to the institution swung wide in 1875 it boasted an Undergraduate College, a Law School, a Medical School, and a Divinity School. The latter shocked everyone to include Christ since the Northerner smelled more akin to an agnostic than a God of Israel fearing religious man. Shock morphed into pristine amazement when the heathen decreed his academic offspring be reared under the auspices of the Methodist Episcopal Church. Pristine amazement turned ripe for scandal when, on the heels of the announcement, the cheapest, richest man in America dropped deader than dust.

Some wagered giving the money away killed him, others reckoned gangrene from wearing the same pair of cheap boots for thirty years, romantics swore he pined away for his furry friend but most of the faithful believed the bishops did it. Little more need be said except the robed ones reared the Commodore's brain trust for forty years until, rumor said; the cheap bastard's spirit came back to its business sense and booted the men in tights out.

With the holy rollers out of the way, the expansion of the University took off like a herd of horny hedonists high on chemically enhanced hormones. Schools and research programs were added like warm syrup to waffles at the Pancake Pantry and by 1925 Vanderbilt ranked as one of the top private schools in the country. The Commodore or "that vulgar sailor" as the Island's socialites still called him had finally arrived, being compared with Harvard, Yale, and Princeton—the academic pride and joy of those who snubbed him so long ago.

Then, the wrinkle rose to the surface.

With his new stature and acceptance came the need for something the sailor failed to acquire during his lifetime: a penchant for propriety, the ability to recognize the full measure of your mantle then mind your manners so as not to bring shame upon the name one wore, in a word, class. To counter this bastard like tendency strict policies and procedures were put into place by prudent men hand picked by polite society; business savvy professionals who made the men in tights appear pretentious Pharisees.

Under their tutelage Vanderbilt became, like its namesake, bigger than life and today remains not only one of the top rated private universities in the United States but also a nationally recognized Medical and Research Center. Boasting close to twenty thousand employees, the capitalistic beauty of a beast clothed as a non-profit pays homage to the Commodore's passion for efficiently making money hand over fist.

That is not to say, however, that issues more ethereal went the way of the wagon with the bishops. To the contrary rumors persist that the perennially ranked money horses: the Owen School of Management, the Law School, the Medical Center, and all the other entities exist for but one reason—to fund the eclectic, paradoxical, highly unprofitable Divinity School program into perpetuity.

And why not?

What higher purpose could the propagation of capitalism clothed as a non-profit serve than to provide funding to spread the propagation of the gospel?[2] Yet the answer to why the cheap hedonist would, through a codicil, decree that a non-revenue generating entity be afforded patronage into eternity remains "the" great-unsolved mystery of Vanderbilt, save the vampire legends, both topics the staid, conservative, revenue-generating entities of the institution would just as soon have ignored altogether but for one wrinkle.

Even as the revenue generators, known collectively as the "corporation" made money and minded their manners the divinity contingent, collectively known as the "community" raised both eyebrows and all manner of hell. It was this hallowed tradition that earned the errant inhabitants of the theology program their nickname— Commie's kids.

Commie's kids ruled in another universe their counterparts coined Trans U and trans was not short for transformation. Transylvania[3] University was, for those in the know, the Bible belt treasure many wished could remain, like an ugly outside child, a family secret. Respected members of the mainstream community found it hard to

---

[2] Of course in order to engage such a question one must first define capitalism, non-profit, and gospel for the purposes of the discussion in order to ensure that all parties are on the same page linguistically, theologically, historically, and sociologically.

[3] land beyond the trees

believe the place stayed in business. The church was, after all, a dying institution. That said what reputable house of worship would acknowledge let alone hire a graduate?

Any local, well read, decently informed Christian who knew God and blessed his holy name also knew the Divinity School was a synonym for den of divorcees, haven for harlots, refuge for homosexuals, and an out and out asylum for every other form of man or beast headed straight to perdition in oil soaked underpants. On Easter Sundays spirit filled Baptists lined up to prophesize from the pulpit that one day saints would rise up and torch the tower of Babel not only in the name of the Lord but also to eradicate the vampire problem that plagued the place.

At Trans U it made perfect sense to appoint an atheist Admissions Director. Who better to objectively analyze the attitudes, attributes, and aptitude of aspiring theologians? But tally a Transsexual teaching Old Testament, a Jew teaching New Testament, and a Dean who's done Dallas, Detroit, and half of Davidson County and some might suspect you have a recipe for unadulterated sin.

The Chaplin, raised as a strict Catholic, was, however, proud to be counted among Commie's kids and took great comfort amid the warm wings of Trans U, a safe affirming paradise where all were welcome: Pentecostals to Orthodox Jews to Agnostics to Wicca's with just one exception, the Church of Christ which had been deemed a cult and banned, along with landmines, in '97.

That said, even the fiercely loyal Chaplain, who doubles as the unofficial greeter of the Divinity School, had to admit that not all the local's concerns lacked any semblance of substance. There were clear, unmistakable signs that all was not kosher as quiche at the southern theological program bankrolled by a Northerner—reason in itself to be suspect.

What *of* the highly respected, much-read, even more published Principles and Practice Professor who neither read nor returned her student's term papers—if that wasn't wicked and evil what was? *Then... there are the unfortunate souls who turn up suddenly, mysteriously dead,* the Chaplain concedes, signing on to check e-mail:

From: owner-vanderbilt-community@list.vanderbilt.edu
To: vanderbilt-community@list.vanderbilt.edu

Subject: Chancellor Gee Dead!

Sent: Fri 2/14/03 6:23 AM

Dear Community,

It is with great regret that we must inform you that the body of our very own Chancellor Gee was discovered at one minute past midnight hanging from the rafters at Benton Chapel. Though the investigation is still in its infancy a (CPI) campus police informant reports that the cause of death is most certainly murder under mysterious circumstances.

Amateurs.
Who would want to kill Chancellor Gee? I mean, other than thousands of service employees who can't get a living wage? Any southern Ivy League informed e-mail messenger worth his editorial weight would have killed Dean Hudnut instead. I mean, what theological student worth his overpriced tuition wouldn't want to line up to execute him on economic principle alone?

----- Original Message -----
From: Eve
To:divinity_students@list.vanderbilt.edu;div-facstaff@list.vanderbilt.edu

Sent: Friday, Feb 14, 2003 8:25 AM
Subject: GALA

The Vanderbilt Divinity School requests your presence at the Spring Gala!

When: Saturday, March 15, 2003stat Tribe
       1517 Church St., Nashville, TN
Tickets: $20 in advance, double at the door
Attire: Formal (all night long)
Hope to see everyone there!

Blessings,
Eve
President, Student Government Association

From: Chastity
To:divinity_students@list.vanderbilt.edu;div-
facstaff@list.vanderbilt.edu
Subject: re: GALA

Attire: Formal (all night long)
Says who? Who died and made you queen for a day?
Give a dyke a title and suddenly she thinks she rules the
world.
Well guess what?
You don't.
While I'm sure you'll show up in a tux and keep it on
all night (we can only pray) that doesn't mean the rest
of us have to.

Blessings,
Chastity

From: Mary (the classy one)
To:divinity_students@list.vanderbilt.edu;div-
facstaff@list.vanderbilt.edu
Subject: re: GALA

Chastity (it's hard to believe your parents named you
that) please refrain from assuming that you speak for the
majority. Personally (and I'm sure I'm not a lone voice
crying out in the wilderness) not everyone in our
community enjoys being treated to poor fashion decisions
and a peep show. Some of us would appreciate it if an
air of decorum and a rare display of dignity could
punctuate our gatherings instead of hedonistic antics
disguised as free expression.

Mary

From: owner-divinity_students@list.vanderbilt.edu; on
behalf of MaryF@comcast.net

To: divinity_students@list.vanderbilt.edu;div-
facstaff@list.vanderbilt.edu
Subject: re: GALA

Dear Mary (the one who thinks she's classy),
You sound like the proverbial pot but I will try to
stay on point. As a democracy we are all entitled to a
voice but somehow it seems we have been overtaken by a
dictator.

Who decided that the dress should be formal and why?
What happens if members of our community cannot
afford the expense - will there be no room at the inn for

14

the economically disadvantaged?

Who decided that everyone must arrive clothed and remain so?

What happens if someone suffers from a snake delusion and starts shedding in the middle of the soufflé?

Personally, I conquered my need to be nude in public in '97 (you should all praise God) but who am I to say others must?

Marilyn Francesca Avery

From: owner-divinity_students@list.vanderbilt.edu; on behalf of MaPapinss@comcast.net

To: divinity_students@list.vanderbilt.edudiv-facstaff@list.vanderbilt.edu

Subject: GALA

Mary F,

Thanks for speaking up. I too have given up public nudity but support the right of others to proudly parade the pound of prized flesh our Savior gave them. I'll buck the system if at least three others will.

Peace, Mary Papins

From: owner-divinity_students@list.vanderbilt.edu; on behalf of luckeme7@comcast.net

To: divinity_students@list.vanderbilt.edu;div-facstaff@list.vanderbilt.edu

Subject: GALA (SO hot in Here)

"Hi all,

As one of the offenders at last years Gala, I figured I'd respond to these criticisms.

First off, for all who don't know me, I am Luc Ke Me, a 2nd year
joint-degree student. I ain't in the face book, but I'll be at Gala and ya'll can meet me and my lovely date then. I will admit to a sordid past in which I have occasionally consumed alcohol and stripped down... I once engaged in a naked sprinting competition against my

roommate around a Cincinnati block. I assure you it was not an attractive sight. There may also be a few pictures floating around in which I am less than fully clothed and (GASP) perhaps less than fully sober. However, at the ripe old age of twenty three I assure you those times are behind me... now I prefer to hang out with the boys at a wine-tasting and make snobby remarks about John Ashcroft's clothes.

I am surprised to hear all the talk about how offensive my show was last year. After all, I had been working out for at least a month in an attempt to be able to bounce my pecks... Although my stomach is not washboard, I had certainly paid attention to my appearance, even shaving my back!

Not a single person approached me before, during, or after the stripping to say that they were offended. I was congratulated by a few people on my show, including members of the div faculty and staff who shall remain un-named.

I did not realize how offensive I look in my boxers, and for that, I apologize, although I will add the caveat that I can now bounce my pecks, so I am probably not as offensive as I once was. Plus, have you checked out Brad? The kid is ripped to shreds.

As for the suggestion that we invite a few members of the Nashville law enforcement establishment to the Gala, I wholly applaud the idea. I am a supporter of the women and men in blue, and think they would have enjoyed my show. I have had a long relationship with the police establishment in Cincinnati and look forward to reestablishing that relationship with the Nashville community.

I'll have to check up on the Nashville indecent exposure regs, but I am pretty sure I am safe on that count... although public intox is another matter.

So here is the story from the point of view of a 23-year-old law/div student with enormous muscles: I was approached by members of the Div school community who explained that there was, yes, a "tradition" that a first year student, preferably male, strip at gala.

I was encouraged in this tradition by many other members of the community, including many women as well as a faculty member who shall remain un-named.

As a matter of fact, I remember there was conflict beforehand... not over whether anybody should strip, but over who got to choose who stripped. It sure seemed as if there was a large portion of the community who supported the tradition.

So, I did the disgusting acts in question... I took off my pants, my shirt, and my shoes (But NOT my socks, mind you... what kind of man do you think I am!) I danced with other men who also were in their underwear. Perhaps there was a little spanking. OK, a lot of spanking. A little butt crack...I think I was wearing button-fly boxers, so there should have been no problems there.

I certainly was not stripping to engage in an act of artistic self-expression or an exercise of free speech.... Instead, I was partying. Having fun. Engaging in a long div school tradition of having fun. Believe it or not, there have been other div students who like to drink and party...there may even be a few among the current crop of students at least if spring break was any indication.

There is obviously a split in the community over this subject. I for one will not be stripping at Gala, but then again, I am no longer a first year and do not fulfill the requirements of the tradition. If some first year wants to do it, I sure as heck won't stop them. I might even smile a bit.

As for not going to Gala, well, I'll be there with my date and my semi-formal wear... I may even bust out a tux. I will have an excellent dinner with my friends in the community and visit with faculty. I'll probably have a few drinks, dance a little, and maybe even offend someone by dancing too closely with my date. I wouldn't be surprised if the DJ played a few songs that mentioned sex and nakedness, perhaps even exhorting the party people in the classic words "It's getting hot in here, so take off all your clothes." (I am... getting.... so hot and I wanna take my CLOTHES ah-ah-off).

I hope this letter is taken in the tongue-in-cheek way it is intended. But seriously, if you wanna see a drunken, offensive formal party, check out the law school formal with its open bar... so many professional students in tuxes, so little time to slam down tequila shots. SO it's settled... Div School is crashing the law school party! Woohooo! I want to take off my pants!"[4]

-Luc Ke Me aka Moses Abraham
----

[4] Male divinity student, Vanderbilt University 2003

The irony of it is, this long, drawn out puppy of an e-mail illustrates a key dividend of my one hundred thousand dollar investment in a Divinity School degree.[5]

From: owner-divinity_students@list.vanderbilt.edu

To: divinity_students@list.vanderbilt.edu;
div-facstaff@list.vanderbilt.edu

Subject: Howard Harrod Memorial Service

"A memorial service will be held at 2:00 pm on Saturday, February 15, in Benton Chapel. In lieu of flowers, donations may be made to the Howard Harrod Lecture Fund (VU DIV School), Gilda's Club Nashville (1033 18th Avenue S., Nashville, 37212) or Alive Hospice (1718 Patterson St., Nashville, TN 37203."[6]

Dr. Harrod had been my favorite professor. He taught Native American Religious Traditions the way Fred Astaire danced. The subject matter, Ginger Rogers, and he flowed like water. With humor and with heart he connected the chasm between Native American, Jewish, and Christian traditions making manifest their common denominator. In doing so he unfolded God for me and all at once I realized I didn't need to *know* who God was. As long as God knew that was more than good enough for me.

A heated debate erupts in the normally hushed Alexander Heard Library. The great gala war, it appears, has tumbled out of cyberspace and into the preferred sanctuary of any spirit thirsty soul sadistic enough to undertake the study of the most written about subject in all of history, who just happens to also be the greatest mystery in history.

"The last thing I ever want to be," the Chaplain whispers, closing down the computer as theological insults start to fly, "Is anybody's minister."

Draining bodily fluids might not sound as glamorous as administering communion or last rights but trust me the dead can be far more likeable than the living. Mortuary arts, as in guaranteed money maker, may be icing on the cake seeing as how my loans, all

---

[5] I *could* read a really long e-mail if it was engaging and entertaining.

[6] Administrative personnel, Vanderbilt University 2003

one hundred thousand dollars of them, will start multiplying like mice the minute I crawl across the stage in May.

"Paper?" a Classmate above the fray offers with a bright smile. I accept a copy of *The Tennessean* with the same.

The headline reads:

Vanderbilt Divinity School Graduate Arrested for Facilitating Prostitution

Poor bastard, he was learning the hard way that chasing God didn't come cheap.

Everything's Coming Up Roses

"It's beginning to look a lot like Christmas" the Man who would be senator, governor, or at a minimum, mayor whispers, masturbating to his new mantra. *Am I just an average upper class Joe or Job on a chessboard wiggling my Willie while Satan whistles and God waits to chastise… it's beginning to look a lot like Christmas… my ass, come on Willie who's your daddy…for Christ's sake does this have to be so hard?* "Darn," he whispers, "Soft again."

Merely another male victim of an over sexualized media or the one dejected soul who has slept with neither the great whore, Madonna, nor an envoy from the Union of Great Liars.[7]
"Honey…"
He hears.
But it sounds like anything but.
"Why are you running the water so long?"

He kills the tap when what he really yearn to do is tell her he can run the water from here to eternity since he pays the bills.
"Don't you hear me speaking to you?"
"I'm praying." *Come on God, just one aneurysm.*
"God will wait but you won't get what you're praying for if you don't get out here."

"I have to go to my office," he answers then sits on the john, hard, so he won't be a liar.

Still, death did not come.

"What are you doing in there honey?"
His head hurts—*maybe it's my aneurysm.* "I'm stuck in the office," he answers, then gets busy wiggling Willie again… *Willie getting you up and ready for your five minutes with fate is my burden to bear so stop hoping for a handout or heaven help us lip service 'cause Ms. Mary wouldn't lay her lips on you if I was dying and an erection is the only anecdote…*
"Honey, now."
We could get laid…possibly well if we slipped outside the institution…"Stop thinking that!" he whispers.
Willie seems not to hear.

---

[7] prostitute

20

Why did we waste last month while she retreated with primitive, evangelical evolutionists when we could've been having sex with a living, breathing woman, "Stop thinking that!" he whispers.

"Honey!"

He hears. But it sounds like anything but.

He flushes, twice, then, for the sake of appearances, washes his hands before exiting.

"Have you seen the roses out front?" she asks, smile dissipating like mist at midday, "Look at that!"

There she is, he thinks, turning around and letting out a fart.[8]

"You're Boss Hogg," she continues, growing more agitated now, "Go over to that mirror and take a good long look at yourself."

He does as he is told, dispassionately analyzing his slightly slumping frame and accompanying pouch. While true his reflection speaks to his affinity for luscious lunches, decadent desserts, and the absence of an aneurysm, Vegas odds say he stands a far better chance of seeing his toes again than Little Mary Sunshine does.

"Are you ready or what?" Sunshine snaps, starting her stopwatch.

He need not peer south to perceive he is not.

Her rolling eyes race across his reflection, "It's just as well honey," she coos, burrowing back in to hibernate, "Heaven knows I can't breathe with you heaving up and down all over me."

I can't breathe either, at least not without the permission of my own fancy, non-affirming, asexual wife with endless attitude and an appetite for the finer things in life which my dick has not been deemed one...wow.

He stops in his tracks.

He had actually said dick... okay, thought it but still...*dick* he thinks louder and Willie flickers. *Dick, dick, dick, dick,* he thinks.

Willie flickers in kind.

He smiles, feeling hopeful as the carefree kid who spent every spare second learning to drive with one hand just in case he got lucky and needed the other one...

---

[8] Okay a fake laugh.

"Hand me the Gas-X honey," Sunshine requests, letting out a long, loud one.

Who knew he would never need that other hand?

"Hurry up, last night's chili is really sticking with me."

He does as he is told then heads back to his office to dress for work. The cream de la crème of Nashville's social, legal, political, educational, ministerial community and his best hope at future happiness hinges on dropping dead after a truly decadent dessert.

"And why not," he whispers, wiggling Willie, "Last night Little Mary Sunshine took out a three million dollar life insurance policy that pays out even if we commit suicide."

@@@@@@

Camille Mariana Leon strode, *some said,* like a gunslinger *but those in the know knew, though they were few, and called it for what it was*—a slither— *but they whispered it— always.* She winds her way round the Capitol stilettos scarcely clicking the freshly waxed floors giving birth to armies of frames fit only to guard poor souls forced to work for a living.

Her slither slows at door B112 behind which one, Detective Samuel Green, stands preoccupied, passionately, purposely pumping his thick cock through equally fat, French vanilla lubricated fingers....he sighs...then sings, in perfect falsetto, "I'm holding *heaven in my own hand, rocking my world, beating my man, feeling, fine feeling well* ...a soft, woeful moan escapes his full lips...*scratching... that...itch,* he squeezes his sweaty scrotum just so, teasing ecstasy until his eyes roll way back under his head... *Riding that...bitchhh...* "Detective Green!" – It was Vic-tor-ree-ah, his superior's boss' snobby assed assistant.

"De-tec-tive Green!" she screeches, pounding the door and his erection ever further into the wrong direction, "Captain Somers wants you now... De-tec-tive!"

"Com..." he sings, pumping for all he's worth "...ming!" And he does, spraying his pride and joy high in the air and onto the ceiling where it forms an aqua tinged rose in full bloom.

"Frustrated artist," Camille explains, arriving at her destination.

She is led first into a sitting room adorned with everything red, white, blue, and country then into a sprawling, lighted filled, cherry accented office that, while more subtle, is just as straightforwardly Republican.

"Vermouth?" the Senator from Tennessee offers.
"Please.[9]"
"Shall I take your case?"
"No thanks, I'm admiring your art."
"God's top ten, a gift from Judge Callahan."
"The upstanding Christian soldier who caught all manner of hell for posting them in his courtroom?"

"Damned shame," the senator says, offering her a seat, "When the very laws Moses brought down from the mountain are deemed unfit for the courtroom."

"I have a few questions about the INC."

"Not much to tell, really," he offers, sipping the forty proof syrup, "The funds were appropriated via the Iraq Liberation Act. It authorized the Pentagon to provide freedom fighters with as much as ninety-seven million dollars in relief supplies and political training."

"Political or propaganda?"
"Your pro is my con."
"I heard of the 97 million allocated only $6,337,421 dollars and 69 cents was spent."
The senator coughs.
"Who's your source, my accountant?" he queries, taking another sip.
"Well I guessed the 69 cents, it's my favorite number" Camille confides, opening her case and turning it towards him, "I understand it's yours too."

@@@@@@

Rena Maria Steinman arrived downtown before eight all bright eyed and bushy tailed but now half past four finds her trolling its outskirts in search of a public servant to escort her to her cousin, Tia's, wedding at the Temple this weekend. As she enters the inn of last resort she adjusts her Perrier logged wonder bra. It took two notarized

---

[9] Who was she to judge the politically powerful for drinking aperitifs in the morning?

notes from grams guaranteeing proper attire and a caveat, an antique silver, rose embedded serving platter, to secure Rena's unwelcome presence at this most joyous event and there exists no way she's showing up without something that wags when it walks super glued to her side.

"Can a girl get handcuffed around here?" she asks the first uniformed officer with green eyes and perky pecks she spots, then flashes her fake reporter's ID for good measure.

His eyes lock on Dolly's daughters. While obviously uncomfortable and slightly asymmetrical they scream former Hooter's hostess wannabe itching to score, "Maybe, follow me and we can discuss it." He leads her deeper into the den of the damned. She immediately scans the room for backup prospects.

With news of her lifted suspension hot off the menorah all eyes will be locked on her so forget the enema and just slap the shit out of her if she appears in that pristine white neoclassical archway without something that screams "screw you" at the bitch bride lurking about the alter, ordinary Joe and garden-variety brides maids in tow.

Jews can be so judgmental, she decides, following perky pecks down a long hallway she assumes leads to the lock-up. Who had she honestly hurt by showing up at her sister's wedding in a pearl embedded bridal gown she got for half price on E-bay?
So what if I was supposed to be the maid of honor? It was all in the family and not half as scandalous as the whole Jacob, Leah, Rachel fiasco and don't even get her started on good 'ole Abraham trying to trade Sara like so much used life stock.

The buns of if not steel at least nicely packaged salami come to a stop in front of a large pool of urine reeking of the motley but otherwise unremarkable crew assembled in cells on either side.

"So, where you from?" Perky asks.

Rena knows, clear to her soul that it took the green eyed gentile this long to formulate *that* question, "Northern Virginia," she coos, pointing, "What's he in for?"

"You might want to lift them a little," the drag queen responds, displaying his own unarguably more impressive rack.
"Put'em back, Pete," Perky warns, pulling out his nightstick.

24

Pete pinches his taut peach shaped nipples, blows them a kiss, and does as he is told.

Perky moves closer, "I caught him giving Hugh Grant a blow job."
"Really?" Rena squeals, searching for her camera phone.
"Naw, but its more interesting than the truth."
Rena giggles.
Not because Uni-brow amuses her senses but because she still needs something that wags in pristine white neoclassical archways.

"What about him?" she asks, pointing to a Brad Pitt like brooder.
"Wife beater."
"Well there's nothing new or novel about that is there?" she suggests, slipping her arm through his as they exit the can and head to the fish tank.

My clock is ticking... she thinks, *no, that's a lie, a frigging Gong Show is going on inside my body. Waggers are contestants and society the judge, standing in front of that giant gong with a cosmic hammer while I lurk nearby without so much as a feather, fervently hoping, wishing, and praying that somewhere a wagger is hoping, wishing, and praying for a tee totaling, Jewish virgin,* no, no, no that's a lie... she admits.

She was no more a virgin than Mary after the birth of Jesus let alone his brother, James. Truth be told, she slept with men too soon. It was a habit she fell into during her college days, which were, as her mother liked to remind her, still not over.

"There," she says aloud, *the truth wasn't so bad.*

It would be her new credo: truth at any cost. And the truth was she knew she had died and gone to sex heaven when she was accepted to the University of Maryland at College Park, the Mecca of all meeting places for Jewish match making.

As guaranteed in the brochures eligible Jews abound but with a wrinkle. Surrounding her like trees in a forest in the fall were flesh and blood life gentiles in varying heights and shades and she yearned to find out if what they said about them was true before she met and married her cream of the crop chosen one.

Anticipating the inevitable, she religiously practiced her *I can never make an honest man out of you speech,* and twelve years later was still waiting to give it. Heathen, she too late discovered, mated and moved on faster than Jewish boys came. So fast in fact that she found herself having sex in parking lots so she wouldn't have to race back to the bar to pick up another one before it closed.

"And why?" she asks aloud.

Because what history said about the gentiles was true and because she practiced that speech and dammit she was gonna give it to someone other than her deaf room mate.

Then, all of sudden she was in love.

With everyone she slept with because she was having sex with everyone she slept with so she must be in love because if she wasn't in love then what did that make her?[10]
Then, last spring when she thought the God of Israel could drive her no deeper into the desert, the Merchant of Venice called.

"Are you ever going to graduate?"
No hi, honey, how are you? No, are you eating? No manna from heaven just pressure, pressure, pressure...
"Well?"
"Yes, mom, as soon as I give my speech."
"It's been twelve years, crawl across a stage or find a job.[11]

She applied to Vanderbilt and soon found herself officially enrolled although unofficially AWOL from a degree completion program at Trevecca, a trailer park of a college where anyone with a brain stem could graduate with high honors in eighteen months. A lambskin was and would be her birthright or her name wasn't Rena Isabella Steinman.

Landing a job however was proving more difficult and she can't fathom why. *I'm just a giving person who wants to share love with the world...*
"No, that's a lie," she corrects aloud.
Truth was she was a spoiled, needy Jewish girl who overate to fill the void in her life...
"No, no, no that's a lie too."

---

[10] She couldn't be a slut, she was Jewish.
[11] see husband

She overeats because she is a realist who not only adores food but also fully realizes every meal could be her last and as soon as she finds an attractive, professional, financially secure hunk who can appreciate this trait in her without turning into a scale tipper himself she will sing *Hallelujah* from the hilltops.

Until then she is grudgingly content to live off her parents.
There. She'd said it.
"Did you say something?" Perky asks.

Thoughts slug through his synapses like sedated sloths, she realizes, squeezing his rippled arm deeper into her aquatic breast, *Meanwhile, mommy dearest moves faster than free tickets to March Madness.*

"What about Jacob, he's a good catch?" the stingy, old Hag hissed last night.
"He's a suspected pedophile when he's not busy being a jailbird junkie."
"He has a job."
"He's an illiterate janitor on the run from Israel."
"He's Jewish," the Hag hissed, tapping on the window and waving him over, "Beggars can't be choosers."
"Why not Son of Sam?"
"Is he still Jewish? I heard he converted."

Rena loved and respected her mother for who she was, the grim reaper of the bank accounts, but that doesn't mean she has to sit back silently and allow herself to be sold short so the selfish hag can have all daddies' money to herself.

She had rights to.

At the same time she is practical enough to know if she doesn't produce a fiancé or some facsimile thereof soon the merchant of Venice will sell her off to the first jaded Jew who promised to light a menorah on holy days and that was no bullshit but it still stunk to high heaven.

Fortunately, the favored fruit of her father's loins has a plan. First, she needs someone close to mommy's breast to convince the lineage

27

obsessed hag that having a heathen for a son-in-law is not the worse fate that can befall a Jewish mother in this day and age. Next, she needs to hook a heathen who isn't married, actively gay, infected with AIDS, or a southern butch packing the biggest penis she's ever seen...

Truth is she ultimately decided it would be a sin and a shame to let all that perfectly good high quality rubber go to waste but sans that wee escapade down the purple path she is an affirmed, optimistic, opportunistic, marriage minded, heterosexual, slightly overweight woman focused on finding gainful employment as soon as possible. Who knows, maybe this perky pecked, green-eyed, uni-browed sloth will come through?

@@@@@@

Harriet Ree-Ree Marie Tubman hurries through the downtown Hilton, pressing her way past conventioneers and little old church ladies so she can spend the next hour trying to flag down something that bears some resemblance to a cab. Forty-five minutes later something more akin to a banana boat bares right, coming to a stop directly in front of her. The banana's no Mardi Gras beauty but the Beast waiting for her is a stickler for time so, reluctantly, she climbs in and heads, she hopes, to Belle Meade.

BM, as those neither rich nor blessed enough to live there call it, is the wealthiest of Nashville's five prestigious satellite cities. Now home to more than three thousand people, it was, originally, one of the largest plantations in Tennessee. Then, one day the head heir decided to construct a golf course and country club on the grounds. Their guests coveted the club so much that they all claimed squatter's rights and the rest, as they say, is history.

Except to say that close to a century ago, the founder of the local newspaper gambled at real estate by founding a company to develop the five thousand acre former plantation. On the heels of rolling that lucky seven he became a Senator and before long found himself poor and wearing prison stripes after being convicted of bank fraud. Meanwhile his lucky toss of the dice, Belle Meade, became home to Nashville's elite health care, real estate, insurance, and banking barons.

The elegant enclave incorporated, electing their own mayor just ahead of the maddening crowds that later invaded Music city in search of stardom, sheepskin, or the sweet escape that comes with life in the big city. One thing was sure, if you were accepted by this crowd there need be no further consensus: you had arrived.

"Well you're not in Southeast DC anymore Dorothy," Ree-Ree whispers as her banana boat glides down the two mile stretch that was Belle Meade Boulevard, turning right at Page Road before continuing to the entrance to Cheekwood.

The botanical garden's fifty-five acre act of nature served as the backdrop to Belle Meade Plantation. On its grounds sat, in addition to all horticulture had to offer, an art center housing century old works heralding the red, white, and blue's 'ode to the masters. The banana boat glides to a stop. Ree-Ree hurriedly pays the driver and disembarks to find herself surrounded by roses encompassing every shade of the rainbow. And then some.

"Focus," she chides, finding herself transfixed by a huge bouquet of roses black as berries burnt by a late summer sun. She scours the sea of faces in search of her new best friend who she comes upon out back. Before she can call out, Camille responds as if she has already heard her name.

"Harriet," she gushes, rising and helping an elderly man to his feet, "I want you to meet, Rabbi Jaffe. I was just sharing with the Rabbi the wonderful work you're doing to continue the legacy of your great-great- grand-mother Harriet Tubman."

This rich girl worked an angle like a pathological liar who's a member of Mensa. Though Ree-Ree had been named after her ancestor, Harriet "roll me another one" Tubman, the woman, while radical and sweet, had been a lifelong addict who lived for drugs and died in a freak outhouse accident.

"That's right," Ree-Ree says, shaking the fragile hand, "Great Grammy Tubman lived for things that make the spirit soar and nothing does that like community based programs designed to show the underprivileged a better way of life."
"Don't waste your breath he's deaf as a doorknob and half as blind just stroke his upper thigh he likes that."
Ree-Ree acquiesces.
The old man smiles.

"Now follow the rainbow but only out the corner of your eyes; to your extreme left next to the black roses are the Wills, Fort, Joyce,

29

Keeble and Dudley insurance heirs of National Life and Life & Casualty; next to maritime blue is Bradford as in brokerage, formerly Paine Webber but now UBS Securities; beside them are the Cheeks' think Maxwell House Coffee."

"You're kidding."
"I never kid."
"Before I discovered Starbucks I loved Maxwell House."
"So did they now shut up grasshopper next to the fuchsias are the Frists, founders of HCA can you say healthcare; Crawford, of Caremark Rx is sniffing peach petals next to the Eskinds, more healthcare money but more importantly the players that helped make the governor a rich man."

"So the governor lives in Belle Meade."
"No, he lives in Forest Hills along with Weien and Kloeppel, Gaylord guys, and Doctor Crants."
"Plastic surgeon?"
"Founder of Corrections Corporation of America, the Wal-Mart of prison farms."
"I guess someone has to keep the slave trade going."
"The extra pale guy next to the crimson is Reed, Gaylord head honcho and neighbor to the governor. The guys bitching near the snow white roses are the real-estate barons who built Nashville: Welch, Matthews, and Palmer."

The Rabbi rises.
"Focus."
"I am."
"You stopped stroking."
"Oh," Ree-Ree realizes and resumes.
The Rabbi smiles and sits back down.

"Near the azaleas is Eakins, he's sold well over a million square feet of commercial space in Nashville, he's smoozing Martha Ingram of Ingram Industries, worth billions and the richest of Nashville's rich who lives in Hillwood not as in the hood but as in H.G. Hill the grocer."

"Where's he?"
"Six feet under but somewhere his heirs are continuing to slide down the hill and there you have it, old money and new money playing together as friends until its time to screw each other over like long time

30

enemies in a winner take all endeavor," Camille concludes, and takes over the stroking, "Ready to dive in?"

@@@@@@

"So how are you doing today Chaplain?" Nurse Nancy asks.

I smile between puffs.

"Well, I'm good but I'll be better as soon as Vanderbilt installs that walking sidewalk I requested—

A stream of obscenities emanating from a nearby room cuts my opening act short.

When the river finally rolls by I look to neighborly Nurse Nancy for answers.

"Mr. Kite wants a drink," she explains, searching for something on the desk.

"Well, I think I can handle that," I say striding into Mr. Kite's room, "Hi, I'm Jack—"

A heaping handful of shit flies my way.

"Shit," I say, because what else do you say if your goal is to be *present*?[12]

I step aside.

Nurse Nancy ducks.

It lands harmlessly, if that's possible, on the floor.

I empathetically fight the urge to pick the shit up and throw it back at him. Eyes masked, I look up and really at him for the first time. The poor soul is as obese and naked as his dick is darn near nonexistent...I try not to stare.

I can't help it.

"Now, Mr. Kite," Nurse Nancy sighs, seeming not to notice, "Are you flashing our new chaplain?"

"Give me a drink," he spits.

Literally.

He rears up and spits again.

I realize he's broken free from his restraints.

"Surely he can have water," I suggest, searching to add something pastoral to this crappy encounter.

"He wants vodka," they snap in unison.

Nurse Nancy and the shit pie kid share a laugh.

---

[12] Fully focused on the person/situation at hand

"You're going to have to take your dirty little hand out of that colostomy bag if you want me to attach a new one," Nurse Nancy cajoles.

A colorful protest commences.

I use this stitch in time as the exit opportunity God surely intends it to be. Alcohol, and its withdrawal, was indeed wretched and evil when it drove a morbidly obese, un-tanned, un-endowed man to strip naked and pitch his less than rose scented excrement at the first evangelical who popped their head in his room.

This whole comforter to the sick and dying gig has been good for both experience and credit but it comes at too high a price; too much pain, too much sorrow, too many regrets, and, in cases like Crappy, regrettable encounters. Graduation rapidly approaches and a new window has yet to open but the door has also not closed but when it does I don't plan to be on the wrong side of it; even if that means risking unemployment and the wrath of a sweet but make no mistake high maintenance woman.

@@@@@

Professor Charles Marion Dates gazes out across his kingdom, surveying his sheep who sit before him collectively shaking in their boots. His reputation always preceded him, a fact he fastidiously ensured would always remain the case. He knew better than anyone that he was notorious among the administration, faculty, students, and staff for flunking, with pleasure, otherwise outstanding students.

His course, Ethics in Society, was a core requirement for every man, woman, or child who planned to graduate with a degree in Theology, Law, Marketing, or Medicine. Rich man, poor man, beggar man, thief, cock sucker, booty boy, or Indian Chief; you didn't make it out of the big V with the lambskin of your dreams unless Dr. Asshole gave you a pass and pricks and proud of its like him didn't make things you needed easy to come by.

Dates didn't love much but he adored ethics, the study of what is good and bad within moral duty and obligation— a bedeviling behemoth bound in a bell jar waiting to wrap its lips around what mistook it for simple.

"Bitches, just little bitches, all," he concludes, placing a limp hand on slim hips as he continues to survey this intellectually motley, but otherwise unremarkable, theological crew.

No, nada, nay, make no mistake; he was the undisputed ruler of this parcel of land. Lock. Stock. Barrel and he planned to tweak those titties 'til the cows came home from whoring.

"Ethics," he begins, strolling the length of the room as if it is a runway and he is Naomi Campbell, "Is the study of morality and can anyone tell me what morality is?"

He scans the room with bionic eyes that come to rest on a groovy little grad student who ducks her head as though shots have been fired.

"You," he decides, pointing and wiggling his finger like she's the lobster he wants de-tanked and submerged in a boiling pot, "You, the shy rabbit trying to hide in your own hole."

"Me?" Mary tweaks meekly, hoping she's mistaken.

He sighs long then leisurely extracts an ornate, rose embroidered fan from his pocket and commences to vigorously cooling himself like a character out of a Tennessee Williams play.

"Yes, my dear, you," he finally drawls, "All day long you, tomorrow, still you, if hell froze over and I pulled out my tutu and performed *Flaming Fags on Ice* it would still be y-o-u."

He curtsies before the laughing class then turns back to the lobster, "Well?"
"The study or act of conforming to an accepted notion of right versus wrong behavior?"
"Is that an answer or are you asking me a question, dear?"

The deer trapped in headlights just nods, leaving him to shake his head in disgust.

And society called gays weaklings.

"One of the things I find most fascinating in the study of ethics is the quandary, the pickle, the wrinkle if you will, of how it can be that man, the creation, is more moral than God, his creator," Dates drawls, fanning himself more leisurely now.

33

A gasp spreads across the lecture hall in a wave that moves from right to left cooling Dr. Date's face like a breeze as his fans acknowledge his performance on the field of life and literary annunciation.

"After all," he continues, pulling up a chair and sitting down, crossing lithe legs clothed in linen Ralph Lauren before smoothing out an imaginary wrinkle and resting his delicate wrists atop each other, "The Israelites, the chosen children, once freed from slavery proceeded to storm into land occupied by people living in peace and slaughter every man, woman and child not once but over and over again across hundreds of years, each time using as their justification, *"God told us to do it."*

He scours the room slowly, seeking eyes willing to wrestle with his own. Finding none, he sighs, "How many of you sin soaked souls would travel from land to land slaughtering every man, woman, and child who crossed your path over and over again?" he asks and when there are no takers, "Then who is more moral, you or your God?"

He sighs seemingly into eternity, fanning his face again for effect. The tips of the embroidered rose petals move faster and faster appearing to take flight while the pitiful, shell-shocked sheep try to chew, without choking, on the miniscule cud he has given them.

"That's enough for now," he decrees, getting up and gliding down the runway and out the room a mere ten minutes after sashaying in.

"Well, I'll be chewing on that cud until our next class," the Chaplain quips, rising and exiting stage left while collective relief is still the only emotion flooding the room.

A Step Back

Fate delivered her to my doorstep.

The Chaplain had not yet died suddenly and under mysterious circumstances and she was the chaplain's girl and everyone knew it. He made the couples acquaintance just before Spring break at a Divinity School dinner hosted at Dean Debbie's new house in the upscale Hound's Run sub division in Forest Hills. Normally, his wife, who was the least social person he knew, would snub such an invitation but this was a special occasion.

"However can she afford a house so close to ours?" she demanded for the third time.
"Hmmm."
"Do you think she made the money starring in porn?"
"Hmmm."
"I heard she screwed every dean and their daddy to get that position."
"Hmmm."
"Make sure you don't touch anything while we're there."

There were always rules when they appeared in public together. He was not to touch anything, talk to anyone, or wander off, unless she told him to go away. All day long he looked forward to this opportunity to spend several hours with his ass super-glued to her side then return home where he wouldn't even get any unenthusiastic sex for his trouble.

"We just did that twelve days ago," she snapped, when he suggested it on the ride over, "Sit up straight and try to have some class for Christ's sake."

He longed to ram the car into a tree but parked it instead before hurrying to open her door. They trudged up the stone driveway in silence...
"Look at this lawn."
"Hmmm."
"Apparently she hasn't found a yard man to bed yet."

The door swings wide and they step into the light filled foyer. He slumps there, super-glued to her waist and waits while she fixates on all the flaws in Dean Debbie's floor plan in order to correct them so she can move forward and find something to compliment.

"Dean Debbie I just love that divan," Ms. Mary says, turning to him, "It works don't you think honey?"
His head hurt.
"Hmmm."

Just then a couple sashayed in wearing Colgate smiles and the unmistakable smell of fresh sex. I gratefully inhale the fragrance knowing it's the closest I'm going to get to laid any time soon. Introductions were made and I learned this was Jackson, the Chaplain, and Jackson's girl, Mary.

Mary, I remember thinking, *what a difference a name makes.*

I still remembered, albeit barely, when Ms. Mary had just been Mary.
I was an eighteen year old corn fed country bred bookworm and a virgin to boot. She was a twenty-four year old first year grad student from Syracuse who was anything but.
I was the freshman center who made the winning shot in our overtime victory against Harvard. She was a babe who didn't know a basketball from a banana but knew a horny corn fed country virgin when she felt one.

We were married by Christmas.
"Hmmm," he says, realizing she has said something.
Life couldn't get any better. I was a four star athlete positioned among the academic elite at an Ivy League School, I was having sex on a regular basis with an older woman who cooked, ironed my clothes, made sure I did my homework, and had sex with me.

The gravy train hit quicksand the year I earned my law school lambskin. I christened it the year the twins came and I didn't. I landed my first job, bought our first house, and learned to masturbate without moving after Little Mary Sunshine woke up, soaked me with flammable liquid, and threatened to start a fire.

It took exactly seven years, right down to the aforementioned Merry Christmas night, for the best of times to morph into the worst of times, and now, eighteen seasons of discontent later there was neither an end nor an aneurysm in sight.

36

"Hmmm."

On our eighth anniversary we met to discuss my "melancholy" and how it was negatively impacting the marriage. At least that's what the memo read.

Defying protocol and all things my sadist held sacred I dove off the deep end, delving into the essence of what made life worth living, "I miss you, I miss holding you," I said, taking her hand, "I miss making love to you, and can we please talk about that first?"

"Okay," she said, putting the agenda aside, "From day one you displayed more than a periodic predisposition towards flaccidity—

I was taken off guard, thinking she'd never noticed, "Well, I always got nervous at exam time…"

She sighs me a river.

"Always know that I adore you but St. Peter suffers from a lot more than test anxiety."

Shame floods me.

I fight back tears.

She pats my hand, "Oh, don't, its okay sweetie, it's not important, I love you for you not for sex, that's what's important, not some silly, saggy, old St. Petey."

Tears now flowed freely down my face.

"How could I care about a saggy St. Petey when God has blessed me with a husband with enough wisdom to worship a good wife? What say I make you some milk and cookies?"

As much as he hated to admit it now, those warm chocolate chips melting in his mouth made him feel like a man again.

"Now, what are you going to get that's better than that?" she asks, patting his head.

"Nothing," he admits, tears starting to flow again.

"Hmmm."

"What are you looking at?" Ms. Mary repeats.

"Hmmm."

His own parents had been married sixty-three years. He often wondered if his dad ever felt like he was sleeping with his mother. He was tempted to ask last Wednesday while he sat watching him dribble but he was afraid. His father was a conservative, God fearing, self taught minister who refused to step foot into a church. Personal questions were a synonym for insults evoking visions of Marvin Gaye not singing but boarding the night train courtesy of an unflinching father who took the Bible literally and figured disrespect deserving of death. While he yearned to ask he instinctively knew it was safer to remain silent and focus on the dribble.

Besides, he was no silly child; he was a respectable man with responsibilities. The big "R" was a serious endeavor that didn't revolve around wants but, instead, your word, your bond, your vow, even if the syllables uttered in youthful innocence doomed you to die a little each time you laid down with the dead weight that was once the girl of your dreams.

These had been his thoughts the night he met the Colgate couple.

They were still beaming an hour later when dinner was announced. He shuffled to the seat Ms. Mary indicated when, out of nowhere; Jackson swooped into the chair next to him. Mommy Dearest, noticeably miffed, moved on when the Chaplain doggedly refused to acknowledge her existence.

For the next two hours, while everyone else engaged in passionate debate about the presence or lack thereof of an omnipotent or not so God, he and his new best friend chatted about everything from evolution to eschatology to Mary, the Chaplain's girl, who continually cast seductive, longing looks her lover's way.

Lucky b— he thinks, catching himself, *maybe I should forget about the aneurysm and just leap from the left ear of the Batman building.*

He chides himself for coveting but for Christ's sake Mary was beautiful, sexy, and had, he could tell and smell, recently bedded the Chaplain really, really well.

He inhales deeply.

"I'm still waiting for my toes to uncurl," the Chaplain confirms, slapping him on the back, "In my last life or early childhood I must have done something really, really, good..."

And while The Man who would be senator, governor, or at a minimum, mayor could not begin to relate, he could and did sneak peeks at the toe curler from the corner of his eye at every opportunity. All night he watched and waited for their paths to cross but they never so much as exchange a word all evening— until she shakes his hand as the Chaplain ushers her out the door.

"You have a secret life," she whispered; then smiled a smile he could not begin to decipher. *Was it pity, empathy, or...desire?* He wondered, and then castigated himself for thinking like that.

@@@@@

Twice decorated Detective Green and his new partner, Opie, were on the bubble, police lingo for next at bat, when the call came in.

"Smeller on the south side."

"We gonna get that?" the rookie asked when he moved but his partner didn't.

This 'lil bitch of a white boy is really starting to get on my nerves, Green observes, flipping the pages of his newest self help manual. *This un-weaned nipple feeder was forever whining about procedures and mandatory reports and shit and now...*

"There's someone waiting for us," the little pussy announces...standing up...and over him like the mother of some virgin he had knocked up.

Whoa... now the retarded, red-haired, freckled face fag is sighing and tapping his size eight, if it's an inch, foot.

"Don't get your draws in a knot," Green advises, removing his own size twelve's from Opie's desk but never looking up from the hot, hairy cunt of Ms. May, winking at him each time he blinked, "He'll still be waitin' when I dive in there."

His days of rushing to and fro like a coked out rabbit were over. He had started out like Junior, all bright-eyed and bushy fucking tailed but then real life stepped in. He was no Clinton fed baby he came of age in the Reagan years when a brother couldn't buy a job much less get hired for one and unemployment benefits, he learned, were only for people who had been employed.

By his twentieth birthday he had been arrested twice: for possession of stolen goods and twice for dealing drugs. He did a little time here and there, holding fast to the only words of wisdom he ever got from his old man—never let your face become familiar to the man.

DC had been his ninth stop in as many years. Word was, crack was the sweetest ticket in town and you could call him a butt ugly buttered up mother-fucker as long as it paid right. After all, he decided, picking the pocket an old hag sportin' a pair of sneakers long on miles but short on rubber, if Uncle Sam could peddle the pipe to the people, surely Sammy could have a toke of the smoke.

His sojourn through the mean streets of Chocolate City wound to an end at the flashpoint which houses all manner of illicit activity—the corner of Malcolm X Avenue and Martin Luther King Jr. Boulevard. It took him ten minutes to find an unoccupied light pole to lean on and take in the lay of the land... observe the players... watch the exchanges...of gunfire being exchanged in broad daylight, in front of a church on Easter Sunday morning...when the rampage finally ended he found himself lying face down in a pile of fliers advertising immediate openings with the Washington Metropolitan Police Department.

The police station at fifth and H opened at eight and he was there, all bright eyed and busy fucking tailed like the coked out rabbit he was. The first several shifts he was jittery as a pedophile priest on speed stripped of his robes and waiting to be cast out like a nun who misplaced her rosary beads but, with each passing day, an ironclad bond developed between him and his training class of fifty recruits. The beauty of this wall of blue, this thin blue line, this blue brotherhood literally blew his mind.

He was a wee bit disappointed at the end of the week to find they were all criminals with rap sheets longer than his. On day eight of his beat, he was exiting the apartment of a babe he'd busted then banged for an hour when a guy ran smack into him and kept running, dropping a gym bag in the process.

He picked it up.
Its owner rounded the corner.
The case was solved.

This twist of fate earned him both fanfare and instant membership in the elite eight, the select fraternal society made up of the eight percent of officers actually responsible for solving criminal cases in the District. He received a raise and was booted up to homicide. On his first night he drew a triple. Just as he wrapped up puking his insides out, the next call came in, and then the next until one shift rolled into another like waves of brain matter where otherwise perfectly ordinary assholes used to be. He lived for down time[13] when murder weary cops got to recharge their batteries shaking down dealers or redeeming get out of jail free cards.

By his third year on the force he was clearing ninety grand and close to achieving independent businessman status. And he deserved every damn dollar seeing as how each night DC turns into a brutal jungle where humans are hunted.

During the day they're just killed.

A scary proposition when you're living la vita loca but praise the Lord he had a really, really big gun and a predisposition towards using it.

At the start of year five he decided, from his house in Mitchellville, that the job with all its drawbacks and drama had been damn good to him. Then, out of nowhere on a perfectly ordinary Saturday in September, the sky started raining bullshit. The front page of the *Post* reported that bodies were piled up at the morgue like politicians at a pork belly retreat in Switzerland, whatever that meant, and suddenly, out of the blue, everybody was pissed off about it.

Reporters dug, politicians danced, and the Mayor inhaled while all hell broke loose in the city. That fancy thing French people used[14]was dusted off and the chief, and the rest of the brass heads rolled the way Ike and Tina sang in a last ditch effort to head off a federal investigation. That should have been the end of it lock, stock, and barrel but Barry, Bonzo, and the bullshit band[15] remained unsatisfied.

The *Washington Post* made sure of that.

They went on and on about accountability and police corruption, digging deeper and deeper up the rank and file's asses like gerbils hired for a Hollywood birthday party.

Every morning there was something new and when there wasn't they filled the empty space with sob stories about "grieving" relatives and shit until they stirred up the already restless natives, inciting their

---

[13] Day shifts
[14] See guillotine
[15] Marion, Ronald Regan, and the republicans

crazy asses to violence. Within weeks three of his blue brethren joined the brotherhood of brain matter.

All took four bullets to the back of the head.

Fired at close range.

The calling card of a professional or a close friend.

The crimes, like most in the District, went unsolved. That, coupled with a minor incident not worth mentioning, motivated him to transplant his ass in Nashville where, he heard, the harvest was plentiful but the bright were few and so far, the 'Ville had been pretty good to him.

"Are we heading to the crime scene anytime soon?" the Bitch whines yet again.

"He'll be waiting for us Opie or my name ain't Sammy Green," he guarantees, winking one more time at the hairy cunt who winks back before closing her legs and sliding into his back pocket.

"See Opie, I was right," he chuckles, when they arrived on the scene two hours later,

"The smelly stiff is still here with his baby sitter in tow, what we got?" Sammy asks the Officer just because TV cops always did.

The rookie glares at them and gets into his cruiser, screeching tires his only answer.

"Friendly sort ain't he?" Green observes, using his flashlight to lift the stiff's chin in hopes of getting a look at what face still remained.

It was Rod Fletcher, a dime bagger from the West End area. He tagged and released the fast talker three times in as many days before the wise ass fell in line with the Samuel Green Retirement program. He paid his respects faithfully for a year then went AWOL a few weeks ago.

"You still owe me" Green whispers, letting what's left of his debtor's head fall back to the steering wheel.

"You know him?" Opie asks all bright eyed and bushy fucking tailed.

"Sure do, meet Rod "hot rod" Fletcher, gang member and prime suspect in three unsolved murders."

@@@@@@

"You want me," Ree-Ree repeated, from her perch at the Mellow Mushroom, "To get thirty girls from Cayce Homes[16] to dress up like nuns and serve Thanksgiving dinner to decrepit, white, senior citizens who might still shuffle around in white sheets?"

"How many shuffling black senior citizens do you know looking to bequeath real estate to clear their conscience before they croak?" Camille responds a little too rhetorically.

Her mentor led her across the street where she introduced her to Loretta Birdsong, who managed the Divinity School Refractory which, Ree-Ree soon realized was just a fancy word for cafeteria. By day's end the two of them drown in a sea of patterns and black material.

By morning they secure permission to use Stratford High's home economics room. By week's end they sew, rip apart and re-sew thirty-three costumes that, despite their best efforts, scream nun instead of pilgrim. That was the easy part. Getting thirty head strong, which is simply a synonym for independent; girls from the hood into said habits and onto a bus had been a whole different matter.

"Do I look like Aunt Jemima to you?" The last Hold-out demanded of Gloria who blocks the doorway, extended black and white head kerchief in hand.

"No, I'm Aunt Jemima but you can be Ms. Butterworth if it'll get your irritable butt moving."
Beyond the bravado Ree-Ree could see their apprehension.

"Will there be racks o'white people there?" Rasheeda asks as the bus pulled away.

"Racks and racks of them," Aunt Jemima assures the now quiet bus, "But this ain't Gone with the Wind, if they slap you, feel free to slap them back."

That seemed to make all the difference in the world as their Mayflower sailed down Shelby Avenue and onto Interstate 24 before barreling along I-65 towards Brentwood.

---

[16]See "the hood"

As they exited the interstate Ree-Ree waited for a sign from the young nuns, some realization they crossed an invisible line leading to another world.

"It's like some kind of fucking fairytale!" Ms. Butterworth screams as they came ashore at the Country Club.

The geriatrics arrived an hour later to a ball room transformed, courtesy of the dollar store, from a stuffy hall and into a festival of fall. Small, candlelit pumpkins and paper Mache turkeys adorn tables covered with the illusion of leaves swathed in all the shades the season offered.

Loretta," Ree-Ree calls, entering the kitchen, "We'll need more mashed potatoes in about five minutes."

"When you need 'em, you'll have 'em," she replies, never glancing over her shoulder.
"You okay?"
"Yeah, I'm fine."

But she wasn't. Her spirit tosses and turns so she suspects her insides seasick but is who to share her concerns with. She was having *if* issues. You know:
If only I had known he was married.
Crazy.
On crack.

She knew to just keep on walking when his lips parted and a string of pearls emerged but he was tall, strong, and better looking and smelling than most men you met these days. So she stopped and tipped her head to the side just so, her spirit's signal it had opened itself up for an encounter with mystery.
Who was he?
What did he want?
What would he give?
Was he funny?
Corny?
Horny?
Was there a wife, job, girlfriend…boyfriend?
The excitement of it all left her feeling spry as Nancy Drew.[17]

---

[17] Teen-age detective, see Nancy Drew Mysteries

Like Nancy, it had been far too long since she lured a man who made her heart skip a beat. Like Nancy she had been far too busy raising a son, making ends meet, spearheading service work at the church... masturbating until her fingers went numb...experimenting with everything not outlawed by the Bible in a desperate attempt to tame the flesh which had, for too many years, gotten her nowhere fast.

Her now adult son, Lorenzo, saw more than his fair share of men pass through. Always just passing through, restless spirits moving from this life to the next bed...in the beginning they were all tall, strong, and better looking and smelling than the average ordinary Joe. Like Nancy she learned, albeit leisurely, that these qualities didn't necessarily equate to commitment which led her to experiment with different formulas.

First she tried men who were a wee bit shorter than most, then less good looking, then weaker, and finally less good smelling until one morning she woke up next to a multi-dimensional midget: a dumpy, ugly, lazy, spineless son of a bitch who smelled to high heaven. Like Nancy she gave her life to Christ that day and committed herself, first to faith, and second to the pursuit and practice of ancient finger art. She and her overworked index had been faithful for fourteen years until last week when she met a tall, strong, good looking, and better smelling man with full lips that dripped pearls.

So she tipped her head to the side and by week's end had been tipped, flipped, tapped, and launched to heaven and back by this gift from above that was tall and strong and better looking and smelling than most men she met these days so you could have slapped her hard and called her honey when her son showed up at her door before dawn.

Quicker than you can say hi, he dragged her tall, strong, good looking, better smelling, rock hard hunk from the bed and, literally, down the stairs before kicking him out into the street butt bald naked.

"So now you screwing crazy, married, cracked out niggahs?" He demanded mugging[18] her like she's a whore who stole something.

And what could she say?

That when he parted his lips a string of pearls hypnotized her?

---

[18] Glaring at

That she forgot to unearth all the dirt before riding him like Old Henry Clay?[19]

That when he came along it had been far too long since someone made her shiver?

That she had forgotten herself and was now ashamed?

…In an instant all these thoughts raced across her brain but instead she said, "You're talking? How many pitiful bitches desperate for a hit have you made suck your little dick today?"

Like Nancy she was cursed with a big mouth.

"I take care of my business okay! I take care of house, my women, my kids, I'd take care of you if you'd let me 'cause I'm a man, okay!" Her son screamed, towering over her.

Then he left.

Left her feeling like a sad, fifty-year old woman far too old to have been so quickly won over by a pretty smile and gentle delivery, left her fearing she had disappointed her Savior, left her feeling ashamed and frustrated that here she sat, half-naked and horny while somewhere beyond the green door a tall, fine, good looking, better smelling, butt bald naked man packing a crack induced hard on was running around with no where to rest his head…

But most of all she was left disappointed that, despite her best efforts, she remained just another single, middle-aged black woman who somehow failed to teach her son how to be a man of both means and honor.

"You ask for mashed potatoes, you get mashed potatoes," Loretta said, joining Ree-Ree out front to transfer fluffy clouds into serving containers.

"First, you make me stay up all night basting turkeys then you force me to dress like a nun to serve them?" Camille complains, joining them.

"You're a pilgrim," Ree-Ree responds.

---

[19]Aka America's National Thoroughbred Trotting Horse or Father of American Trotting Horses, foaled 1837/Long Island

"And you're crazy, Ree," Loretta adds, "Paleface Willy would kill you if he knew you were glorifying the rape of the Indians. Where is whitey anyway?"

"At the Capitol protesting a government-sanctioned holiday glorifying the rape of *Native Americans*."

"Meanwhile I'm here in a habit serving ham flavored turkey to retired klans people."

"Please Cammy if you dressed as a nun you'd spontaneously combust."

"Ain't that the truth" Loretta agrees and leaves.

"Besides" Ree-Ree continues, "They aren't ex-Klansmen; they're just elderly, asset ridden white people."

"You make me so proud," Camille gushes, then slips into the kitchen, "Are you okay, honey?"

"Yes," Loretta answers, wiping away tears with the hem of her habit, "It's just that this is the ugliest thing I've ever worn."

"Well," Camille comments, coming over to give her a hug, "I've decided it's a keeper, a divinely multi-functional outfit."

"Dare I ask?"

"No, but you can witness if you promise not to judge," she answers, displaying strings of pearls, "Let's shed this skin and join the party."

And they did, mingling in with then disappearing into the exactly 300 people fire code restrictions limited the Brentwood Country Club to; where a host of nuns from the hood and asset laden ex-klans men drink together, eat together, and, as the evening wears on hand dance together to Sinatra and Nat King Cole.

@@@@@@

"Why do niggas always have to fiddle with your high?" Mary mused aloud.

"Did you say megas—what's a mega?" Mary Papins asked, bringing her a fresh cup of coffee.

"Not megas I said niggas."

Mary Papins giggled nervously, "But why do they have to be that? Why can't they just be meanies or megas? Why do you have to place a racial connotation on it?"

"It has nothing, in the end, to do with race," Mary began impatiently, "Niggas are neither defined by color, class, nor the classlessness within which an offense is perpetrated, no, nada, nay, it is instead found amidst the gray."

Mary Papins wasn't getting it.

"In other words anyone anywhere at any time can be a nigga. And people notice, note it, and love them anyway. Hitler was a nigga but there were people who loved his sick little ass. Julia Roberts was a nigga in *My Best friends Wedding.* Captain Kirk in episode 63 of *Star Trek* —mega, Heathcliff in *Wuthering Heights*, Brad Pitt in *Legends of the Fall* and *Thelma and Louise,* Ashley in *Gone with the Wind*, Rhett Butler in GWTW, Scarlett O'Hara, hell, damn near everybody in GWTW—all megas. Robert Redford in *The Way We Were,* Jack Nicholson in *One Flew Over the Coo Coo's Nest,* Bill Clinton in real life but Black people love him anyway because he knows and they know and he knows that they know and they know that he knows that they know that he's a mega too."

"Oh, so you mean a putz is a Jewish mega?"
"Exactly."
"So why can't white people say mega?" Mary Papins ventures nervously.

"Because it has too many layers and we don't run that fast. You see, say a black person says *"mega please"* to a friend, relative, or acquaintance. Now the interpretation could be *"you're crazy"* as in you're really tickling my ass with that one."

Mary pauses to remove a stack of index cards from her purse, "But then come the layers within those two words, *mega please*, it could also mean:

- Don't even start that crazy shit (I'm not in the mood or I don't even have time to hear all this— which can be humorous or serious)
- That shit was crazy, I remember that shit too (Humorous)
- I ain't in the mood to be dealing with your crazy shit today (Not humorous)

48

- I don't even know why you trying to tell me this dumb ass shit (tolerating you/pissed at you but love you anyway).
- I'm about ready to fiddle you up (tolerating you but not feeling much love)

Mary takes a sip of her tea, "By the time we tried to flip through all these cards we could be all fiddled up."

"How do you know all these things?" Mary asked, gazing at the cards in wonder.

Mary was tempted to tell her because she could be a mega too but instead said, "Let's get back to my mega, I was thinking about sending him packing..."
"Again." Mary adds, nodding.
"Again and asking him to give me time to evaluate this latest turn of events..."
"What events?"
"To start with questionable charges on our credit card statement," Mary leans in closer, "I went out to get the mail..."

"Don't get the mail," Mary Papins squeals, "Make margaritas or masturbate but don't go near the mail."

"I opened the statement and there they were, questionable charges, I called him several times on his cell but and he kept saying he was in a meeting but not half an hour later roses showed up from *Joy's*, now if that's not a sign of cheating I don't know what is..."

Mary nods.

"So you agree," Mary pushes, pressing the point, "He's definitely cheating..."

"Oh gosh, I don't know, men are like mice, just plain scary, but," Mary Papins continues, patting her hand, "Don't worry, sooner or later a mega will always show their stripes."

@@@@@@

Athena was at home in Virginia, naked and more than perfectly comfortable when. Reverend Fisher, a prophet from Nashville she counted a friend, called.

49

"And you call yourself a friend," she chastised as soon he told her why, "I don't care how old Ms. Clara is, tell her it's not gonna happen."

And she hung up.

Not two seconds later, Ms. Clara called, on Athena's back-up private line.

"I'll pay double if you'll humor an old hag, just this once."

"Don't be silly, Ms. Clara but what did you promise about the "H" word?

"I'm sorry honey."

And it sounded like just that.

"Okay sweetie I'm on my way."

She calls Reverend Fisher back, "I arrive at eleven; be ready to bargain."

"But I can't just give you a body," is the mantra of the Davidson County medical examiner who was uncommonly distracted by the enchantingly nude body of the blonde cheerleader lying on the slab. Athena can understand; the unfortunate former Mary Jo Sunshine *that can't honestly be her name* has the whole Sleeping Beauty thing down to an art form.

"I have to thoroughly examine the body, extract and weigh the vital organs, check for seminal fluids…"

"In what order?" Athena asks.

"I understand procedures," Reverend Fisher diverts, diving in, "But this young man was shot four times, in the head, at close range, it's pretty obvious what killed him."

"Then there's ballistics…"

"Look, we both know you routinely skip autopsies altogether."

"That is just a vicious lie and a rumor to boot," he snaps, turning beet red, "I'd like to come face to face with the person uttering such slanderous…"

"Pleased to meet you," Athena says, handing him a business card, "I'm an attorney licensed in several states to include Tennessee and…she hands him another card, "The owner of Monroe Memorial Services. Perhaps you've heard of us? We have a local office just down the street and we keep meticulous records on all our customers, photos to boot."

"Well sometimes the cause of death is obvious," he agrees, "but you'll have to wait until I extract *a* bullet— just in case we find the gun."

Her general manager, Tony was waiting with the hearse when the body finally arrived. The party left Sleeping Beauty with the butcher and made the journey to Monroe's where Athena was surprised to find three employees waiting.

"I called in extra help to make sure we made the deadline," Tony explained.
"That was sweet," Athena says, addressing the group, "But I'll do this one."

Their mouths dropped and nobody bothered to pick them up. Why everyone knew it had been at least forty years since a Monroe woman took a "hands on" interest in the business. Could they, in good faith, leave someone's dearly departed in her inexperienced, meticulously manicured hands?

"You're sure?" Tony asks because someone sure as hell needed to.
"Don't worry, I know how to do it," she says and shoos them away.
Six hours later, the young man was bathed, shaved, dressed, transported, and lying at rest just as Ms. Clara had insisted must be the case the evening before.
"He must be free to fly with the doves at daybreak," she whispered.
"With the doves at daybreak," had been Athena's vow then she bowed and retreated from the dance.

@@@@@

"I will get this job, I will get this job, I will get this job, I will get this job… " Rena repeated incessantly, trying to breathe and not hyperventilate at the same time.

All happy hours should be damned to hell. Because of one she didn't receive word of this interview until midnight, leaving her less than eight hours to sleep, treat her hangover, exercise her way into her little blue suit, and knock the socks off the interviewer.
By six she was showered.
By 6:05 she was throwing back fur from the dog that mauled her.

51

By 6:45 she had shoved herself into three pair of control top hose, two girdles, and her little blue suit.

By seven she was on 395 north headed for her date with destiny. By seven eleven she sat, trapped by fate, evil, or pure happenstance behind an overturned tractor-trailer that had, until Irish eyes stopped smiling, been otherwise occupied hauling a double load of mid grade liquor.

Why had the God of Israel conspired with the two Jacks[20] to deprive her of this once in a lifetime opportunity to turn her world right side up?

"Heaven or Nashville," she screams.
Repeatedly...
Until her passive, pathetic fellow prisoner's car horns drown her out.

Heady aromas from spilled spirits drift into the air; snakes enchanted from the pavement by charmers, beckoning her to drown her cares in their eighty proof promises...or had the Jacks been watered down to seventy five percent? She was halfway out the window when a blaring horn snaps her back to her senses.

"You bastards! You won't sabotage me," she decides, steering right and onto the shoulder, "I'm rolling now!" she screams, throwing back her head and cackling with glee, "Cement suckers!" *Only suckers and losers sit, bumper to bumper like fresh biscuits while their destiny gets sucked dry by a merciless sun...*"of a bitch!" she screams as flashing lights fill her rear view mirror, "I will get this job, I will get this job, I will get this job," Rena repeats, closing her eyes and ramming the accelerator; a madwoman with a mantra and a mission.

---

[20] Bean and Daniels

Happy Anniversary I/the Dead Zone

When you think about it, every commemoration—birth, marriage, death, salvation or garden variety ego event is really an anniversary of some sort—an occasion to mark for remembrance an act that is out of the ordinary. Take Rena Maria Steinman, today is the second anniversary of the day, when, determined to make her date with destiny she made a mad dash down I-395 north in Alexandria before crossing over into DC.

"We bigwigs here at channel 5 were very impressed with the tape you sent," the VP of Programming said when she arrived.

All breathless.

"Thank you," she manages, heart racing from the excitement of the chase, the hunk interviewing her, and the likelihood armed officers would be bursting in any second.

"How did you come to find her?"

"Like all good reporters I have my sources, which must, of course, remain anonymous."

"Of course," he agrees, offering her bottled water, "We're always looking for aggressive new talent here at five and I have a feeling you'll make a wonderful addition to our family."

"I would," she gushes, bubbling over, "I really, really would."

"Wonderful then," he says, extending his hand, "You have the job."

Rena instinctively hugs him… long and hard.

A little too long and a little too hard. It had been a little too long since she hugged anyone who was this long and this… hard and it feels a little too good to let go a second too soon, "You won't regret this, I promise."

"I'm sure I won't…unless you refuse to let me go."

Pink, she reluctantly complies, "Sorry."

"Think nothing of it," he assures, leading her to the door, "I understand you won't need business cards."

"Excuse me?"

He reaches into his pocket and pulls out one of her black market channel five business cards, "You can recycle this one if you're running low."

"I can explain that."

"No need," he assures, pressing the card into her hand, "Fake it until you make it a wise man once said, now go find me a story."

Find him a story, find him a story, and find him a story... Rena repeats on the elevator then all the way to her Camaro, *find him a story, find him a story, find him a story, but where, where? Find him a story, find him a story, where, where...* she echoes again and again, crowding her brain with the phrase 'til her fingers tap, ever so slightly, on the horn in rhythm to the mantra, moving ever faster words run together in time and touch until all that matters is the mantra calling out to eternity beckoning the big story that, while not discovered, was already written and waiting to be birthed into the world by a busty brunette princess...

"You need help, miss?"

Rena opens her eyes to find an undercover officer flashing his badge.

"Heavens no," she smiles, recycling her business card, "I'm Rena Steinman, a reporter for channel five, I'm sorry if I startled you."

"Get out of the car ma'am."

"I was just calling out to my next story, channeling if you will," she explains, exiting with the card still extended, "Rena Steinman."

"Detective Samuel Green," he responds, "So you're looking for a story?"

"I am."

"I heard one over the radio about some white woman with a wild hair up her ass who raced through an accident scene like it was Indy her last name was Earnhardt."

Rena drops her business card, forcing her to step closer to Sammy. Bending to retrieve it, she watches him watch a preview of what lay beneath her little blue skirt.

"Really?" she prods, the tip of her nose, lips, then breasts brushing his crotch as she rises to re-extend her business card to him, " "I'd love to arrange a private interview with the officer or driver involved."

Sammy whips out shiny handcuffs.

"Your car or mine?" Rena asks, extending her wrists.

She broke her first big story for channel 5 News that evening, "Yes greater Washington Metropolitan area you heard it right, Rena your channel Five Roving Reporter has uncovered evidence that supports a woman's claim that a DC detective detained her in a deserted downtown garage, handcuffed her then engaged in intercourse with her in the victim's Camaro…"

It was also her last as she fled aboard the last flight of the night to Nashville.

"It was the most embarrassing moment of my life," the old Hag wails, at the second anniversary communal dinner commemorating her greatest shame.
"It only aired in local markets ma," Rena snaps, turning on the lights, "And I got air time can you at least give me credit for that?"

@@@@@

The Man who would be senator, governor, or at a minimum mayor is swimming in anniversaries and planning to lap up every second of it. It is the twenty-seventh anniversary of the date he met Ms. Mary. That is the good one should hold onto, he decides, that life brought you something new every day. It mattered not that it also commemorates the event he most wished to erase—what good could that part of the puzzle do?

No good at all, he decides and files it away in a giant drawer in the *dark cave where he retreats to stow away the waste that had once been his wife…life…stop thinking like that, he thinks.* And does. It is the five-year anniversary of the date he joined a most prestigious firm. It ranks as one of the fastest growing law firms in the country and he is perfectly positioned to make partner. That was the good one should hold onto if one was to lead a productive, purpose driven life.

It matters not that it's also the six-year anniversary of Ms. Mary closing his firm, plunging him into a cesspool of depression from which he has yet to fully recover. *It matters not that here stands a functioning misery addict who wakes each morning detesting every waking second he'll spend that day helping someone else's firm become the fastest growing litigation machine in the country.*

What good could thinking about that part of the puzzle do?

No good, at all, he decides and files it away in a giant drawer in the dark cave where he retreats *to stow away the waste that had once been his wife, life…stop thinking like that,* he thinks.

55

And does.

It is the four-year anniversary of his unsuccessful race for office. It had been a good, clean, competitive run affording him a rush like few he'd felt. It was as if all his hard work, good decisions, and difficult choices raced together towards a destiny that would confirm he was, indeed, living a morally productive purpose driven life. That was the good one should hold onto if one wished to achieve said state.

It matters not it also marks the one year anniversary of the resignation of the victor of said race, prompting a run-off for the open seat spurring his wife to vow divorce if he so much as thought about inching toward said seat.
He thought about it anyway.
She knew immediately.
He stopped thinking about it.
What good could it do? Absolutely none and that was the good one should focus on if one wished to lead a productive, purpose driven life.

It is the two month anniversary of official confirmation the Colgate Chaplain was, indeed dead. It is the one-month anniversary of the first spontaneous, un-artificially inspired erection he experienced in the grieving widow's presence, and the one-week anniversary of the same said Mary officially moving in with he and his knife oops wife.
And that is the good he will hold onto as he aspires to engage in a productive, purpose driven life.

@@@@@

Orpheus Gray, Opie to officer's at the precinct and others of little perception or understanding, yearned to be in law enforcement his whole life or at least since he was eight. That was year his dad rolled away like a stone down a mountain except they lived on an island, Staten Island, and his already overworked mom had to take on another job to make ends meet.

His older brother, Bradley, was assigned to watch and otherwise nurture the nuisance he called nuisance, unless something better sprang to mind. The idiotic names, however, were the least of the young Orpheus' worries; he was far more concerned with his older brother's career aspirations.

"I've wanted to be a cat burglar since I crawled out of the crib," the fourteen-year old said for the fifteenth time.

56

"But they're criminals," Orpheus says, squinting against the sun, "You'd go to jail."

Bradley launched his eyes to heaven, "Holy Moses, Opie, thieves and crooks are criminals; cat burglars are professionals. They go to fancy parties, drink fancy beer with butlers then rob the rich bastards blind after they fall asleep."

"Kind of like Robin Hood."
"Exactly, except you'll never catch me wearing green tights."

Cat burglars needed practice so Orpheus tagged along that night on Brad's pioneer training mission.

Mom listened and apologized, listened and apologized and listened some more to the officers who collared them before explaining, "Their father said he was going for a walk and kept on walking."

They nod as if she said the magic words then gave us another lecture for good measure before releasing us. Mom was quiet as a church mouse as we followed her out of the police station and home where she wished us good night and went to bed.

We woke the next morning to the smell of sizzling bacon and leapt from bed.
"It's been too long since I made you two breakfast," Mom said, when we materialized like magic, "Run and wash up, these are almost ready."
It was the first time she used the waffle iron since dad rolled away on an otherwise ordinary day and soon, the cat burglar and his assistant dive into golden piles of heaven topped with whipped cream and strawberries.
"Leave the dishes for me," she warns, planting a kiss atop their heads before disappearing down the hall.

They were only too happy to oblige, stuffing themselves like blowfishes until everything in sight was gone. Full beyond their wildest dreams, they waddled outside to share their illegal adventures with friends, who stood, salivating, faces pressed against the kitchen window.

Their fan club begs Brad to retell the story for the third time. Their mother pulled up beside them in the old white Chevy their father had, like them, left behind, "Hop in my loves."

They climb in, beaming, while friends turn green with envy over why some guys got to have cool moms who were proud to call criminals her sons.

@@@@@@

It came together so seamlessly that neither could recall who proposed the mourning Mary move into their mansion. At the end of the day, the offer appeared as benign as sand and simply what pillars of the community did in unfortunate situations such as these. After all, the twins were adults off doing God knows what young people their age did, they more than had the room, suites, in fact and why not provide respite to a shell shocked soul crumbling in the aftermath of a bloodbath that's transformed her life.

His wife, who suffered flashes of maternal instinct, approached the poor dear, who she privately pegged Casper,[21] to discuss the idea. When the weeping widow resisted, I was enlisted to help the distraught damsel see the wisdom of our wishes.

She politely declined.

Unwilling to be stripped of our right to provide relief to the needy, we next enlisted the aid of Reverend Fisher, our current minister, to help the poor dear understand the sad truth: sometimes you have to surrender and let others take care of you.

Presently she acquiesced and settled into the blue or tranquility suite, named after the Lincoln bedroom at the White House, on the main level.
"Our quarters are upstairs and the den is down, I love to eat but I don't cook so don't expect to see me much," Ms. Mary explains, "When I'm not out you'll usually find me upstairs reading so call me, on one of the intercoms, if you need anything."

"Thank you," Casper whispers then disappears.

The next eve the trio attends a candlelight service honoring victims of crime at the Divinity School. As they enter Benton Chapel classmates swarm around Mary, whisking his widow away. Ms. Mary points. He is about to sit when Reverend Fisher gestures... *thank God*... "The reverend needs me."

---

[21] See the Friendly Ghost

He watches Mary from his post near the pulpit, the way she moves, drifts actually, feet barely touching the ground, the way her lids descend masking eyes that make his bellybutton quiver... even when they fill with tears. He fidgets as the organ moans its initial melody filling the hall with woe *is me I came here to be near the widow,* he thinks over and over, anxious to make his move.

A keen sense of caution warns him to wait... but there the widow rocks, crestfallen, fragile, and looking finer than a honey soaked spiraled ham. He abandons his post near the pulpit and, in full view of and the entire congregation, commandeers a seat next to the weeping former Little Mary Sunshine, places his arm around her shoulder and pulls her close while she sobs...body, bones really, shivering... firm peach shaped breasts brushing against his flushed skin.

He inhales deeply but discreetly, rocking her more and more gently while the spiritual community looks on approvingly, Ms. Mary sleeps, and he prays, *As Christ is my cloak let me not soak my suit...*he strokes her firm arm, bones honestly, brushing against her peachy left breast rhythmically with the rock also known as often as humanly possible...and exhales, praying something new now that St. Peter gushes like Old Faithful. And suddenly life feels akin to something he might actually want to make it through alive.

Having a mourner in the house proves his theory; it is, indeed, the next best thing to having orgasms in church. Last month' tomb is this month's social club as concerned classmates and friends come to call. Mary, an undercover southern girl, has her own suspicions. Some based on lore about food not furnished to guests being the shortest road to hell, "Outside of a lie," the widow shares, removing two apple pies from the oven, "besides, cooking always makes me feel better."

"Funny, you don't look like the kind of girl who would be able to cook," he observes, leaning across the island with a contented smile.

She returns his smile and for the first time, it actually reaches her eyes, "That's funny, that's exactly what Jackson used to say."

"Then it must be true, I—
"Honey," he hears, but it sounds like anything but, "Is that you?"

He furrows his brow, closes his eyes, tightly, as if against an assault, purses his lips, takes a pained breath... clenches his fists, parts his lips and practically hums, "Yes, honey, I'm coming..."

59

What the fuck was that? Mary wonders, pretending not to notice.

"See you later," he whispers and scurries up the stairs.

He enters the suite ahead of his heart which is still pounding when it finally arrives.

"You're late," she notes, never looking up from her book, *Falling Out of Grace.*

"The chamber of commerce meeting ran long," he explains, shedding his shoes.

"I was going to ask you to bring me a glass of water on your way up."

"Hmmm."

"Something smells good, what's Casper cooking down there?"

"Apple pie I think."

"Apple pie you think," she snorts, turning the page, "You never met a dessert you didn't recognize."

"Hmmm," he says heading to the door.

"Where are you going?"

"To get your water."

"Thanks honey, bring me back a piece of whichever pie looks most perfect."

He re-enters the aroma rich kitchen with a smile that evaporates as soon as he sees the picture perfect pies cooling on the marble island. While hospitable to pleasantries over pastries Casper otherwise preoccupied herself running, apartment or job hunting, or hiding out it her room hindering his carefully orchestrated attempts to engage her when he is not otherwise occupied working, teaching, meeting, or volunteering.

"Honey," he hears but it sounds like anything but, "What's taking so long down there?"

He refuses to answer[22] and concentrates on cutting her pie just so before scurrying back upstairs.

"What took so long?"

"The pie was still hot so the first piece broke up."

"You know I detest messy desserts—

"That's why I cut you another piece," he assures, shedding his suit in favor of battered shorts and a t-shirt.

"You forgot the water."

---

[22] okay he does answer

"Hmmm," he says and heads back downstairs.

He'd carefully orchestrated yet another opportunity to run into his angel before he crawled into bed with the beast from eternity. When he reaches the island the strains of Forensic Files float from her room joining the heat still drifting from fragrant apple pies, it was her favorite show. At the freezer, he debates his next move. He could just knock on the door, pop his head in and say hi or goodnight or how's it hanging...
He chuckles.
He made a funny.
"Honey," he hears, and heads back upstairs with the desert and two pints of peach ice cream.

"I wanted to make sure you didn't need anything before I turned in," he says breathlessly, bursting into Mary's room following another carefully orchestrated excuse to spend more time with her.

She drifts like a dream from her place at the window, "No, but thank you," she says then hovers, waiting for him to leave so she can slip back between the covers.

"Goodnight then," he says, crossing the room to pat her on the head before planting a light kiss on her forehead.

"Goodnight," she answers with a weak, yet, he intrinsically feels, affectionate smile, before walking him to the door and softly closing, then locking it behind him.

@@@@@

The door had barely closed behind them before the hot sun, quiet hum of the car, and the heavy breakfast lulled the aspiring criminals to sleep and when they woke they found themselves parked in a dark yard in the middle of nowhere.

"Bradley, Opie!" Grandma Tate exclaimed when, afraid and uncommonly hungry, the boys finally worked up the nerve to get out and feel around for some form of life.

"Your mom is out like a light, it's a long ride from your neck of the woods to Nashville," she reports, grabbing his hand which then grabs Brad's, "I guess you two tulips are hungry?"

She could see their enthusiastic nods even before she turned the lights on.

"So, what will it be meatloaf, chicken, or chess pie?" All three was the answer and the next hours were spent eating, doing Elvis impersonations, and playing word games in the room Grandma Tate called the parlor. We finally fell asleep in our banana splits and when we woke the sun was high and the smell of bacon was back but the old white Chevy was long gone.

"Your mom headed home," Grandma Tate explained pouring cod liver oil atop bacon flavored Purina, "The way we figure it a summer in the middle of nowhere might just keep you little criminals out of jail."

And so began our season in the dead zone, a seemingly endless stream of days during which Brad prowled empty unpaved roads in search of excitement or even a cigarette butt while I drowned myself in black and white westerns.

"It's our anniversary," Grandma Tate announced, entering the parlor after another Purina fest.

It had been three days.

She turned off the fuzzy tube, "Your mind is mush," she explained, dragging us kicking and screaming to the Police Boys and Girls Club, a dungeon in the basement where cops outnumbered kids, boys' outnumbered girls, and a pig always guarded the door.

Brad was ready to kill himself.
 I was in hog heaven.
And frankly Grandma Tate didn't give a damn.

@@@@@

Camille decides to loop around the city by way of I-40, exiting at Church Street to cruise by Play to check out the crowd. The lot and side streets overflow with aluminum, a very promising sign. Winding, swaying bodies slither past Tribe and down the street then around like headhunters welcoming prey while arriving partygoers brave three city blocks to join the fray.

Pleased, she U-turns and cruises back down Church and through downtown before ripping across the chasm separating the coliseum from its neighbor, Shelby Avenue. The historic district had seen better than worse then better then worse and now, getting better again

62

days on the coat tails of young white couples who, beamers and strollers in tow, were moving in like the mafia.

Soon this area will morph into a version of so many before it. Cops would crack down to make way for the good middle class folks. Reinforcements would arrive as clockwork, pushing the disenfranchised further into obscurity, where exiles wait to be accepted into neighboring suburbs before bomb rushing the wall as if it has Jericho stamped all over it. That made this the time to act.

She steers the black Benz into Cayce homes, the belly of the beast. She breathes deeply, sucking in the soul of her surroundings, makes peace with them, and heads down along the beast's buttocks where the abandoned apartments lay. Shadows dance by the foggy windows animated by some semblance of support, they were the walking dead, always witnessing, wandering, some aimless, others with a single-minded mission; to search out those who might serve as prey in this, the valley of dry bones. Camille kills the engine. Immediately its windshield is tapped upon twice.

"What's your pleasure?" Reggie begins, then, recognizing her, "Hey Chip a Hoy you lost or just feening?"
"Neither, I have a meeting with the Dog."
He rounds the car and hops in, "I'll lead the way."

@@@@@@

From his throne at the head of the mahogany conference table, the Dog closes his eyes to wave after wave of bills hundred dollar bills... flowing...flowing, flowing... *no dancing...dancing bills kicking their legs high...man, look at the thighs on those phat...*

"Ahem," his henchman, Birdie, hums.

The Dog opens one eye to a fine, phat babe that would look real good all naked and wrapped in hundred dollar bills.

"Mr. Birdsong," Phat begins, extending a luscious hand.
"Shout out to the Big Dog, all my friends do."
"Shout out, big Dog I'm hosting a business diversification dinner for a couple of your colleagues and I thought you could be the guest of honor."

A broad smile crosses the Dog's face, "I guess that means I get to dive in first."

"As deep as you dare."

The smile takes over the Dog's face.

It is not for Camille but instead Evander, his head henchman, who bears an uncanny resemblance to the boxer right clear down to the chewed off ear. Half an Ear acknowledges the affirmation with a mighty roar that refuses to be drowned out by the wailing slip of a man being dragged behind him.

"Well, if it ain't Lester the kiddie molester," Big Dog sings in perfect pitch then winks at Camille, "Let's take a little ride."

The ten of them pile into cars and set off.

"This Benz is the da bomb."

"Well that's high praise coming from you Dog."

"Damn straighty, my lady, stop right here."

They have traveled half a block.   The vehicles holding the henchmen come to a stop behind them. Big Dog and Camille exit da bomb and head for the front door.

At their Alpha Male's signal, the pack extracts Lester from Camille's trunk.   Evander hurries ahead of them to open the rickety front door. A horde of rats scurry in the face of upright predators.

"Give me some light, Lenny," the Dog barks.

And there was light.

"How long you been out this time Lester?"

The wailer just whimpers.

"How long Lester?"

"Twooo…twoo..two days buuttt…"

"Shhh…I know," the Dog whispers, massaging the man's quivering shoulder blades, "Buuttt that's what you s-s-said when they caught you raping little Mary Sunshine,"

"When was that?" he asks, turning to his Head sans ear.

"Seven years ago today," Evander answers without hesitation.

"Strip him," the Dog barks.

The once again wailing, stammering, molester is stripped bare as the day he was born before you can say it then dragged to the center of the room where they bind him, lotus style, to a sturdy beam.

"I-I-I di-di-did-n't do i-t-t"

"Lester, look at me," Camille instructs, and he does, "I'm here, you're not alone but you must speak truthfully, we're all family here."

"The hell you say!" Big Dog barks.

"L-L-lorrrenz-ooohh"

"Did he say Lorenzo?" Evander asks.

The Dog barks.

Literally.

The pack joins in

"There is no room for falsehoods here, Lester," Camille says above the din, "Fate is knocking."

Lester wails.

The wolves laugh so hard they can barely howl.

Camille addresses the assembly, "The sun has already set on anger, allowing the devil his foothold, let us engage in no further unwholesome acts but only what benefits all involved."

"The hell you say?" Big Dog asks, wiping away tears.

"Lester?" she prods, then waits until he looks up.

When he does, he swims in an ocean of compassion and sympathy.

"You didn't mean to hurt her did you; you're just not well..."

"I'm sick I tell them I'm sick the little ones they make me sick Go-ggood dammitttt!"

"Shhh, " Camille whispers, "Do not grieve the holy spirit with whom you are sealed."

"You heard the man," the Dog barks, snapping his fingers.

A paper sack materializes.

"Lester," Camille advises, "Close your eyes now and take a deep breath. Breathe in peace, hold it, then release it along with all bitterness, rage, anger, and every form of malice or thought of ill will."

Big Dog takes a large jar of Peter Pan from the sack and sinks his huge paw deep into the peanut butter, "Somebody come hold this limp thing up for me."

The men look at each other then to Camille who steps forward and kneels down, gently searching for then supporting the limp appendage. The Dog slathers Peter Pan all around it, coating it, as well as his crotch, several times over.

Lester begins to sob again.

"Don't cry," Camille comforts, "Pray and you will be forgiven as Christ forgives all who call upon him."

"The hell you say," Big Dog chuckles, licking leftover peanut butter from his fingers, "Kill the light!"

And then there is darkness…and Lester's screams as a rat reunion gather to feast.

@@@@@@

Dr. Professor Charles Marion Dates, his date, his ex, and the love of his life[23] were all out for a night on the town at Blackstone Brewery.

"Just look at him," Dates decides, peering from behind his cognac, "He's beautiful, sinfully so, and still single surely a sign he really wants to come back to me."
And why wouldn't he?

Sure there were gay men with even gayer hardware around every corner and under every bush but primo wasn't like pussy.
It wasn't all created equal.

Sure any Joe or Joanna can find that "special" someone if they were willing to go piece meal. Trade a little personality for a little passion, a little less libido for a little more comfortable way of life, a little ugly for a little more love— piece meal.

But a package, now a package is something different. A package wasn't pussy, you weren't just gonna find it around every corner or under every bush. A package was personality, passion, and a pork barrel full of other things positive, pretty, and starting with "p" but pussy was not counted among them.

He and Remington Steele[24] were a couple for twelve years, seven months, twenty-four days, six hours, eighteen minutes fifty six, no seven seconds. More or less.
They were the toast of the cultural, theological, and intellectually elite. They were Taylor and Burton, Bogart and Hepburn, Ben & Jerry's, Jurgen and Elizabeth,[25] they were madly in love with each other and knee deep in life and the pursuit of all things intellectually and physically stimulating when the beautiful, big balled, bigger dicked bastard came home and dropped the fucking bomb—he was dumping me for a beauty school dropout.

---

[23] all of whom are the same person
[24] God, can you believe that name?
[25] heathens see Moltmann

Can you say grease or at least Vaseline? It was like some sadist plunged me into the dead zone without sticking dynamite up my ass first and the shit was really fucked the hell up— I mean what do you do when a tongue stops spinning and it's your turn to hop on and ride? *Just look at this bitch* he thinks, gratefully accepting a fresh cognac from his date, his ex, and the love of his life.

They did this dance every year, same time, same place— like clock fucking work. You know just to exhibit to each other and the entire gay and straight world that they could, that it was completely possible for homos to have a hard yet horribly cordial, messy, compassionate break-up and remain good friends… *Oh great,* he thinks, draining his fifth, *the bitch's cell phone wants to ring now.*

Remington answers in that deep throaty voice that still makes his bellybutton quiver.

"You hard as steel bitch," he hissed[26] for all he was worth, *I'd give anything to turn you over, spread your cheeks wide and—*"What?"
"I said that was Tyson trying to find parking," the Steel Bitch says, standing his fine ass up, "Just stay there, I can't wait for you two to meet."

"Fuck," the suddenly dizzy Dates mutters, signaling the waiter for a refill while the fine asshole saunters out of the restaurant.

The bitch was forever wanting to wave his newest fine, packing, fucking package in his face knowing full well the former love of his life was beginning to fear he would soon find himself labeled among the pieces instead of the packages…the very thought of it all makes his head and heart hurt so much he feels in fear of fainting or farting.

"Charles?" Remington whispers in that deep voice that still makes his bellybutton quiver.

What the fuck, he decides, lifting his heavy, seasick head so his date, ex, and the love of his life can parade his pride and joy package before his pathetic piece meal eyes.

"This is Tyler," the Asshole announces, introducing him to a fucking pussy.

---

[26] inside

@@@@@@

"I told you it wouldn't take long for something to kick off in there," Green crows, snatching up the last doughnut, "You can't buy this kind of entertainment."

"No truer words were ever spoken," Opie observes.

An unbelievably beautiful man smashes through the glass window followed by a petite blonde with a guy's hands still wrapped around her neck.

"I guess we better break this up," Green says, getting out of the cruiser, "You coming bright eyes and bushy-fucking tailed?"

@@@@@

Mary was running for her life.

Personally she always fancied herself partial to something more peaceful like pills but popping was far too obvious—the insurance policy would never pay out. She pondered drowning but ruled it out for the simplest of reasons; she was a control freak who couldn't swim.

Though she hated guns she could really fall hard for a hollowed out bullet right about now but, alas, she is in Forest, not Green Hills so she would have to settle for the next best thing—running alone, midday, at Radnor Lake where, it is rumored, Janet March is buried and bats begin circling at sunset.

Her newfound addiction to the activity is, she recently realized, a piece of the puzzle, part of a master plan that will, ultimately, hopefully, as in sooner rather than later, reunite her with the love of her life. *The sooner the better*, she repeats, lest she be overcome by a legion of Commie's kids high on Hummie's empathy laden pastoral counseling courses.

While their intentions are honorable they conjure images of an evangelical Jerry Springer audience peering over walls, around corners, and from beneath rocks watching and waiting for her to crack, to start *ranting and raging about faith versus fair, the ex love of her life or the late love of her life or the anything but what they were actually thinking which was the somewhere dead and decaying love of her life...*"Stop thinking that!" she snaps, bringing the car to a screeching halt at the Granny White market.

Where was she going?

To Radnor Lake to run she remembers and puts the car into gear again, pulling out and in front of an eighteen wheeler which catapults onto its side to avoid wiping her out. *That was almost extremely lucky or not depending on how you look at it*, she theorizes, cruising by the Purity Milk truck, wheels still spinning, *I could be dead and reunited with relatives reaping insurance rewards or just non critically crushed and covered with white stuff that's going for four bucks a gallon.*

What the fuck! She thinks.

And fights back tears. Here lay the wrinkle with this whole suicide disguised as death thing—if not done properly and with proper foresight the first time, you were just kind of fucked. By fate, family, friends, or just poorly paid strangers who check on or fuck you late at night as you lay, not quite dead, but in a persistent vegetative state brought on by your own piss poor, lacking proper backwards planning and foresight the first fucking time failure.

What the fuck! She thinks.

And fights back tears, first pulling into then reversing and backing into a parking space.
Twice.

I made it, she thinks, fighting back tears. *This phenomenon is either a good or a bad sign depending on how one looks at it. I'm here now so I may as well run even though running will hurt like hell but I already hurt like hell already, all over, but mainly on the inside but at least if I run I'll hurt all on the outside as well but I already hurt so much inside but if I run it'll hurt all over the outside as well as the inside and maybe that'll give me balance besides the sooner I start running the sooner I run into a sociopath itching to put me out of my pain...*

What the fuck! She thinks, fighting back tears before finally giving up then getting out of her car an hour later.

Drying her tears, she reties her shoes for the fifth time and starts to run, past the leisurely, elderly, and assorted folks that frequent the fragile forest where death and life intertwine like lovers lost in their plan. She had been dragged to Lover's Lane first by Ms. Mary who fancied the trails.

"I'm not a hiker," Mary had insisted.
"You'll enjoy it, plus I promised Jeri we would meet her there today."
"I'm really not predisposed towards mystics…"
"Oh she's not like that, she's highly spiritual but she's also one of Vanderbilt's most respected financial analysts so, trust me, her head is firmly grounded on her shoulders."
Because she was living rent free and couldn't say no she grudgingly agreed.

"There you are," Jeri, whose head sat, literally, on her shoulders gushed, grabbing her as soon as she stepped from the car, "Come to momma you poor baby." The busty midget wrapped her arms around Mary's thighs while her hostess looked on with unabashed approval.
"Sorry, but your nose is tickling my bellybutton," Mary finally says when the embrace shows no sign of ebbing.

We hiked four excruciatingly slow miles through steep trails where death and life lay, rose, or hung in gentle balance like ballerinas frozen in time. It was exquisite art that only nature could produce and the only thing that kept me from beating my brains out against the nearest boulder while my captors droned on incessantly about china, spirituality, and New Testament trivia…
"What do you think Mary?"
"Hmmm."
It worked for her husband.

Ms. Mary looks exasperated, "Do you think you could whip up a couple of those luscious punch bowl cakes for my lesser half's law school dinner, if you're up to it that is?"

"Sure," she said and…actually she really couldn't remember any more about that day. It was as much a fog as her previous indeterminate outings in the dead zone since her soul mate did exactly what it had sworn never to do.

Increasing her pace she passes the second parking lot and heads up a series of small hills encompassing a much less traveled portion of the park leading to Franklin Road. There and back, an orthodontist training for the next Music City Marathon told her, equaled eight miles. .She has never run that far before but she has never survived dying before either. *What the fuck!* She thinks, really starting to feel the run.

She can't get her rhythm together, her chest is tight, her breathing ragged as shards of hell *but hell is just a state of mind* she reminds herself, pounding one foot firmly on the ground in front of another. *At least it's one of its states and I'm firmly trapped in it hell how am I supposed to do this live I mean when I'm dead the walking talking running dead and nobody seems to notice?*

Well, that isn't entirely true, she admits, fighting to quicken her pace.

There are people who know she's not really there and those are the people she must avoid you know the ones that look at you with complete all consuming pity as if saying, "You poor dead dear would you like to lie down?" *When any bastard worth his birthright knew that lying down was the last thing the dead wanted to do because eventually they would have to get up which is the absolute hardest thing in the universe for a dead person to do especially when said dead is popping pills and chasing with Pinot in order to slip ever deeper to death so the next day the rotting shell that used to be her life can pretend to still live until dusk settles like sand on the Sahara and her chenille draped coffin calls once again from the shadows...*

"Where the fuck did that come from?" she whispers, pushing the tomb to keep moving when what she really wants is to stop running but she can't because the pain on the outside has yet to equal the pain on the inside which means she still has no balance but why would a dead person need balance?

"Do not stop running," she yells. *You're running for your life; if you stop your heart will stop and you'll lose all hope and didn't Jackson always say that depression was a hope deficiency in disguise but so was death, the great destroyer that sprang from the tree of life like a lamb but was a beast, reality that was a dream drenched in blood, but death was just an illusion, eternity masquerading as a last breath so why wouldn't it just yank off it's mask and—*"Show yourself!" The weary, wailing, sprinting Widow screams into the fragile forest.

And the long shadow of Death steps from the trees, stopping her dead in her tracks.

71

Cry Freedom

"I am Mary the Marionette and I am guilty of my crimes:
Of once being God
For being a daughter of Eve, Sophia, Hera or whoever was originally evil
thus dooming us all

Of dwelling in a body that is not mine belonging to others
 some cruel, some kind

Of daring or of yearning to be free for grabbing holdst of life
 Instead of
Letting it
dangle
 me

Of warring, of whoring for causing strife for loving
 for hovering of bringing
 forth life

For fucking, for faking, for reaping
 What's sown for having or failing to have
A mind of
 My
 own.

Of fishing of flying for laughing for crying for cradling, for killing, of
helping, of healing, of
Lying of loving when all hope seems
 lost.

Of being subjugated, raped, and murdered en masse
Of crying wolf, for cutting or smoking my grass
 whilst all the while my soul
 Cried Freedom

For failing to fall
For being more manly than many
Of surrendering the ghost for did not my soul cry
Freedom?

Of asking why must there be one and why must it be man?
Why must power rest within hands?
Does it not also
Cry freedom?

Of eating apples or oranges or running out of time
I am Mary the Marionette,
I am guilty of my crimes."

Flocks of reporters circle the Capitol like vultures at a Vegas hit man convention. Some, to include Rena the Roving, are still in sleeping bags but the majority make the most of the networking opportunity, courting tips and confidential sources over coffee and warm Crispy Crèmes.

Rumors had been flying for weeks about the downfall of the Governor who, it is rumored, wears a girdle, abhors the uninsured, aids and abets sexual harassment, and generally fails to uphold the ethics of his administration. His long time friend, the Mayor, while supportive in private has his heart locked on the poor bastard's job so publicly avoids the approaching anathema.[27]

That said, he is none too happy when the Joe shows up, announced, in the dead of night like a knocked up whore looking for a welfare handout. Thinking him merely on the run from feminists or the terminally ill, synonyms in the Mayor's mind, he reluctantly and under cover of darkness provided him refuge only to wake to restless descendents of Brutus camped out on his front lawn.

How had he, a man who prided himself on intricacies, missed a fucking bomb?

"Are they gone yet?" the Yellow Belly asks as his Spokesman, Andy, approaches.
"No way, they're dug in deeper than a gerbil up Richard Gere's—
"I get the idea."
"They even ordered port a potties," Andy continues, amused by their fore planning.
"Any new leads on the bomber?" the Governor asks.

"No, but overnight polls say 6.2% of the public think the bomb should have exploded in your bed," The Senator from Tennessee quips, stepping from the shadows.

"Can I have the good news first?" the Governor responds and they share a laugh.
"That was the good news," Andy adds, slapping his boss on the back.

---

[27] abomination

After placing a call to the Director of Homeland Security, Andy strolls down the walkway leading to the press; a look of practiced concern on his face. Sleepers spring from bags while Rena fights with, then scurries from, a port a potty. Completely unrehearsed and un-orchestrated, cameras flash and lights come up as soon as Andy's size eights hit the podium, "The Governor has pulled a muscle and will be unable to run this morning" he quips and waits for at least polite appreciation from his audience.

"Forget fatso, we came for the bombs!" A bullhorn booms.
To appreciative applause.
"The TBI and ATF are on the scene, gathering evidence on the cause of the explosions but we're not going to speculate until all the facts come in."

"Forget the facts you little mouthpiece, tell us what you think!" The bullhorn bellows darn near blowing him backwards.

Hearty laughter ripples across the mutinous mask wearing media that, just months before, crowned him one of the buckle of the Bible belt's most eligible bachelors. "Who said that?" he demands, mentally taking on his boxer's stance, "We maintain an air of mutual respect and civility here that will not be compromised."

"You're no George Stephanolopos, you little hobbit!"

The jackals are openly enjoying themselves now. Andy scans the crowd, searching for the eyes belonging to the buzzard feeding on him right here in full view of the public while the cameras roll...he clears his throat and continues, "We expect to learn shortly who is behind this most grievous act and rest assured, they will be dealt with swiftly and accordingly, thank you."

Turning, the Governor's mouthpiece walks swiftly and a bit too stiffly, in Rena's opinion, away and disappears into the hole from which he was obviously pushed by his superiors. *I rattled the hobbit's cage pretty good* she decides picking up her bullhorn and heading off in search of the nearest port a potty. This was her first foray into the political press pit and while she snagged no exclusive she definitely made her voice heard.

Her questioning revealed an important truth, the mouthpiece, Andy, is an issue laden, blindly ambitious son of a bitch but, she decides, getting back to business, he's single, employed, cute, and, rumor said, possibly convertible.

This was going to be a good day.

@@@@@@

Green and Opie cruise Shelby Ave. toward Lillian Place to drop off their impromptu passenger who, according to Green, gave head like nobody's business but knew how to keep her mouth shut.

"What the hell you mean, you ain't got time to take me to lunch *and* give me a ride home?" the Mute demands, needlessly rearranging perfectly coiffed hair she dared him to touch while he banged her from behind, "I don't bust nuts to go home hungry *or* hoofing it."

"Okay, I'll drive through Krystals."
"Krystals? I ain't no midget, shaughty," she flicks her frozen hair, "You know, it's mud stumper[28] day at the Silver Sands."
"Krystal's."
"Sweat's."
"Krystal's."
"Harper's and that's my final offer."
"A Big Mac and a ride home."
She nods.
Show him a seventeen-year old slut who couldn't be bought for a Big Mac and he'd show you a fish fillet lover.

"There's Reggie…Reg-gie!" the Mute screams, waving wildly and hanging from the window at the same time.
"Shut the fuck up, this ain't no hog calling contest," Green screams.

Opie feigns invisibility while his partner glares in his rearview mirror at the disappearing young men. *What the hell was Reggie doing out this time of day?*
"You're gonna pass McDonalds," the Mute warns, flicking her hair.

Dolly didn't start kicking 'til dusk and rarely spread her legs before eleven so why were they out so early…who gives a cunt? He

---

[28] pig's feet

75

decides, tossing a bag containing two Big Macs into the back seat. The slut catches the sack midair and digs in like a shovel. *This heifer is chomping hard as a cow on cud*, Green thinks and laughs at his choice of words.

To this day he didn't know what the hell a cud was. It was the favorite phrase of his eighth grade American history instructor, a fat ass cracker with a fake accent and funky ass farts. He drove that fat freak crazy: sleeping in class, blowing spitballs, yawning from the front row while he carried on and on about the great Christopher Columbus or some such shit.

"What do you know about American history?" the Cracker challenged, waving his pointer.
"Everything I need to."
"And what precisely is that Master Green?"

"That the white man has been screwing the black man since he dragged him here in chains."

The fart was so angry he lost his accent and slipped into some Cajun ass shit that had to be straight outta Louisiana. It shocked us but it fucked with him so bad he excused himself and didn't come back for three weeks. When he did however he came packing a new approach to higher education.

"You're never gonna amount to nothing," he'd hiss in his fake ass British accent then waddle away like the fat Cajun cracker barrel fag he was.

I wish I could find him now, Green thinks, bringing the undercover cruiser to a stop in front of the whore house, *I'd kill to show him how wrong he was*, "Come on Shrek, un-ass that seat, this ain't no ride at Disneyland."

The Mute shoots him an ugly look, flicks her frozen hair, and gets out.
Yeah, he thinks, driving away, *I should look the psychic up.*

@@@@@

Ree-Ree took the afternoon off from her job as Director of the African American Cultural Center at Vanderbilt to evaluate a vacant house on Shelby Avenue. *Damn*, she observes, arriving at her destination. She can't help but notice the young drug dealers congregating on the corner, "Lord could this place be a *little* closer to that imaginary line?" she whispers.

Knowing one needed to make a few friends in a new neighborhood before acquiring enemies, she chooses to ignore them, concentrating instead on keeping her footing as she climbs crumbling steps. Locking what little there is of a door behind her she takes out the high-end video cam her boyfriend, Ricky, surprised her with the day before. She turns it on. Rats scurry across the floor. "Damn," she screams running head first into a beam in the middle of the room. "Damn," she mutters, feeling her way to the musty, mildewed curtains she pulls down to allow light into the hovel of her dreams.

Startled rats run around like blind mice inspiring Ree-Ree to retreat she by way of exploring the upper level. She is pleasantly surprised to find the stairs leading to the second floor quite stable and soon discovers a large, though battered, bedroom with huge windows and loads of potential, "Well, praise the Lord," she exclaims, settling on the floor for a smoke to celebrate. Sixty seconds later she relaxes, savoring the pungent smell and trying to con herself into taking a look at the basement.

@@@@@

Green predicts the punk bitches will be gone when he cruises down Shelby... but there they are, shootin' the shit. He brings the car to a stop and gets out. Two mutts melt away but Reggie and his running dog stare him down.

"I know you two saw me glide down a few minutes ago so why y'all still here, you tryin' to disrespect me?"

"Ain't no crime to stand on a sidewalk and socialize," Reggie answers, and turns to resume his conversation.

@@@@@@

"So now you're gonna be a Pussy! You were a tough guy a minute ago," Ree-Ree hears.
Then, silence.
Rising to her feet, she takes in the scene below through the lens of her video cam. A hefty officer aims his nine millimeter at the base of a

kneeling young man's head. Another young man stands, his hands behind his head, being guarded by a tall, red-haired, freckled faced officer.

"You know what I oughtta do?" The chubby Cop asks.
She can only assume rhetorically.
Silence answers.
"I oughtta bust my size twelve's up 'yo punk ass!'"
Well, who would look forward to that? Ree-Ree wonders.
He presses the gun deeper into the kneeling boy's neck.
She can only assume for emphasis.
Ree-Ree pans the scene taking in the undercover cruiser with flashing lights, zooms in on its license plate then back to the young men, one standing…
…the other still on his knees.

"You bitches are all the same…" Chubby continues.
Ree-Ree lowers her camera and raises the rickety window, "Hey! why don't you try talking to them with a little respect?"
"…Running your mouth when you know it's only good for one sucking thing…"

"Hey!! Why don't you try talking to them with a little respect!" she yells, louder.
And then there is silence.

So she settles back in and is about to relight her joint when the rickety door commences rattling like heavy chains on the deck of an old slave ship. She hurries down the surprisingly stable stairs, waving stagnant, slightly weedy air as she goes. The door threatens to separate from its last hinge just as she reaches it.
"Yes?"
"Were you directing your comments our way?"
The red haired, freckled faced officer asks, turning ever so slightly to the side so, she assumes, his holstered glock shows.

She stares at him blankly.
He returns her stare.
"Miss…"She finally prompts.
"Miss?" He repeats, perplexed.
His partner and the two young men look on.

"My name is Ms. Tubbman and what I said was," she repeats, raising her voice so his chubby partner can hear, "Why don't you fine officers speak to these young men with a little more respect?"

"Miss Tubbman," Freckles offers, "I think you'd do well to stay out of this, we know these guys—

"And knowing them means its okay to call them little pussies? How would you like it if someone called you little pussies?"

"Mind your mouth," Chubby snaps, walking away from the boys and towards her, "We know these boys."
"You mean you're homeys? Cause when you're homeys it rolls off your tongue like, *man, you gone be a lil pussy now?* And everything's cool but this," She waves her finger for effect, "Doesn't appear to be cool."

By now a small crowd gathers.

"I bet you don't just roll up on white kids talking on the street in Green Hills or Belle Meade and dare them not to be a pussy."

"Correction, little pussy," Camille observes, stepping past the observers to join Ree-Ree on the past well worn porch.

Green glares at the natives in disgust, "Get your asses outta here."

They, like spirits, melt away while he mounts the crumbling steps, "We communicate just fine with these hood rats," he hisses, "We understand them and they understand us…"

"And just what do they understand?" Ree-Ree challenges, "That if you're young and black cops, no wait, an undercover cop can just yank you up, degrade you, press a gun to the back of your head and say, "So you're gonna be a *pussy* now."

"Correction, *'lil pussy now,'*" Camille supplements, "Do you have a predilection for little pussy detective?"

@@@@@@

Mary recognizes the gift for what it is—a miracle. It arrived in an unmarked package on the anniversary of the 91st day since Jackson was murdered, done in, indeed, by vampires. Its cover is stamped *Good Grief* and she cracks the binder to find:

79

for Boodie written in Jackson's flowing script.

She melts into the marble floor right there at the door and sobs like a babe for its bottle until she, laden with tears, dribbles down to the bottom basement stair some hours later. Only then does she begin to read:

Good Grief

ARE YOU SUFFERING FROM SHELLSHOCK*

1. How many much time has elapsed since the loss?
a.) 2wks – 1 month
b.) 1-3 months
c.) 3-6 months
d.) 1 year
e.) 2-5 years
f.) 10+ years

2. Do you know what day of the week it is?
3, Do you care what day of the week it is?
4, How long has it been since you changed your underwear?

5. Do you feel like the walking dead?
6. Are you talking to yourself often?
7. Do you still cry:

1. Never stopped
2. hourly
3. daily
4. weekly
5. occasionally

8. When you cry do you still question why this happened and/or blame yourself?
Yes   No

9. If you blame yourself, is it because you killed them?
Yes   No

* Post-traumatic stress disorder resulting from combat

Good Grief

ARE YOU SUFFERING FROM SHELLSHOCK?

1.   It doesn't matter how long it's been since you suffered the loss, you're still suffering so get over it.

2.   Who cares?

3.   If you answered yes, good for you. If you answered no, even better for you. Death causes you to move in time with a different drummer. Warning: following this drummer too long will lead to unemployment.

4.   Allow your dearly departed to guide all funk issues.

5.   A sure sign of shell shock. You *are* the walking dead but don't worry—there's a new wave of pain heading into shore any second to revive you.

6.   Only a sign of shell shock if you're answering yourself in threatening tones.

7.   Tears are a sacred language, be as fluent as you please.

8.   Cut it out.

9.   If you answered yes, you're reading the wrong book, pick up my new title, *How to cover your Ass and kiss it at the same time* due out in April.

GROPING

Perhaps, you are taking this opportunity to literally grope yourself. If you are and its making you feel better, go for it—full throttle. The groping discussed here, however, is of an internal nature as in groping for answers. This may be especially true if you are; indeed, the person who has murdered your dearly departed.   If you did it is probably best to remain quiet, and, if circumstances warrant, start groping yourself.

If you did not kill your dearly departed you might still find yourself groping. How did this happen? Why did this happen? How could I let this happen? How could God let this happen?

Demand answers, from anyone and everyone to include people who don't know who the hell you are or who your loved one was either, demand and keep on demanding, of the ocean if necessary. You may not get any answers but it'll sure tire you out after a while.

COPING

Okay, Freddy's dead, yes, dead, just like the song said. Or maybe it's Frieda, Frankie, or Frosty the Frigging Snowman. The bottom line is _____ is dead. So, how are you coping?

1. Are you sitting in a corner?   Yes   No

2. Are you pissing on yourself?   Yes   No

3. Are you shitting on yourself?   Yes   No

4. Are you sitting in a corner pissing and shitting on yourself?
                                                    Yes   No

❖ If you answered no to at least one of these questions you are doing as well as can be expected.

❖ If you answered yes to all these questions you are still doing as well as can be expected.
❖ If you answered half and half you're sitting on the fence: piss, shit, get off, or put on a diaper.

@@@@@

"I didn't need your help."
"I might've believed that before you arrived at a Belle Meade meeting in a banana boat."
"Bitch."
"Believe it or not, jail is the last thing I had in mind when I told you to meet me," Camille states for the record, smoothing an imaginary wrinkle from her black Armani suit.
Silence answers.

"In fact I have a meeting in exactly 2 hours, thirty-six minutes and twelve seconds," she continues.

"With who? The official timer for the New York City Marathon?" Ree-Ree quips.

"Bitch. With the Dog."

"So that's why you're dressed like death?"

"As opposed to?"

"An untrustworthy white Wall Street Powerbroker trapped in a black woman's body."

"And where's that white body of yours?"

Silence answers.

"The pussy power wearing off?"

"Never."

"So where is he, off trying to broker an audience with Bin Laden?"

"I thought you got paid to resolve disputes," Ree-Ree accuses, trying to flip a switch.[29]

"It was peaceful; you're not shot are you?"

Silence answers.

"I hope Ricky makes it here to bail us out before dark," Ree-Ree finally says, sitting on the hard cot, "The freaks come out at night you know…"

"So you gonna be a 'lil pussy now?" Camille dares, joining her.

@@@@@@

"So you're going to walk away from six figures and a three day work week to teach math to kids in the hood?"

"God told me to do it."

"God told you to do it."

"In a dream, he said go back to school, earn a PhD in math and teach my poor lambs calculus in inner city schools."

"Is this the same God who told you my lamp lady was a pagan symbol that screamed torch me?"

"Her shoes are curled at the ends."

"Well that settles it."

"Okay, I was a little carried away with the Nostic Gospels at the time."

"And the sign of the cross in holy water over every window and door?"

"Dead Sea Scroll flashback."

---

[29] Change the conversation

83

"Did God mention you're the one human in the western hemisphere who's worse at math than me?"

"The Lord works in mysterious ways."
"Don't throw my words back at me."
"They worked for you."
"They had to, I was debating an atheist."
"I was an agnostic."
"Same thing."
"I already signed up for the classes and wrote them a check."
"You didn't."
"I did."
"Without talking to me first?"
"Rise up like a lion to do the work of the Lord."
Mary's hands hit her hips.
"Do you think Moses asked his wife's permission before he went to Egypt?"
"No he took his cues from a spontaneously combusting bush instead."

@@@@@

It seemed forever but had been, in actuality; just a few hours before the steel bars swung wide. Ree-Ree bolted from the cell, outside, and into her Paleface's arms, kissing him long and hard before slapping him, "What the hell took so long?"
"It was a long ride," he answers, with a smile.

"It's nice to finally meet you Ricky" Camille says, extending a welcoming hand.
"When can I get my money back?"
"Well as long as a check will do—
"When I extend cash, I expect cash in return."
"Okay, Sunshine, I'm sure there's a cash machine down the street, where's your car?"

"You're looking at it," he says, unlocking a top of the line mountain bike from a pole,
"I'll meet you there," he informs Camille then turns to Ree-Ree, "You riding with me?"

Ree-Ree tries to avoid Camille's amused eyes.
"No, we'll meet you there."
Rick rides off and the two tackle the short trek to the cash machine.

84

"A bike?"

"He's energy conscious"

"So he pedaled all the way down from the mountain to pick you up?"

"Apparently."

"How long has the tang[30] been locked up?"

"Two months."

"No wonder he's on the rag."

In the near distance they see him, a lanky, tense figure with a mass of blonde curls atop a head wagging as fast as an excited dog's tail, "He's sweating that puppy like the $300 I owe him is the last in the entire machine," Camille whispers, and takes her place, second, in line. The patron ahead of her leisurely presses the keys, ultimately initiating the printing process. The ATM spits out the receipt. The man studies it carefully then tosses it on the sidewalk.

"Look you tree killer," Rick rails, turning red, "That's the third you've tossed, good God man, how many do you destroy in a week? A month? A year?"

"Who knows?" the tree-killer responds.

Rick tramples all over his personal space. He seems not to notice, pushing more buttons, and tossing more paper before collecting his cash, printing one last receipt, and tossing it to the sidewalk before walking away whistling Dixie.

"Watch my back," Camille whispers, stepping past Rick and to the ATM.

She answers the machine's inquiries quickly and is instantaneously rewarded with: *This machine is temporarily out of funds.* Camille doesn't know which is funnier, the look on his face when she reads him the message or the look when she tosses it to the ground.

"I'm horny," Ree-Ree reports without preamble, climbing onto the bike.

Rick throws a dismissive look in Camille's direction then joins her. The two pedal off into the sunset.

"And they say romance is dead," Camille observes, looking at her watch. Though she missed her meeting with the Dog, the day was still young. If she hurries she can pick up da bomb, shower, pack, and still make her meeting with the Cat.

---

[30] sex

"Earth calling, please pick up."

"I'm serious Boodie, God told me to leave it all behind and apply to Divinity School."

"The same God that told you to become a PhD in math and teach hood rats in the inner city?"

"Maybe that was a—"

"Aberration in the atmosphere that lasted all of a week?"

"A slightly off key signal but I heard clearly this time and it all makes sense; I don't hate what I do I mean writing code and crashing systems is a pretty okay gig but it's not what I lie awake dreaming about at night and you absolutely hate your job…"

"So God told you I'm supposed to quit my job too?"

"No, but I want you to come with me."

"Where are you going?"

"Harvard, Yale, Chicago, or Vanderbilt."

"Cold, cold, cold and where the hell is Vanderbilt?"

"Nashville."

"As in Tennessee?"

Jackson simply nodded.

Always a bad sign.

"What the hell is in Nashville, I mean outside of hicks, hee-haw, and country music for Christ sake, you can't be serious."

"I'm serious."

"Well you've seriously bumped your head if you think I'm leaving DC for the Deep South."

"It's the Harvard of the South and much more than just country, it's Music City."

"I'll buy you a banjo, two lessons, and see you after your next epiphany."

Jackson took my hands, sat me down, and sank deep into my eyes—always a bad sign, "Boodie, I love you more than life but God loves you more and me more and God is calling and I have to follow even if that means leaving or losing you."

"Then go. You don't want to keep the big guy waiting."

We spent a lovely winter in Venice, spring brought cherry blossoms in full bloom, summer unrelenting heat spawning steaks in the backyard and long hot nights spent making luscious love amidst candles and stars, shadowy figures flickering in sync with flames dancing against the walls of our haven, hearts joined with heaven, heavy breathing, and the halo effect but on the heels of July August rode in hauling a moving truck, tears mixed with thinly disguised envy, feelings of betrayal, and garden variety abandonment.

Jackson headed to Hee-Haw land leaving my love and my envy to vie for what lay between thee and me. The next two years brought seven seasons of long distance dating, six weeks each summer, five days in the hospital for stress related illnesses, four prescriptions to battle an anal affliction from hell, three trips to the proctologist, two weeks notice, and a one way ticket to Nashville.

@@@@@

It had taken four years of research and nearly five years of letter writing and spontaneous protests in the lobbies of the EPA, Kennedy Center, and the offices of congressmen from California, Alaska and Washington State to convince the Environmental Protection Agency to investigate the possibility that Air Force F-16s were releasing toxic gases in the Earth's ozone layer. It took another year to get an audience with the investigative panel put together by the EPA.

"And you suspect that this will pose a long-term threat to public health?" the Chairman inquired at the conclusion of Rick's testimony.

"Definitely," Rick finally answered when he realized he was serious, "But the gas can be eliminated by merely altering the fire suppressant in the jets' fuel tanks."

After a five-year investigation, the EPA recommended that the Pentagon alter the fuel tanks. Two weeks later, the towers fell and the number of F-16s in the air increased three hundred fold. When confirmation that the EPA closed the case reached him, he began a heated letter writing campaign that spurs results, months later, in the form of a four word e-mail: *it's not a timely issue.*

Now, years later they refuse to answer his inquiries personally, opting instead to cut and paste the same aforementioned response regardless of the ecological issue introduced: global warming, power plant pollution, anti-missile silo construction in Alaska, urban sprawl, increased logging in national forests...all received the same cut and paste response straight from the Secretary of the Interior: *It's not a timely issue.*

Rick was no dummy. He understood politically and intellectually how Interior Secretary Daisy Duke might think it wasn't a timely issue. He wasn't immune to the need for national security. It was the timeliness of the issue Green Freaks (as the elitist media referred to them) were being sensitive to when they muted both their criticisms and their legitimate concerns while the issue of oil and gas exploration in Alaska's Arctic National Wildlife Refuge sailed through both the house and Senate.

He was no dummy. He realized for partisans protecting the environment and being unpatriotic went together like uncle and Sam.

But what had their silence gotten them?

✓ A plan to pillage Alaska in search of oil the Administration knew was a synonym for a needle in a haystack.
✓
✓ A five year delay in the administration's promise to reduce power plant emissions.
✓
✓ Not a not a single altered fuel tank though fighter plane missions continued to multiply like mice.

And there was no end in sight.

He held on, hoping the release of the international report from a forum of leading scientists from over a hundred nations would serve as a wake-up call. The commission concluded that the potential for unchecked pollution causing wide range climate changes was high and would inevitably result in drought, hurricanes, and other natural disasters.

Copies of the findings report were forwarded to the White House, Senate, House of Representatives, and the American media. Rick received ten responses; nine said: *it's not a timely issue.* The other said: *Eat the Rich.* And Rick, for reasons he himself was still unsure of, responded to the one and within a fortnight found himself, through an intermediary, in a cyberspace meeting with the mysterious head of the Earth Liberation Front.

ELF, considered by the FBI to be the number one domestic terrorist threat, prided itself on its body of unconnected cells, each independent, and each covert with no individual within the organization knowing more than a few faces. Over the past decade the group claimed responsibility for more than three hundred million dollars in economic damage encompassing everything from freeing minks to resort area arson.

Despite appointing a domestic terrorism task force, in the past ten years not a single EFF member had been apprehended.

"It sounds like you're running a well oiled machine," Rick types into the encrypted program, "Why would you be interested in a pen to paper pacifist like me?"

The rich have ravaged, raped and pillaged the mother who birthed them forth in protest and groaning forcing the whirlwind to arrive to feast upon the first fruits and provide meat for many.

Rick read the response and for reasons he still can't fully fathom, accepted it as an adequate answer to issues exponentially mushrooming out of control.

The crowd today is large and growing both pleasing and troubling him. While good for print it proves just how obtuse people were about the obvious. Runners, sunbathers, sightseers, carefree college kid, and garden variety baby boomers, some still living the buzz life all drawn to the ever warmer weather as bees to honey, too stupid to rise to action in the face of incontrovertible signs of a deteriorating atmosphere.

"We will no longer sit silent while this administration and Interior Secretary Duke break promises about preserving and protecting the environment," Rick declares into the bullhorn to cheers all around, "We will fight them without fail, using as our weapon language they will understand!"

He approaches a giant effigy of Interior Secretary Daisy Duke, meticulously stuffed with garbage in various stages of decomposition. Once there he douses Daisy with all-natural kerosene then strikes a match to light the torch that longs for rose red lips opened wide mouthing Edvard Munch's *Scream*.

The flame's tongue teases her outer lips before sliding into her mouth kissing long and hard, setting them both ablaze while protesters, sunbathers, sightseers, runners, daydreamers, pragmatists, idealists, and college kids cheer, court melanoma, sightsee, run, space out, wig out, cool out, say, "Way out" or "You're environmentally hindering your own cause, cut it out stupid."

@@@@@

How could she be so stupid which is quite often just a synonym for hopeful, expectant, or believing the Universe is aligned along something resembling balance or at least let me know its coming beforehand also known as fair. How had she allowed not only the love of her life but also herself to sashay away from six figure incomes to commune with commies, embrace wiccas, and join hands to sing *Cum Ba Ya* with basket weavers from Nigeria?

What the hell had she been thinking?
Oh, that's right, I wasn't thinking, I was following my heart, a garden-variety synonym for hope, hormones, and hemorrhoids the size of peaches fleeing the fiery pit from which revelations past and present spring.

And what had following her heart, hope, hormones, and hemorrhoids gotten her?

Widow hood or some facsimile thereof, heartache, debt, and alone or at least as alone as you can be when you're surrounded by future preachers wearing their own pain like ordination robes prepared for just such an occasion and what can we do for you dear, and you're wasting away right before our eyes and is it true that your Diner's Club, mortgage, and tuition are due and you really need to get out and get some fresh air dear…

What need did the dead have of fresh air?

Besides, since when was the air outside fresh and she can argue with the ocean round about now because she feels afraid most of the time, and she isn't even sure why. She feels raw, naked, totally exposed, with no center; pure nothingness; a vacuumed black hole in a nicely decorated tomb cursed with shapely legs amid a valley of dry bones.

90

When you were dead and raw and scared to death the last thing you needed to get was out. You were already out. All over the place like blood and guts and rivers flowing along the Rhine winding through Shem where Jacob, Joseph, and the boys are hanging out harassing Hitler or doing heavy lifting that ladies are above unless they're lesbians looking for a good time or a woman to love in all the wrong places but where was the right place?

Where *did* the walking dead go for good time and with whom?

The phone rings again and again. She does not move, cannot move.

"Mary," she hears from the intercom and has to move.

"Yes, Ms. Mary?"

"It's Jeri on the phone and don't say no or else."

The intercom goes quiet.

Calls from her hostess' spiritual advisor had become a daily if not bi-or tri- occurrence. At first, Mary found her irritating at best and a condescending pain in the ass at worst but the self proclaimed, self-appointed messenger of mercy began to grow on her.

"Hey."

"Hey honey I have something special for you."

"You shouldn't have."

"I had to, the spirit told me to and I always obey the spirit but you have to come out with me to get it."

"Out with you?"

"O-u-t with m-e, the spirit told me I'm supposed to take you out on the town and provide you a night of pleasure."

Mary laughs, "Thank the spirit for me but I'm not up to it."

"You don't have to be the spirit will take care of all that, I'll see you at six."

"Wai—

But nobody's there. Just like her.

I'll call her later and cancel, she decides, returning to what was either a lover's last gift or a fellow theologian's idea of a joke.

Good Grief

People to AVOID while GRIEVING

1.) Anyone you couldn't stand in the first place.
2.) Clinically depressed people*
3.) Relatives who want you to mediate long running family disputes.
4.) The same who suspect you've hit the lottery.
5.) People suffering from Jerry Springer syndrome**
6.) People who want to know how long it's been since you got humped well.
7.) Avoid #6 at your own discretion.

* See finally someone's life is worse than mine syndrome.

** They want to know every grisly detail.

DOPING

Many who have lived through the experience of losing a loved one recommend it highly as do many friends and spouses of same said people. So with the question of whether to essentially answered, the issue of how best to dope need only be addressed. Some swear by the mild tranquilizer to take the edge off, others report that getting laid really well has the same effect, still others go for the real knock out drugs but many of the same report that getting laid really, really well offers the same effect.

SCOPING

It's not your imagination. It's not hormones, hysteria, or even the halcydol you inhaled on the way to the wake—you're being checked out like a black market copy of Dean Debbie does Dallas. Parents, siblings, relatives, friends, co-workers, classmates, and perfect strangers all seeking solace in the assurance that you're grieving at an appropriate level.

In addition to the aforementioned scoundrels you are being stalked by a freak or two. They always fancied you the cat's meow and have endlessly entertained fantasies in which they help the horny mourner moan a new tune.

If you have, in fact, killed your loved one now would be a prime time to grieve at an appropriate level. Afterwards you can deal with the freaks. You are free to say fuck them figuratively or literally do so—same basic premise but with subtle variations.

The tolling of the doorbell rouses Mary from a deep sleep. *My face is falling off*, she notes hazily, sitting up. It falls to the floor, leaving her unfazed.

"Oh, that's not my face," she giggles.
The bell continues to toll.
She wipes the remaining glob of slob from her face.
"Coming," she calls, and hopes she is as she tries maintaining her equilibrium across the marbled floor leading to the beveled front door.

She is irritated, then surprised, then embarrassed to find Jeri, the mini mystic there, all bright eyed and bushy fucking tailed. Sans any semblance of further encouragement the neck-less lead financial analyst slash spiritualist walks in and heads for Mary's suite. Mary trails, puzzled by her inability to keep pace with such a wee wobbling person.

"Jeri, I'm so sorry, I tried to call you to cancel but I fell asleep…"
"Good, you probably needed the rest."
"Yes," Mary agrees, removing pill and wine bottles from her bedside table and into the bathroom, "I don't sleep well at night."

"Good, then I don't have to worry about getting you home early." Jeri responds, making herself comfortable on the bed.
"Look Jeri, about tonight—
"There's no if, ands, or buts about it, the spirit has spoken and I'm not leaving here until we've been obedient to it, I'm your angel tonight."

@@@@@

I've seen better, Athena decides sitting in the parking lot that doubled as the Key Bridge. Just ahead she can see Georgetown. Usually as alive as an army of ants, it sat, deadlocked as any jaded jury without so much as a bassinet moving. On days like this she'd give anything to be in Nashville where rush hour meant just that.

Turning off her ignition she turns on 107.5 and smooth jazz courtesy of Grover Washington Jr. joins her in the fully customized Expedition. The soothing music acts as chamomile, soothing her frayed nerves and allowing her to let go of things she can't control—like the shipment of caskets lost that morning on a Knoxville highway when a of chicken decided to cross the road.

Animal lovers, she thinks, turning up the music, was the life of one of KFC's finest worth not only the cost of the caskets but also the inconvenience caused by closing the roadway for the better part of a morning? Who could say? So she didn't say a word. She looks at her watch…four, and she was scheduled to meet Camille Leon for an early dinner downtown at five.

She dials the number with regret. She had been looking forward to the meeting since last month when the vixen, out of nowhere, appeared at her side at the grand opening ceremony for Monroe's new mausoleum community near Harpeth Hills.
The voice answers before the first ring.
"Hi Panther."
"No, it's Athena Monroe."
"I know."

"I'm afraid I'm running late, actually that's an understatement. I'm stuck on the Key so I guess we'll need to reschedule…"

"Actually I'm running behind schedule myself, why don't I meet you at your DC headquarters later, say around nine?"

"Nine it is." she agrees, and hangs up feeling much better than a moment before.

She bides her time for another hour then makes the first U-turn that won't get her arrested in three states. She arrives home in Reston two hours later and is more than a little pleased to see iron gates swing open at her request.

She spends the next hour luxuriating in the lilac fragranced bubble bath her live in maid drew while Sade sings of love lost and found and lost again. By quarter of eight she is dressed in black and climbing back into the Expedition of the same. The gates swing wide and she's back on the road by eight urging Parliament to tear the roof off the mother. Accelerating, she turns up the volume, merges onto I-66, and finds lines to rival Disneyland.

When she reaches Monroe's two and a half hours later the white pillared mansion sits dark save the one interior lamp always left burning, Monroes' ode to the eternal flame. She parks in front of the French doors. How could someone born with an antenna up her ass have forgotten her cell phone?

Although the grounds are obviously unoccupied she goes inside anyway, stepping into the marble foyer and locking the door behind her. She enters the main parlor, a huge hall where up to seven guests were usually on display. Tonight, however, a single shiny black casket sits on the far side of the room, evidence of the power of a chicken to change the productivity of an empire.

"Damn."
She looks at the antique grandfather in the corner.
"Damn."
Damn near midnight and she is one tired fool who doesn't feel like driving back across the bridge.
"Damn."
With her luck the Hindenburg would be on exhibit there.
Outside, the sleek black Expedition beckons in the moonlight, as sick a joke as just say no. Inside, the empty black coffin starts to look more and more appetizing... Hindenburg... coffin... Hindenburg... coffin...it all sounds the same so she sheds her shoes and scurries across the room reaching the silver lever just as the eternal flame goes out.

@@@@@

Mary shields her eyes against the blinding light, oops sight, confronting her. Unable to sustain focus she shuts them again, tight, as if against an assault and tries to find then take a deep breath.

"More champagne?"
"No, I just need air," she answers, seeking a wall.
"Then you might want to open your eyes dear, walking is easier that way."

Mary reluctantly complies.

Yep, a knee high, neck less, round African Buddha as naked as the hair hanging from her crotch is long, *braided, and beaded at the ends...* Mary glances away quickly lest the native think she's interested in anything other than a National Geographic sort of way and asks, nonchalantly as possible, "Why are you nude?"

"It's the way people outside the west often wind down but if it makes you too uncomfortable?" The freaky spiritualist coos, twisting unruly clumps of crotch hair around her stubby fingers.

"No… I'm okay but I only agreed to let you rub my shoulders…"
"Relax sweetie" she says, pressing Mary back onto the bed, "We're just going to work that tension out."

"I don't know, I'm not feeling so well—
"Shhhhh."
"Just my upper back, all my stress, goes right to my—
"Back," she says in a soothing voice, "Lie down."
Mary reluctantly complies.
The hefty hump hops onto her back.
"How's that?" the Hump whispers in her ear— then licks it.

Mary bolts upright sending the horny hump tumbling to the floor.
"I'm okay," the Hump assures, struggling to get back to her feet.

Oh, my God, there's something crawling in her crotch hair Mary realizes, "I really have to go home… "Now," she adds when the petulant Pigmy refuses to move.

"Okay, but let's pray first," the sweaty Pigmy insists, kneeling (though who could tell the difference) and waiting for Mary to join her, "Give me your hands."

Mary reluctantly complies keeping her mouth open in case she needs to chew them off.

"Lord, thank you, we just want to thank you for being you and for presence and your holy spirit which guides us if only we are open. Lord, help us to be open to your love and your spirit, and experiences, and bodies and Lord, help Mary learn to be comfortable with bodies in whatever form they come for I am simply a vessel sent to do your will. Amen."

@@@@@

"Amen."
Athena concludes and feels her way through the dark to the mahogany secretary where she finds a small flashlight. Turning it on, she heads downstairs in search of the main fuse box which lies closer to a good night's rest than Reston.

Three floors down the beam reveals a door you would have to know existed. Beyond it lay the green door, a room housing the most opulent of burial supplies: marble divans, slate coffins studded with cat's eye, and her personal favorite, an authentic, double-wide Egyptian sarcophagus. She locates the breaker and flips the switch. Light floods the room and she withdraws, using her key to take the elevator instead of the stairs.

She returns to the parlor only to find the room still dark. "Damn," she says then notes she's used the word far too many times today. Before backtracking she opts to try the ancient kerosene lamp in the foyer, which acquiesces, illuminating the parlor just enough to provide the peace of mind she needs to climb into the casket destined to serve as her resting place tonight.

She pauses, sojourning to the summer she was eight and irritable after a long day spent shadowing her father who never stopped moving. She took a nap on the floor while he worked nearby only to wake hours later in a powder pink coffin crowned with a tacky, oversized carnation spray. She screamed like a mentally ill Pentecostal, falling out and onto the floor in her fervor to get out.

Tonight, all she wants in the world is to climb in, she realizes, swinging the lid wide. Someone was screaming like a Red Sox fan.
Wait...
She was screaming like a Red Sox fan while the most beautiful girl in the world sits up and smiles like its All Saints Day.

"What kind of twisted sicko are you?" Athena demands when she can stop screaming.
"Don't you mean what kind of twisted sister am I?" Camille responds, climbing out and stretching as if a contented feline.

"You're crazy, do you know that?"
"Why, because I'm not afraid of the dark?"
Athena laughs despite herself.
The Nut joins in.
"Let's start over, I'm Camille Leon, my friends call me the negotiator."
"I hear you're good."
"The best."
"Athena Monroe."
"The Panther."
"No Panther," she insists, "Possibly a spider, spinning webs."

97

"Sorry I hold that title—

"Please, you're no spider, you're a snake."

The pause is both pregnant and barren.

"So… are you planning to drive back across town tonight or what?" Camille finally inquires, stroking the coffin, "It is of course yours but if it's going to be empty …"

"You've kind of spooked me," Athena admits, "But I don't think I can survive one more second behind the wheel."

"Well, I took a tour while I was waiting for you," Camille responds taking her hand, "I spotted an Egyptian double-wide three floors down."

The room goes dark once more.

"If you're not afraid of the dark."

Damn, what a day, Athena summarizes, as, hand in hand, they descend into darkness.

@@@@@

While Ethics Professor Charles Marion Dates is indeed dateless, dirty, and morbidly depressed over the less than pretty picture of him that appeared in the paper he bows down but most assuredly not out.

First of all he won the fight okay let's just get that straight from the jump who do you think you're dealing with and for that matter who did that beautiful motherfucker but let us not fail to mention the blonde;

Okay;

Who did that pussy packing blonde think she was stepping to not me, oh—

"No!"

Now, here I am sitting here all alone, unwashed and unshaven like some mountain man waiting to get banged by Paul Bunion except I'm not waiting for Paul or Peter but instead for that goody two shoes bitch, Mary Papins, to come and bring me that special hemorrhoid cream they only carry at Metro Medical supply over on Church Street.

He hated it when his anus acted up which it always did when he got extremely angry or horny which usually happened when he got extremely angry because he was extremely horny.

98

His head hurt.

Not only because he was extremely horny and angry and plagued by hemorrhoids but also because owns a hangover the size of Oprah's ass after she's been eating alone too long.

Hell is a hemorrhoid you don't want to hump and if I have to explain that screw you too— where the hell was Mary Poppins or Papins or whatever the hell that pussy called her ass?

Good Grief

Hump Day

Hump is defined as a rounded protuberance, mound or mountain range, a difficult, trying, or critical phase or obstacle, can also mean to copulate with—often considered vulgar.

In the world of work, hump (as in day) is synonymous with Wednesday, that recurring wrinkle in the middle of the week most likely to wear you down. But just over that hump, hope springs eternal for Thursday is a synonym Happy Hour day rolling into Friday which every working stiff knows is the pot of gold at the end of the rainbow, if, and here's the wrinkle, you can make it over the hump.

When the reaper comes to call any day can suddenly morph into hump day. If, by chance, you are fortunate enough to lose your loved one on a Wednesday, welcome to double hump day. Hump defies all borders and is home to stay like mice, worthless men, lazy kids, and flies don't give a damn about calendars.

So what constitutes a bad hump day?

Repetitious never ending periods in which the entirety of your essence threatens to not only devolve but also drip through cracks or crevices left unfilled by despair.

We leave you with the top five coping suggestions from *Humping for Dummies*, due out next spring:

1. Hump
2. Hump well
3. Have a few glasses of wine, have a friend over, hump friend?
4. Have a few glasses of wine, have hostess' husband over.

5.   Have a few glasses of wine, have hostess' husband over, hump hostess' husband well.

@@@@@

At first Mary thought the book a miracle, then a bit crass then downright sick yet overly perturbed she was not. What could she expect from Commie's kids? It wasn't that they set out to exhibit bad behavior but instead intrinsically realized the party was over as soon as their feet hit the pulpit. Tradition dictated good sportsmanship but this crap was over the deep end...

... and she's being tossed on a troubled sea where she rises and falls and feels she knows not what or why the sea parts and swallows her whole while a hump floats by...reading a book about humping...was it helping... humping....helping... humping... humping... humping ... then waking or some facsimile thereof and realizing, all at once, the book is not some sick joke but instead prophetic literature sent to guide her through this topsy-turvy, twisted, pain soaked journey.

And how does she know? Because at this very moment she finds herself humping the hell, and well, out of her hostess' husband...

...and loving every second of it.

"This is Rena your Roving Reporter reporting from outside the Capitol where the Director of Homeland Security and Interior Secretary, Daisy Duke, have arrived from Washington DC to meet with the Governor, Senator, Mayor, and, it's rumored, their Counsel."

"As you can see," she continues, lifting her camera phone and scanning the area, "There's a huge crowd gathered outside, easily double last week's as regional and now, national coverage descends on the city following the second bombing of an unoccupied housing development, this time in Franklin."

Inside, the Governor sits, in the conference room with the rest of the invited, trying not to tap his fingers while they wait for the Director of Homeland Security to climb out of his "date"[31] and make it to this most important meeting.

"I told you we could secretly meet this morning instead of slinking around in the dead of night like cattle rustlers," the Senator from Tennessee chides.

"He might have surprised us by being on time, stranger things have happened," Daisy defends, picking up her needlework, "Do we know anything more about the terrorists?"

"You mean other than that they're the home grown variety?" the Head of the TBI clarifies.
"Precisely."
"No."
"This is the last thing we need," The Senator from Tennessee, decrees, bringing immediate agreement from the Governor and Mayor.

"Did the administration think the truce would last forever?" Andy demands of Daisy, "That the green freaks would just lie down and die while you guys plowed through their tulips and daffodils?"

"Green space," their Counsel corrects, "I hear its trees that have them up in arms."

---

[31] See Dean Debbie

"You might need increased security Daisy," the Senator suggests, bringing vigorous agreement from the Governor and Mayor.

"They're harmless," she answers, never missing a stitch, "All smoke and mirrors."

"And bombs," Andy adds.

"They only hit unoccupied buildings."

"So far, are you planning to ignore them to death?" Andy poses, picking up her scent.

"Of course not," Daisy snaps, never missing a stitch.

"Then give them something," Andy prods.

"It's not mine to give you little imbecile, I'm the Interior Secretary not the fucking tooth fairy, I do as I'm told," she continues; stabbing her embroidery as if it has stole something, "I follow my leader to the Lincoln bedroom just like everybody else then bend over so my personal convictions can get shoved up my—

"Nice of you to join us sir," Andy enjoins, over her shoulder, as the Director of Homeland Security enters the room.

"I read your briefings," he says, taking his seat at the head of the table, "Good work, now, have we caught them?"

"No, but they sent us a fax a few hours ago," the head of the TBI offers.

"Bold little devils aren't they," the DHS deduces, "I don't suppose they told us where to find them?"

"Unfortunately not, but the theory from Washington is they're a recently established cell of a national group called ELF. They've been operating along the Northwest Coast and Alaska for years."

"Don't forget that our country's entire cache of top notch feds have failed to arrest a single elf." Andy inserts.

"Not even one?" the Senator from Tennessee echoes, astonished, "So this group has been dug in deeper than a gerbil up Gere's anal opening for ages and you've never zeroed in on a single un-American elfish asshole?"

All eyes race to the man seated at the head of the table.

"Well, these are some of the first documented attacks under my watch, which, as you well know has been completely inundated with other issues since September 11th. I can't speak to why my predecessors were unable to apprehend—"

"That's right, pass that buck," Andy adjoins, enjoying the action.

"Shut up, you little masturbator," the head of the TBI hisses, rising from his chair.

"Catfight," Daisy crows, finally resting her ice picks.

"Do you really want to have a public discussion about sexual proclivities?" Andy challenges.

The head of the TBI, to everyone's astonishment, backs down, "As I was saying," he says, turning back to face the Senator, "My office will work hand in hand with homeland security to bring these domestic terrorists to justice."

"Do we really want to be calling them terrorists?" Daisy asks, ice picks clicking again.

"Call a spade a spade, I say," the Governor asserts.

"We've been waging a *war against terrorism* for years now and it's taken a huge toll on the psyche of the public," Daisy responds, the picks picking up pace, "Now we're going to start labeling fellow Americans terrorists too? How can the public feel safe?"

"So you think it's better to sugarcoat the slop?" the Governor asks in disgust, then addresses the men, "McVeigh was a terrorist and he got what he deserved, the public demanded it. These vermin are worse than garden variety criminals or cowards, they're terrorists, plain and simple; if I could I'd kill every one of them myself I would."

"And accomplish what?" The Director of Homeland Security queries, "Daisy has a point. An outside enemy unites a country, internal ones crack you like walnuts."

"So, what do you suggest?" The Senator solicits.

"That we sit on this information until we round these guys up."

"Will they be rounded up anytime soon?" Andy asks, "Vultures have been circling me for weeks."

@@@@@

I am a corpse The Man who would be senator, governor, or at a minimum, mayor thinks and wills himself to lay motionless as the main course at a vulture convention, wishing, hoping and praying his wife has some early morning pressing business to attend to whether a committee, class, or a cliff to conveniently drive over. Not because he hates her, no, nada, nay, make no mistake, he finds her far more bearable these days, but needs the bottomless pit up and out so he can get in.

You're awake I know you are, he thinks, breath held, *I hear you scratching...maybe its ticks*, he decides and fights off a surge of giggles bubbling clear down to his toes...while he just...lies here... *I'm dead...in the center of the Vegas desert waiting for my guests to arrive for the feast...*as does she, repetitively breathing... breathing...breathing until he yearns to scream, "Die already or get up!"

He hears a door.

It's her door...he hears footsteps heading...down... the stairs...the alarm as the door to the garage is activated....the hum of an engine ...a car door closing...the garage door clanking shut like the gates of hell.

Fugg, he cogitates[32] and farts.
Really.
"Oh!" the Pit gasps, leaping from the bed, "What do you have to say for yourself?"

My timing sucks he thinks, but instead says, "Hmmm."
"I'm running late," she announces.

His downtrodden heart races once more. *It's still early*, he realizes, settling back in to hibernate, *chances are, Mary went for a run or out to meet a classmate for coffee...* she did that sometimes, left the house early, altered her schedule, trying to stay away until both the Pit and he, he finally had to admit, were gone....

Still, their earliest interactions had taken the greater orchestrating by far: brushing against her while they were all in the kitchen together, pressing his hand, ever so slightly, into the small of her back even as Ms. Mary stood nearby. Initially it was as much excitement as poor St. Peter could handle but soon Willie demanded more.

At first he was unsure how to proceed.

He was, after all, the hunter and she the fine but frail prey...*Stop*

---

[32] thinks

thinking like that he thought and did. *She's at most a wee fragile but is, he knows, equally, unconsciously seeking companionship in the form of a faithful friend and so is he and surely she was in need of a friend but how can I get to know my new friend better if she keeps shifting like shadows on an icy dance floor?*

The question was still with him when he arrived home that fateful evening all un-bright eyed and bushy tailed.

"Reverend Fisher called twice today to remind you that you're delivering the sermon on Sunday and don't forget to write the check for the Women's Day Retreat."

"Hmmm."

"Did you see Casper on your way in?" Ms. Mary asked, never looking up from her book, *The Crucified God.*

"For a second she was walking into her room."

"How was she?"

"I don't know, she didn't say."

"The girl's far too quiet…"

The phone rang and then again.

"What are you waiting for, Christmas?"

"Hello…hi Jeri… peace be with you too, uh-huh, hold on," he covers the mouthpiece, "She wants to speak with Mary."

To his shock and awe the Pit gets up, walks over, and turns on the intercom, "Mary honey, someone's on the phone for you."

"Okay."

She picked up and I hung up but Ms. Mary somehow forgot to turn the intercom off.

"How are you feeling today?"

"Lonely."

"Now we know," Ms. Mary whispers with a giggle, crossing the room to join me on the bed.

"I don't know think I'll ever get accustomed to sleeping alone…"

You won't have to, I vow sending her psychic assurances.

"Poor Casper," Ms. Mary sighs, snuggling in closer, then "Shushhh!" when his

"Hmm"

Interfered with the reception.

After that he usually knew whatever he needed about how she felt, wanted to feel or planned to do. The phone rang and he was Johnny on the fugging spot, collecting intelligence as if Einstein issued it. His unabashed devotion to his work would have made Hoover proud as St. Peter rearing like a prize cock and why not? Mary's oral meandering detailing her and the chaplain's love life affords him the most active sex life he'd had in ages.

Armed with knowledge the two had been religiously committed to riding each other like prize stallions one could reasonably presuppose that sooner or later young Mary would commence to missing her saddle. Inspired by passion and proximity, a multiplier stacked in his favor almost guaranteeing grief sex, so long as he manned his post like a Marine at Guantanamo Bay, masturbating and praying lest he be caught with his pants down.

He was loathe to leave, even to go to work, but fortunately his new best friend proved equally hooked on their new pastime and took great pleasure sharing everything she just happened to overhear why he was away.

"Casper didn't sleep at all last night."
"Hmmm."
"The poor dear is planning to buy a body pillow to keep her company at night."
Progress! "Hmmm."
"What's next, a blow up doll?"
Close! "Hmmm."

He was delighted to the point of orgasmic to discover that as he slipped phrases from her monitored conversations into *their* conversations her guard relaxed and she surrendered the smile he loved so well.

"That's exactly what Jackson used to say," she'd say.
"See, then it must be true," he always responded and felt the bond between them grow.

He honed his initiative taking skills by searching her suite whenever she was out, rummaging through closets, lingerie drawers, and even the trash, a small action affording additional insight. Though his new best friend long ago shared details of poor Mary's dependence on anti-depressant medication, she was apparently uninformed when it came to her predilection for Tylenol PM, sleeping pills, and red wine.

106

"I know I shouldn't" she finally confided a week later, "But right now unconsciousness is my best friend."

"I know," he said, placing a fatherly arm around her shoulders, "All the more reason for you to grab hold of something firm to help you ride this out."

He took the plunge by dipping his toe ever so judiciously after she was unconscious taking care to ensure they were never naked at the same time lest he abandon all sense of propriety by diving in too soon. His preliminary success spurred Willie to broaden his horizons but before long he noted she seemed increasingly uneasy when awake.

He watched from the shadows as she drifted about the kitchen preparing meals and wrestling with random thoughts flashing and fluttering across her face before fading back into the fog. One morning soon after he overheard her tell Ms. Mary that Jackson visited her during the night.

"The hug was so warm and tight... I didn't want to ever let go..."

"I'll be back tonight," he called out, heading off to teach his Foundation of Ethics class.

He arrived home that evening with one hell of an erection only to discover his widow whisked away by a spiritual advisor who obviously didn't give a damn about his poor tortured soul.

"What exactly does a night of *"pleasure"* entail?" he asked as nonchalantly as pulsating Willie would allow.

When his new best friend tells him he knows Little Mary Sunshine will be popping pills and guzzling wine like a suburban housewife as soon as she walks in.

A few hours later he *stumbles* upon the trembling lamb in the kitchen drinking Jack Bean straight from the bottle.

"How was your evening?"

She laughs and he delights in the experience even though it doesn't reach her eyes.

But it does, later that night when he slips, naked, into her bed, gathering her ever so gently in his arms then whispering, "It wasn't pretty was it Boodie?" ever so softly in her ear. Silly, sleepy laughter spills out of her like water swallowing us both so completely that by the time she stirs to find she's naked he's nearing orgasm and she's not sure if she's moaning or dreaming and neither of them are quite sure how he came to be inside her or who's to blame but they're both there and it's done and it's good.

In the cold light of day Mary was, of course, mortified to the point of moving out but his new best friend would have none of it. "You can leave after the holidays," Ms. Mary insisted when they cornered Casper in the kitchen, "Christmas makes me morbidly depressed and you promised to cook for the holiday party, you wouldn't disappoint the entire community let alone us now would you?"

And of course she wouldn't, not after everything we had done for her.

@@@@@

While Ethics Chairman Charles Marion Dates is indeed dateless, dirty, and morbidly depressed over the less than pretty picture of him that kept appearing in the *Tennessean* he is down but most assuredly not out. Propriety dictated it indeed an issue to be dealt with but the more pressing problem at hand is where in God's name was Mary Poppins or Papins or whatever the hell that pussy called her ass?

Doesn't she know hell, hemorrhoids, and queens wait for no man? Okay that craps not true but hell this shit is getting Biblical. God's treating me as an errant Israelite or petulant prophet instead of like the poor, dick whipped, and sore assed but intellectually brilliant ex package I am.

"Stop thinking like that girl" he snaps and slaps himself just on gp.[33] He was nobody's penniless princess he was the most respected Ethics Professor outside the pearly gates of Princeton which is precisely where he was headed as soon as his ex beautiful fucking package un-assed the chair there that was rightfully his as was his very figurative and literal rear end.

---

[33] General Principle

But that justice would come to pass as soon as he dealt with the first furry mother fuckers on his list— the bitch ass cops who pulled him off the blonde before she was completely bald.

Bitch.

See what happened when you were white?[34]   She better ask somebody but back to this fat, conniving bitch cop and his flaming sidekick, Dopey Opie.

They pull me off Blondie's ass and into the back seat of the undercover lover while they try to calm down the beautiful motherfucker who's flapping his perfectly pink lips about how he's gonna kick my ass.

My ass.

Can you believe that shit after what he, in concert with rent-a-blonde pussy, tried to pull on me…in public?

Pleassse…

I know he knows we both know he has to get up earlier in the morning than that to tickle my ass and tell me I'm ready.

So Bull and Shit send the merry couple on their way then Bull sends Shit inside to check things out and meanwhile I'm calming down to angry because I'm really horny and I know my hemorrhoids will be showing up any minute so I'm in a hurry to get home but instead of setting me free so I can take care of this shit Bull proceeds to leisurely waddle up and down side streets scoping and roping like I don't know what's going on.

How was Bull going to just disrespect me like that? Am I not a man? So Shit comes back outside and gets in the car and I'm like:

"Excuse me but could you please bust me in or out because my hemorrhoids are hell on wheels and they're headed this way."

---

[34] Your momma didn't teach to take off your earrings, pull your hair back and put on Vaseline before you went vamping in another bitch's camp.

"Keep your shorts on."

"Thankfully, gratefully, no pray tell prayerfully, I'm not wearing any but that's beside the point—"

"What's he doing?" Shit wonders aloud.

While Bull stalks the skinny.[35]

"You're yanking my dick, right?"
. Shit's mouth falls open, "Watch your mouth."
"You really are from Mayberry[36] aren't you?"
"Look mister."
"Dr."
"Dr.?"
"Yes, Dates, Dr. Dates dear and do close your mouth your tongue is rather unattractive."

Shit closes his mouth.
Bull opens the back door, "Look Cinderella, the prince has decided his preference has blonde pussy stamped all over it so hail yourself a pumpkin and get used to playing with your own dick like a lady, okay?"

"Okay."
Was all he'd said and they parted like perfect gentleman.

But now, after licking his wounds, he is more than ready to show Bull what real balls look like. How could another brother try to play him like that, conducting his dirty little business in public while I sat right there in the back seat? Who did the bitch take me for? Cinderella?

I'm no blonde.

The blonde went hobbling down the street with one shoe, half a head of hair, and his whole life wrapped in one beautiful delusional package.

Everyone who wasn't a pussy knew all about the dirty cops in the

[35] Gather intelligence
[36] See Andy Griffith, Patron Saint of the South

110

"squeaky-clean" Nashville PD, knew they supplemented their income by shaking down dealers and socially straight dick that curved to the side every now and then.[37]   It was an old game played out in the District a decade ago when he there finishing his thesis.   Cops swarmed around gay bars like flies on fish searching cars for seats or grams as in crackers— a you can take your money to the bank sign someone without a dick was getting screwed.

Hush money bought amnesia; buyouts bought pictures, and ongoing payouts kept it out of the papers. A faction of the local gay community had been up in arms over it for years while he watched from the sidelines more amused than anything. He viewed it as the principle of the matter and had no patience for drifters. After all, the Bible said be ye hot or cold but lukewarm, like pussy, was to be avoided at all cost.

Paradoxically, he felt empathy for their pitiful plight. These poor souls who, simply by virtue of gender, found themselves bound like hemorrhoid plagued hostages to pussies, a synonym for hell on wheels sans the fun. Dates stands, who can sit with this shit, firmly convinced that straight men are merely mutations of nature brought on by spoiled fruit and fathers who fail to share the secret that could save their very souls.[38]

Which was exactly what Bull dug for not only himself but Shit as well when he made the mistake not only of doing what he did, right in full view of him[39] but also of calling him Cinderella. He might be dirty, unshaven, and morbidly depressed over the less than pretty picture of him that kept appearing in the paper but he was no blonde pussy princess wannabe— he was a queen.

@@@@@

Big Dog didn't like the changes he was seeing. Buildings, once abandoned, were being renovated which meant the value of real estate was rising in the hood. Every third corner was empty, further evidence that the eagle was starting to fly in the wrong direction. Maybe Chip a

---

[37] Professional, married men who crave a real hole and some pipe to put in it.
[38] That really scary stuff lived in non-anal holes.
[39] Was he not a man?

Hoy was right; maybe he better learn a few new tricks and make it out of the game alive.

It was Chip a Hoy who insisted he collect Lester's bones and cremate them.

"Who hit you in the head with a shovel?"

"I held it up for you" She echoes before witnesses, "You owe me."

The sick dusty freak now rested in a pink flamingo shaped urn in his family room. Chip a Hoy christened the bird 'da bomb.

Truth be told he holds a soft spot for the lady. There was something about her that reminded him of his dead grandma but that wasn't gonna stop him from banging that drum slowly. To that end he was here to make the Chip happy or at least to shut her the hell up. Last night she had lost her ever lovin' mind and called him a whiner. He wanted to whip her ass, but because his dead grandmamma raised him right, he took the time to explain.

"Look, I'm not sinking good mother fucking money into some unprofitable fucking goody two shoe program to feed fish only fit for dick food."

"I'm a businesswoman, it's all about green," the Bitch parrots like a broken ass album.

But he isn't so sure.

He gets out of the Benz and heads across the street where Ree-Ree waits for him, a super glued smile on her face.

"I hear we're going to be neighbors."

"I don't know about all that but I guess I could do worse."

"Well this is it; it's a mess but come inside so you can see the potential."

Big Dog follows her into a house he knows better than most, grinning wide when he catches sight of the sturdy beam that served as Lester's cross.

"You can see it's really nice," Ree-Ree says, sounding like a real estate agent, "High ceilings, big windows, large rooms, good light...a little love and it'll be the perfect safe haven for troubled girls."

112

"Still tryin' to reform hoochies, huh?" he says, shaking his head like she just said stupid out of the blue, "You can take a hoochie outta the hood but you gotta scrape the hood outta the hoochie."

"I can scrape."

"I bet you can."

The newly installed doorbell rings.

"Show yourself around," Ree-Ree offers and gladly goes to answer it.

She swings it wide and is surprised to find the red-haired, freckled face cop on the porch.

"Good early evening Ms. Tubman," he begins, extending his hand.

"No, thanks."

"I wanted to come by and say I'm sorry about what happened. My partner can be a bit pompous but he has seniority and I'm just a newcomer."

"How unfortunate for you."

"I was hoping maybe I could take you out to dinner and make it up to you."

Big Dog appears behind her and the two men, in an instant, sum each other up as pig and criminal respectively and interchangeably.

"I'm sure your male non-minority ego told you I'd get all weak at knees at the prospect but my tastes run in a different direction."

Camille appears out of nowhere, walking up the steps and past the officer, "Hey babe," she greets, pausing to plant a kiss on Ree-Ree's cheek on her way inside.

Officer Grey takes note, wondering what direction, exactly; Ms. Tubbman's tastes ran in.

"Good day, detective," the object of his desire says and slams the door in his face.

"So you like your crackers with strawberry jelly?" Bid Dog barks.

"None of your bus—

"Actually," Camille interjects, "The lady prefers blondes."

Big Dog shudders.

"Like you haven't dipped your little dick in the dumb pool," Ree-Ree returns.

"So, what do you think of her?" Camille asks, locking arms with Big Dog and leading him away, "True she's hell on wheels but you can't beat her with a stick."

@@@@@

"I booked it as a birthday surprise for him," Ms. Mary shares with Casper, who's trying to make a beeline for the stairs, "But we don't leave until after his birthday, a few days before Christmas actually."

"That's wonderful," Mary says, with a nervous smile, "I guess that means you won't need help with the big dinner."

"Actually it means I need to move it up to this weekend, that won't be a problem will it?"
"No, anything I can do get you two on your way…"

"Don't tell me you want to get rid of us," The birthday boy exclaims, engulfing Casper in a bear hug he invites his wife to join.

"Of course she doesn't" Ms. Mary says, joining in, "Next week will be one to remember."

And so far it has been. Having made his credit cards as accessible as air his best friend clandestinely camps out in a hotel across the street from the mall leaving him ample opportunity to help himself to their houseguest who's enjoying one hell of a hard time keeping his hands off her.

"I'm sorry, I can't help it," he repeats yet again when she stirs to find him using his master key to keep her from oversleeping.

"You said you'd stay away and keep your hands to yourself," she insists, trying to make it out of bed before he can make his way into it.

"I said I would but then I amended that statement to say I would try but you would have to help me," he counters, pressing her back onto the pillows.
"I'm trying," she assures him, trying to squirm away.
"I know, I know," he pants, covering her body with his own and kissing her, "That's why I have to try harder."

And he does, three times in the four days preceding the Divinity school's holiday party, which goes off without so much as a single streaker, stripper or hitch.

The following day, the anniversary of his birth, he wakes before dawn like a newborn—naked and in need of a tittie to suck. He skips downstairs in search of a feast to stave off the famine inevitably interlaced in the upcoming Christmas vacation in Cuba. He pauses just outside her door and sends up thanks to his Savior for supplying this slice of heaven here on earth then unlocks the gate to happiness.

But the ghost is nowhere to be found. He wanders, aimlessly, around her suite, his own personal corner of paradise, searching for tangible evidence that she had, in fact, ever been there. He stumbles upon it an hour and countless tears later at the rear of the rose hued commode. With trembling hands he extract it out and holds it close, inhaling deeply in an attempt to breathe in what remains of her scent before opening it:

Good Grief

12 Ways to Encourage Relationships with Others

1. Accept an invitation to lunch.
2. Insist on picking up the tab for said lunch.
3. Repeat this process with everyone you know.
10. If this gets you to #10, you have no friends.
11. Truth is knowledge, embrace it.
12. If you live to let stiffs ride you like a trick pony pick up my new book, *Dating the Dead,* due next fall.

@@@@@

Police Chief Somers, summoned to the Capitol for a meeting with the bigwigs, knows he stands a far greater chance of falling back than springing forward by its conclusion. Folks in Nashville changed chiefs the way religious women changed their underwear and it didn't help his son was committed to getting arrested, at minimum, once a week.

Fifty years with old man winter taught him one thing—that it was one year too many. The buckle of the Bible belt might not be Miami Beach but it's a far cry from Chicago where a frozen ass was also your closest friend. Besides, the Mayor had recruited him on all but bended knee, entrusting him with the safety of Nashville's slightly

115

schizophrenic citizens and he plans to see the job to its end or his name wasn't Somers.

"Winters," the Governor says, rising when he enters the room.
"It's Somers, sir."
"Of course it is" the Mayor agrees but doesn't sound quite sure.

"Take a seat, son, things are really kinda hellacious around here right now, you know with all these pesky explosions and the like," The Governor begins like the good ole boy he is, "But, not to worry, it's just a few pissed off passionflowers with wild hairs up their ass—"
"Everybody loves foreplay," Andy interjects, slapping his knee.
"But still…"
He pauses.
The Mayor twitches nervously.
"… These pansies have folks in some of our finest communities sleeping in their cars for fear of getting their faces blown off."

"I've put my men on overtime; they're patrolling the areas around the clock."

The Mayor shakes his head, "That's not the right answer but how could it be when you didn't even let the Governor get to the question?"

"Never played Jeopardy have you son?" the Governor queries, placing a fatherly hand on his shoulder.

Is that some kind of rhetorical question or am I supposed to answer that? Somers wonders, weighing his options.

The Governor opts to continue, "So seeing as how an important portion of our constituency is currently confronted with the possibility of facelessness the last thing they need is the Queen of the Pansies running around like an African Headhunter with its head cut off threatening to divulge clandestine and otherwise classless intelligence that might cause our already fearful constituency to lose face in the community."

"Come again?" Somers says.

The Governor throws his hands into the air, sighs wearily, and collapses into an overstuffed chair. The Mayor is poised to take over the helm when his colleague's midget of a spokesman steps over him.

"One of your little piggies pissed on the wrong queer, said queer is jumping up and down hanging from a chandelier waving a leather Louis Vuitton day planner bursting at the seams with notables from the house on the hill to hell in it like a king kong sized rainbow flag."

"Don't forget the Jew," the Governor whispers, motioning to the Mayor.
"We were accosted by a young Jewish woman," the Mayor begins.
"Who jumped out of a port-a-potty," Andy adds, "Don't forget the port-a-potty."

"Who jumped out of a port-a-potty someone placed just outside the exercise room. This potty hopper hoped to extract information about an extortion scheme involving the closeted gay community—

"Perpetrated by the police department," Andy reminds the Mayor with a smile, "Don't forget the police department."

Fall on the first day of winter, Somers thinks fighting back tears spawned by chills racing down his derriere.

"But that's not it son," the Governor says, rising again, "Don't' worry about the gays, they get off on running around with their drawers in a knot—

"Everyone loves foreplay," Andy quips.

"We all know you inherited some bad eggs," the Mayor explains, "But we need to do damage control."

"How hard is it to gag a fag these days?" Andy asks.
"A little less salt for an old sea dog if you don't mind," the Governor snaps, "But what we do mind, Winters, is when one our brightest turn up missing then murdered and no one in the police department seems to have their drawers in a fucking knot over it!"

As much as it pains him, Captain Somers finds himself forced to finally say, "Come again, sir?"
"Roderick Fletcher," the Mayor offers, as if it's the magic password.

"Roderick Fletcher?" Somers repeats, feeling a bit punch drunk.

"Did I stutter?" the Mayor demands, "Or are you really this uninformed?"

Is that another rhetorical question, the Chief wonders, weighing his options.

"Well let me educate you," His Honor hisses.

And in short order he learns Mr. Fletcher was a nineteen year-old from New Jersey attending Vanderbilt who, according to a statement released by his department, had been murdered just off Shelby Ave. while sitting in his car.

"Unfortunately there's nothing terribly unusual about that," Somers says, ready to educate the big wigs, "Young African American males execute each other for a myriad of reasons: drugs, a few dollars...because they never knew their daddy."

"Well, young Mr. Fletcher's daddy," the Governor interrupts, "Is a statesman from New Jersey as was his daddy before him."

"His momma runs the chamber of commerce," the Mayor adds, "And his aunt is some reporter for the Washington Post."

"Collectively," Andy concludes, "They're kicking up a storm that would put a mess of sand monkeys to shame."

The Governor sighs deeply.

The Mayor joins in.

Somers feels a fall coming on.

"They claim to have filed several missing person's reports yet got no follow-up."

"The parents never received official notification their son was found murdered," the Mayor continues, in a tone bordering on morbidity.

"Let us not forget the piece de resistance," Andy implores, animated now, "One of your detectives accused our well connected buppie, post mortem, of being a serial killer."

"Are you beginning to get the picture Winters?" the Governor asks gently.

"Yes sir I am," Somers answers in an unwavering tone, all the while sweating the climax to this first day of winter fall.

@@@@@

The Man who would be senator, governor, or at a minimum, mayor spends the Christmas holiday in Cuba reading a humorous treatise of grief and sobbing into the monogrammed handkerchiefs his wife gave him for Christmas. When he finished *Good Grief* he immediately began plotting his assassination by the communist regime. What else was he supposed to do while his wife got her back waxed and tossed tequila with Fidel—stick his recently resuscitated St. Peter into the canned substitute they sold at the bistro downstairs?

For the record, as well as the sake of confession, and his sanity he scores twice before the bistro sells out stranding him on the verge of overdosing on vitamin V[40] in a last ditch effort to prop St. Peter up long enough to push him into a hole that holds no hope of happiness.
"Did you say something?"
"Hmmm."
"Are you going to get it in sometime today?"
"Hmmm."
"Get hard or get off already."
Like I can do either with you.
"Did you say something?"
"Hmmm."

As the days wear on the waves call out, beckoning him to abandon both the stagnant confines of his cabin and the hopeless hole and just drown already. On day eight, following his third trip to the buffet table, he rises, hits the dessert bar and when he can indulge no more heads to the upper deck to meet his maker. He is at peace and ready to take the plunge when salvation arrives in the form of a text message from the bistro downstairs.

Recognizing this as manna from heaven he hurries below where he buys all three cases then reports his credit card stolen to cover his tracks. For the next seven days he saturates St. Pete in canned goods, engaging in an aluminum orgy to put Octopussy[41] to shame. *Who*

---

[40] Viagra
[41] See James Bond

119

knew salvation came in a can? He thinks, closing his eyes and plunging into a fresh container, "Who's your daddy?"

"What part of the woods were you raised in?" Ms. Mary screams, ripping the comforter from the bed, "You are sick!"

"I'm not sick," he answers, shifting to conceal a mound of used cans.
"Then what are you?" she demands, discovering the last case and dumping all hope overboard.

"Satisfied," he whispers, raking the pile under his pillow and praying they're reusable.

As soon as his feet struck the ground deemed Nashville he initiates a mission to get runaway Mary back aboard the love boat. Several weeks of sensual, if groggy, sex followed by a week of canned happiness has his nose opened wider than a parachute and he plans to jump again on a regular basis. Faculty and Face book[42] in hand he sets off in search of his human slice of heaven. Loath to waste time when Willie is whistling, he decides to start where he suspects she had.

The door opens and The Man who would be senator, governor, or at a minimum, mayor manages to keeps his composure in light of the smile flooding his eyes. The face, while not a stranger, is also not familiar but reassuringly warm and affirming nevertheless.

"Is Mary here?"
"Mary doesn't live here anymore."
He remembers.
"Francesca, right?"
"Yes," she says, extending her hand, "We met, just briefly, at Dean Debbie's—
"Last spring."
"Last spring, that's right," she agrees with a soft smile, "But like I said Mary doesn't live here anymore."

"Oh right," he says feeling suddenly sad again.
"Would you like to come in for a minute?"
"I would," he decides a full minute later, on the spur of the moment.

---

[42] Directory of staff and students

She listens with the patience of Job while he tells her all about the hellish birthday slash Christmas trip to Cuba, the last place he would ever want to go to in the first place.

"So what did your wife actually give you for Christmas?"

"Handkerchiefs, can you believe that?"

"And your birthday?"

"Tube socks, can you believe that?"

"I can't, but are you still accepting gifts?"

"I am," He decides a full minute later, on the spur of the moment.

And just like that she gives me the second, third and fourth blowjob of my life.

And swallows each time.

Need I say more except to say I've decided to put my search for Mary on hold while I explore this new opportunity that has, overnight, turned a widow loving can man into a carnal future congressman who steers with his left hand down West End Avenue while using his right to caress the silky hair of the siren paying enthusiastic homage to Emperor Willie... I pause to wave to well wishers who will someday be my constituents.

—Priceless.

Home on the Range

He was an abused puppy, petrified to poop let alone make a wrong move. The antithesis of adequate with an average erection cycle of just under sixty seconds but hope for the bush hangs on—when high on his drug of choice breaks his record keeping the poor bastard up and pumping for almost three minutes—prognosis: chances of igniting let alone experiencing orgasm grim to none.
"Just relax."
Instead he instantaneously tries to make himself useful.

He succeeds like a developmentally challenged quadriplegic defusing an intricately triggered time bomb while William Hung[43] sang *Home on the Range* for the hundredth time.
"Who set this little puppy on repeat?"
"Hmmm."
"Did you say something?"
"I said am I too heavy or taking too long or going too soft too soon or—
"Shhhh, just relax."
Instead he shifts uncomfortably.
"Lay back, relax and repeat after me… it's not the destination that's important it's the journey…"

Which was, of course, an abomination but as usual it works and soon the fledging, flapping, flailing swimmer wobbles his way to a gentle wave caressing then pulling away whispering *relax* before dripping honey on wings folding and beating against shutters trapping wind and whirlpools filled with foamy funnels casting him out then dragging him in and down to float on an ocean floor where breath has yet to be birthed waiting patiently until their ship finally washes ashore some two hours and six orgasms later.

Simply saying he was a happy camper is akin to saying snakes smile on Wall Street when stocks close high. Our winter run of countless orgasms on ice, an idyllic adventure rolling merrily along towards eternity rolls on until, high on my histrionics and his ego, Erection-man ventures to the vaginal love hut Vitamin V free.

---

[43] See American Idol

A legion of aborted erections later he lays, aghast, while giggles pour out of me like oil.

"You're laughing at me," he says, welling all up.
"Only if you don't laugh too," I say, never dripping a beat.
After several moments he does and finds it really is quite funny.

When oil stops flowing some five minutes later, the erectually challenged undertakes something vaguely resembling garden variety foreplay.

"Let me help you," I say, running my lips along his lip line and every line in between before wrapping St. Peter in my tongue like a prize tortilla prepared for just such an occasion and stroking, afterward worshipping it at the alter of everything and nothing not even Santa or an upside down cross can keep the cock from flat lining before I crow.

In the end, as in too many hours to count later, we opt to simply hold each other and talk and rock, then try yet again, and again until we finally wind up leisurely dry humping each other home like seals on a white water raft—a *straight* lesbian encounter without the ecstasy but perversely enjoyable none the less.

Giggles pour out of her like oil again.
He joins her, "Wow, is this what unconditional love feels like?"
"Sure it is baby," Francesca whispers and rests her head on his beaming shoulders.

"You know," he ventures, hesitantly; "Before we met I may have been a bit depressed."
Giggle pour out of her like oil again.
"No shit Sherlock, Mary said after the chaplain died you were the only person she knew who could make her feel like a barrel of laughs."

He laughs despite himself, "You know," he confides, completely comfortable now, "I was telling my family the other day that if Ms. Mary dropped dead I'd probably remarry within six months."
"Quite doable when the replacement is already in the wings."
"That's what my family said," he says incredulously.
Blood rushes to his head like hammers on heroin she realizes and snuggles in closer.

123

"Ms. Mary spends all her time upstairs like something out of Flowers in the Attic and it's as if I'm heading for the firing squad every time I hear that dirty five letter word."

"Honey—

"Exactly," he continues, "a perfect example of how something pure can be perverted—

"Couldn't we be making better use of our time?" Francesca interjects.

"I'm okay but thanks."

"Who are you now, your wife?"

He giggles then flops onto his back like a beached whale, "Are you sure, it's been a while," he parrots in falsetto then lays there, spread eagle and dead as a doornail.

"That's tempting," Francesca giggles, "But I gotta go."

"Get me some water and wipe my ass before you leave" he hisses.

"Okay now *you* gotta go."

They giggle like little girls on a schoolyard.

"I'm feeling brave," he decides, springing up.

The bed rocks like a hammock.

Francesca smiles, "The deer and the antelope stop reigning and discouraging words are cast to the winds in favor of two people admitting failure and proposing they give it one last try."

"Hmmm."

"Did you say something?"

"I said St. Peter is ready to reign."

"But will the cock finally crow all the way in?" Francesca asks, oil threatening to pour again.

"Let's pray on it," he suggests.

And so we do leaving heavy hearts, soft appendages, and the past behind and pressing forward toward what lies ahead.

Amen.

@@@@@

Reverend Fisher stands unable to explain why he has returned here. He had, in nineteen years as a minister, officiated countless funerals offering everything from comfort to antidotes to eulogies embodying anything and everything the left behind, the cast, required

124

to bid farewell to that which remained, the remains, reclining upon a lavish divan framed by friends and family gathered to commemorate their fine or not so final performance.

Nineteen years and he has never returned to a resting place for one reason, no one was there, what sprang forth when all that was unnecessary was left behind was already in a place across which the Holy Word declares existed a great gulf, fixed and inaccessible. But the death of this young man remained with him… weighing on his spirit until he finally rose from his desk to step outside for a breath of fresh air only to find himself first behind the wheel, driving he knew not where until he was, it seemed, deposited by God in this place where Roderick Fletcher lay waiting for him.

Was it the surreptitious performance of the service on a Sunday or Easter? He knew as well as the next Job that holding a funeral service before dawn on a Sunday morning was an almost unheard of occurrence and conducting one at sunrise on Easter many might argue outright blasphemy. Sunday in general and Easter in particular was a day of reverence, a Holy day when anything could wait, especially the dead.

Let the dead bury the dead.

Jesus himself said and while personally it was a trick he'd like to see the sentiment at the heart of the saying was not lost on him.

But Ms. Clara had been a member of the congregation for sixty years, she was mother of the church, a bona fide boat tipper, but when he arrived all bright-eyed, bushy tailed, and plenty wet behind the ears she cast amen down like manna from the front row, organized fish fries, rallied the women, and never failed to support when the congregation screamed silence at the pulpit because the message came wagging a little too close to home.

The same silence surrounds him now as he takes in an ocean of tombstones rising from the earth like witnesses standing in collective testimony. All he knew of this young man was that Ms. Clara named him among her "nephews."

At the time that had been enough.

Her only request was that he be laid to a peaceful rest at sunrise.

He didn't realize she meant the very next sunrise.

"He's tired," she repeated to each protest regarding processes, paperwork and propriety,

"The sun has set on anger; there must be peace by sunrise."

125

"I'm a minister not Moses, Ms. Clara."

"I know I can rest now 'cause I can count on you," she said and fell asleep, snoring lightly even before he let himself out.

While living Rod Fletcher had been, like all of us, just a vapor, now, dead, a memory serving as a greeting among acquaintances, a warning among enemies, and a veritable storm in the making. Reverend Fisher scales a steep hill crowned by a mound of unmarked earth, a dark belly full with life heralding the inevitability of birth.

"Ashes to ashes, dust to dust," he whispers.

And it hits him.

There was not a tear.

No sobs, no gnashing of teeth.

No falling out or into or out of the coffin, no screaming, no late appearances, no depressed friends, spurned lovers or complimentary representative from the Legion of Wailing Women, funeral crashers on a mission to make complete strangers feel properly mourned, no girlfriend swearing undying love, no orphaned child wailing inconsolably without any idea why.

He sinks, bearing the realization, down next to the woman heavy with child and searches his eulogy, prayers, and the expressions of the regular sunrise worshippers who sat, in respectful silence, too polite to ask the obvious questions while Sister Loretta sang Amazing *Grace* with the voice of an angle and the coffin was opened and later swung shut... *every eye to include my own remained dry as death valley sand.*

What did that say about his sheep? But more pressing and to the point what did it say about their shepherd? When had he gone from being a man of promise to one who mocked the earnestness of Ezekiel? How had he become the watchman who blew not his trumpet as the sword descended upon the city; in his silence inciting blood that flowed down the heads of the unsuspecting; giving testimony to tyranny?[44]

"How Father?" he whispers, feeling the first wave of pain flow from the laborer to that which is now heavy laden, "Will you require his blood at your watchman's hand?"

He remains, waiting for an answer, until dawn breaks across the horizon but a sign appears from neither above nor the belly and when

---

[44] Ezekiel 33

he finally rises from his knees he is angry, dirty, and painfully aware he still can not weep.

@@@@@

Mary is weeping her way through the reformation session of a workshop for sinners sponsored by a covert wing of Our Sister of St. Cecilia's at the Cool Springs Marriott in Brentwood.

"There, there, my girl you are among friends here," Sister Sarah assures, smiling serenely, "Throw open your heart and share your sins with us."

"I was taken in by a husband and wife who had no child of their own," Mary murmurs.
"Like Abraham and Sarah," a fellow sinner chimes.

"And before long the man came to lay with me while his wife slept…"
"Like Abraham and Sarah," a Methodist sinner notes.

"Like Abraham and Sarah except he came bearing this," Mary explains, reaching into a sack.

"Is that, canned meat?" Sister Sarah inquires leaning in closer.
"Artificial, so officially I guess, it is…" Mary pauses, fearing she cannot go on.
"Speak up child!"
"It's pussy in a can."
"For the love of St. Peter," Sister Sarah whispers, making the sign of the cross.
Mary pops the lid.
A fishy odor fills the air.

Mary waits, albeit impatiently, while the shell shocked women collect themselves, "And while I was yet woozy with pills, worry, and wine he crept into my bed and placed a can between my thighs—
Sister Sarah's assistant, Faith, faints.
The others press her to continue.
"He drowned me with wet kisses and pleas for understanding…I reached down…rammed his penis in the can and he exploded."

"Exploded?" Sister Sarah echoes, incredulously.
Mary nods, "Then he whimpered, wept, shook, shivered, let out a

sigh of relief, and fell asleep faster than a newborn babe."
"Just like Abraham," A Jewish sinner[45] intones.

"This went on for weeks, then, overnight, he would be satisfied with the can no more."
"The soul of man is never satisfied," Sister Sarah affirms, shaking her head.

"I was weak with wine and worry and pills and he was full of passion…"
"Just like Abraham," the Jew whispers into her cell phone.

"…And I kept trying to pull away but he kept saying it was safer to stay in the hole than to tell his mommy the truth, which I didn't quite understand because I was far too woozy from worry, wine, and pills to worry about holes as well!"

"That's because you're a WHORE!" The Southern Baptist bellows, "A stupid, cheap whore who's gonna burn in hell!"
"Who let her in?" Sister Sarah asks, glancing around.
"I have to go home," Mary announces, rising and searching for her Bible.
"I hid it," the Baptist cackles.
"I've had that Bible since I was five," Mary cries, frantically canvassing the room.

"You're   cold…cold…cold…warmer…colder…you're   free-zzzzzing…"

"Who let the Baptist in?" Sister Sarah demands again.
 Mary scurries in the other direction.
"Warmer…warmer…warmer…you're getting hotttt…" the Baptist hisses, fanning herself feverishly, "Hotter…hotter…you're burning up!" she cackles, dissolving into tears.

Mary pulls her charred Bible from the wastebasket.
The Baptist rolls out of her chair and falls to her knees, "Forgive her father for she knows not what she does, save our souls from the fiery depths of hell, redeem us and make us pure, wash us that we may be whiter than snow…"

"Just like Abraham" Rena whispers.

---

[45] Rena the Roving Reporter

"Someone is going to confess they sinned and let her in here," Sister Sarah insists, extracting a cell phone from her habit and dialing security.

Mary races from the room and into the arms of an angel arrayed in white, "Welcome to RVs of America," the Angel says.
Mary feels in fear of fainting.
Seeking to be *present* she chooses not to fight the feeling.

"Retroactive Virgins of America are committed to the recovery of stolen or otherwise misappropriated virtue," the Angel explains when she regains consciousness, "At this very moment an army of sisters comb the countryside in search of your virginity."

Mary looks to Sister Sarah for confirmation.
"It's true child."
"We can't grant you full membership without it," the Angel continues, "But fear not, they won't return without it. Meanwhile, you are to assist Sister Sarah."

The next morning Mary sets out with her mentor, Sister Sarah, a 75 year-old virgin with rheumatoid arthritis, astigmatism, and a wooden leg. Together they scour Belle Meade neighborhoods like Jehovah Witnesses, watching, waiting, and praying until they spot a young man emerging from a bedroom window, the scent of newly relinquished virginity still on his breath.

"Halt you unholy heathen in the name of the Father, the Son, and RVs of America!" Sister Sarah commands.

Realizing he's busted, the bandit leaps to the ground and sprints across the lawn.
"The heat is on!" the Nun cackles, giving chase. She gains ground spurring the spry young whippersnapper to jump the fence. Not to be outwitted, Sister Sarah hikes up her habit, pulls off her leg, and uses it as a projectile, cutting the unsuspecting misappropriater down at the knees.

Mary helps Sister Sarah hobble over and together they strip search him.
Sister Sarah reaches down his underwear and lets out a triumphant whoop, "Another virginity recaptured!" She declares, holding it high, "You can't see it yet because you haven't been re-virginated but it's a wondrous sight to behold child."

Mary nods.

She is afraid to do anything else.

"I always hide them in my pouch for safe-keeping."

"I—

"Not that I don't trust you," Sister Sarah assures, her fevered excitement evident, "It's just this is the most priceless of treasure."

The dynamic duo[46] return to St. Cecelia's well after dusk, delighted with their booty: six virginities re-captured in one day—a new record. True, they bear their fair share of war wounds. Mary has misplaced a favorite earring and Sister Sarah is missing a leg. The protégé pulls the mangled prosthetic from a sack and places in on a pew. It will take the Jaws of Life to straighten it out.

That last guy should've dropped the virginity, Mary thinks noting splotches of dried blood on the foot; *the sex couldn't have been worth the pussy whipping the virgin gave him.*

@@@@@

The sex was worth any whipping he might have to take socially, economically, or politically, The Man who would be senator, governor, or at a minimum, mayor decides, taking his seat up front at an important Metro Council meeting being held at the Capitol. For the first time in history large screen televisions lined the halls and were set up outside on the lawn to accommodate the overflow crowds gathering like maggots on a decaying carcass.

The air hangs heavy, pregnant in fact, with tension fueled by rumors of secret cells and wee green men who sent things blowing up in the night, the most upsetting news to hit the since the king fell dead off the can and citizens were up in arms. Tennessee was, after all, is the. Volunteer State, christened so because enlistment tallies proved again and again more men volunteer to serve during times of war than anywhere else in the States.

You didn't get more apple pie patriotic than people round these parts. Tennesseans weren't cowards creeping around destroying things under the cover of night. When they want to blow something up they sign with Uncle Sam and head overseas where they can torch things in broad daylight like real men and get paid for it.

---

[46] See Batman and Robin

No, nada, nay, make no mistake, Tennesseans are simple, friendly, God fearing folks who believe in keeping the peace even if it means going to war. Hard working people who respect an honest day's work and take pride in a job well done: the last variation of deviant they expected or would tolerate among them are freaks with hearts intent on blowing up perfectly good American real estate …why, the very idea shook the foundation on which Music City rocked.

Yep, everyone who was anyone and every nobody in between wants to know about the bombings but the Man Who knows what few do—they'll need sleeping bags. *Before they ever get within fifty feet of the meat of the matter this jittery motley crew will endure a procedural dog and pony show to put a half century of Grand Ole' Opry performances to shame.*

For as long as anyone can remember although nobody knows why, the agenda has been conducted alphabetically. Before we ever make to "B" there waits a gaggle of appointments to announce, affirmation of posts, appreciations to be given, and the anthology of the latest antics of Commie's kids, the latter requiring several hours alone.

The Senator, Governor, and Mayor are in attendance; the Senator simply for the sake of appearances since he has his on eye on a house as in White. The Governor hankers for the Senator's seat so as long as this circus remains confined to Davidson and Williamson County he's content to sit back and watch the show. The Mayor covets the governor's mansion, a mission impossible if fate prevails allowing all hell to break loose.

And me?

I'm here just in case the poor bastard needs legal counsel before being cast face first into the fire of voter opinion.

@@@@@

The seat Rena has been able to secure at the Capitol is on a port-a-potty in the parking lot. You had to know someone to get a seat on the lawn. Knowing someone who knew someone got you to the steps. Knowing someone who knew someone who knew someone got you inside. Knowing someone who knew someone who knew someone who was in the know got you front row. Knowing somebody who

131

claimed to know everybody got you what it got her—a seat on a port-a-potty in the parking lot.

"You can't park here lady," a cab driver who has to be from New York screams, pounding the aluminum door, crumpling it like a can.
A can.
I made a funny she realizes, giggling, "Yes I can," she insists, holding on for dear life, "I know somebody!"

Presently, after what seems an eternity, the potty stops quaking.
Rena peeks out, "What took you so long?"
Perky Pecks slides in, engulfing her in a bear hug, "They had me playing usher inside."

"Good, good, what're they saying, what's going on?" She asks, activating her mini-recorder and pulling his pants down at the same time.

"Not a damn thing," he laughs, sitting on the warm seat and whipping out what has her whipped at the same time. He lifts her like a log, spreads her legs wide and places her atop that which has made many a woman whimper.
She moans.
"Believe me," Hook whispers, "You've got the best seat in the house."
Only if you haven't had high quality rubber Rena notes, enthusiastically accepting second best.

@@@@@

The sex is worth any whipping he might have to take socially, economically, or politically, The Man who would be senator, governor, or at a minimum, mayor still thinks at eight the next morning when they finally make it through the "A"s.

"Initially we suspected some sort of gas leak," the Governor says, "Now, we are no longer sure. One thing we do know for darn sure—
He pauses for effect.
"These little freaks sure as heck aren't from around here."
He is rewarded with enthusiastic applause all around.

The Mayor takes the lectern while the Senator snores nearby, "With the exception of the last agenda item addressing complaints filed by the Coalition for Gay Rights, this concludes this evening's meeting."

"What about Commie's kids?" the Church of Christ constituency cries.

"Change in wording leads to re-alphabetizing and unfortunately C-o-a precedes C-o-m so anthologies will be tabled until the next meeting."

The Capitol empties faster than Yankee Stadium during a lopsided loss. The Mayor signals to Chief Somers who rises to a hearty chorus of boos. Literally. The Man who would be senator, governor, or at a minimum, mayor sighs, *Why do these simple bastards keep accepting the most replaced post in the City…perhaps they visit in the springtime when life springs forth in Nashville as if from the womb…perhaps no one tells them the family secret*[47] *…perhaps it's all part of some cosmic character building exercise…perhaps it's an opportunity for an ordinary yet extraordinary Joe to leapfrog ahead like a well laid man on a mission…*

The sex is worth any hanging may have to take socially, economically, or politically, The Man who would be senator, governor, or at a minimum, mayor decides, grimacing for this simple masochist, Somers, who's taking it up the ass straight from a less than gentle gay crowd that, while small, launch verbal attacks to make George Carlin proud.

When they can decimate him no further they politely thank him for attempting to pitch a well prepared but piss poor statement then compliment him on his choice of tailors.

"Thank you," Somers says and navigates back to his seat.

"Hang in there," I whisper as the Eunuch hobbles past.

The sex is worth any beating I may have to take socially, economically, or politically, The Man who would be senator, governor, or, at a minimum, mayor notes, changing his clothes and driving at the same time. The Vanderbilt Board of Directors Meeting started twelve minutes ago and though listening to a bunch of stiffs is the last thing he longs to do after spending the night listening to the same, duty calls as does the light at the end of a tunnel he is destined to travel.

---

[47] Violent crime rates in Nashville are almost identical to rates in Washington DC

The sex is worth any beating I'll have to take socially, economically, or politically, he confirms, mouthing a forty-minute oral report on the meeting at the Capitol the night before.

"Thank you," the Chancellor says when his mouth stops moving.
Pause for polite applause.
"Next we'll open the meeting to final debate and ratification of our new Ethics in Private Education Policy…"
"Excuse me," The Man who would be senator, governor, or at a minimum, mayor whispers, exiting the room.

Popping a breath mint he scurries down the long corridor leading to Chancellor Gee's office. Slipping past his web surfing Secretary he slides into the meticulously ornate suite where Francesca waits atop the glistening conference table, the school flag wrapped around her otherwise naked body.

"Welcome home," she whispers.
He dives in headfirst—
Limbs spread wide to welcome him.
"Wave world," he requests, preparing for takeoff.
"Wave world it is, honey."

His driver takes him places the Board of Directors and Chancellor Gee can only hope to go rocking, rolling, working, wiggling, and grunting their way up and down the conference table like pigs in slop, bumping, grinding, sweating, and ultimately climaxing their way to paradise all over the proposed *Ethics in Private Education Policy.*

"It's good to be home," he sighs and simultaneously springs to life again amidst warm all engulfing waves that propel him higher and higher towards the horizon and his new mantra, "There's no place like home, there's no place like home, there's no place like home…"

@@@@@

"The pickings are pretty slim over here as well," Perky warns, leading Rena back to the fish tank in search of a fresh story after last night's bust at the Capitol.

He was right. A couple of hookers, a housewife collared for lifting engagement rings, a Croatian teen arrested for gang banging, and, in the corner, when they shift like ghosts, an elderly black woman reading a Bible.

"Who's she?"
"Ms. Eula."
"What's she in for?"
"Assault."
"You're kidding, she has to be eighty."
"Ninety but looks can be deceiving; she tried to beat one of our detectives to death."
"You're kidding."
"I'm not."
"Is there any way I can talk to her alone?"
"Sure," he says, opening the cell, "But it'll cost you," he gestures to the other perps,[48] "Get lost."
Their hearing and comprehension skills are above average.
"Can you just do that?"
"I know somebody."

Rena enters the cell and sits on the bench next to Ms.Eula in what has to be the grimiest jail cell Davidson County offers, "No pan over there, then to me," she directs.

Perky takes direction well, using the camera phone with video feature to capture the worn Bible laying on a battered blanket, the practical Red Cross shoes, the sturdy cane carved in the shape of a tree.
"Now, zoom in on her then include me."
The screen fills with the ample, elderly, female inmate in an orange jumpsuit.

"I'm Rena your Roving Reporter reporting from this absolutely miserable place where Ms. Eula Williams, an eighty nine year-old asthmatic, tax paying widow being held, without bond, charged, she insists unfairly, with assault."

Rena motions with her foot.

Perky takes two steps back to get a better shot of the two women. Rena, pleased with the positioning, turns back to the widow, pats her

---

[48] perpetrators

hand empathetically and smiles, "Ms. Eula, honey, why did you, in your own words, jump the trifling, shiftless ass motherfucker?"

@@@@@

"Misery always loves company, remember that shit," Detective Green counsels his partner who, he has decided, isn't such an unbearable pain after all.

Opie nods.

"When things are good people line up to kiss your ass but when shit starts droppin' from the sky everyone starts aimin' for a duck."

"Why are they aiming for the duck?"

Green refuses to answer, just on gp, instead cruising past Fisk, stopping the car near the corner of Jefferson and D.B. Todd before turning to face his still next to stupid partner, "Never get caught in the trap of feeling guilty about knocking hustlers up. These guys at fifteen and sixteen; they ain't like we were, they're career criminals."

Putting the car back in gear they navigate a slow cruise down the animated street.

"Now this stretch of real estate," Green instructs, sweeping his hand in both directions like a broom, "Is mine but those three side streets across from TSU[49] are up for grabs, but," he cautions as a wide smile crosses Opie's face, "Like great sex, it won't last long."

His protégé gets out while he watches from behind the wheel. As instructed Opie identifies himself, isolates the leader, puts a lanky arm around his shoulder and walks a little further up the block with him. Green smiles, proud as a father; he has broken his pup in not only quickly but also well though, he can't take all the credit—the Albany State grad was lazier than any crack head he knew.

Less than overnight, bright eyes and bushy tailed took to collecting taxpayer paychecks to loaf like foot freaks take to feet.

"Punk only had two hundred bucks," Opie announces, climbing back in, "I let him keep forty."

"Your loss," Green answers, snatching a hundred, "The house still collects half."

---

[49] Tennessee State University

The radio cuts into Opie's attempt at protest.

"Green," Chief Somers snaps, "Get your black ass downtown, now."

@@@@@

Ms. Eula, as she insisted on everyone outside her ever shrinking circle of contemporaries call her, had lived in her house for sixty-eight years, raised a child in it, nursed her husband, Harvey, on his deathbed in it and, finally, retired to it. Once upon a time she expected that she would, like Harvey, die a peaceful death in it. These days however odds dictated she was far more likely to be beaten to death during a robbery or raped then subjected to garden-variety asphyxiation or strangulation.

When she was young old black women were the safest souls in their communities but now they were hunted by drug heads and crazies who, often, were their own children, or their sister's children, or their friend's, or neighbor's burden to bear and you better believe it all became too much so she and her best friend, Clara, finally took to visiting only each other.

Usually Clara came next door to Eula's because she was an extrovert and polar opposite in most every other way. Eula believed when you made your bed hard, you must be forced to lay in it, nails and all. Clara thought it far more prudent to simply find a new bed. Eula wouldn't give a bum a cold biscuit while Clara lived to listen to sob stories from knocked up girls needing money for a prom dress or young hoodlums too lazy to be ashamed to show up with their hands in their pockets and out at the same time asking for money for everything from baby food to bail.

Just when Eula thought she'd seen everything, Clara started loaning them her car, gladly giving her keys to any low life knocking on her door with a lie about running low on milk.

"Let me get you some money for that," Clara says, shuffling off to the dining room.

Eula shuffles behind her, keeping the spare eye in the back of her head locked on the shiftless loser the whole time, "Is your name Clara or Susie Sausage head?"

"Is that a rhetorical question or do you need an answer honey?"

"Don't you give that little heathen your car; thieving is in his genes his granddaddy would steal his own pecker if he could find it."

"I can't drive it anymore and it's just sitting there besides he moves it across the street for me every Monday morning, saves me a parking ticket."

"And now the hustler is collecting his paycheck don't you know you can get in trouble with the tax man for paying people under the table?"

"He's not under the table honey," Clara says then takes to humming some song or another while counting cash extracted from its hiding place, fancy white dinner linens unused for many years.

"You're gonna go broke behind these shiftless folk faster'n you can say sucker."
"Sucker," Clara says with a smile, throwing in an extra twenty for gas.

They went on like that for the better part of the summer, cooped up tighter than chickens, Clara playing welfare warehouse with Eula prophesying it would land her in the poorhouse. The prophet was perfectly content to stay inside but Clara began to go stir crazy. It was weeks since they went anywhere other than church or the grocery store so, mind made up she drags Eula, kicking and screaming, two blocks to a bus stop where they board the same.

"Drop us at the nearest Catholic church, would you honey?" Clara requests over the Prophet's protests and the driver acquiesces, delivering them to Our Lady of Perpetual Health just as a group prepares to depart for Harrah's, a floating casino just outside Paducah.

Clara slept like a baby all the way while Eula kicked and screamed with anyone willing to listen to her for more than five seconds.

"Are we here already?" Clara asks, stretching four hours later.
"Yes!" the fellow passengers respond in union.
"Testy little buggers aren't they," Eula whispers to Clara then sets about kicking and screaming her way off the bus.

Over the next hours she kicks and screams her way through blackjack, poker, three Jack Daniels, and four slot machines before finally falling still when they sit down at the complimentary all you can eat buffet.

"I can't recall the last time I had so much fun and the people," Eula says, feeling in fear of tearing up, "They're all so nice, do you think they'd let me live here?"

"Someday," Clara assures then resumes counting money like a dealer, "Well, it looks like we won just over two thousand."

Eula chokes on her turkey leg and starts kicking but, much to the delight of her fellow diners, not screaming.

When the grizzle is ultimately dislodged and the paramedics leave Eula finishes her meal and they board the bus for home, "That chili cheese casserole was just what I needed," she confides, settling in.

"Well, the Lord always provides," Clara responds, then drifts off to sleep before the bus departs the parking lot.

As the bus glides to a stop back at the church, Eula is unable to rouse Clara who's sleeping deeper than the dead.

"Are you gals Catholic?" The driver asks, when they are alone.
Eula, loathe to lie simply nods, securing she and Sleeping Beauty a ride right to her front door.

"Come on, let's get your tired old bones to bed," Eula scolds, ushering her usually spry friend upstairs, "Lord knows I never thought I'd see the day I tired *you* out."

"Enjoy it, it'll be the last time," Clara assures, sitting on the bed, "Be a honey and give me that pink gown in my top drawer, it'll help keep these old bones warm."

A minute later, clad in the powder pink gown and fuzzy red booties Eula gave her the Christmas before, Clara looks a little girl suffering that weird aging disease. Eula tells her so and she just smiles falling asleep before she can be properly tucked in.

"Lord knows I never thought I'd see the day I tired her out," Eula muses, wobbling down the stairs and letting herself out after checking the doors, twice, to make sure they are tied down tight as a tent at revival.

She crawls, literally, up her own stairs shedding shoes, hose, girdle, dress, bra, and garden variety accoutrements along the way before collapsing into bed in a slip to meet the sand man. She drifts a thumbnail away from slumber when she all at once comes awake. She lays there, trying to figure out why when she hears a crash out back. She rocks forward twice, gaining just enough momentum to get her body moving in the right direction. Wobbling her way to the window she peers out. Her cherished lawn ornament, an angel in repose, lies broken in her backyard. Knowing a statue that survived a tornado would not simply tumble without assistance she dials 911.

When the officers finally arrive, one comes inside while the other stays in the car. Eula walks into the kitchen and, glancing out the window, sees a figure run by. She screams for the officer and grabs the phone to ring Clara. No more than a second later the cop returns to the kitchen, not even breathing hard.

"He got way but my partner's calling for other units in the area."
Eula hangs up the phone, "Okay but we need to check on Clara."

He seems not to hear, choosing instead to head for the front door where his partner waits.
"We need to check on Clara," she repeats, louder this time.

"Ma'am, her door isn't even open; robbers don't close doors when they're on the run. You can't' want me to bust in and give her a heart attack so stop kicking and screaming, lock your door and go back to bed."

Guess Who's Coming to Dinner

Ricky and his right hand man, Harry, a hacker extraordinaire and quite hairy to boot were up to their elbows in red listed residential development blueprints. The bombing of the buildings in Brentwood and Franklin had gone like clockwork. The ATF and TBI were, as usual, oratorical imbeciles running around like chickens with their heads cut off while they waited for a citizen to deliver the perpetrator to them on a silver platter.

The Unabomber was a prime example.

Here you had a guy, a raging lunatic according to the press, who for eighteen years sent booby-trapped packages to everyone from University Presidents to computer executives; who wrote long missives to the masses setting off, according to the ink, the longest manhunt in history yet, in the end, it was not the ATF, CIA or the FBI but his own flesh and blood baby brother who polished off the fine silver that sent him to prison.

Ricky didn't have to worry about that.

He was the only child of only children who had been orphaned at any early age, a family tradition than made him more than relatively safe. Knowing the big dogs would never connect the dots themselves, he sent a fax in hopes of setting the hounds on the right trail. It was an act not of arrogance but of garden-variety boredom born of listening to the imbeciles lip sync *we don't have any definite suspects yet* which is simply *sometimes the truth is just too pathetic for words* played backwards.

The mastermind in the making is shaken from his reverie by banging at the door. Stunned, he looks at Harry whose long arm hairs stand on end.
No more need be said.
Rick grabs a bat, marches to the door, and peers through the peephole, "Are you trying to give me a heart attack?" he demands, pulling Ree-Ree inside, "What the hell is she doing here?"

"I have information you'll want to hear," Camille answers, before Ree-Ree can.
"All I want to hear is the door closing behind you *after* you give me the money you still owe me."

"First things first," she answers, and, on cue, a gleaming environmentally decadent vehicle with tinted windows skids to a stop.

"Are you expecting someone?" Rick asks Ree-Ree.
"I ordered pizza," Camille answers before she can, walking into the cabin like company.

"What brings you out to these parts?" Rick demands of the emerging figure.
"My truck" Athena answers, striding to the passenger side and taking out pizzas.
Harry strolls past him and makes a beeline for the food.

"Have them out of here by the time I conclude my meeting with John," Rick snaps at
Ree-Ree who merely raises an eyebrow.

Rick exits the can five minutes later to find the four huddled over the blueprints like old friends, "What the hell is going on?"
Silence answers.
Rick fears his head will explode. How can Ree-Ree and his right hand chew at a time like this? "This is a private place!" he yells.
She raises an eyebrow, "Are you screaming at me?"
"Only because Harry can't hear and chew at the same time."
Her hands head south—
He knows they're gunning for the hips, "Honey," he whispers, rushing over and taking her hands in his.

"While you're whimpering like a bitch hawks in the administration are convincing the President to launch a strike against an outside entity in response to the bombings you coordinated," Camille informs Rick nonchalantly, "Pizza?"

Harry stops chewing.
"Close your mouth man," Athena suggests, "That's kind of nasty."
"That's impossible, Rick says, recovering, "They know we did it, I sent a fax."
"Oh, they got your fax."
"Then why would they bomb?"
"Because the fight against terrorism is the only thing keeping the economy afloat."

Rick shakes his head, chuckles, "You want me to believe they'd

142

drop a bomb on someone minding their own business when they know we did it."

"Not a bomb," Camille assures quietly, "Bombs. You really aren't this naïve are you?"

When silence answers she turns to Ree-Ree, "Is he?"

Ree-Ree shrugs and pops another pepperoni in her mouth while Harry's hair continues to stand at attention like privates at an inspection ceremony.

"I have to confer with John," the Mastermind in the making says, melting away as if a mirage.

@@@@@

"Let us bow our heads in prayer," Methuselah intones above the fray then waits, albeit impatiently for the thirty- two attendees at Big Dog's first annual fried turkey cook-off to settle down and come to some semblance of pseudo-reverence…"Gracious Father—

"Shit," Hook shouts leaping from his chair.

"Shush," Marvella, the mother of five of Big Dog's kids' scolds.

"No, shit," Hook insists.

Methuselah opens one eye.

"One of these furry little rug rats just shitted all over my brand new wing tips."

"No shit," Evander laughs, getting up and coming over to take a look.

Methuselah opens his other eye and sits back in his chair while Wilhelmina, the mother to two of Big Dog's kids, one of which is the rancid Rayquan who's crawling around the base of the burnished paw foot Mahogany table, gurgling, and the other women argue over whose fault it is that the child's stomach is sick.

The men meanwhile move back to the living room where Air Force licks their wounds through yet another ass whippin' at the hands of anyone willing to spend more than five minutes on the field with them.

"They ain't been worth a damn since the Admiral[50] left," Hook observes.

"That was basketball," the Dog barks.

"Don't matter," Hook answers, donning a new back-up pair of wingtips.

"You right."

"He's clean," Big Dog's still pregnant girlfriend, Kiesha, announces from the doorway.

The contingency, with Methuselah bringing up the rear, return to the dining room and take their places while Marvella coats the room, liberally, with Febreeze.

"Let us pray," Methuselah intones solemnly over the crying and squabbling that permeates the packed room, "Gracious Father in heaven," he begins.

The doorbell rings.

And keeps ringing.

"Get the door," Marvella says to Wilhelmina who looks at her like she'd rather slap her mother.

"Forget it," Evander says and heads to the door.

A minute later he returns to whisper in his boss' ear.

"Take the kids in the kitchen," Big Dog barks.

"These kids are hungry and ready to eat," Marvella snaps, tearing off a drumstick and handing it their three year old son who's throwing a tantrum to rival his daddy when he wants to suck her titties.

Silence answers.

The women and children evaporate like snow on a balmy day.

"Bring them in," Big Dog barks when only the men remain.

Methuselah hears the shuffle of feet and opens an eye...Red Crosses, Hush Puppies, battered Nikes, black and white Zebras, Stride Rites, and Wing Tips.

"Peggy!" Big Dog shouts out to the battered Nikes who step forward, "I ain't seen you in ages. Peggy used to give the best sucking head this side of the South Pole."

Evander and several Henchmen concur.

"You could drain a camel couldn't you Peggy?"

The Nikes nod.

---

[50] Robinson, David

"You still in business?"

"Naw, Big Dog, I'm clean now. I got a job and everything. This here's my momma, my grandmamma, my niece, Tee-Tee and her baby Boo-Boo, and this is Reverend Doctor Pastor Fisher."

Each of them, to include Boo-Boo, nod in turn.

"So why yall here, you a Jehovah Witness now?"

The Nikes fall to the floor, "We came to beg you not to kill my son."

"Only stupid sons of bitches steal from me. The penalty for stupidity is death by hammer."

"Boom!" Evander bellows then blows imaginary smoke away from the barrel of his gun.

The Red Crosses and Hushpuppies whimper.

The Nikes reach across the floor and wrap their arms around Big Dog's ankles, "I know he's stupid but Bug is all we have left," she sobs.

The Wing Tips step forward and bend down beside the battered Nikes, whispering words of comfort in her ear then helping her back to her feet. As soon as he steps away the Nikes fall back to the floor and reattach to Big Dog's ankles. The Wing Tips look away. Big Dog glares first at Methuselah then Hook then at his crew before finally settling on the Wing Tips, "Maybe if the good man of the cloth bows down, I might consider it," he offers, lighting a Cuban and settling back in his chair.

Methuselah opens his other eye and meets the gaze of the Wing Tips, a man already wrestling with demons of his own trying to deliver a prodigal son back to a fold of four women and a fourteen month old whose hopes and dreams lay hopelessly intertwined with their lone surviving male, a two bit teen-age hustler who left them long ago.

"I don't bow down to another man unless he's a brother in Christ whose feet I'm washing," the Wing Tips finally say.

Only Peggy's sobs break the silence.

"Stop slobbin' on my shoes," Bit Dog finally barks, pushing her away, "Hell, I never had a whole family come to see me before so your wish is granted, I won't blow that stupid son of a bitch away."

"Christ is king," The Wingtips, Red Crosses, Hush Puppies, Nikes, and Zebras exclaim, clapping and cheering like fans at a fucking football game.

"Yall gotta take that shit outside," Big Dog directs, waving them away, "You plannin' on prayin' anytime today?"

Methuselah closes his eyes, "Gracious Holy Father in heaven…" he begins.

While Evander runs in the kitchen to rustle up the other halves of their whole and soon the room re-erupts with the sound of laughing, crying, arguing, and Hook complaining about the aroma once again wafting from the giggling Rayquan who's once again crawling across his shoes.

"Amen," Methuselah ends, and dinner begins.

@@@@@

"It's not that complicated," Camille explains, munching on a breadstick outside Rick's office, "You go public, schedule a press conference and announce culpability."

The toilet on the other end begins to flush uncontrollably.
"Through a spokesperson," she yells over the gurgles, "Someone not directly involved in your organization that won't crack under pressure."

"That might work," Rick grudgingly agrees, opening the door, "They can't very well decimate somebody else if we tell the world we did it."
A smile creeps across Camille's lips.
"What's in this for you?"

"I'm the negotiator for a group with a potential membership in the millions with economic resources in the billions who have a vested interest in global warming, sprawl, and wildlife preservation."
"Cool beaners," Harry says, joining them, "Let's sign'em up."
"You idiot, that's the total number of blacks in the US."
"That's African Americans, thank you very much," Athena corrects before Ree-Ree can.
"Today," Rick shoots back; they glare at each other, "What's your angle?"
"I have no angle; I'm here as a guest."

"This is my place and I didn't invite you so who did?'

"I did," Ree-Ree replies before anyone else can.

"Oh," Rick says," So what do you do Ms.?"

"Monroe. I'm an attorney and the owner of Monroe's Memorial Services."

"The godfather of the funeral home industry?"

"One and the same," Athena answers with a measure of pride.

"Do you know how much land your people waste by burying instead of cremating?"

"We've already been scattered plenty but thanks."

"What about marketing mass graves then?" he challenges.

"Since a plot is the only land many of them will ever own, I'll bow to the status quo."

"Are you serious?"

"Are you blonde?"

"You two need each other," Camille intercedes, slipping past them to visit John.

"Why?!" Rick demands, "I already have space reserved in the family mausoleum."

"Hypocrite."

"Land whore."

"Blonde."

"Black woman."

"Excuse me?" Ree-Ree retorts, before Athena can.

"Athena is organizing an American Empowerment Party," Camille informs from the other side of the door, "You have the Environmental Liberation Front, alone you plateau, together your numbers explode overnight."

"Maybe I'm blonde—"Rick enjoins sarcastically.

"Maybe?" Athena challenges.

"But I don't see any common interests, blacks—

"African Americans," Ree-Ree corrects testily.

"Double A's," Rick amends, "Are as interested in land conservation as they are in joining the Klan."

"Just because the majority is forced to spend their existence worrying about how to preserve themselves—

"Preserve? What are they, fruit?"

"In the hood," Athena continues, "Doesn't mean they don't realize they need clean air and water to survive like everyone else."

The cabin is quiet for the first time since they arrived. The Negotiator, usually willing to surrender the floor to silence for as long as it wishes to speak, knows this is an occasion in which she cannot afford such a luxury. "Now is the time," she counsels from beyond the green door, "For the three to converge; civil liberties, environmentalism, social justice. The three must become one if victory is the true goal."

John swallows in agreement.

"A stitch in time," she adds, emerging, "Has opened and we must step through it now."

Her cohorts, to now include Harry, nod as if hypnotized but Rick remains unmoved, "And if I say no?"

"I will regretfully accept your decision," Camille assures, "Then offer you up like your own flesh and blood brother."

@@@@@

Eula called Clara, a friend closer than anything flesh and blood, again on the phone in the kitchen, this time letting it ring a full minute. She thought to dial 911 again but, impatient, waddles as quickly as she can back upstairs where she puts on sneakers before opening the top drawer of the nightstand and taking out the .357 magnum her dear sweet Harvey left her along with everything else he owned.

When she reaches Clara's back door she finds it ever so slightly ajar. She steps inside and locks the door before becoming aware of a sound above her heartbeat. Turning on the light she sees the faded pink telephone receiver lying on the countertop. She puts it back on its cradle, opens the drawer next to the refrigerator, takes out Clara's carving knife, adds it to her arsenal and waddles on, "Clara?" she calls, in a shaky voice, from the bottom of the stairs.

Lord, let me give her a heart attack she prays, climbing stairs that multiply exponentially with each step, *showing up in the middle of the night packing heat but no teeth or wig*...breathing hard and feeling twice as heavy as her two and a half hundred pounds she arrives at the bedroom door. *What should I do next? Turn on the light or call out to her?* "Clara?" Eula calls, turning on the light.

Clara lies in bed facedown, a white bed sheet wrapped around her neck, a single red bootie still on her foot. Eula drops everything, rushing to her side where she loosens the twisted sheet, "Oh Clara," she whimpers, taking a deep breath and blowing life into her best and only friend.

But she would not accept it.
She was gone.

Eula closes the once twinkling but now terrified gray eyes then gently places her head back on the pillow. Moving gingerly she searches the ransacked room, looking for the other red bootie. Finding it, she places it back on Clara's foot then calls 911 again. .

When the cops arrive Eula scours their faces, searching for the lazy son of a bitch who, in the end, doesn't even have the decency to come back. She complained, bitterly, to the officers that if help had come sooner, Clara would still be alive. They promised to find her killer, walked her back home, and made sure she was locked securely inside.

The months immediately following Clara's death were spent calling the police several times a day to check on the status of the investigation but she got transferred around so much that eventually she gave up. These days she spent most of her time weeping, eating, and watching news reports filled with violence creeping in from all sides.

The shiftless drop like flies, her kind is being butchered like cattle, and the cops keep repeating, *"We're actively investigating the cases,"* as if that'll make Dorothy come home to Kansas dressed as a candy striper. Personally, Eula suspects the pigs are committing the murders.

She turns off the TV, ready to waddle her way to the kitchen to commit hari kari on the chicken lying in her sink, when she hears knocking on a door down the street. Peering from the lacy white curtains Clara gave her the Christmas before she spots two dirty bastards pretending to canvass the neighborhood.

Unwilling to waste time watching the illusion of progress in action she continues to the kitchen where she seizes Clara's carving knife and makes the instrument live up to its name. Chicken joins the onions, garlic, and jalapeno peppers in the sizzling skillet. Their magic take hostage the air inspiring her taste buds to flicker then catch fire, "That's right baby, blacken for mama," she urges, anxious to enjoy the bird before the Ray of Sunshine Church bus arrived to pick her up for Bible study.

She is adding the finishing touch, parsley, to the fiery skillet when a sharp knock on the back door startles her. Unwilling to burn her blackened masterpiece, she grabs an oven mitt, picks up the skillet, waddles to the door, and swings it wide to find herself standing face to face with the same sorry motherfucker who responded to the first 911 call the night Clara died.

"Afternoon ma'am," the Asshole begins, not even remembering her, "My name is Detective Samuel Green and this is my partner, Opie, and we're trying to gather information on a murder that occurred a few days ago."

"What are you going to do about Clara's death?" Eula demands, sending praise up to God for leading this shiftless son of a bitch back to her door.

"Who?" he asks.
"Ms. Clara Angelica Mason, my next door neighbor, the woman who was robbed and strangled while you fiddled your fat little fingers right here in my kitchen, what are you gonna do about Clara?"

"Lady," Detective Green explains, trying to control his temper, "That woman was old, she lived her life, and everybody's gotta die from somethin—

That's when one hot bird jumped a trifling, shiftless ass motherfucker.

@@@@@

Francesca signs for the roses then rips up the card without ever opening it. There was no need; it would be generic and unsigned. *What a little mutt* she thinks, placing the bouquet in the bathroom with the others, *aspirations of statesmanship but afraid to scribble his name.*

She isn't surprised.

She knew he was a mutt the first time she met him.

Not only because his soul was shouting it from the rooftops, but also because it fit him as well as a cheap suit. There he was on display last Spring, a shuffling, flesh and blood human Disney caricature drooping next to Dean Debbie's tacky divan, a solitary dried out sunflower fast losing what little was left of its petals...

A mere ocular shift right revealed the source of his desolation— a wife packing a face that would melt butter and a body that enjoyed it often. Amid brief forced pleasantries he continued to shed, right onto his wife's shoulder. She brushes it off and walks away in search of a socially acceptable colleague.

He keeps his eyes on his feet and follows, head bobbing in sync with his wife's gait...stopping... standing patiently but with a pained look...*is it constipation or a bowel control problem*, she wonders while his wife expounds on the finer points of Protestant Post Colonialism as it relates to religiously conscious regional areas in Sub Sahara Africa.

"What are your thoughts on the theory that God exists for the disinherited?" Dean Debbie asks Goofy.

We all freeze on cue like an E.F. Hutton commercial.
"Well," he chuckles, "I'll tell you as soon as my wife tells me."
Theologians and those in training fake affirming laughter.
After all, what would Jesus do? Ask which of them was waiting for the other to die—not that we weren't thinking it.

A Maccabee[51] in the crowd drew near until Francesca could feel his warm breath against her ear, "The mangy gentile mutt will excuse himself after dessert and commit hari kari all over Dean Debbie's God awful divan."

The Chaplain rescued the upholstery's life by entertaining the suicidal diner throughout dinner and dessert. Francesca wasn't surprised; Jackson had a weakness for underdogs ...*along with a wicked sense of humor.*

A smile emerges as she remembers the two of them, huddled together in the corner like little old ladies at the Divinity School's Spring Fling, whose theme, *Hoedown at Hog Happy Heaven,* inspired

---

[51] See Book of Maccabees

pigs, costumed or not, to parade merrily around…many displaying way too much pink….

A cheerful, heavily snorkeled but still undisguised newly divorced couple approach them, hand in hand, "Praise report; right after the party we and our new significant others are all headed to Harrah's to swing for the weekend."

"So the four of you plan to cash in your chips and roll around in adultery like pigs in slop?" the Chaplain clarifies, with a smile, "I'm not judging just witnessing."

"We know," the giddy pigs reply, square-dancing away.
"Men."
Francesca almost choked on her cherry.
"You're talking?"
"Look at him, neither you, I or poor Nurse Nancy would ever guess he's gay."
"Gay? He's way too tall."
"The longer their legs the higher they throw them over their heads," the Chaplain stated flatly and for the record then dared me to square dance and try to dance at the same time.

Seven thirty and still no word from the spineless mutt who would be you know what. *This is the silliest stunt he's pulled since he showed up artificial preservative free.*

"In case of emergency," the Chaplain shared as we slow danced next to newly divorced swinging swine, "Stimulate the nerve endings around a man's anus, it'll get a preacher pulsing and butt cheeks parting wide as the Red Sea every time."

I stroked the mutt's rectum.
His legs flew up and over his head like adrenaline high hummingbirds bringing me face to face with an unbelievably large asshole.

This was not what I had in mind so I pretended not to notice.

Several minutes later he asked me to help him get his legs back down, "I don't know what happened," he explains, looking more than a little sheepish.

"Relax, sweetie we'll get them unlocked."

Five minutes and three relapses later, his legs finally stayed down. "That never happened before."

"Well," I said, as nonchalantly as I could, "Why don't we just go out to dinner?"

And they had, stuffing themselves to the gills and giggling throughout like pig-tailed girls on a schoolyard. Which is what makes his current error all the more unacceptable.

That weak-balled bastard is more than three hours late for dinner, Francesca realizes, giving the clock a withering glance. *What has the Butter Melter required this time that has him running so late…a children of Israel trek around Radnor Lake, a last minute yen for ripe pineapple, or just another pesky back hair that would give her no peace?*

"Why am I surprised?" Francesca demands of the overcooked beer butt chicken, "His head is so far up her ass that when she farts he tumbles out onto the floor."

@@@@@@

Camille was being called on the carpet for far from the first, second, or third time. In fact she fast approaches seventy times seven, the rod by which men and means are measured. That, alone, called for a banana.

"Camille," the Senator says, rising, "Thank you for agreeing to meet us, we realize it's the dinner hour."

She smiles in response at the contingent who, with one exception, has obviously enjoyed an afternoon of golf.

"We have a question for you," the Senator begins.

"Thank you for inviting me," Camille interrupts, accepting an un-offered seat.

"Sorry," the Statesman explains, "I forget my manners when I'm late for dinner."

His compatriots concur.

The Suit opens a leather expandable file and extracts a picture, which he hands to the Governor's Spokesman, who hands it to the Mayor who hands it to the Governor who hands it to the Senator who smiles his thanks before placing it on the shiny mahogany table in front of their guest, "Do you recognize the man you're screwing the hell out of in this picture, Ms. Leon?"

"The quality isn't the greatest," Camille responds, looking up and into the eyes of the Suit, "But I'd recognize St. Peter anywhere."

The Suit leans forward, attempting a smile of familiarity.
"Ms. Leon—
"Call me Camille."
"Camille," he obliges, enjoying the way it rolls off his lips, "Do you know what the term misappropriation of funds in the financing of a terrorist enterprise means?" His eyes wander down.

His instant familiarity does not shock her. These days any banana with a peel was aware of and took comfort in the bias that affords them the luxury of being infatuated with themselves simply because prophecy is always validated through time.[52]

"Let me guess," Camille muses, "You would be the goofy mutt?"
"Excuse me?" the Man who would be senator, governor, or at a minimum mayor, asks, suddenly flushed.
"Never mind."

She is here to witness not judge. He sits, after all, an intellectualized animal genetically separated from a banana by a mere three percent. Take a banana, add a dash of differential DNA and what do you get?
A man.
Your Man.
Any man.
Men doing exactly what she would be doing right now if she was a banana packing heat.

After all, what manner of beast with a brain would say no to the walking, talking, *and* employed parade of pussy the media reported shortage of men spawned? Hell, if she were a banana she'd be singing:
Free love, free ride,
Free pussy on the side,
In her house, in her bed,
Free side pussy by the keg,

---

[52] Isaiah 4:1/ and in that day **seven women** shall take hold of one man, saying, we will eat our own bread, and wear our own apparel: only let us be called by thy name.

Had one piece now I got seven
Praise GOD I've died and gone to heaven.

Literally.

But for the time being she's stuck with a clit and a slit and plans to milk it for all it's worth.

"Do you know what it means to start whistling Dixie honey?" the Senator asks while the rest of the Bunch smiles.

Ah, the part of her life she disliked best. More than playing mediator, more than donning masks, more than wearing high heels and lace thongs that irritated her ass to no end, she hated sitting pretty in a room full of bananas like an overworked waitress praying for a tip. She, however, seeks more than a tip. She seeks truth, justice, and the American Way a synonym for she shouldn't have to waste time trading pleasantries with these narcissistic sons of bitches if what was really gonna get this party started was some good old-fashioned cunt.

@@@@@

It was her party so she could cry if she wanted to but what right did she have? Sure, she was in mourning but so were millions of others. People, she now realize, die every day, every minute, in fact, every second, just like flies. Her Crisis Counselor told her so that very morning.

"There's no way I can make it through this," she wailed.

He hoped, for the last time, "Yes you can."

"I can't I can't people think I can but I can't live through this I can't."

"You can because people do it every day, every hour, every minute, every second, the same way they die just like flies."

She stopped crying, "Is that supposed to be some new spin on looking on the bright side or laugh and the world laughs with you, cry and you cry alone?"

The Grief Counselor shrugs, "That you must decide."

Thanks a lot Mary thinks thanking him for his time. He expects a decaying, suicidal sex slave from Belle Meade to trust her decision making abilities? And her insurance paid him for this? If she could trust her decisions would she have found herself navel to face with a naked reject from National Geographic? If she could trust her decisions would she still be trying to escape the pit of exile, her resting place since Jackson abandoned her to jack off endlessly or praise God ceaselessly or whatever the hell you did when you crossed over to the light?

"Don't get preoccupied looking for them to be in the dark, they're far more likely to be right out in the light, and remember—they're not like dicks, they really do come in all shapes, colors, and sizes" Jackson shared as if they were discussing tulips or daffodils, "So don't get too close."
"How close is too close?" she whispered.
"You tell me."

But she *had* gotten too close; not to the vampires but to love, to hope, to relaxing…she had melded into and been engulfed by the gray and in the gray there was no day or night or decisions just union wrapped in joy….which was pretty damn cool, while it lasted, because the complication, the wrinkle if you will lurks in black and white hanging out on either edge of the eternal nebula, fixed and inaccessible, a synonym for in the end or in other words someone is eventually fucked.

"What shall we do this eve, end it all or die trying?" Jackson liked to ask whenever they found themselves hanging on for dear life.

Die trying…she imagined she would have died trying to save the other half of her soul but she never even realized she stood in the very place she need fear most. Who knew the vampires would all be so respectable, that a starched sea of renown was the wrinkle that would rise to the surface?

Had Jackson known and if so how had she been locked in the dark when they kept counsel with each other always…even now…
"Running for your life suits you, your legs look fabulous."
Mary hears just behind her right ear.
They're my grandmother's; she promised to give them to me when she died.
"I know what I'd like to give you."
Mary giggles.
"Come on, let's get out and live a little."

It is especially lovely tonight, she decides, *peaceful as a stream flowing through a full moon lit with a hint of laughter—but in a blue sky.* Was it a Tennessee novelty like Walking Horses but what was so special about that? Horses usually walk...then there are the lawn ornaments; pigs and garden variety poultry dressed in red white and blue for the fourth or ties, tails, and top hats for President's Day...still Nashville was like poison ivy and fire ants,[53] for why lingered she here when her reason for coming was long gone?

An hour later Mary enters the Vanderbilt Loews Hotel. Music drifts down the hall and to the lobby bidding her follow it home. She enters a candlelit lounge where Dean Debbie lies atop a baby grand piano slamming back dirty martinis and belting out a pretty good rendition of *Are You Lonely Tonight?*

How appropriate, Mary thinks, making her way to a table in the corner, *Lord knows I'm lonely tonight for why else would I venture out in search of vampires?*

"I can't wait, I'm excited to see what's behind that door," Jackson stated flatly and for the record a day before death came to call.
"But what if it's not all great and wonderful like the books read?"
A swill of Rolling Rock, a shrug, a smile, "At least it'll be different."

What hadn't been lately?

@@@@@

The Suit tries on a different smile.

Penis laden specimens master a repertoire of three, between them, while women amass variations with the same veracity with which they shop for shoes at a double red dot sale...
The Suit tries on his last one.
No, nada, nay not many surprises with bananas, you can pretty well tell what they're like on the inside by a cursory glance at the outside...

"Ms. Leon," the Goofy Mutt ventures, "This situation is not a pretty one to say the least. At the same time we're not interested in torching the baby with the bathwater so we need to know, here and now, how far you are willing to go—

---

[53] It grew on you whether you wanted it to or not and was all over you before you knew it.

"How far would you like me to go?"

Balls, the one thing her kind and bananas have in common.
Jesus wept.
Bananas babble.

The Dwarf rips off her clothing, the Senator enjoys a sound licking, the Governor bends her, the Mayor masturbates, and, across the room, the Suit and she change positions for the twelfth, no, thirteenth time.

"Balls anyone?" she offers, extracting rum soaked, gold foiled, treats from her bag.

Eyes confess what mouths will not, that the bunch can neither individually nor collectively rally their balls together a syndrome coined CBD.[54]

"Anyone?" She repeats, unwrapping a ball and popping it into her mouth.

The Bunch decline, eyes telling each other, and finally, her, no further words need be spoken, that they all understand one another, and have, in good faith, reached at least a preliminary agreement.

"Perhaps we should get together individually to discuss the particulars," The Mutt suggests, rising to formally end the meeting, "I'm sure each of you has a preference as it pertains to how you'd prefer to proceed so I'll act as mediator to ensure all of your, and of course your," he adds, reusing his first smile again, "Needs get met."

Only pleasantries remain, which Camille conducts without regret.
"So Ms. Leon," the Suit says as soon as they are alone "What *are* you willing to offer?'
Camille stands, "Thanks so much for asking. Above all tangible considerations I'm willing to offer evenings during which you will be sucked, fucked, blown, owned, licked, tricked, teased, pleased, nibbled 'til you're weak in the knees... " she inches closer, "Cheered on like a warrior while Willie swells, yells, flies, dies and goes to hell; wakes up climbs up, hooked like crack, poking me for re-runs in my back, moaning, groaning, screaming, feeming, looking for more every

---

[54] Communal Ball Deficiency

evening, mastered, captured, strung out like smack, pussy-whipped crazy and begging me back."

Balls anyone?

@@@@@

Mary camps out behind a column in a corner trying to relax and casually scan the piano room at the same time. "There you are," she sighs, greeting the warm current sending orgasmic sensations coursing through her body. She shivers, closes her eyes and flows with the experience.

"Who said there was no sex after death?"

Apparently the same person who said life is fair.

Spirit to flesh love rocks like a mountain cradled in eternity manifesting the Holy Ghost[55] referenced in the book of Bar Kays.

And therein lay the wrinkle.

Eternity is just that, neither surpassed nor matched in purpose a synonym for flesh to spirit=too everything, too beautiful, too painful, too satisfying, too soaring and too searing, ending, as it inevitably must, with her body yet anchored to earth by fettered feet a synonym for fucked. *Spirit and flesh, pain and beauty, hope and fucked—forces as deeply and irretrievably intertwined as air and breathe, heart and beat, life and death...*

"This is an emergency," Mary announces to the next waiter who happens by.

The man in white understands 911.

"Apple martini with extra olives instead of cherries, loaded potato skins, and death by chocolate for dessert."

"Right away ma'am."

Dean Debbie begins her set with a classic, *"Lets get it on,* she implores, *"Let's get it on—you know what I'm talking about, come on baby...*

A beefy trio in the middle of the room endeavors to eat their adjective into extinction.

"Let your love come down...

---

[55] R&B hit 1978

Customers at the bar conduct business.

"If you believe in love lets get it on, you know what I'm talking about come on baby...

In the opposite corner, a large family reunites for an occasion after many years spent apart.

Mary is captivated. The group, already grand in number, add new members faster than bugs fleeing exterminated woodwork; each greeted identically, with warm Colgate smiles and sincere hugs Mary can feel clear across the room. Four adult generations mingle; gracious silver haired matriarch to spiked hair punk rockers outfitted in couture they should've bought off the rack at Wal-Mart.

The uninvited guest spends the next hours dancing, drinking, laughing, sharing stories, and unconditional affirmation—it is love and the intruder drinks it in, deeply, resolving to neither waste nor miss a moment of it, treasuring each smile... melting into each embrace... accepting any hint of humor drifting her way...when she lifts her lids, she knows not how much later, she floats in bottomless pools belonging to the unofficial greeter of the clan.

She knows my secrets Mary realizes and looks away, *they all do*, she realizes now, seeing them as if through new eyes.

"I saw your light from across the room, I'm   Sophia."

Mary rises from her chair as if from recovery, "I was enjoying your family, the love you share is quite beautiful,"she offers, collecting her shawl.

"That's very beautiful Mary" Sophia compliments, reaching out to finger the fine silk.

"Thanks, the Love of my Life bought it for me in Venice."

"I know."

Mary is taken aback.

"I have one just like it myself."

"I better be going, thank you again for sharing your evening with me."

"Thank you for feasting with us Mary, I hope to see you again soon."

"I as well," Mary concurs, shaken yet strangely pleased with her evening spent in the company of vampires.

The Book of Praises

I have no enemy &
No enemy has me.
Selah!

To be a savior you must also be a martyr—
I choose to be neither.
Selah!

Where will he bend?
Where shall she break...?
-- It doesn't matter.
What matters?
Me.·
I matter. Selah!

Just breathe...
S-E-L-A-H-h-h-h...

I've been rigid &
I've been warm
I've been bitchy &
I've been charmed
I've been naughty &
I've been nice
I've been to hell and
Paradise
Selah! Raise those feet

I've been weak &
I've been strong
I've been right &
I've been wronged
I've been cool &
played the fool
Been on bottom but
'Oft on top
But this middle shit has got to stop.
Selah!
1-2-3
 Selah
Pray for me!

Just breatheee...
...□Σ–E–Λ–A–H–η–η–η□...[56]

---

[56] S-e-la-hhhhhh...

The Calm before the Storm

The podium overflows with the Metro Nashville Police Department's finest—Chief Somers to the latest officer to attain the rank of Detective, Orpheus "Opie" Grey, who stands, albeit uncomfortably, with his back to the legion of beat cops he leapfrogged past, in a show of support for their beleaguered brother.

"Have you located the body of Roderick Fletcher?" A Reporter from the *Tennessean* asks, before the last light comes up.

"Not yet," Chief Somers replies confidently, "But we're aggressively working in partnership with the coroner's office to discover what went wrong in this case."
Cameras flash.
Film rolls.
"We again apologize to the family of this young man and are committed to reevaluating our internal processes to ensure this never occurs again."

"Detective Green can you explain to us again why Mr. Fletcher was only charged with these murders after he died?" a News Channel 5 Reporter requests.

"We were always aware that there were witnesses to the murders who refused to step forward," Detective Green reads from a prepared statement, "The investigation was sty…mied by their silence."
Cameras flash.
Film rolls.
"In the course of time an eyewitness, Jeffrey Burns, fingered Mr. Fletcher but was himself killed shortly after that."

"Do you suspect that Roderick Fletcher killed Jeffrey Burns?" a Reporter from 4 asks.

Green catches himself before the smile in his heart spreads to his face, "We're currently investigating that possibility," he responds.
Chief Somers takes an audible breath.
Green's heart threatens to flood, "Are there any more questions?" he asks, graciously.

"What about the case of Clara Mason?" A bullhorn blares from the back.

"Clara who?" he demands when the ruckus dies down.

"Ms. Clara Mason," Rena repeats moving through the crowd and towards him with a bailed out Jailbird in tow, "her next door neighbor, Ms. Eula, here discovered her body and was subsequently arrested by you."

Cameras flash.

Film rolls.

"She's here with me today seeking answers from the lead detective in the case."

Cameras flash.

Film rolls.

"That would be you wouldn't it detective?"

Cameras flash.

Green wrestles against an intense urge to beat the living shit out of this bitch Jew.

Film rolls.

"That case is still open," he says, recovering his composure, "Unfortunately it's also colder than a stiff packed in dry ice but we'll continue to pursue any new evidence that presents itself."

"That's a bit hard to believe," Rena pushes, feeling her big break squirm, "Since you failed to protect poor Ms. Clara when she was being strangled to death right under your nose with her own freshly ironed—

"And starched," Ms. Eula adds, snatching the bullhorn, "She always starched her bed sheets; said if she could do it for rich white folks she could do it for herself."

Chuckles ripple through the crowd.

Now it is Chief Somer's turn to smile inside. He won't have to fire this sorry son of a bitch; the press will do it for him. He casts a sidelong glance at the Mayor who's fighting off hyperventilation. Somer's heart threatens to burst, his buns are nice and toasty, and his money says the Mayor would sooner murder than be cast face first into this fire himself.

"I'm a detective miss not a fortuneteller," Green states flatly and for the record, "I responded to her call even though it wasn't my responsibility because I was in the neighborhood. I checked out this lady's house and even chased the suspect on foot; there was no evidence her neighbor's house had been entered."

"And that excuses your failure to at least follow up on a phone call?" Rena presses.

Green steps towards her, "Am I supposed to call every grievin' old hag to ask how she's hangin'? Do you want me to stop by the morgue to say hi to the stiffs too? People die everyday, every hour, every minute—

"Just like flies Detective? That is one of your favorite sayings isn't it," Rena probes, nearly orgasmic.

Cameras flash.

Film rolls.

Time stops...nope, it's just him.

"All I'm sayin' is I don't have time to go back and care about each one," Green continues, calming down for the cameras, "Because there's new dearly departed folks that need my undivided attention."

"Thank you, Detective," Rena coos, "For your most enlightening comments."

@@@@@

The mountain of food covering the buffet table could feed a small army: potato salad, Cajun collard greens, fried chicken, barbequed ribs and feet, macaroni and cheese, baked beans, green salad, vegetarian lasagna, string beans, apple pie, peach cobbler, strawberry cheesecake, and a highly spirited rum cake. Nashville's top kingpins make their way around the spread, loading plates like it's the last supper.

"This is some crib you got Chip a Hoy, what you doing hanging out in the hood?"

Hook, the ruler of heroin, opium, and ecstasy asks gazing out from dreamy green eyes birthed from long black lashes curling just so atop lids that laugh at the world.

You didn't need to be psychic to know he got plenty play, poon, tang, head and yah yah even before he knocked off Wild Willie to become king of heroin hill. Light of skin, fine black men with cat eyes and a whorish nature always got laid much and well. They didn't have to chase the bush; legs flew open for them as if they were on fire and an ego the size of a mountain was the only antidote.

164

"And don't sling us that same shit Athena tosses around about how that's where her peeps are," Big Dog barks.

Good 'ole Athena, Camille thinks, smiling. She knew they would fit together like a question and its answer moving in sync to a symphony playing in real time, "Athena spends her time in the hood because her peeps are her passion," she answers, popping the cork on a bottle of champagne, "For me it's business, a means to an end and we're all actors in a universal play whose time has come."

The doorbell rings.

"Excuse me just a moment."

"Damn, she's fine," Big Dog barks as soon as she's out of earshot.

"True, true…." Methuselah muses, bypassing the mudstompers and ribs in favor of vegetarian fare.

"Two g's say I hit it," Hook wagers, bright eyes gleaming.

"Five g's say I hit it first," Big Dog barks, upping the ante.

"Bet."

They bump on it.

Camille re-enters the room, arms bursting with roses, "You shouldn't have," she says, giving Big Dog a kiss on the cheek.

"Beautiful flowers for a beautiful woman," he gushes, winking at the green-eyed monster.

@@@@@@

Francesca is beginning to wonder if the pussy power is wearing off when the goofy Mutt finally shows up at her door.

"I'm sorry about not being around much lately," he explains despondently, body drooping ala sunflower last spring.

"That's okay," she assures.

But of course it isn't. There were explanations to be given, excuses to be made, restitution to be allotted, apologies to be accepted…"I just assumed you ran out of cash or condoms."

"No, that wasn't it," he says, missing the sarcasm altogether, "I've been feeling really torn about all this…"

"Well, you're still looking pretty torn, and tight," she observes, leading him to the couch before settling in on the loveseat.

165

He gazes at her with sad, puppy dog eyes, "Can I come over there with you?"

"No, sweetie, you stay over there."

"The truth is," he says sitting on the very edge of the couch and using long limbs to cross the chasm to her hands, "I'm falling in love with you."

"…And that's a bad thing?"

"I don't know…that's just it…I don't know what to think about what I'm feeling…how do you think I should feel?"

"Well, only you know that sweetie…does it feel good?"

"Oh yes, God yes, the best it's ever felt, ever, ever, ever into infinity."

"But that's bad?"

"Yes…no…I don't know I mean the more I'm with you the more I want to be with you…"

The wide-eyed, bushy fucking tailed Mutt confesses staring at me with tortured yet hopeful, hungry, puppy dog eyes.

"That's how I feel about you too."

He falls to his knees and licks her feet.

"Okay, that's enough honey."

"I was hoping you would say that but I was afraid you wouldn't."

"Well that doesn't sound good," she answers, getting up and heading to the kitchen, "Would you like something to drink?"

"Sure."

Francesca opens the fridge, pours two glasses of tea and turns to find him standing right on top of her. *How does this goofy mutt creep around so quietly?* She hands him the glass, drops back out of the pocket, and passes off to the right.[57] He rolls left and around wrapping her up immediately.

"I've missed you," he sighs, burying her face in the cubbyhole between his breasts and stomach.

"Really," she says, sliding away and into a chair, "You sure fooled me."

"I should have called but I've been really confused and Ms. Mary has been really suspicious with me being so much happier and all."

"And that's a bad thing?"

---

[57] ask any football fan

"Yes."

"Because?"

"Because I'm beginning to worry I might not be able to live with Ms. Mary until I die a not fast enough death."

"And that's a bad thing?"

"Yes."

"Because?"

"Ms. Mary said no divorce under any circumstances but she also said she would divorce me immediately me if I ever cheated again."

"So you've cheated before."

"Once, well twice, well are we counting individuals or instances?" He waits not for a response.

"And my family...a divorce would kill them."

"So no one in your family is divorced?"

"Half of them are but I would be the tiebreaker..."

"I see...and that would be a bad thing?"

"With my parents parked in the pasture it would perturb them no end to have the morality of the family tip irretrievably south before they march off to meet their maker."

"I see," Francesca says, rising to her feet and waiting for him to do the same.

Instead he pulls her down on his lap, "But now I just don't know if I can keep going through the motions with Ms. Mary until I die."

"Well, let me know when you figure it out," Francesca responds, trying to stand.

"I think I am figuring it out," he insists, pulling her back into the cubby hole.

"Honey," she gasps, trying to breathe, "This is a hamster wheel and you're burning time."

"This time it's different."

"Because?"

"I had an epiphany at the firm retreat—

"Honey epiphanies are like sperm, necessary but messy, call me when you have an e-fucking-piphany," she suggests, trying to slide from his grasp, "They're far more refreshing."

In her fervor for freedom she falls to the floor.

He reaches for her.

She rolls.

He follows, like toilet paper, clinging to her at the front door, "Listen, I was stuck on this ship watching all the other couples and maybe they all deserve Oscars but they all seemed genuinely happy then, inexplicably, I found myself thinking how much happier I would be if—

"If I were there?"

"If I pushed Ms. Mary overboard."

@@@@@

Presently, Camille's guests are stuffed to the gills and topping it off with cold brewskies[58] she matches bottle for bottle, "Hook, what did you want to be when you grew up?"

"What the fuck kind of stupid question is that?" he asks, draining his bottle.

"The only stupid question is one that doesn't get asked."

"And that one," Big Dog adds, "I made a funny."

The men enjoy a laugh while Camille waits, patiently.

Soon only silence fills the space.

"What did I want to be when I grew up?" Hook repeats, his agitation growing, "What the fuck difference does that make? I thought we were supposed to be here to talk business, what the hell did you want to be when you grew up?"

"A hit woman for the CIA," she shares without hesitation.

"Damn," Methuselah muses, shaking his gray head.

"So are you with the CIA?" Big Dog barks, springing up, 9mm glock in hand.

"No," she answers, shining eyes locked on the gun, "I've always wanted one like that; can I play with it?"

The men stare at her for a long second.

"I wanted to be a hit woman because I could kill people and get paid for it."

"You could come work for me," Big Dog offers, handing her the gun.

"These days I'm more interested in business diversification as it relates to the inner city drug trade—"

---

[58] beer

"Man, she is one crazy fucking bitch" Hook summarizes, as if she's absent.

"Slowly," she continues as if he is as well, "And in such a way that you gain instead of losing money or if you decide you don't want to give up the trade, I'll assist you in relocating it out of your own neighborhoods."

"Why the fuck would we want to do that?" the Invisible Man demands, "We're rolling in cash, rides, bitches, we got everything we need."

Camille strokes the gun as if a kitten, "Where's your house on the Vineyard?"

"Fuck the vineyard!"

"You use that word a lot," Camille observes, "Are you at a loss for words or not getting it right?"

Big Dog lets out a howl, literally, and slaps his knees.

"Whitey has it, that's where it is," Methuselah muses, uttering the word he hopes will divert the green eyed monster itching to slap their hostess, an action that, judging from the way she's stroking that gun, could result in them carrying him to the car, a gaping hole accenting his emerald eyes.

"That's right," Camille enjoins, "They're sailing around in the light of day clothed in respectability while you creep around hiding crumbs, terrorizing your neighbors, and offering your brothers up for blood sacrifices and free labor for a capitalistic prison system." She pauses, engulfing them in her gaze, "Do you three own mad stock in Corrections Corporation of America or are you serving your people up on silver platters and not even gettin' a cut of the skinny for it?"

The once light-hearted party bows now, heavy with tension. The men sit, anger encasing them like a tomb. They wait for Camille to speak but she remains quiet. It was the mistake people so often made; rushing to fill an uncomfortable silence with apologies, with praise, with placation, with anything to soothe the discomfort stillness delivered... but in silence there lies strength, peace, and remembrance. Eyes closed, Camille breathes it in, strokes the gun, and feels it warm to her touch; thanking her for remembering that it too longed to be caressed from time to time.

"What's your business plan?" Methuselah finally asks, rubbing his gray head.

169

Camille smiles.

She knew he would be the first to follow the beacon, to open to the possibility of something new. He is an old spirit, a life-force long restless, a servant weary with traveling across time and space, seeking solace but finding none, seeking justice but finding it lacking, seeking love but finding usury; resorting to a path that offered some measure of relief in leaves that grow in pungent clusters empowering its possessor to press on, to dream on, to hold on and hang in there.

"Yeah, what's the plan?" Big Dog barks, following his lead, as she knew he would.
"Yeah hit woman," Hook chimes, "What's the plan?"

Things of power and purpose always traveled in threes: pain, death, renewal...all things of substance came in threes, "It's a threefold plan," she begins, handing the well loved gun back to the Dog, "Brilliant in its simplicity."

@@@@@

"Well..." Francesca offers, caressing the eyes her Confessee has slammed shut, "You didn't push her overboard you just thought it."
He opens his eyes, "I wanted to."
"But you didn't, you just *thought* it...so...how did it feel?"
"Really, really good," he admits, shuttering his eyes as if against an impending sandstorm, "Which is why I'm thinking maybe I need a change, what do you think?"

"Open your eyes honey."
And when he does.
"It's what you think that's important."

"Counseling won't work," he says, trying to take off her dress, "Too little, too late."
"Not if you want it to work, look at Bill and Hillary."
"Bill has his Hillary, but I have my hell" he responds, wiggling out of his pants and underwear without any hands.

"How do you do that?" she asks, giggling in spite of herself.
"I can change clothes while I drive," he announces, trying to pull up her dress.

170

"Slow down Alf."[59]

"I've made up my mind, Ms. Mary and I are getting divorced and that's all there is to it."

He tries, in vain, to gain entry.

"What gives you that idea?"

"We talked about it when we walked at Radnor this morning."

"Talked about it how?"

Silence answers.

Twelve position changes and accompanying attempts on his part later he amends his position, "We agreed that we have nothing in common, that she hates sports, politics, my family, my friends, basically anything and everything I'm interested in," He tries to kiss her.

"And?"

"And she said she realizes we'll probably eventually divorce and that's okay as long as she gets two thirds of the money, her allowance, the life insurance policies, the river cottage in McMinnville, and the house in Belle Meade."

"You're joking."

He shakes his head.

"Wow, did that hurt your feelings?"

"A little but its okay…"

"Gee golly Kunta[60] I thought you'd have to chop off your own foot to get away."

"Me too," he giggles, trying to get it in again.

"My money says you'll still have to."

"What else do you want?"

"Tell me what you want," Francesca answers, stroking St. Peter for the first time in far too long.

"I want to go home," he whispers, fervently praying it might happen, "I want you to take me to the river, wash me down, drown me then revive me again," he confesses with wide, pleading, puppy dog eyes.

And her sea parts, drawing him nearer the whirlpool…deeper then deeper, pulling away only to suck him in again like anger and fear and

---

[59] canine ambassador of Pluto, see NBC
[60] See Roots, Kunta Kinte, Haley, Alex

dreams too long deferred, eaten alive by loss and liquid love and I who was so long lost am again found and at home and hell is far, far away from this affirming journey filled with joy and he has learned.

Learned that he can, with a compatible partner, go from soft to hard to harder to hardest to soft to hard, harder, hardest, to soft to hard, harder, hardest to soft to hard, harder, hardest and back again, on this side of eternity, without ever having to exit the hole from which this never ending happiness sprang.

To those who had, like him, stumbled upon this miracle of life, he offers his sincere congratulations. He was tickled pink to call them friend. To those who failed to be so fortunate, he can only offer his happy ass to kiss from now 'til such time as they crossed over and came, literally and figuratively, to the fucking light.

@@@@@

Captain Somers searches all night and finally finds the illegally confiscated file of Roderick Fletcher at four a.m. What should be thick with investigative notes is instead thin as skin, bearing only a form 252. His heart experiences hot flashes while shivers race down his spine towards their final destination. He sits on a heating pad to halt the hell that is an icy hole.

One of his many predecessors instituted the little used Rule 252 years earlier after being lured to a department suffocating beneath the weight of the crack wars. Unlike Chicago where drug lords banned the cheap product, crack hit the streets of many cities, to include Nashville like a tidal wave, swallowing whole communities the way whales swallow whiting.

Dealers were better armed than police, willing to kill with abandon, and unafraid of death driving veteran cops and detectives, unable or unwilling to fight these types of criminals, into early retirement. The situation offered no easy answers but the public, press, and political pundits demanded them anyway leading officials to sanction Rule 252, an emergency action instituted on the East Coast.

Under Rule 252 officers could close cases administratively if a suspect was killed, committed suicide, confessed on his deathbed, was already in jail, or fled to a country that failed to recognize extradition agreements. For the first time, in history and en masse, police departments solved hundreds if not thousands of cases without making a single arrest.

It seemed a beautiful compromise that made everyone's life easier: cops on the street, overburdened public defenders, and especially citizens, who, informed of the dramatic increase in solved homicides, were not only able to sleep better at night but also spared the taxpayer expense of trials or incarceration; a win-win situation, perfect in common sense simplicity except for the wrinkle, that unforeseen shift in the atmosphere that screws everything up.

In this case the wrinkle's label read: lazy law enforcement officers unwilling to do the required follow-up necessary to close out the files. It was this failing, their refusal to follow standard documented police procedure without any conscience or semblance of principles that spurred department after department to outlaw the practice. In reviewing the scant file of Roderick Fletcher the only thing that surprises Somers is that the lazy bastard, Green, filed a report at all, "Tagged him with four fucking murders!" he screams, beating the file against the desk.

Even when Rule 252 was in its heyday any cop worth his balls knew you never attached more than two stiffs to a stiff but that refusing to follow proper rules and standard procedures glutton Green got greedy and tagged four. *There's nothing more disgusting than a masturbating homicide detective who refused to do his homework. The lazy bastard figured Fletcher for just another throwaway but he was way off base; now the kid's classmates, devoted family, a host of relatives, and many sorrowing friends are kicking up more fuss than fags at Ms. Gay America the funeral ...*

His snobby assed assistant, Victoria, appears in his doorway, "You might want to take a look outside sir."

A huge though remarkably quiet crowd gathers around the stairs. News vans and reporters circle while sound crews set the stage in anticipation of a lynching, "Where the hell is Green?" he demands repeatedly of everyone in general and no one in particular racing through the station and outside to cut off the press.

"I want to know where my son is," Mrs. Fletcher is already saying, "We reported him missing last November but heard nothing, now—" tears overtake her.

The cameras catch sight of Chief Somers.

Miraculously, she collects herself, "My son was no saint but he never got into trouble for anything more than dealing a little weed, off campus, which we can all admit was wrong."

Her daughter leapfrogs past her and to the mike, "Roderick didn't kill anybody," she states firmly for the record, "Officers from cities less honorable than your own are sometimes trained to pin a murder on anybody just to say they closed a case. First they wouldn't look for him, then they said he was murdered, now they can't find his body but they're claiming he killed *five* people," She holds her hand high, spreading her fingers wide for emphasis, "Five. "

"FIVE!" Somers screams.[61]

"Yet they never questioned him once, about anything?"

Somers prepares to fall on his own sword.

Green cruises by like a saint on a Sunday drive-by.

"There he is!" Rena screams, sprinting toward his car, news crews on her heels.

Green is a mite more than tempted to run her ass over. And over.

"What of these allegations?" the Jew Bitch demands, sticking the mike in his face, "If you suspected Roderick Fletcher of five murders, why didn't you arrest him?"

"I'm not at liberty to make a statement at this time," Green offers, getting out of the car and heading toward the building, "But rest assured the cases were investigated thoroughly and the right man held responsible."

"Where's my boy's body?" the mother cries, "He wants to rest in peace."

"Where's your evidence?" His sister demands.

"When *can* we get a look at the evidence?" Rena asks.

"As soon as I finish manufacturing it," Green says.[62]

"You haven't answered the nice lady's question," Chief Somers whispers, taking him by the arm and turning him back to face the cameras.

"We're currently in the process of wrapping up our investigation,"

---

[61] silently
[62] *okay* thinks

174

Green says, forcing a smile, "I'm sure the information will be made available to you shortly."

"Is it true Detective Green," Rena presses, "That you knew the identity of the serial killer mowing young men down like grass but never bothered to tell anyone?"

"I had witnesses who gave me information off the record but the cowards would sooner kill themselves than appear in court," he responds, turning away again.

"My son never killed anyone," the Mother screams, "But you have."

Sensing calamity, Captain Somers steps in, "It is my understanding that Detective Green was in the process of obtaining a warrant for the suspect—

"No one regrets more than the NPD that we didn't get to bring this killer before a jury of his peers," Green interrupts.

Captain Somers grabs his arm and attempts to usher him inside.

"Gentlemen, do you have a suspect in Mr. Fletcher's killing?" Rena inquires of their rapidly retreating backs.

"Not yet," Green answers over his shoulder, "But rest assured, I'm working on it."

@@@@@

The one-year anniversary has been creeping up on Mary for weeks, inching in like fog threatening to descend all at once, like death. She repeats the now memorized message sent by the classmate the Chaplain loved most; *"Grief is a tidal wave that overtakes you, smashes down upon you with an unimaginable force, sweeps you into its darkness where you tumble and crash against indefinable surfaces, only to be thrown out on an unknown beach, bruised, reshaped, and unwittingly better for the wear.*

Grief means not being able to read more than two sentences at a time. It is walking into rooms with intentions that suddenly vanish. Grief is 3 A.M. sweats that won't stop. It is dreadful Sundays and Mondays that are no better. It makes you look for a face in the crowd, knowing full well, there is no such face to be found in that crowd. It

175

humbles. It shrouds. It blackens. It enlightens. Grief will make a new person out of you, if it doesn't kill you in the making.[63]*"*

But it had killed her in the making; the her she knew anyway, and left in its wake neither a widow nor a widower but instead a widowee weeping, running, and dying for three hundred and sixty four days, eight hours, six minutes and twelve no thirteen nope fourteen seconds and counting, counting, counting not on a real life but instead some garden variety facsimile thereof nestled in the arms of Death.

So why did she feel so uneasy?

...Because you still have to get through this anniversary you silly rabbit, she decides, burrowing deeper into the cubby hole between his breasts and stomach...but feels no better.

Anniversaries especially but garden variety ordinary days with Jackson were always filled with laughter and frolic whether spent visiting castles in Slovenia or buried up to their eyeballs in Maccabeens, Moses, and *How to Efficiently Hunt Vampires at Mardi Gras...that's it*—she realizes, and relaxes a bit, *the bloodsuckers are still under my skin.*

For months now she prayed and meditated and publicly and finally privately promised both herself and others that she would, on the advice of counsel as well as for her own good, walk away from what they had done to her.

But how could she?

They lured the love of her life in as a lamb to the slaughter, promising, if not eternity at least a long life by history's standards— barring, of course, a garden-variety car crash or the like.

"And you trust them?" She asked, repeatedly, because her spirit was not at peace in their presence.

"They're some of the nicest, most caring people I've ever met," Jackson always answered with a wide smile devoid of hesitation

---

[63] -StephanieEricsson, *Utne Reader*47(Sept.-Oct. 1991): pp. 75-79.
    From Morton Lieberman, *Doors Close, Doors Open: Widows, Grieving and Growing* (New York:G.P.
    Putnam's Sons, 1988) 24.

"You *really,* really trust them?"

"With my life."

Had been both the final answer and the outcome.

What followed was the meat of nightmares, a stitch in time where just that and space and reason took flight leaving behind her life lying in a river of blood, drained of breath, light, and the laughter she pledged and planned to live out her life with. How could she just walk away from that and hope to ever really live again?

Should it matter that on the other side of the line lay suckers instead of something less frightening, like a garden-variety Pentecostal? Would Jackson just walk away and marry the first political hopeful who would be senator, governor, or at a minimum, mayor and pretend vampires hadn't absconded with what was once a *real* life? *Right now the filthy parasites are probably parading around Belle Meade or* …flying past her window…

Dr. Davis was indeed the noted author, tenured professor and Chair of the Principles and Practice department at the Vanderbilt Divinity School who had never read a student's paper she didn't regret.

So she stopped.

Why continue the practice when so few defendable principles were contained therein?

Beyond that her reasons were her own business, secrets she would sooner take to her grave than share with a single solitary breathing soul.

It was, indeed, true that she was really, really angry but weren't all women named Angela Davis? She'd met a number in her day, even attended a convention of the same name—all angry and all with a story:

I was an abused child.
I was raped.
I was discriminated against.
He hit me.
I killed him.
She'd heard it all before.
It was the title of her last book.
Groupies. She hated them but they were great for sales.

It was nothing personal; she hated, in fact, most people, especially her husband. He was prettier than her. And slimmer.

And more likeable.

And wittier though hers was sharper but somehow didn't go over quite as well...

He had more friends.

He had relatives.

Even their foster kid, who, according to her four inch file, detested all things male, liked him better.

Plus, she was the only one in the house being hunted by vampires.

It was bad enough she had to work with them. It was worse that you didn't always know which ones were suckers.[64] Take Hummie who was only called Dr. Humfordstein by first semester freshmen and

---

[64] vampires

MDiv-5's in fear of failing after investing over a hundred grand. All five feet of him was forever humming while wasting his existence sitting around in high water kakis, laboring over books no one would ever read, and teaching feel good courses depressing enough to send folks jumping off high buildings that aren't on fire.

The knee high loser was still paying off his school loans and a sucker right down to his stubby, untalented bones. No one[65] used vampires any more. It was discriminatory; an anal exercise in labeling designed to make those in the minority feel bad about themselves and bad karma to boot. It was disclosed, years ago, by committee they were okay with being called suckers since it was, organically, their natures.
Vampires suck.
See?
Sure there are other things that suck:
Babies
Men
Men who don't suck
Men who suck at it

You get it. Plus suckers offers far more auditory appeal. Even when used in a derogatory fashion it subconsciously triggers memories of something hard you put in your mouth and enjoy for hours.

And if the suckers, the kid, and her husband weren't crappy enough her neck was disappearing. She suspects it is a survival reflex. The suckers might have a bounty on her neck but they'd have to find it first. Call it karma but she finally feels empathy for that scary little pygmy masquerading as a spiritual advisor. For years she refused to acknowledge, outside the occasional autograph, the little National Geographic escapee privately pegged *no neck Nelly*.
Was it karma?
Karma Sharma if what went around came around it was her turn to be not only brilliant but beautiful, sucker free, *and* as rich as these spoiled rotten ass wipes around here.
"Daddy just bought me a Bentley."
"We just bought the Hamptons."
"I just got laid."
Screw you, you, and you. Why didn't the suckers do society a favor and drain a few of them?

---

[65] See educated, informed, in the know

179

She glances around, grudgingly, at this facade masquerading as a coffee hour, the divinity school's ritualistic Friday at ten opportunities for shepherds to pretend they actually gave a damn about their sheep's theological experience. Every year the committee she manned voted to ban the free crispy crème orgy. She was sure the measure would pass after a Gold Level donor's obese daughter died of sugar intoxication but theological self interest won out over restraint and the party raged on.

"You look tired Angela," Hummie coos in that concerned comforter tone he teaches in his Death and Dying course.
"Call off your dogs you little sucker."
"So nice to see you too."
"Why don't you drain a few of these idiots?"
"They pay the bills."
"Learn to write."
"I just finished a collection on Pastoral Care to the Poor."
"Something that'll sell."

"Excuse me, Dr. Davis," Mary Papins, who Dr. Davis personally thinks could use a prolonged slapping, interrupts meekly, "But I checked my mailbox again today and my paper still isn't there."

"Maybe someone stole it dear."

The walking, talking helium tank pauses as if that might actually be possible, "But wouldn't that be a violation of the honor code?" she asks the Sucker who also serves as her advisor.

"Well," he muses, turning to Angela, "Why don't we ask our esteemed Principles and Practice professor."

She has to get out of here, fast. If a prick penetrates a wall the horde descends as if Jericho is stamped all over it. Even now sugar high ass wipes with necks are approaching their mailboxes en masse while flamboyant anals[66] from the hood circle nearby.

Need she say more?

Any second they would be in a java bean driven, sugar induced hissy. Fingers would start waving, hips would sprout hands, and, inevitably, one of them would be crazy enough to challenge her.

---

[66] Gay guys

Damn.

They're heading her way already blabbering about the principle of the matter.

What did they know about principles?

"Before you expound on principles perhaps you might want to practice self control," Dr. Davis advises as they near Jericho, "Only suckers venture where fools dare."

The hussies melt away like butter.

"Creampuffs," Hummie summarizes, munching on the same," Shouldn't you be off somewhere reading Angela?"

Who has time to read? She thinks, exiting anyway. Suckers are circling, she hates her husband, her foster kid hates her, she's losing her neck, *and* she has a new book to write.

@@@@@

It was a fear of vampires that had drove Little Mary Sunshine, barefoot and bare-chested, out into the hot Florida sunshine. *Dark Shadows,* her mommy's favorite soap opera, was filled with people in a small town who sucked each other's blood. The show caused her many a nightmare since they were people and they lived in a small town too.

Seeing no one in the street she ran to the backyard and smack into her brothers engaged in battle. Teddy was using a sausage to drown Timmy who was using a little pig without a blanket...no, it had a blanket but it wasn't helping him any. Mikey was rolling around on the ground laughing, his saggy piggy picking up sand as he went.

"Can I play?"

Their meat disappeared faster than you could say fast leaving her feeling, for some strange reason, incredibly shaken. Where was her meat? Did they know she didn't have meat—was that why they never played with her? She couldn't ask them because then they would know for sure she didn't have one.

"Come on, let's go." Teddy says.

Timmy and Mikey follow.

"And don't follow us," Teddy adds as she begins to do just that.

Confused and alone Mary turns on the water hose to take a drink while she thinks about her newfound problem. She drank 'til she thought she would pass out then raced inside past vampires disguised as ordinary people. Once inside the can, as the cowboys called it, she climbed atop its mouth and exhaled while warm liquid gushed out. Done, she got about the task of fishing for her meat, sticking her inquisitive head as far between her legs as she could.

All she could see was her own pee in the bowl…so she started fishing around with her fingers and finally found a little bump that tingled when she touched it…cool…but where was the meat…nope it wasn't there. Peeved, she walked out and past the vampires barely noticing the old blood suckers at all.

She returned to the back yard, this time peeking around the corner. The three of them were playing with their meat again; Teddy writing his name in the sand, Mikey squirting pee into the air like a fountain, and Timmy watering an orange tree. *Maybe it's not time for my meat to show up*, Little Mary sunshine thinks and all at once feels much better. Until it did she would practice which made perfect then challenge them all to a meat fight… *but how do you practice when all you have is a little bump … should I ask mommy…no she's busy with her vampires… besides why would she care when she had a huge one of her own?*

@@@@@

China is already suffering," Rick shares[67] with his Department Chair at the meeting he was summoned to, "The drought is in its third year, grain production is off by 30 percent…you know as well as I do that we are the second-biggest producer of greenhouse gases."

"As a nation we are off meeting our targets, but there are timelier issues at work here," the Chairman answers.

"I left MIT to join Vanderbilt because you made it clear this was an environment that vigorously promoted radical thinking and boisterous debate."

"We do Rick and I esteem you far above any professor in my Metaphysical Sciences department but with the nation's attention continuing to be focused on one issue not even private universities can afford to be champions of free speech gone wild."

---

[67] like they were magic passwords

"So you want me to say trees are a leading cause of pollution?"
"We would prefer that you said nothing."
"So you want me to take it up the ass straight *and* silent."

"Well I hadn't considered all that," the Chairman muses, "But now that you mention it your suggestion will do nicely... that's all," he adds when the worn brown hushpuppies do not realize it is time to exit. *Etiquette*, he thinks, turning back to *Science Weekly*, it had become a lost art.

"Do have any idea who you're asking to bend over and take one up the 'ole hole you decrepit bag of dry bones?"

"Excuse me," the old man repeats, confused.
"I said," the young Whippersnapper says, "Do you know who you're asking to bend over and take one up North for the good 'ole South?"

"Well now, why don't you enlighten me," the Bag of Bones invites, settling back in his worn but well maintained leather wingchair.

"A Yankee," the Whippersnapper announces as if it explains everything.
"A Yankee."
"And Yankees don't just turn tail, play dead, and take it up the ass; Yankees stand up, stir things up, and see who's still standing on principle at the end of the day."

"Are you done?" the Bag of Bones asks quietly, reaching for his cane and attempting some facsimile of rising only after the Yankee Whippersnapper indicates the affirmative. His legs rattle with each step, slowly making his way to this brilliant young man whom he personally, and on all but bended knee, recruited from MIT.

He places a frail, fatherly hand on the young man's left shoulder while using his right to bitch punch the brilliant, vulgar, yellow bellied Yankee Whippersnapper whom he personally, and on all but bended knee, recruited from MIT.

The idealistic punk falls to the floor.

"Who the hell do you think you are, one of Commie's kids?" the Chairman demands, giving him a kick to the balls for good measure,

"This decrepit bag of bones bent over and took one up the Erie after you instigated that uproar over renaming Confederate Hall," he reminds his protégé, poking him with the cane.

"It was the principle of the matter," the Whippersnapper wheezes, trying to protect his prized pound of flesh from this geriatric psycho.

"*It's the principle of the matter*," the Chairman mocks in falsetto before slowly rattling his way back to his worn but well maintained leather wingchair.

He settles comfortably in before leaning forward ever so slightly to convey his continued interest in his most talented recruit, "It is war, you ungrateful imbecile which leaves you with this choice, get the fuck out of Metaphysics or park your St. Peter at the door and assume the position."

@@@@@

Little Mary Sunshine crept down the long, dark hallway that led to her destiny. Ducking inside, she closes the door and ever so gently presses the silver lock. The click echoes endlessly in the small space, loud as any gong singing why'd you show up for the show .
She freezes, her small feet frozen to the floor.
An eternity later her heartbeat slows only to race once more at sight of her porcelain oppressor.

It sat, unforgiving, dressed in its Sunday best whites. Mary steps backward, touching the door.
"There is no retreating now."
The vampires say from the other side.
Mary takes slow measured steps forward until she faces her foe.
"Don't look down!" Barnabas, the king of the vampires, warns.

She does anyway not on principle but because she just can't help it.
The vampires laugh.
So does her opponent, mouth opening ever wider each time she blinks 'til she fears she'll faint, fall in, and be swallowed whole.
"Don't be afraid," Barnabas counsels.

Snapping her eyes shut, she pulls down her panties, "In the name of the Father the Son and the Holy Spirit," she prays, assuming the position, "I command you to...Damn, Damn, Damn!" she hisses, stamping bare feet in the growing puddle until her porcelain enemy cries.

"I too have shed many tears," Barnabas shares, "Yet remain as white as snow."

Not so white now are you? Mary giggles then gets busy cleaning the mess.

"You and I are far different from others," Barnabas says over and over, voice fading away to mad, terrifying laughter.

Maybe I'm different...but that would be horrible...I don't want to be the only weird one...maybe mommy is weird too...

. Half a roll and an fool proof plan later Mary skips past mommy and parks on the front porch pretending to play jacks, ear tuned to the TV ...waiting for the creepy music that signaled the vampires were flying away until tomorrow. When the vultures are gone she counts to twenty then laughs like the Count, who, strangely enough, is the only character she can stomach on Sesame Street.

Opening the front door, she hears the water running and just above it, mommy humming. When all is quiet she counts to twenty, laughs like the Count then creeps down the hallway before bursting into the bathroom. Water splashes, bubbles leap, and mommy looks like a beached whale.

"The vampires scared me," Mary explains tearfully, closing the door and taking a seat atop her arch enemy.

"Sometimes they scare me too," Mommy confides, closing her eyes and sinking deeper until her huge bump disappears beneath a sea of bubbles. *Damn dish liquid to hell,* Mary thinks, itching to kick the tub.

Instead, she makes small talk about mommy's favorite subject, vampires, inching ever closer to the tub's edge...but still the bubbles would give her no peace. *I have to see what's between her legs,* Mary decides, falling off the toilet and into the tub...

Almost.

"What in the world is wrong with you?" Mommy snaps, catching her mid-air and restoring her balance.

"I was looking for the soap for you."

"Well, I can find it myself now get out of here before I make you assume the position."

Having seen her brothers "assume the position" she scurries out. That night, asleep in the snoring whale's bed, Little Mary Sunshine has a dream:

It was high noon in Dodge City[68] and the damsel in distress needs a cup of sugar. I get the nod. I step outside and am pushed backward by the hot sun. I am barefoot. The smoking meat, that was once my feet tell me to take the shortcut to Ms. Kitty's. As I round the corner at full speed, I find myself caught in the crossfire of a gunfight. Realizing an intruder has crossed their mist; they join forces, pointing all their weapons at me. Determined to go down fighting, I whip out my own weapon only to find the barrel missing. Turning tail, I run, furiously, toward home. I am reaching for the door when I am gunned down, from behind, and die a wet, yellowbellied coward's death.[69]
Mommy shakes me awake. "I'm hungry."

The whale hates eating alone so while my brothers sleep the sleep of dead men we load hot dogs high with relish, onions, and mustard; mommy dips her fries, I drown mine in a river of red. There remains just enough sweet tea for two so we drain the container then collapse back into bed to sleep the sleep of pigs…
Almost.
Mommy shakes me awake, "My water broke," she says like she wants me to assume the position or something.

@@@@@

"I'd like to start out by thanking you all for showing up on such short notice. My name is Methuselah and I will be reading from a short statement:"

For many years the Environmental Liberation Front has been involved in diplomatic attempts to educate both the government and the public to the very real threats facing our ecosystem. Our efforts have consistently met with indifference, double speak and outright lies and deception on the part of the present and well as the past administration. Because the universal truth of mother earth "non omnis moriar", translated "I shall not wholly die" must be preserved, we have now been forced into a position in which we must defend the very lifeblood of our existence both for ourselves and for the generations to come."

---

[68] See Gunsmoke.
[69] Without her boots on.

"I stand before you, the spokesman for ELF, to confirm this organization was solely responsible for the bombings in both Franklin and Brentwood."

Pandemonium takes over as members of the media fire questions at the old man. Silence answers and the room goes black. Pandemonium reigns as members of the media look for lights finding them in the form of pin lights, cameras, and cell phones but the elderly man, old enough to be someone's grandfather twice removed, is nowhere to be found.

@@@@@

When mommy is released from the hospital a week later, Little Mary Sunshine races from her aunt's house to Ms. Kitty's to buy her a candy bar with the quarter she has been saving since the night her mommy's water broke, making her big bump hurt something awful, and sending everyone hurrying around like someone was having a baby.

At the store masquerading as an ordinary house, her hands longingly touch the Snickers and Milky Ways before surrendering George Washington for an Almond Joy, which she thinks tastes like anything but. She arrives home sweaty and breathless to find mommy keeping company with vampires and her new baby brother sleeping…so while Barnabas sucks and mommy munches on chocolate covered coconuts and almonds Mary waits, albeit impatiently, for the wee creature to open its eyes… finally tickling his tiny feet to hurry him along.

She watches with fascination as he stretches, yawns, then lets out a wail to wake the dead…
"What did you do?" Mommy hisses, sounding just like the vampires.
"Nothing, maybe he's hungry."
Barnabas fades into an Ivory soap commercial.
"I fed him before you came but maybe he's wet."
"Can I hold him?"
"Not yet."
"Can I change him?"
"You can watch," Mommy says, pulling off the diaper.
Mary suddenly feels in fear of fainting, *the wrinkled, screaming creature has more meat than me!*
She falls to the floor.

187

The room goes black.

From the distance she hears mommy calling cowboys who lift her as if she's a sack of flour; *that's right lay me on a bed I need rest and maybe a cup of water but first I*—"Damn!"

"Oooh... mommy!" Timmy screams.

Teddy turns the cold shower on full steam.

"Stop, stop, stop," Mary gasps, struggling to escape the tub.

Mikey and Timmy hold her down.

"You kids better stop playing with my water," Mommy yells while Barnabas laughs.

Tommy kills the tap.

The three of them giggle like little girls except they're pushing and shoving each other.

"Where's my meat?" Mary wails at the top of her lungs.

"What meat?"

"My weinie!"

"Silly rabbit, only boys have weinies," Teddy says when they finally stop giggling.

"But what," the former Little Mary Sunshine gasps between sobs, "Do girls have?"

@@@@@

Methuselah knew the TBI, FBI or something that ended in "I" would be arriving soon so he prays then enters the parlor where he pours ginseng tea to keep him both warm and company while he meditates on why he allowed a Snake to talk him into playing possum in such a fool hardy venture.

When the doorbell rings, his servant, Hop Sing, leads the agents into the library where they stand, evaluating the lavish surroundings.

"Are you Methuselah...what is your last name anyway?" Agent Anderson asks, looking down at his notes.

Silence answers.

They display their credentials, introduce themselves as agents Anderson and Baker and repeat the question.

"There is no last name, just the one you speak, would you care for tea?"

"No thank you," Agent Anderson answers, "As part of our ongoing investigations, we need to ask you a few questions."

"Of course"

"Are you a Muslim, sir?" Agent Baker asks.

"I am of the house of Adam."

"So does that make you just plain black, a black Jew like Sammy, a Christian, a Catholic or a Communist?" Agent A asks.

"Last I heard Catholics still consider themselves Christians."

"Do they really?" Agent B asks A.

They call a time-out to consult.

Methuselah is drifting off to sleep when the session resumes.

"You're right, officially if not morally, Catholics are still unofficially Christians."

Methuselah massages his bad leg, "Well, in the end what do any of these labels mean?"

"What's your religious affiliation, sir?" Agent A asks.

"The house of my fathers walked with God, I believe in God."

"Do you believe in Jesus Christ as well, Mr. Methuselah?" Agent B asks.

"Is that the test for Christianity?"

"Are you a militant?" Agent A demands.

"A militant?'

"A militant." Agent A repeats

"What is a militant, Mr. Anderson?" Methuselah asks.

Silence answers.

"I am a watchman," the Old Man finally says.

"There are among us Americans, Mr. Methuselah, targeting civilians or hiding those who are targeting civilian populations and refusing to bear arms openly."

"What has any of that to do with me, Agent Baker?"

"Do you have other family in the area sir?"

"I have no living relatives by your standards, Mr. Anderson but by my own we are all interconnected and thus related."

"How do you make your living, Sir?" Agent B asks.

"Investments, trading, good old fashioned capitalism." Methuselah says, sipping his tea.

"Of the drug dealing variety?" the two ask in unison.

"Herbal remedies for things that ail the soul date all the way back to antiquity which, by the way, includes America," Methuselah muses, rising to water his plants, "Tobacco, alcohol—"
"Cannabis, Hashish, Mary Jane, Crunk—
"Don't forget the black pot."
The agents go stiff as concrete.
"And Caesar has always received his share."
"But has the tax man while you've been trying to wrap yourself in respectability," Agent A returns, elbowing B.

"As the bastard descendant of Caesar Sammy receives his cut right along with the rest of the rat pack," the old man answers, pouring more tea, "As to respectability, cha•cun 'a son gout."

"Come again," the two prompt in unison.
"Everyone to his own tastes."

@@@@@

A woo-woo. She...has...a...woo-woo. It rhymes with boo-boo which can only be bad. Her woo-woo is a boo-boo. She is beyond comfort. The injustice of it all is still too fresh and, for her counterparts, too funny. Like Alice, her whole world has flipped upside down masterminded not by a devious rabbit but by a meat shortage that could only be blamed on Mother Nature.

"Don't' cry just 'cause you can't be a cowboy," Timmy says, comforting her, "You can be a damsel in distress."

Mary wants to drown him in a dirty toilet. She tries but the little bastard outruns her.

Little Mary sunshine lays in bed with mommy that night feeling anything but bright eyed and bushy fucking tailed knowing she has been robbed of a prized possession everyone ought to be entitled to...all that practice...if nothing else it was the principle of the matter...practice makes perfect Grandpa Henry always said but he never bothered to tell her she didn't have the right equipment. Would he still love her when word got out she'd never have meat?
Someone calls my name. I wake up. Grandpa Henry is dressed, as always, in his overalls and standing in the doorway. He motions to me to follow him. I get up and join him. He takes my hand and we fly

190

away, sailing high over treetops until we arrive at a cemetery where he points out a freshly dug grave. He reaches down, lifts me up and dumps me into the hole. I scream for help. My family arrives, fried chicken and sponge cake in hand and stuff their faces while Grandpa Henry shovels dirt on top of me.

Waking in a sweat, Little Mary Sunshine lays there, feeling like anything but, heart pounding, breath held, waiting for vampires to swoop down and eat her alive while mommy sleeps hard as the dead. Just before dawn she finally dozes off:

After years of rigorous practice, she has finally made it to the World Championships. The stadium rocks with cheers as the three contestants step onto the field.

Contestant A, a six-foot tall cowboy, pulls out his meat and writes his name, **Mac**, *in the noonday sand. The crowd applauds appreciatively.*

Contestant B, an even taller cowboy, whips out his meat and writes, **Wieners Rule!** *The crowd roars.*

I step onto the field, dressed in a green tutu and ballet shoes. The crowd boos. I motion to the linesmen who roll a pummel horse and springboard onto the field. The audience holds its collective breath as I race down the field and spring off the board.

As I sail high into the sky, I spread my legs wide and write in flowing cursive:

Damsels tread where cowboys dare!

@@@@@

"We suspect you're financing insurgents," Agent A says, fishing for body language.

"I'm sure you know regulations instituted following 911 allow us to indefinitely detain, without trial, people we deem potential threats to national security," B adds.

"Anyone covered by this order cannot seek remedy in any court, anywhere," A adds, only too pleased to parrot the words that were his personal favorites.

"But we don't want to torch the baby the baby with the bathwater," B assures, "Just tell us what you know."

"There is a generation that are pure in their own eyes, yet not washed from their filthiness; a generation, whose teeth are as swords, and their jaws as knives, to devour the poor from the earth, and the needy from among men," Methuselah begins, closing his eyes, "There are three things that are never satisfied, yea, four things that say not, it is enough: the grave; the barren womb; the earth that is not filled with water; and the fire that devours all"

"And what exactly, does that have to do with this investigation?" A asks, rhetorically.

"The Lord shall bring a nation against thee from far, from the end of the earth, as swift as the eagle flies; a nation whose tongue thou shall not understand; a nation of fierce countenance, which shall not regard the person of the old, nor show favor to the young.
It commences with an immense raging cloud of fire enfolding and engulfing itself, a ocean of brilliant light out of which springs four living creatures, malevolent and metallic moving as fast as lightning on their mission to resolve the malady of the maladroit. Their four wings touch each other as they fly in formation, their cloven hooves a silhouette against the sky. Glowing coals of fire frame their midst illuminating their four faceless heads which fan out from the fire appointed for earth which has been held in reserve for judgment by a fire that will fill the skies, casting a shadow upon the sun and muting the moon and stars."
A and B exchange glances before answering, in unison, "We're going to have to ask you to come with us sir."

"It is the day of the Lord, gentlemen," Methuselah says, opening his eyes again for the first time, "and we are the house of Judah."
A and B see him to his feet.

"I'll just need my walking stick," the Old Man says.
His servant, Hop Sing, appears as if out of thin air holding his request, a jeweled cane with an ivory handle carved in the shape of an eagle, bull, lion, and lady.

Behind the Scenes

"How long has your church building fund been in progress?" Camille asks the elderly woman polishing the pew.

"Officially, eighteen months because that's when we hung the banner," she confides pointing at the giant white sheet that was impossible to miss, "But just between me and you since you know what froze over."

That said she disappears leaving Camille free to leisurely survey the aging structure. She takes note of the damaged rafters, the long neglected ceiling, and the stained glass windows with patches of new cloth sown into an old garment, taking away from instead of adding to the tapestry; new wine in old bottles, running free while what held it together perished slowly.

"You're early," Reverend Fisher notes, entering the sanctuary.
"I'm a time freak and we are advised to measure it, are we not?"

"Where are you from, Ms. Leon?" he questions, fishing instead of answering as he leads the way to a center pew sitting like a wide brown lady dressed in red.
"Call me Camille, Doctor, and I'm from all over."
"A military brat?"
She shakes her head, "International affairs."
"That must have been lonely."
"You learn to settle in a little at a time."
"The art of easing into being a stranger in a strange land."

"Build ye houses, and dwell in them; and plant gardens, and eat the fruit of them; that ye may be increased there, and not diminished and seek the peace of the city whither I have caused you to be carried away captives, and pray unto the Lord for it, for in the peace thereof shall ye have peace."

"Are you an exile seeking peace?" Reverend Fisher inquires gently.
"Aren't we all?"
"All places are not equal, Ms. Leon," he responds, extending a beautifully bound package, "The lamb was loving but he drove the moneychangers out of the temple."

"You are afraid that your hands will not be clean?" Camille queries, refusing to accept it, "Things from outside do not defile but what is within."

"Would you make me Simon, Ms. Leon, offering to sell salvation for money knowing that its love is the root of all evil?"

"If they love money as much as you think, they won't be willing to give it up in which case all you've done is brought the good news to some who might otherwise not hear it."

The Reverend shakes his head in disagreement, "They've heard it, trust me, they simply choose not to listen; and whosoever shall not receive you, nor hear your words, when ye depart out of that house or city, shake them off like the dust of your feet."

"Are you planning on moving Pastor?" Camille asks with a smile.
"I'm sure you understand the spirit of the Word."

"I do," she agrees, "But is not faith without works dead think fast young people are dying all around you, I passed six liquor stores, a pack of pushers, and housefuls of homeless people in the two blocks from my car to your church so are you really a servant of the Master or just lip syncing?"

Reverend Fisher places the binder on the pew between them, "Let's not bandy about Bible verses as volleyballs, Ms. Leon, it is an exercise in vanity."
"Don't be shy, Reverend, let's be frank with one another."
"There are other concerns," he begins, then stops short.
"Be swift to hear but slow to speak Pastor?"
Silence answers.
"Do you perceive in me the gall of bitterness and the bond of iniquity?" Camille offers then smiles at his surprise, "Or is it simply a mirror into which you stare?"

"Are you a Christian?" the Fisher demands in a tone commanding an answer.
"I'm a negotiator," she responds softly as if that is in itself an answer.
"But are you a Christian?" He insists, searching her eyes for truth but finding in them only his own.

"It is only wise to question the allegiance of a stranger," she

194

assures him in a tone, that, for reasons he cannot begin to fathom, irritates the hell out of him, "I visit the sick and shut in, those locked away in prisons; I tithe ten percent of all I have, offering the first fruits. I have no patience for falsehoods; I speak truthfully to my neighbor. I believe we are all members of one body. I do not allow the sun to set on my anger knowing it gives evil a foothold. I believe that those who steal should steal no more but must work doing something useful with their own hands that they may share with those in need. I endeavor to allow no unwholesome talk to escape my lips but only what is helpful for building up others according to their needs that it may benefit those who listen. I seek not to grieve the Holy Spirit with whom we are all sealed, I strive, daily, to rid myself of all bitterness, rage, anger, and slander along with every form of malice, endeavoring instead to be kind and compassionate to others, forgiving as Christ forgives us all so you tell me, Reverend, pastor, doctor Fisher am I a Christian?"

@@@@@@

Professor Dates waits for his date, a young man of age, an intellectual, and a virgin to boot. Did life get any better? Out with the rude, prude, and please let me intrude who can all be summed up as haters or some reasonable reputable facsimile thereof—you know the ones St. Paul was preaching about when he spoke of those who cause dissent among brethren over stuff nobody knows all the answers to anyway.

Everyone might love a happy ending but megas and ministers can't stand a mystery. No, nada, nay, make no mistake; Paul was calling the men in tights out. So was Christ every chance he got, calling folks out like couples at a child custody hearing. But he wasn't calling out ordinary Joes, or average garden-variety sinners, no, nada, nay, make no mistake, he was doggin' out Pharisees, the modern day equivalent of popes, pastors, and deacon possessed folks climbing into pulpits to cast down curses from it.

If you ever want to hide something from simple church folk put it in a book that doesn't have Bible, Bible study, or Hymnal stamped all over it. Every Sunday and Wednesday night worshippers and Catholics are the most intellectually lazy people you'll ever meet in a parking lot let alone a church pew but it's easier to look to the pulpit for answers, affirmations, and garden-variety rationalizations than to crack open something that might bite you in the ass by giving you answers you're afraid to know.

195

These are the poor souls who are really in the closet, stacked so high atop each other they can almost reach heaven expect they spend all their private time in hell and want to take others with them. Lord bless their souls they spend half their life worrying about dying and the other half obsessing about what people with real lives are doing while they walk around spreading less joy than the dead.

And why?

In the end it's all a mystery.

But what of hell? What of eternity? Better yet what of an eternity in hell? What of fire and brimstone and misery for endless days? What of reading a few books that don't begin with "B"? They won't disembowel you but it really does bite to repetitiously stroll, slide, walk, shuffle, stagger, stumble, drag, slink, or slither into a pew to be verbally affirmed or ruthlessly lashed by someone who does this for a living but is, in the end, just as clueless as the next person in the face of the Great Mystery.

This seeks not to bash those who seek after this Great Mystery for what manner of man since the dawn of time has not? Forever there has been the seeking but the Great Mystery remains just that. I know your minister knows everything so he sure as hell knows this: If Job didn't get the skinny after all the shit God let him go through your garden variety man of God sure as hell ain't getting them either.

Its one thing to realize it's all a mystery but another to treasure that, to keep reminding oneself of this enlightening yet at the same time really disturbing truth every day...hour...second birthing it into consciousness as you morph into a child unable to stomach meat. In fact it can be downright hell, inspiring many to consciously or un—say screw this shit and revert back to pretending they know every damn thing and pulpit parkers gravitate towards the profession because they pretend better than most.

Out with *do you know where your child is* do you really know who your minister is?

You should. Ask them some really hard questions. Better yet wait until they're in the pulpit primed to preach. You know, after the singing, after the praying, after the offering, after the testifying, after the next offering, after the falling out, after almost falling into sin right there in the church, after the Deacon promotes the upcoming men's day fish fry, after the Pastor asks if there are any other announcements—

196

After they say praise the Lord.

Stand up.

At the very last second and say, "Pastor I have a question that torments me each time I crawl into my secret closet to pray and pastor it's about you."

And watch that joker sweat.

Invite him to abandon the pulpit like Jesus did and answer to the matter then open the floor to other pew parkers but be prepared. Should the cowards desert you in this, thy hour of need, count thyself faithful for did not the apostles do the same to Jesus? Fill the uncomfortable silence by confessing your own sins beginning with lusting in your own heart then ask the pastor if he has lusted, with who, and how recently?

Out with being afraid to challenge politicians in robes; this is not Rome, there is tea in China, and there's another church looking for tithers right around the corner so why are you being led by the brain by, at best, a savant without a book fetish or, at worse, a savant with a book fetish who rigorously engaged in theological study, crossed the scary threshold, climbed into the pulpit and pretended to forget everything they learned?

Out with being afraid of anarchy ensuing and heads rolling because one who would chase God now dares to share the Great Mystery with pew parkers seeking affirmations disguised as answers.

In with messengers or masochists, you decide.

@@@@@

M & M, as the e-mail message was now being called, was birthed into cyberspace by a known yet unknown source during the Bible belt's sacred hour, a southern, Christian communal tradition and the sole reason Rena's cell didn't start ringing off her hips 'til ten after six. The old Hag's starts chiming at 6:11 and to her family's shock and awe she answers it.

"Hey sweetheart, do you want me to massage your feet or suck your toes?" A seductive male voice asks, "All the triple-X mud stomper talk you can handle is only 99 cents a minute so lay back, spread those piggies, and prepare for liftoff!"

"Don't you realize it's the dinner hour!?" the Hag snaps ten minutes later and hangs up.

Her phone chimes immediately.

To her family's shock and awe she answers it, "Later," she whispers and turns it off.

When she turns it back on at 6:20 it tolls like the Bells of Notre Dame reverberating from City Hall to the hole in the wall over on White Bridge Road. Everyone from Elvis impersonators to the Governor's mouthpiece want to talk to Rena about the first bomb to hit the city since elves sprang out of the closet and rained all over the Interior Secretary's parade.

Who was this Man who would be senator, governor, or at a minimum, mayor and even more pressing and to the point what manner of madness had driven him to get involved in an affair with a woman who could not only read and write but who also had internet access? This error alone, Music City political blogs suggested, was enough to cast his judgment and therefore his potential for a political future in doubt.

--Any consensus on whether the viability or lack thereof is still up in the air (though probably not literally).

--obviously the letter writer is a nature lover; the references to rivers speak to someone in tune with the symphony of life.

--she seems to be someone who likes to bang her own drum.

--Correction: male drum.

--Does this make the guy who wants to be our next Senator, Governor, or at a minimum, Mayor, gay?

--does haste make waste?

--he was only hasty with his wife.

--how do you know, did you write the e-mail?

"Well did you?" the old Hag hisses, now, in the middle of her second cousin's bar mitzvah, "Are you Mary the Messenger?"

"It said Mary T. Messenger, clear as day, ma," Rena answers, turning her cell phone off and sitting back down, "And of course it's not me."

"Don't of course it's not me when you, I, and the God of Abraham know it could very well be you," the Hag hisses, signaling for a fresh plate of quiche.
"It's not me."
"Then tell these people to stop calling."
"I can't.
"She can't," the Hag hisses in falsetto to her father.
He seems not to notice.
"They'll stop calling if I tell them the truth."
"And what *is* the truth Rena Steinman?"
Silence answers.
"It's you, I know it's you, I knew it was her, I knew it."
"It's not me ma."
"Then who is it?"
"I don't know.
"Then why are they all calling you?"
"Because the e-mail said to."
"And I guess your name dropped from the sky like manna?"
"Who knows ma, can I please eat now?"
"Quick, confess your sins and save your soul from Shem," her sister, Sophia giggles, enjoying seconds... or was it thirds?

She couldn't count when she was hungry, "How long are you going to be bitter behind a little white dress?" she asks condescendingly.

"It had a twelve foot train," Sophia spits, literally, before breathing deeply and regaining her composure, "But I've breathed Selah and it is well with my soul."

"Just like the e-mail said or did that just slip past you ma, did you hear the way that *"it is well with my soul"* just fell from your favored daughter's lips like gold coins."

"Don't try to confuse me by bringing money into this, that's your father's job."
"Darn skippy," her Father says and no more.

"I think she wrote it," Sophia says, looking Rena square in the eye, "Are you telling me," she continues, waving the Hag over, "And ma that you've never had occasion to handle high quality rubber behind closed doors?"

"First define handle culturally, socially, and theologically," The Poor in Food challenges, helping herself to quiche.
"What manner of madness is this?" the Hag demands of her husband.
He responds not even with, "Hmmm."

"Well, Rena Steinman, answer me."

"After you answer me, culturally, socially, and theologically, in that order," Rena insists piling potato cakes onto her plate.
"Rena Mary Steinman, put that platter down and answer your mother," the Hag hisses, snatching the plate.

Sophia starts choking on her fourth helping of matzo balls, *or was it her fifth* ...Rena wonders. She couldn't count when she was hungry. Sophia plummets to the floor at her feet. "How long *are* you gong to be bitter over a little white dress?" Rena asks condescendingly.
Sophia doesn't answer choosing instead to simply turn blue.

"Play nice," daddy says and no more forcing Rena to employ, half-heartedly, the Heimlich maneuver. Matzo balls spring from her mouth like breasts from a water bra and drop, whole, to the floor.

What a waste, the Poor in Food thinks, helping Sophia to her feet and handing her water to soothe her throat.

Sophia takes a sip, "So your middle name is Mary and you still expect us to believe it's not you?"

@@@@@

It's easier to be a pulpit parker than a poor soul standing on the precipice of endless mystery just as it is easier to sit than to stand to hear than to listen to pray than to study to pretend than to know to run than to face the fact that you don't because if you do you confront foundational change which is scarier shit than AIDS ever was or will be which is why this whole situation with the most blessed angel of anal relief is shocking his ass to no end.

200

He sits, pensive, uncomfortable, and for the past hour, given present circumstances, lighthearted throwing back tequila shots at the bar from an upright position, neither his preference nor choice, worrying over the poor dear when he wasn't too busy cursing her out or musing over how someone morphs from half of a couple that mates more than minks to cold turkey without so much as an uncontrollable outburst of anger or even an attack of hemorrhoids.

He coins the phenomenon CSK, Coretta Scott King syndrome. You got hold of some stuff that was next to Holy and your hole dried up, disappeared altogether, or was still too busy smiling to be bothered.

Any person in her condition and right mind would be parked at the wailing wall making it live up to its name but instead she was forever running around smiling like the cat from Alice in Wonderland when there was obviously little to smile about sans her being one of the most photogenic pieces of pussy, the only quantity they come in, he knew, "Who's she trying to fool?" he asks the air, *The love of her life is dead, she's destitute as dirt but still skipping around like in public like Little Mary Sunshine while likely in private*—he glances up from his chaser of whiskey and out the window.

Little Mary Sunshine races past trailing a fat one legged nun swinging a pre-historic club…beating the living crap, literally, out of a hairy animal. A card carrying member of PETA[70] Dr. Dates exits to offer both assistance and an escape to Trans U's newest dethroned saint, a delusional traitor who rewards his generosity by arriving minus his special hemorrhoid cream they only sold at the medical supply place on Church Street. Then the lying, unsympathetic pussy packing no special hemorrhoid cream pretends there's nothing amiss with this little nun and pony show.

"Tulip, you're trying to blow smoke up the ass of an official Ambassador from the house of Commie," Dates informs, smacking the clueless chickie on gp alone.

The silly little bitch breaks down like a Catholic and confesses that she's been hanging out with crazy[71] nuns from a secret order of Our Sister of St. Cecilia's who run around recapturing virginity from males who have stolen, accepted, or unfortunately found themselves cast

---

[70] People for the Ethical Treatment of Animals
[71] as in virgin

into the pit which the Bible proclaims a woman's you know what to be.

Dates surveys the old chick. Poor babies...didn't they have anything better to do? He didn't have anything against them dressing as pilgrims, praying without ceasing, and pining over the Pope but pleaseee...chasing after virginity that's been stole, sold, traded, given, or good old fashioned stuffed down some poor Joe's throat?

That was like trying to catch the fucker who fucked you over forty ways from Friday the first time you fucked up and called the motherfucker a friend.

It wasn't happening. It was gone and not just with the fucking wind. It was gone like the past and make no mistake that shit is gone no matter how hard your ass might try to hold on it is vapor cradle it if you will but at your own cost. It is gone with that first cherry and all the titties in China ain't bringing it back.

"So you mean I'll never get it back?" the poor devastated widowee who's been running around like Little Mary Sunshine for the past year asks, weeping.

"Sometimes it's so hard to believe you're not blonde honey," Dates comforts, checking her roots just on gp.

Disappointed by the results and short on time he confiscates the nun's club, calls her a cab, and watches her hop her hefty lil one leg ass to it.
The nerve!
What was she saving that saggy mothball infested hole for—a bunker when they dropped the big one? Does that hearty, ungrateful trunk of bones have any idea how many unfortunate souls get snatched away before or during their sexual prime?

Poor of Sex souls die exponentially every day without adequately getting their grove on[72] and here you have Mother Superior Methuselah assaulting folks behind consensual sex acts occurring in the middle of the day.

---

[72] Having enjoyable sex

Of course if life was perfect and he was God there would be a guaranteed minimum number of really good lays a person was entitled to before their ass shipped out. This small change in the universe, he is convinced, would drastically reduce the number of souls arriving in eternity with an attitude about any and everything because they walked around wasting a perfectly good pit or pound of prized flesh while they had it.

Losers.

He is determined that when he dies it will be with his odometer turned over and his ass tank full.

"ummmuu…"

Dr. Dates looks down to discover he has completely forgotten about the victim of all this madness, the poor, hairy creature. Cousin It[73] is climbing out of a drainage ditch, "Please don't hurt me anymore," It whimpers when it catches sight of Mary.
"I'll handle this," he assures the creature then turns to Mary, "You can apologize over lunch which is on me."

Dr. Dates escorts the duo to the Po' White Trash Café so they'll feel more at home and directs Cousin It to the men's room. It emerges thirty seconds later looking like a hairy breck girl. Dates is as shocked as a blonde with her finger stuck in a light socket. Hair bouncing and behaving, It was really quite handsome: full lips, big eyes, big hands…big feet.
Really, really, big feet.

Introductions are made and I learn that my hairy new friend's name is, appropriately enough, Harry and that he is something of a hacker extraordinaire.
"Even if I do say so myself," he says shyly, looking up from his soda.
"Come to Momma," I think.
Ask and you shall be given the Good Book says so I do and discover he is a virgin to boot.
Be still my heart.
Do you know how hard it is to find a virgin? Some claim it some shame it so by whose standards do you name it after all if you go

---

[73] see The Adams Family

Biblical think it done it damned whether you do or don't.

"A virgin?" Dates repeats.

"Are you sick?" Mary asks.

'Cause somebody damn well needed to.

"Thank you sweetie," Dates says, kissing the top of her head.

"No more than anyone else, I'm just really busy, I'm one chapter away from completing my thesis and I work full time and I'm something of an activist…and a violinist, which doesn't leave a lot of time for other things."

"You poor baby," Dr. Date purrs, cutting up his veggie burger.

The waitress arrives with their drinks. The well tipped hostess slips sending Harry's pina colada south. The frothy white concoction flows all over the Breck girl's lap. "Either of you want my cherry?" Harry asks, lifting the invitation from his foamy crotch.

Be still my heart.

@@@@@

Ree-Ree runs around the room like a chicken with its head cut off, trying to stay on track to reach the Sky Show[74] line by four.

"Ricky, it's almost three, come 'on," she urges zipping black leather boots that rest, just so, below thighs that rocked and an ass that knew how to roll.

He never looks up, ""I have to have this ready by tomorrow."

"So finish when we get back, you never sleep anyway."

He never looks up.

"You promised."

"I promised because you made me promise but I'm not going, I'll be the only white guy there, they'll think I'm a cop."

"Jeepers creepers can it get any worse?"

"Okay they'll think I'm Eminem."

"Call the press; are you afraid of getting your ass kicked?"

"Hardly," he educates never looking up, "I researched stats on the internet, I'm far more likely to get shot or stabbed."

---

[74] See Tom Joyner morning show concert series

She laughs, "You're talking? Look, my friend fronted the money and dresses for that dinner—

"You mean the one glorifying the massacre of Native Americans?" He asks, never looking up.

She rolls her eyes, "Where I dressed up plain as a pilgrim and dished out dinner for three hundred pale faces."

"I bet some of those pale faces were darker than yours," he says, looking up.

And he knows he has fucked up.

"Look all I'm trying to say is you're my queen, I take you to mountaintops and I just don't think you should ask me to jump off one."

Silence answers.

The hands slap the hips.

He knows he has really fucked up and that he better not stop looking up.

He lays his tools of the trade aside, rises from his workstation, bends down and gives her a butterfly kiss, the kind of kiss that starts with a single caress then en masse, nibbles the bottom lip forming a wave around smile lines, teases the tip of your tongue, touching, tasting, intertwining, dancing a tango, entangled, drifting down and into Eve's deep darkness before diving, unrepentantly, into the pit...

...Ree-Ree relaxes against the wall, hands finally falling from hips to melt into magic white landscape that rises like mountains in *The Sound of Music* sending Julie Andrews climaxing across the countryside as waves of clouds roll over us both wishing us well, "Baaaby," she coos, joining him on his knees and giving him a fevered kiss before sighing the sigh of the well loved, well eaten, and Rich in Contentment, "That was soooo good, now, get your blonde ass up and let's go."

@@@@@

Daddy was no blonde but he when he was around he drove a blue Mustang that sprouted wings when we went over hills at a hundred miles an hour. It was nineteen seventy, the year before seatbelts were safe when you didn't drive unless you drank and Little Mary Sunshine crowed, too naive to know her life was in danger at every curve and crest.

205

All she knew was that daddy was handsome and gave hugs that turned into helicopter rides all the way from the front yard to the living room where he collapsed on the couch bringing up wind while she waged war with his dusty boots. They were old, smelly, and a sight to behold but they were also daddy's, the same boots that came bearing the biggest, most beautifully wrapped box her eyes ever saw early one Christmas morning. She tore away enough paper to cover a wall and was rewarded with Polly, a life sized baby doll who walked when you held her hand.

Polly had eyes dark as night with bright specks that twinkled when her curled just so lashes blinked, bright red led lips that smiled without ceasing, and shiny black hair styled in pixie curls held back in a bow but it was her dress that captured Mary's eyes and heart: a red, satin dream with embossed velvet roses atop a fluffy white petticoat and ruffled underpants.

Inside of thirty seconds pretty, smiling Polly with the pixie curls and bright red lips lies in a corner, naked as the day she was pressed in plastic, while Little Mary Sunshine prances around the Christmas tree in the prettiest outfit she has ever seen.

Later that morning they all piled into an old van daddy borrowed wearing their Sunday best, and drove away leaving Polly naked and still laying in a corner. Daddy sped down I-4 like the hounds of hell scaring mommy, who praying aloud, to death while Al Green sings about love and happiness on the radio.

It was the days before seat belts were safe when you didn't drive unless you drank so Mary, who was always a little excitable, stood up front with her parents, in the space between their seats where she could not only see but also feel the van begin to spread its wings as it ate up the ground. All at once, out of nowhere, a red mustang roars past their bird like lightening leaving dust in its wake and Mary sobbing while the rest of her family looks on in utter confusion.

"You let that man pass us," she wails, as if Jewish and her daddy's shoulder a wall.

"Hell, we can't have that now, can we?" Daddy howls, flooring the gas while the cowboys smile, Mommy prays, and Mary dances around in Polly's red dress.

That night, lights from the tree twinkle in the background, forming Mary's backdrop while she the Dialing for Dollars movie, a nine A.M five day a week staple, Santa left behind for people he missed this year. She gazes at the screen, transfixed, as the giant rolling bin spins round and round, tossing telephone numbers. When it stopped some lucky person would be called and asked: *What is the Dialing for Dollars movie of the day*? If they knew the answer, they won the money.

Mary always held her breath, hoping their number would be called even though she knew they didn't have a telephone. Today's lady, shocked to be called at night, doesn't know the name of the movie. Neither does Mary but it's about a pretty, young girl with blonde curls who gets a beautifully wrapped present for her birthday. She tears it open to find a pretty little doll with blue eyes and curls as blonde as her own. Four commercials and two spins of the giant wheel later the doll grows up, learns to walk, steals the girl's dress, stuffs her in a box, and takes over her life.

Mary shakes like a leaf, convinced that Polly, now lying naked in her bedroom closet, is out to get her. What doll wouldn't get a selfish little girl who not only stole her red satin dress but also swore never to return it? She dashes to mommy's room only to find the door locked, "Dammit, daddy's home," she hisses, desperate to scream, "Plastic Polly is after me!" her but she cowers afraid.

Summoning all her courage she scurries to her room, throws open the closet, grabs naked Polly by the neck, and drags her to the hall closet where she buries her beneath sheets, towels, and assorted odds and ends. Mission accomplished, she runs back to her room, climbs into bed, pulls the covers over her head, and holds her breath; listening for sign that Polly is trying to dig her way out.

In the darkness Mary can hear, just above her heartbeat, the beast in the shadows quietly moving about, waiting to leap upon her as soon as looks out… or she closes her eyes, sighs, and breathes deeply…

The beast's breath is hot and heavy while she had none at all… running through the woods then finding herself on Interstate four not in a van but in the dark, naked, and running through the night but not on a road but on dirt and she's sure she'll run out of time running out and slowing down until all that's left is her neck barely above water drowning in the dirt that welcomes her weak and weary body being dragged back to the waiting van by Barnabus, the king of the vampires, who, as she wakes… Mary can just make out standing next to her bed, naked as poor Polly.

@@@@@

The festive in Spirit is pleased she wore the black leather, appreciative of the way it binds itself to her like a second skin, melding, moving; pure pitch drawing light from its surroundings and swallowing it whole.   She enters the building, regards the space, breathes it in then searches for the Panther but finds, instead, a wrinkle in the darkness; a lone white Ranger hiding out in the nose bleed section, I-Pod in hand, alongside his trusty sidekick, Ree-Ree.

"Apparently the pussy power is still in effect," Athena observes, joining her, "The mad professor seems to having a good time."

"Probably sending me another e-mail about the two hundred dollars I still owe him," Camille predicts with a grin.

"Do you need a loan or are you just looking to get your little cocoa butter ass whipped?"

Camille bothers not to answer. It is electric in here, addictive even, a sea of shades— burgundy to burnt purple to pale as bleached whale, warm to swallows all to damn near whiter than snow all moving in unison not to a wave but to a fierce, primal beat breathings, sighing, then raging, longing to rest, whimpering then growling, then crying, demanding to be fed; rocking on a sea of black, long dead but still hungering across hundreds of years, thirsting but finding only saltwater for

Justice
Drowned in tears
Blood, woe, and innocence
All lost,
Rising from graves on waves
Shaking off
Frost.

…Except they don't know it yet.

As the music ends Big Dog bounds past them[75] and onto the stage. In the midst of the cheering pandemonium he holds up his hands—and

---

[75] not to mention Tom Joyner, Jay, Sybil, and Ms. Myra

there is silence; or a reasonable facsimile thereof given there gather more Negroes than the law allowed all crammed inside the Titans football stadium without so much as permission let alone a permit, "As saltines like to say," Big Dog says over the din, "We're gonna pause for a few words from our sponsor…"Now!"

Evander and the Henchmen, automatic artillery in hand, drop out of the sky and onto the stage behind Big Dog. And then there is silence as opposed to some reasonable facsimile thereof. Ricky looks up from his I-Pod for the first time, "Are those the Temptations?" he asks Ree-Ree who responds by wrapping his arms around her waist and backing that ass up.

"This whole party was put together in large part due to the generosity of sistah Athena, owner of Monroe's Memorial Services," Big Dog barks, "With fifty locations there's sure to be one ready to service your ass if can't give her five minutes of yo fuckin time in return."
Silence answers.
"Yall better show Sistah Athena some love," Big Dog growls, passing the mike to Athena with an embrace while the crowd claps like confused thunder.

"As I look out across this room," she begins, after Big Dog puts up the hand, "I see so much beauty, passion, and grace. I see strong, black men and women, the descendents of kings and queens and I thank God because the fact that you are here tonight to party with us means you survived another day, so give yourselves a hand."

They do, and the band, directed by Evander and the Henchmen, joins in, pumping out the fierce tribal beat.

Athena breathes in the beat, her body instinctively responding to the pounding as the crowd joins her in the jam, jumping, heat pumping, power pulsing, heartbeats rushing towards time, space… towards a beat that won't be erased, alive, a beat that marches on towards death…death? *Where the hell did that come from?* She wonders missing a beat then losing her rhythm altogether like buckshot lacking a shell.

"Let me help you find that," Camille whispers, bumping her slightly and knocking her back on beat.
"You saw that, huh?"
"Who didn't?"

209

Camille points to the giant flat screens surrounding the stadium, all locked squarely on them.

They crack up.

"Try to stay on beat," Athena advises.

"You're worried about me?"

And the band rocks on and on for hour and hours and later, across the stadium, as sirens chime in the distance, from deep within the bowels of the pit of his desire, the Lone Ranger, distracted from the task at hand long enough to glance up at the a screen, spots the two of them still dancing on stage.

"Is that a Taste of Honey?[76]" He asks Ree-Ree who never looks up, responding instead by wrapping her hands around his head and backing that ass up.

@@@@@

---

[76]Sukiyaki, see

Department of Ethics Chairman Dr. Charles Marion Dates is camped out at Club Chili's on West End awaiting his prey, a candidate for the associate professor position that posted a little over two years ago. The long vacant opening was yet another example of why you couldn't trust bosses or bitches especially if they were one and the same.

Two summers ago while he was otherwise engaged on a sojourn to Jerusalem the Israelites called a closed door meeting and appointed him chairman of the associate professor of theological studies search committee not because there was a funded position but because it was all about appearances, Princeton was posturing, and West was setting Summers up for a fall.

Never mind his Ethics program was understaffed, never mind it was darn near impossible to recruit a ripe theological ego unless you had a position of equal stature for their equally educated ego laden wife or, never mind.[77] Never mind the last candidate was a theological search committee's wet dream: well published, single, and quite unattractive.

The dinner interview at F. Scott's was going along just lovely when, over dessert and light hearted debate over whether the church was a dying institution, the candidate spontaneously imploded for why else would he suddenly blurt: "I'm a forty-eight year old virgin."

With the exception of the Representative from the Board, some jack of all trades part-time professor with delusions of political grandeur, everyone paused, fork midair. Not because it was a surprise—I did say quite unattractive, but because we could not, individually or collectively, discern whether his posture reeked of depression, pride, or an open invitation for one of us to rectify the situation.

The last was simply out of the question, not only because he was quite unattractive but also because we have our principles even if we don't practice them religiously but back to the meat of the matter— never mind they let me bring in damn near a million candidates before

---

[77] sweet, salty semen if you must know

anyone bothered to tell me there was no job let alone a funded position but it was all about appearances and Princeton was posturing making manifest the eleventh commandment: The one getting screwed must always be the last to know.

But none of that matters now. After his prey date waits a real date, with hairy Harry, his new love interest who just so happens to be in possession of a pristine virgin butt. Do you have any earthly idea how long it's been since *he* had a virgin? Can you say *never*?

But it was more than that.

Under all that hair and there's plenty of it, rests a hairy, fine, intelligent, witty, well endowed son of a samurai who hates not only clothing but also Uncle Sam and everything he stands for a synonym for rabid sinner so why is he so torn about spreading those cherry cheeks wide and bringing Junior home to momma?

He had done worse. His brief yet passionate affair with Hoover's grandson reeks about as far from practicing principles as a gay and proud of it St. Peter could stray without deserving to be hung upside down by his head and nailed to a cross...perhaps, just perhaps he's feeling something kinda freaky that runs a little deeper than your garden variety hankering for a piece of pecker food.

He is, in fact, starting to suspect he might have in his sights that very thing he had despaired of ever being in receipt of again this side of eternity—a package. He was talking love here okay? L-u-v-v, love and it was the last thing he was going to risk losing when he now stands a damn skippy chance of living happily ever after then dying with his tank full of Harry.

It's a hairy thought but a persistently pleasant one nonetheless, especially given the many advantages of humping hairier humans. First, the obvious: a little less evolved equals tad more animalistic;[78] more hair equals more easily stimulated equals far more easily excitable equals not only more sex but more of it than most can handle equals his beautiful, big-balled, bastard ex-boyfriend, Remington Steele,[79] would be fit to be fucked.

A virgin!?

---

[78] with tad and animalistic first being defined in cultural, social, theological, and historical contexts
[79] could you believe that name?

Men still chase that cherry long after they've been on more tops than bottles of Coke which is why he's sitting here, wasting his time waiting to interview a candidate who doesn't have a prayer in hell of getting a job that doesn't exist.

"Where are you, you little loser?" he asks aloud, turning around just in time to see a pale, lanky, blonde drink of something leisurely strolling towards him like it's Palm Sunday and his name is I don't have anything better to do Polly.

"You're in whiteface right?" Dr. Dates asks, then waits for an answer.

And black women wonder why they can't keep a man Rick thinks, taking a seat. *Make no mistake, it isn't easy to look myself square in the eye after being bitch slapped by a bag of dry bones old enough to be dirt but it is yet possible if I resolve to hold fast to my principles and practice what I profess to preach thereby undertaking the first step on a sure path to restoring one's dignity.*

"So you're interested in the ethics of physics as it relates to theological study?" Dr. Date's finally begins, over Courvoisier chased by Corona times two.

While scientists are renowned for their egos these theological assholes are in a league all their own. Sure, my theories can wipe out the western hemisphere but these clowns think they can too via their "connection." Worse, they think have the corner on wisdom—that God talks to them. Big deal. God talks to me all the time I just don't go around broadcasting it. I mean who would take you seriously? Look at him, dissecting me as if I'm some deficient specimen on a slab... "Harry sends his love."

Maybe he's not a spy of the establishment trying to invade Commie Land, Dr. Dates decides, "And your particular area of interest is end time study?"

"He also asked me to tell you that he's really, really looking forward to your date later this evening."
"Really?"
"Really, he's even thinking about shaving for the occasion..."
"He better not!"
"That's exactly what I told him."
"Really? You're not..."

213

"Gay? No, no, I'm into women…black women actually."

"You poor dear, strictly prickly, but back to business, end time study…"

"As it relates to nature intertwining with theology and quantum physics," Rick explains.

"An intriguing, under-researched field…"

"That's what I'm counting on."

"You're hired."

They shake hands.

It was one of the few, correction only, thing Hoover's grandson taught him: when it's principles that matter it's more prudent to ask forgiveness than permission. He has accomplished the task so unceremoniously dumped on him by the clandestine committee single-handedly, with aplomb, and without so much as verbal approval let alone administrative or electronic authorization or in fact a position and he is proud as hell.

His backstabbing Israelites bestowed upon him bullshit and he has taken it by the horns and thrown it to the winds along with every standard principle and legal hiring practice outlined in the University's Standard Operating Procedures. There would be uproar among the Committee, the Dean would exact answers, and when Chancellor Gee caught tail of it, feathers would fly but who gave a gerbil's ass?

"It's high time the pompous, overpaid Principal learned— they don't call us Commie's kids for nothing."

@@@@@

Reverend Fisher, Camille, Athena, Ree-Ree, Big Dog and Hook gather around a less than mahogany conference table in the conference room that doubles as the dining and study hall for the sparsely attended tutoring program held in the basement of the Ray of Sunshine Presbyterian Church in southeast Nashville.

"The feds wouldn't allow me see Methuselah," Athena begins opening the meeting, "So far, he still hasn't been charged with any crime."

"They did allow me five minutes for spiritual counseling," Reverend Fisher adds, rubbing his hands together like kindling, "He's in good spirits, he said not to worry, he'll be fine."

214

"It'll take more than balls in suits to crack that nut." Big Dog barks.

The Gathered concur.

"The heat however is on," Camille informs, "The feds feel he knows more than he's admitting which, fortunately, he does not but that means we need to drop the curtain on his contraband."

"I told you she would try to start telling us how to conduct our business," Hook crows.

Big Dog hands Hook five Bens, then turns to Camille, "With the wise man locked up, folks are gonna be tripping to crouch in on his territory."

"Methuselah realizes that," she answers, "And he's not ruffled."

"It'll never work," Hook insists, "Too much chaos, niggahs are crazy, they'll lie, steal, cheat, fuck your woman—.

"You talkin'?" Big Dog growls.

The two men glare at each other.

Reverend Fisher holds his breath. The women simply shrug, more than willing to wait for them to work it out.

When cold stares threaten to crack the surface Camille decides it's time pull them back to basics and off thin ice, "Time is money, gentleman. Eagles don't stop flying because you're flexing your St. Peters."

"My shit ain't no saint but he'll sure make you wanna sin," Hook guarantees.

Ree-Ree grudgingly concurs while Reverend Fisher mumbles intelligibly under his breath.

"The next order of business," Camille continues, reluctantly "Is our participation in the upcoming environmental slash peace march slated for next month."

Now it was Athena's turn to bitch and moan.

"I don't know that I can sell this. People want jobs, fair pay, young black men want to be able to talk bull and shoot craps or play some hoops and feel safe at the same time. Black folks want someone of authority in this country to finally say we were wrong and we're sorry—"

"Didn't Bill do that?" Ree-Ree asks.

"And maybe once they get some fundamental needs met they'll have time to give a squirrel's ass about some damn trees," Athena concludes staring Camille down.

"I guess she told you," Hook says, slapping the table.

"You need this" Camille answers, glancing neither left nor right, "The fastest way to win friends and influence enemies is first to care about the things that they care about. They have what we need: money, expertise, and most importantly, cover."

Silence answers.
Hook's smile grows wider.

"Look, we're on a strict timetable and nothing covers rear ends like a rally and time is money and running out so are you in or not?"

"In." Athena answers.

As do the others as the affirmation circles the table enfolding the Green Eyed Monster.

"Good," Camille says, spreading a map across the table, "Reverend Fisher and Ree-Ree will stay here; the rest of us will head for the borders: Athena and Big Dog to Canada, Hook and I to Mexico or some facsimile thereof."

Big Dog frowns. Hook sends a wink his way.

"Remember," Camille reminds, folding the map, "No wrong moves."

@@@@@

Little Mary Sunshine lay in the dark, refusing to move. He remains quiet as well but she knows he is there, she can smell him and there is no mistaking the smell of vampires. They reek of sticky sweet molasses and battered spirits mixed with blood, sweat and tears born of closed in spaces and restless nights.

He spreads his wings of shackles clanking instead of flapping like feathers but they lift anyway parting to reveal something hanging… heavy… but suspended midair like a dark harbinger of things to come. She opens her mouth to scream but only silence answers beneath the claw covering her mouth.

216

Is this how my porcelain enemy feels? She wonders, gasping to breathe, *Anger and darkness but no air*?

Her arms and legs kick wildly only to be covered by shackles weighing down her already breathless body.

"Stop fighting me," "Barnabus hisses, hot breath dripping onto her neck which no longer knows her. "If you make me wake your mommy you'll be sorry," he promises, preparing the way himself before plunging fangs into Mary's flesh, "It has been too long," he whispers, disemboweling her once again.

At the rush of blood the horde flies in feverishly; forgetting they ever knew her, feasting on her fruit sans mercy or famine. There are no watchmen or soldiers standing guard, no legion of angels with arms stretched high toward heaven, no hope on this day of our Lord rising from the ashes to grant a reprieve... just a dark winding forest filled with vampires, cheering themselves on as they drink deeply from the scant life left of her before bringing her back from the dead.

@@@@@

"Was your house broken into?" Reverend Fisher asks his right hand Deacon who he suspects harbors delusions of political grandeur.

"No, this is what always happens when Ms. Mary leaves town, the twins go crazy," he responds, picking up clothing and wine bottles as he goes.
"I thought they were still abroad."
"Hmmm, you're right the twins and their broads."

"What's that?" The unusually observant wise man asks, indicating the rubber appendage dangling from a leisurely rotating ceiling fan.

"Frat party," he answers, turning the fan on high in hopes it'll merge with the blades, "So what can I do for you?"

"Well, I have great news— I just saved a ton of money on my car insurance by switching to Geico."
"That's great."
"But seriously, I've located a source of funding for the church renovation project."
"Hmmm."

217

The wise man pace as is his custom, "I yearn to build a truly Christian version of what that heathen Hillary proposed. That *is* what the gospel of Jesus Christ is all about, don't you think?" He continues without waiting a response, as was his custom, "I mean when you come down from the mountaintop and get metaphysical about it I am you, you are me, he is she, we're really all one and that means everything revolves around not only me but also around a great ray which is hope and I'm determined, and God is my Witness, we're gonna get it done to the glory of our Lord Jesus Christ."

"Hmmm."
"And that's where you come in."
"Hmmm."
"I have a handle on the main sanctuary but it came to me in a vision, a prophecy if you will, we need a non-profit to fund an additional wing called the Village where the entire world can come together but we first we have to fund it, now how can we do that?"

"Fish fries?"
"I knew I smelled fish," Reverend Fisher declares, walking toward the kitchen, "I was wondering when you were gonna offer me some, you got fries too huh?"

"I meant to fund the Village."
"It's gonna take a lot more than fish and fries to fund this puppy; I'm talking the Taj Mahal of Christian communal rooms, nothing but the finest for my God."

"I guess we could approach Christian businesses…"
The Wise Man gives him a condescending slap on the back, "Have you ever tried to get money out of a Christian let alone a business son? No, I'm talking practical here which means you have to take the problem to the people."

"The parishioners?"
"Are you kidding, have you ever tried getting money out of a parishioner?"
"Hmmm."
"Well it's like trying to turn tail and run without any legs, hey is that a leg lying over there in the corner?"

"It's an antique," his Deacon says, steering him back towards the front door.

218

"That wife of yours always finds the oddest things on her travels but back to business. When I say the people I mean the world, the capitalists, the unrepentant Christians in disguise who need to clear their consciences."

"Hmmm."

"Hmmm," The Wise Man agrees, nodding.

"No," his Deacon and right hand Man corrects, "I mean hmmm like that could be a problem, God, non-profit, yes, all that plus religious affiliations, taxes, church and state…"

"So, you're suggesting God gave me an illegal vision?"

"I'm saying we better have the right separation of church and state."

"That's why they pay you lawyers the big bucks."

"But I'm really short on time…"

"God is the creator, I'm the big picture guy, and you're the architect," the Wise Man says with a wave, "I'm entrusting all the minor details to your capable hands."

@@@@@

"Not everyone can handle a package," Camille advises, removing Hook's hand from her thigh yet again as she negotiates a sharp curve in the road, "You strike me as a piece man."

"You like playing hard to get don't you?" Then, when silence answers, "Educate me."

"A piece anyone can handle but a package is like running headfirst into a truckload of dynamite, it either blows you away or leaves you wishing it had."

He laughs despite himself, "Hook daddy can always tell, beneath those starched shirts and sensible underwear, when there's a tiger begging to scream like a bitch."

She laughs despite herself.

"You see you had to laugh yourself," he says, laying a hand on her thigh.

"I'm sorry; I know you prefer doing that alone."

"Is that supposed to be some kind of insult or something," he asks, moving his hand.

"Not judging just witnessing."

219

"Not witnessing just bitching," he corrects in perfect falsetto.

"You're really cute when you're an intellectual."

"Let me out.

"Let you out?"

"Let me out, pull over now."

She pulls off the highway, stops the car, and waits.

As does silence.

"It's my turn to drive," he finally announces, getting out.

"Okay."

Hook slides behind the wheel. As soon as he re-enters the roadway Camille closes her eyes. He studies her out the corner of his. *She's far more attractive with her eyes and mouth closed* he decides.

"Cat got your tongue?" she inquires, "Or do you just have stage fright?"

Sure she's eyeballing him, he turns to face her only to find her eyes still closed, her mouth slightly open…her breathing soft and even.

"You have a nice mouth."

She opens her eyes.

"Does it work as good as it looks?"

"Do you have to hump every hairball that rolls your way?"

Hook laughs despite himself, "Damn, I thought brothers were hard on women, you consider yourself a hairball?"

"Some days, others I'm just an ordinary asshole like you."

He laughs despite himself, "Don't make me stop this car."

"You're what happens when girls throw it at boys before they crawl out of the crib."

"Got my first piece at five, enjoyed my first double at ten and haven't been without all I can handle since."

"Because of the way you work that thang?

"Not thang, triple T, Mr."

"Mr. Triple T?"

"Tried true and all up and through you."

"Sounds like a snake."

"It'll clean you out."

. She laughs.

"My stuff is tight," he continues, "I bet yours is too but ready to open wide and sing the ballad of the prime pipe."

"No thanks."

"I can make it talk to me," he promises, green eyes twinkling, "I can make it talk to you too, what you wanna know?"

She giggles.

He knows he has her going now. Once you get them giggling you're already halfway in the hole. She's one of those siddity high maintenance bitches but, fortunately for her, he likes them like that... *makes it all the sweeter when you take all the shit they took you through back out on their asses the old fashioned way. A honey like her has had her share of power tools but you haven't been properly twisted until you've by screwed by a hook.*

"Its not gonna happen," Camille sings.

"Why?"

"You missed your window of opportunity."

"When?"

"The dinner meeting," she answers, patting his hand like he's a cancer patient, "If you held out I would have been forced to fuck you to tip the scales but, my loss, you said yes and you're turning a wonderful profit to boot."

"Good, we'll fuck to celebrate."

"Sorry, I don't fuck and face when financial considerations are at stake."

Hook laughs, "So you're worried about having to look me in the face after you've been turned out?"

"Not quite," Camille confesses, running her hand up his thigh, "I'm afraid I might have to kill you when you can't stop screaming like a bitch."

@@@@@

Francesca floats in the luxurious bubble bath wrestling with something akin to an attack of conscience even as the Temptations' *Ball of Confusion* blares in the background. In the vein of garden variety female she realizes what she really needs is another woman in whom to confide but therein lay the wrinkle. She never ran in packs the way so many women do, feigning familiarity and satisfaction when they're merely keeping company on the hunt in case something interesting strolls by. Give her a man any day.

Testosterones were trips but women are wild as ticks in winter; ready to feast on each other at the drop of a fork or a fucking man without regard to which came first, the friend or the dick. Men might precede words that give women heartache but they don't envy women, clits already have the market cornered on that—and clits, with a slit, as a rule, hated her the second they caught wind of her leaving her with quite the dilemma: work to win this perfect stranger over or enjoy a perfectly lovely event with the overfriendly banana the poor heifer was hoping to lure home tonight.

A prophet once told her she possessed a seducing spirit. The kind that chimes out to men while they slept, sermonized, or slithered inside their souls searching for the affirmation of angels blessed with a black hole that led back to the womb. After she climbed out of him she knew what he had, that she *knew* men in a way most women were afraid to. Knew not only what they wanted but intrinsically how they desired it, for long long, in what denominations and to what end and was not afraid of the power that held.

Knew that to hold a man a woman or some garden variety facsimile has to commit herself to a lofty sexual work ethic, criteria deemed too much work by legions quite comfortable doing little to nothing when it comes to making a man feel like love and lust are one and once is never enough to stop me thinking of loving you like this again real soon.

And men loved that shit.

To love a man's dick is to love that man for he is that dick and that dick is he and to try to have it any other way is to have an unhappy camper endeavoring to, if you are lucky, gnaw through his own leg to get away from you since the 'oft used alternative, death by husband, is damn near impossible to make it through alive.

No, nada, nay, make no mistake in the end, with men it's all about the sex which is sad since they tend to marry their aspirations then sleep next to their worst nightmares, tossing and turning their horny little heads while their wives avoid, attempt to locate, or wipe, literally, their trifling ass. A fortunate woman, in Francesca's book, was one wise enough to embrace this truth and love her man through that thing which he loves most while making him love her thang more than he ever thought he could.

An unfortunate one is, well you know enough of them so take your pick. If the disillusioned were allowed to throw back the fish that hooked them Jesus could feed the five thousand from now till eternity without ever needing to fry up that second fish. Meanwhile women have finally recaptured the emancipation of Athens and a married man will have sex with a sheep to avoid copulating with his wife and if you don't believe me ask any condom about its ancestry a synonym for the Holy state of matrimony can be some sad shit.

Francesca floats in the foamy, marble bubble bath, able to empathize with the pain of both sides. Having said "I do" one time too many she knows it is indeed a tricky feat for fish to successfully mate with creatures that rip out their insides, never cover bowls, and harbor an aversion to water. At the same time all she could say was God bless any man who could live with a woman because most women sure as hell can't.

Floating in her heavenly whirlpool Francesca realizes, right down to her seducing soul, that her ability to look these truths squarely in the face is what makes her what she is— just another clit with a slit whose ass was in a sling if her affair with this married fucking mutt got out.

@@@@@

Camille woke from a catnap when they reached Truth or Consequences, New Mexico where they conducted the first phase of their business under cover of darkness. The pair then drove on arriving at their destination just before dawn. They then reversed course, driving back in each direction twice then inexplicably changed course three times until Hook can take no more and calls a halt to what is, obviously, this bitch's own special madness.

"I'm gonna lie down in a real bed for at least five minutes before you drag me kicking and screaming a mile further down a road." He states calmly, getting back into the car after exiting it five minutes earlier in an attempt to kick his own ass for coming with her in the first place.

"Here, honey?" Camille inquires, "In this two horse trailer park?"
And it was.
Two horses and two trailers, a single and doublewide are all that litter the county side for as far as the eye can see.

Hook seriously enjoys the discomfort he senses in this unusually serene bitch. *The ice cold cunt shivers at the prospect of bedding down in a trailer in broad daylight.* "Let's cruise to the next town," he suggests, turning down yet another dirt road, then another and another until they happen upon Fred's Trailer Town USA, the land of the forgotten where generations of white folks are on food stamps and Fred lives in a Dodge Caravan where beer flows and flies gather like fish thrown back by men who used to be able to circle their catch three times if they wished to cast it back at the loins from which it sprang.

"You've got to be kidding," Camille snaps, when Hook brings the car to a stop in front of a hexagon shaped trailer with a horse shaped Motel sign hanging on the door, "Big Fred's Mustang Ranch?"

Hook gets out and stretches like a mountain lion before leisurely raising the car key high in the air and dropping it down the front of his pants. The key pops right back out. He catches it midair, "That's what you call a muscular controlled knee jerk reaction to third leg stimuli."

"That's what you call having too much time on your hands," Camille responds, extracting a spare key from her bra and locking the doors, "Sweet dreams."

@@@@@

From her heated heavenly bubble bath Francesca scans the *Living* section of *The Tennessean* before flipping to the *Society* page. The Greater Nashville Chapter of Un-humped and Happy or Not Housewives of North America were having their eighth annual gala to benefit the Deflowered Daughters of the Confederacy. The DDC, the bastard stepdaughter radical arm of the Daughters of the Confederacy, weary of teas and taxidermy, have sworn to take back the night by outing whores spending too many of them with Confederate husbands who had better things to do than their wives.

Haters.

It was simple supply and demand. The very foundation on which capitalism was built so when were women going to get it in their heads that other clits were not to blame when their husbands went astray? When were angry, un-humped and happy about it wives going to rise up and realize there was a price to be paid for failing to faithfully fuck their husbands like it's the first time he made *A Million Ways to Leave*

Your Lover a number one hit or learn to faithfully fake that fucking shit?

Instead, they spend their time shopping or watching Oprah or paying someone to lurk around looking for signs of seminal activity to prove their husbands are not only getting laid and lying about it to their face but also laughing about it behind their backs when their time would be far better spent humping their husband until not only his back but also his dick hurt.

And men love that fucking shit.

That said she floats guilty.
She has broken the rules. She has slept with the husband of a friend, colleague, classmate, acquaintance, or whatever she chooses to call this other clit for the most practical yet impractical of reasons—convenience[80] in the process invading every square inch of the mansion his wife named Prime Belle Meade Property.

She has slept, loved, and lain in the bed of another, riding her husband to high heaven and back before opening like a butterfly to begin again until they overflowed with both laughter and each other, languishing, savoring, and loving without end while sharing everything, except his wife, with each other.

Her only saving grace in this cheap soap opera is that it has been conducted in private, behind the scenes, with curtains drawn while time stood still. *Otherwise that might well be my face plastered on the Society page with a scarlet letter stamped across my forehead...*knocking invades, bringing her out of the reverie that's as close to cloud nine as she dares go when it's time to plant her feet firmly to the ground and clean house.

She places wet oily feet on the marble floor and scurries from the bath through the master suite and out the French doors to peer over the winding spiral staircase leading to the beveled front entrance.

"You're home early."
"I know," he says, entering the mansion, arms overflowing with church files.
"But you're never early."

---

[80] With *convenience* of course first being defined in cultural, social, theological, and linguistic terms.

"It couldn't wait," he says, shedding his shoes as if they're on fire and sprinting up the stairs, "I'm about to make you an offer you can't refuse."

@@@@@

Hook cursed Camille long, hard, and in three different languages before admitting to himself that it wasn't going to bring the Bitch back any faster. Exhausted and none too comfortable being seen alive in a place like this, he rents the room all the way in the back that boasts a private shower made possible by a water hose and stolen milk crates blocking the hall leading to it.

After cursing Camille long, hard, and in three different languages Hook sheds his clothes and takes a shower not because he wants to but because it is a longstanding custom then collapses into the bed and a fitful sleep.

Everyone in the world is nude, uninhibited and having sex except him. Everywhere he goes there are naked bodies, limbs tangled together like braided rope, rising and falling like icing on the red sea flowing through him like fire on fire, hot, hungry, he's searching for someone to quench his thirst but there is only a sea of saltwater washing over the open wound where his hook used to be waiting for what was naked with legs spread wide for him...legs, thighs, labia, lips spreading wide, wider, wildly laughing over the hole where the family jewels were once buried....

Hook wakes frantically reaching for his middle man, the most trusted of allies and mediator who let right hand know what the left was doing. "There you are," he sighs, relieved as his namesake snakes up his stomach and around his waist, "Come to daddy."

The beast, long and muscular, pulses forward in response bringing with it lips *wrapping around to encircle, slow like a lazy sigh, squeezing ever so gently before drawing back so her slither rolls around massaging vessels moving in rhythm to the icy peak, the penthouse whose elevator collapses plunging down to the base until his balls echo nipples of nothingness zooming up again, casting his hope toward heaven where sweet sticky saltwater swirls clockwise then counter...*

"That's what I'm talking 'bout."
...Sliding down a pole down a silk sinkhole wrapping, wrestling,

226

slipping along a high red hill with a hook tickling the back of her throat where lies the heart of him, hanging on but yearning to release a river from it's resting place filled with water moccasins feasting on the family jewels—

"Christ!" Hook screams, waking and grasping for the headboard but finding instead more milk crates refusing to move half as fast as he needs them to while the room swirls, quakes consume his body, and an anaconda threatens to swallow him whole, "Wait, no, no, stop!" he screams...

Like a bitch, all the way down.

τακινγ ιτ υπ τηε Ασσ[81] *Straight*

The Man who would be senator, governor, or at a minimum, mayor was at his favored place in the entire world: on all fours facing a wall of mirrors, taking it up the ass, straight. Mary had alluded to it teasingly; Francesca had gone so far as to parade around in one throughout their Final Four Foray. And still he waited... in vain as Israelites or Utah fans after Karl[82] left the mountain, not behind a burning bush but a championship ring that was not to be.

Who could blame him?

What mouse let alone man wanted to be the sixth man on a team boasting Ewing, Barkley, Stockton, Jackson, and Iverson[83] as starters? Malone was no freshman and there was no fab in front of that five[84] when the name of game was rings and champions was what prophets early on declared each to be.

The aging workhorse wages war against the Timber wolves, reaping rewards from skeptical LA fans who can respect a man chasing behind a ring like a knocked up bitch as long as he came in strong off the bench.

He loves this game.

Loved Garnet, the Timber Wolve's upstart player of the year who would soon learn, like a Bull before him, that no man is an Island until he finds himself babysitting a tattooed defensive animal decked out in wedding attire in a last ditch attempt to add yet another ring to an already impressive collection.

He waited while Kobe ducked the press and posted bail or whatever you did when you were trying to play ball and beat a rape charge at the same time. The ego maniac is distracted, Shaq is sarcastic, and Karl cries foul on the sidelines for just as sure as Queer is queen, defense is king and Kobe stands a better chance of beating that rape charge than shutting down a masked man shooting the lights out in the city of stars.

---

[81] Taking it up the ass, Straight
[82] See Malone, NBA
[83] prophecy is validated by time
[84] See University of Michigan: Rose, Howard, Webber, King, Jackson

"Holy Moses," he exclaims, in joy as his favorite team gets their haughty little bottoms not only spanked but straight up pistol whipped by the Pistons.

It matters not he bet several thousand dollars on the boys from Cali. It matters not that his arch enemy, the man currently occupying his Vice-Mayor seat, hails from Detroit. It matters not that Ms. Mary will kill him when she finds out…he moans long and louder than any bull giving birth then sighs softer and sweeter than any garden variety pussycat, "A little to the right," he requests, and the magic hook responds in kind.

"Inter spem et metum?"[85] His new best friend asks.
"Hmmm."

Not even God could have told him life got better than bumping, grinding, and banging your way through a buzzer beater between Duke and UConn but truth be told there is a light at the end of his tunnel and its love is shining down, up, in, out, and through him, "Holes" he sighs, ready to give birth yet again, "God bless them every one."

@@@@@

Reverend Fisher scans the assembled crowd and immediately sends up another prayer to his Father in heaven. The pews overflow for the first time since 9/16 when, it was rumored, even Satan was at the church on time and sitting in the front row, prompting religious leaders to proclaim a spiritual awakening in the making.

Within weeks the awakened fell back to sleep along with their father, Lucifer, who never cared much for formalized worship anyway. His hopes and dreams for the temple-rebuilding project went the way of the dinosaur with them except there was no oil waiting to rise from those ashes. This church, which had gradually withered over a hundred years would soon, on his watch, die; the victim of an aging congregation that failed to tap into the fountain of youth.

He looks out across the bursting crowd. Among them in this house of God he suspects lurk murderers, thieves, fornicators, liars,

---

[85] Between hope and fear

backstabbers, whoremongers, rapists, drug dealers, and miscellaneous, garden variety deviants.

And it troubles him greatly.

Troubles him because he lives close enough to the Spirit to know great darkness and danger sojourns in his midst. Troubles him because he doubts he measures up to this task, this beast of looking death and destruction and denial square in the face and bearing witness against it.

Troubles him because beyond this very real darkness lies a gray area not easily identifiable and he is a man who brokers in black and white. A man, who, from his youth loved and followed God, dwelled in truth and immersed himself in the Word, soaking in his glory, living to share the mystery of

The life-changing story;
In the beginning was God.
And the Word with him,
Creating, molding,
Fashioning a beginning;
Where Word became flesh and dwelt among man,
Teaching him love, sharing the plan;
Of salvation, of rebirth, of truth evermore
Of a Father and a Son and a Holy Spirit which bore
Witness to acts joining time, space, lifting the veil,
Unleashing
the grace that
Communes with spirit, face to face;
A Son, so loved yet sacrificed, a lamb,
So we might know Him, the Great I AM.

And for him faith is a black and white issue just like race. GOD is, GOD was, and GOD would always be, omnipotent, all-powerful, without error, infallible, the truth, the light, the way, the beginning, the end, the answer, the question, the cure for all sin, the recipe for righteousness, yada, yada, yada.

The wrinkle was, righteousness wasn't simple and neither was sin or your garden-variety existence or some facsimile thereof. It was all a complicated web of nature and nurture and timing and circumstance and flesh and blood and principalities and rulers in high places. And here, in his church, this crumbling temple he pined for and whored behind until the assembly appointed him sovereign seven years before, he notes and recognizes among the audience demons, minions, and all manner of descendants of fallen angels; remnants of a battle fought long ago.

A battle fought and lost with the defeated still denying defeat, opting instead to continue waging war against the heavens for reasons their hosts neither remember nor can begin to comprehend but it is not these otherwise ordinary people who worry him. He is accustomed to seeing people's demons, their underlying spirits. He saw them all the time, especially in white neighborhoods: at Harris Teeter's, at Titan's games, at the Governor's Ball, everywhere, like fire ants in Texas.

Demonic spirits lurk just beyond the surface, hiding from veiled eyes, deceiving individuals into counting them figments of the imagination; the stuff of fairy tales and porn but he knows better having bore witness to the true nature of man the moment he rose from beneath the water following baptism on his thirteenth birthday which just so happened to fall on Easter Sunday.

Elijah made the long walk to the alter while the gathered crowd applauded like confused thunder not only because he was the son of a con man but also because he held the title most suspended boy in the seventh grade. His pastor, a man he religiously referred to as Porky, asked him the customary questions then directed the deacons to prepare their new brother in Christ to join the brotherhood.

They whisked him away; stripping him of his clothing faster than you can say wait then wrapping him in a white sheet. The Deacons shepherd Elijah out and to the baptismal pool, a tub of stagnant water that sat, always, in a giant tin tub dividing the choir loft for just such an occasion. Elijah and the Pastor climb into the pool.

"Elijah Fisher," Porky booms, "I baptize you in the name of the Father, and the Son and the Holy Spirit!" bending him back like Gumby[86] and into the dirty water for what seems an eternity before snapping him back to his feet.

And he feels different…

…lighter, and cleaner, and freer… and filled with knowledge and an awareness he had not possessed before.

Images pop in high definition Technicolor and its all so beautiful

---

[86] See Cartoon character, see Murphy, Eddie (Saturday Night Live)

that it hurts and the music is high resolution, and the choir is digitally wired to reach right out and into your heart and what was once lost was now found and it's love baby and it rocks big time. Grateful as all get out he turns to his new best friend, the saint disguised as a pig, to thank him for saving his soul from the fiery pit of hell, "Sweet Judas!" he screams instead, shocked as Pastor Jenkins and the congregation to hear such words escape his lips.

Porky's face turns gray; a miracle in its own right since he was a blue black man.

@@@@@

Mary long ago gave up the idea of weed as a coping mechanism. She also gave up on the idea of miracles leaving her in quite a quandary that inevitably morphs into hopelessness abandoning her in deep danger an inch away separating her from not surviving this *electric* experience called life which, according to the Book of Prince[87] meant forever and that's a mighty, mighty long time.

Like anyone needed to tell her that.

For years a recreational user she yearned to drown in a mound of the most potent marijuana money could buy when Jackson croaked but she couldn't, first, because she was broke but beyond that because she knew leaf escapism would simply delay the inevitable. After all a decade spent with a person whose chief duty most recently involved ministering to the dead, dying, and those left behind exposed her continually to the five stages of grief:[88]

S1: **shock and denial**. People are numb and often deny that a change has even occurred. They blame others and do not recognize the need to make decisions.

S2: **Anger.** After realizing the loss has occurred they may begin to feel

---

[87] see Roger Nelson/Purple Rain. Rock icon
[88] see Kubler-Ross'grief cycle Worden, William J. Grief Counseling & Grief Therapy: A Handbook for the Mental Practitioner. New York: Springer Publishing Company 1991.

anger at the loss and the unfairness of it. They may become angry at the person who has been lost or anyone in the vicinity.

S3: **Depression**. Individuals experience an overwhelming sense of "the blues" and a lack of energy. Individuals desperately need the help of family and friends.

S4: **Dialogue and bargaining**. People feel a need to tell their story in order to make sense of what has occurred. Good listeners can be critical.

S5: **Acceptance**. Individuals don't like the change, but they are beginning to accept reality and are willing to work it into their lives.

And while she didn't look forward to the experience she anxiously sought to rifle through the stages as quickly as possible.

And she did, over and over, a gerbil on a wheel with no end in sight. *Weed takes the edge off the most wicked of experiences* her inner voice whispered but she pressed ahead, denying, crying, grieving, bargaining, and accepting without so much as a blunt, joint or doobie until she woke up riding Death as if it became her.

Who could fault her for giving in when she continued putting out all the while hanging from a cliff where only a sea of leaves could comfort and hanging was, was it not, what people advised you to do at times like this—to *just hang in there*...they counsel over and over, mouths stuck on repeat without ever really considering what they're urging the discouraged to do.

Hang: to be suspended in the air, without any means of support; as in to lynch.

An electric word, hang, it can mean forever and that's a mighty long time... unless you're an Eternist or a Resurrectionist and we won't even try defining those terms at present.

Hanging only rings fun if you're fit and have a monkey bar fetish but beyond that its essence lies somewhere between sadistic, satanic, and sucks leaving weakness, according to the Good Book, strangely, synonymous, with strength and something just short of hashish later she finds herself calmer, him slightly more tolerable, and the sex at least minimally entertaining but what more could she hope for when she was just paying the piper?

How, she wondered, humping him later that night while his wife slept upstairs, *did anyone in their right mind take him seriously straight?*[89] Mary understands, even through the weed, that here humps just another trip around the grief wheel. That said who cared? She was beyond tired of trying to just hang in there with rage, vampires, and words she's unable to even whisper to her own soul.

She refuses to play the role of Job, suffering quietly through everything from hemorrhoids to the wipeout of one's heirs only to rise from the ashes and demand answers of the great Mystery. She stands neither Judith nor a virtuous beauty waiting to join a tyrant's head to the earth with a tent spike but instead she accepts herself for what she is: a garden variety morbidly depressed traitor grasping at life by sleeping with death. *E*lectric words *life* and *death*; they both mean forever and that's a mighty long time…

@@@@@

Calling a man of God Judas in the middle of his own church makes time stand still. The Pastor and the thirteen year old stand in the tub, feet glued to its' bottom, eyes to each other. The congregation sits, butts glued to their pews waiting for a shepherd to lead them. The ninety year old church mother struggles, quivering all the way, to her frail, arthritic feet, "Stone the bastard," she yells.

And all hell breaks loose.

Reverend Jenkins sprints from the pool leaving Elijah wet, shivering, and trying like hell to outrun saints itching to crucify one of them.

He stumbles upon the man of God much later that night, cleaning up after the Easter fish fry to benefit the church building fund. He wept while sweeping crumbs from the concrete floor. Elijah picks up the spare broom and together, they sweep and cry and pray after Pastor Jenkins confesses he has been stealing money from the church treasury and pocketing it in the church building fund. Elijah, in turn, confessed, "I got baptized this morning to win a three dollar bet."

---

[89] sober

So no, minions and petty demons in this gathering do not trouble him but this woman, if indeed that was what she is, who should be sitting to his right but who has, like Elvis, left the building.

She is the missing piece, a black hole taking in everything and nothing all at once, appearing as light but carrying an equal amount of darkness.

She was gray.

The nefariousness that quickened almost from the beginning, an inhabitant of the garden, a witness to the play recreating the unfolding of eternity, full of mystery and secrets and lies and deceit...or a purveyor of the light yet to come?

He can not yet tell, she is gray and it troubles him, gravely...

"Reverend Fisher?" Loretta repeats.

Apparently.

For he opens his eyes with a start only to a sea of eyes watching and waiting, albeit impatiently, for him to wake from the dead and tell them where he was coming from when the real question is where the hell is he going?

Reverend Fisher rises.

"See he is alive," a child chimes from the back.

The church cracks up while he steps, slowly, into the pulpit, "Well, Jesus says a little one will lead them," he mummers, and waits while they get it all out of their systems and silence steps to center stage, "Please look with me in your Bibles," he looks up and over the rims of his glasses, "Your Bibles are those black books with the word Bible stamped on front."

The Fisher follows the lead of at least a third of his audience, folding his arms across his chest and waiting for the cows to come home, chew their cud or comply with whatever fancy tickled the titties of its owner.

After a few moments the mass, albeit with attitude, complies.

"And turn to the book of Jeremiah."

"Jerry who?!"

A contingent from the center demands.

The situation devolves into confusion as the tadpoles flounder, many unsure how to spell Jeremiah let alone navigate, without rhyme or reason, through a sea of prophets and saints, big and small, fishermen all, themselves still learning to swim.

This is going to be a long day, Reverend Fisher realizes again giving Loretta, his trusted friend and Choir Director, an increasingly exasperated look even as the church swells with the sound of wailing babies, flipping pages, and flapping gums all racing around searching for the ever elusive Jeremiah.

Loretta passes the exasperated look to her left, and he follows suit only to see the gray, bright as day, seated to the right, where she had not been seconds before…

The gray simply smiles and shrugs, more than well pleased with the way the morning is progressing.

"Turn to page 692," the Shepherd directs, able to stall no longer, "Chapter 20, starting with verse 14, reads in part:

Cursed be the day I was born, cursed be the man who brought my father the news, may he hear wailing, wailing in the morning and a battle cry at noon, for he did not kill me in the womb, with my mother as my grave. Why did I ever come out of the womb to see trouble and sorrow and to end my days in shame?"

@@@@@

Eventually, the Man who would be senator, governor, or, at a minimum, mayor surfaces for air and when he does it is as a new man. Having been to the mountaintop and tasted from the tree of the sweet fruit of freedom he vows to chew off his own leg sooner than dig in for the duration with a slice of death that just keeps on breathing. For the first time in two dozen years he likes himself, he really, really likes himself and he plans to mate and marry someone who madly adores his middle man whom Francesca christened Mad Dog this morning during their sacred dick dipping ceremony.

Kicking back[90] on the couch he turns on the telly and the widescreen fills with Bill Clinton, his secret hero, being interviewed by Oprah, who looks like someone has been doing her really, really well. Bill, it turns out, is on a promotional tour for his autobiography, *My Life*. Oprah, who looks like someone has been doing her really, really

---

[90] Getting comfortable

well grills Bill over Lewinsky-gate, Hillary, and the hell that ensues when you combine cigars with an ultra absorbent not so little blue dress.

"Well, you know," Bill answers, "The whole thing was kind of sleazy…"

Just like my current situation, he notes, engrossed.

"But you have to remember, our twenty-second President, Grover Cleveland, had a child out of wedlock *and* there was a rumor that W's daddy spent twenty years working on top of his secretary and no one batted an eye…"

And suddenly, his minor-league indiscretion doesn't sound so bad.

"I never thought," Bill continues, "Not for a moment, that Hillary would leave me…"

And there lay the fly in his ointment as well. While he doubts Ms. Mary covets this marriage any more than he Vegas odds say she plans to endure a wrenchingly drawn out death duct tapped to his side.

A notion dawns on him as if a dream though it's a nightmare he would have never dared dream—he must divorce Ms. Mary. The very idea leaves him delirious with delight yet heady with fright to the point of fainting. "Will I actually get to cry freedom on this side of eternity?" he asks Bill who simply fades to a commercial along with Oprah who looks like someone has been doing her really, really well.

He spots the *Society* page lying on the table. He picks it up. The Deflowered and Un-Humped Daughters of the Confederacy are hosting a ball and silent auction at the Lipstick Lounge to benefit the newly formed Bounty Board which begins hunting on the first of the month…*Stop reading that,* Mad Dog warns and he does, *I won't let random possibilities pee on our parade*, he promises, as Bill resumes talking while his fingers do the walking.

@@@@@

"You know him?" The Staten Island cops asked fellow officer, Orpheus Grey, on more than one occasion after busting his older brother, Brad, for burglary, not of the cat but instead garden-variety kind.

237

Jimmy Carter had his Billy. Hillary had her Bill and he had his Brad.

"I know him," he responded, time and again, bailing him out by trading the kind of favors that bind the thin blue line at its crossroads.

"I could bust my balls to detective faster if you could stay out of handcuffs longer than a shoplifter on speed."

"Where they teach you to talk like that, Colombo Academy?" Brad quips, enjoying his own joke enough for both of them, "I'm putting in the real work junior, wait and see, you're gonna ride my coattails to the top."

"More like save your ass from the fire," he answers, dropping him off at their mom's house before heading off to pull the latest extra shift bartered for the fledgling cat burglar's freedom.

The day Orpheus made detective he met Delores White, the beautiful daughter of the largest egg farmer in the state and she liked him, she really, *really* liked him. The night he made detective Brad attempted the biggest score of his career, the White house, only to be cornered in a henhouses by Delores' dad who mistook him for a fox and fired.

When the responding officers deposited his body on the slab at the morgue the medical examiner unearthed the family jewels stashed in his designer underwear. Mr. White was outraged, Delores was inconsolable, the police department was aghast, and Opie demoted and placed on administrative duty where he was forced to answer phones and make coffee like a testosterone drained Barney Fife[91] vacationing in Mayberry.

@@@@@

This is Qatar," Rick informs, clicking to the next picture, "An oil rich Middle Eastern desert kingdom where liquor is banned and women walk around swathed in veils."

He clicks again.

---

[91] See inept Deputy, Andy Griffith show

238

"After the Battle of Seattle and other successful protests the World Trade Organization voted to subvert our cause by hosting their meetings in places where protesters are made to feel less than welcome," he continues, clicking again.

The screen overflows with corpses, headless, and otherwise attired, hanging from the walls of the city.

He clicks back twice, "This is Qatar," he says, against the backdrop of the idyllic picture that kicked off the slide show, "The site of the next World Trade Organization meeting."

"Damn," Dr. Dates says, whistling, "They're gonna go Biblical on your little asses."
And black women wonder why they can't keep a man, Rick thinks.
"Nice," Camille comments.
"Anyway," he continues, "A peaceful meeting would no doubt elicit orgasms in the trade ministers from the WTO's 140 member countries but because we," he clicks again, "Like aliens, are everywhere, they will, despite their best efforts, find themselves flushed out of their hiding place."

"You go GI Joe," Dates encourages, settling back in his chair and pulling out his rose embroidered fan.

Rick reaches across him and starts the projector. An animated feature fills the screen:

@@@@@

Orpheus Grey was christened a uniformed, badge wearing; shield carrying, gun packing District of Columbia police officer the day after his brother's funeral. Who knew a cop could be hired on the spot by an automated recording? At the fifth precinct station the following morning he drew the smallest straw after roll call and was assigned to walk a beat with veteran officer Pierre Smalls, a three hundred pound asthmatic with a predisposition towards beef and bean burritos purloined[92] from sidewalk vendors.

"You been eating rotten eggs?" Grey asks when they stop yet again so Smalls can burp, catch his breath then release substances soaked in pure unadulterated evil.

---

[92] stolen

The funky cop pants his way to a short retaining wall where he waddles his way onto the same.

"That's not a rhetorical question, I really need to know."

"Man, don't make me laugh, I can't breathe," the Funkster says, giggling like a five year old until a fart sends him tumbling off the wall and down a hill, screaming like a bitch all the way, a gaseous ball of bad burritos barreling toward Constitution Avenue.

The following day Grey picked up the *Washington Post* and came face to face with a younger, slimmer Pierre Smalls smiling from a headline that read:

Decorated Officer Dies in the Line of Duty

Grey resigned from the Washington Metropolitan Police Department that evening after serving just one day in uniform.

"You know him?" Grey asked his new partner, donning gloves and taking plastic bags from his pocket.

"Sure do," Green replied, but with a smile, "Meet Rod "hot rod" Fletcher, gang banger and suspect in two murders."

But he knew months ago that was a lie.

As the responding officers it fell on their shoulders to guard Mr. Fletcher's remains until the medical examiner arrived to bag and tag but the wagon was running late and his partner had a date with a stripper from a tittie establishment that boasted not only beautiful girls but bragged about several ugly ones too.

"He's not going to get up and walk off," Green promised, walking to their car, "But that's what your bright eyed bushy-fucking tailed ass'll be doing if you don't hop your happy hump in this car before I pull off."

He had gotten in.

"Besides, your time will be better spent filling out all that paperwork you're so damn fond of."

Green dropped him off down the block from the station. As soon as he entered he pulled out his notes and headed to the records room where he requested files on the unsolved cases his partner rattled off. He read then re-read the scant information contained in the files of Henry Rhodes and Rayshaun Oglesby only to discover less than a single shred of evidence linking Roderick Fletcher to either murder.

But that didn't deter his partner from processing the Form 252. He showed up later that evening high on lap dances and with the scent of sex still on his breath and committed pen to paper with abandon, weaving a tale of multiple murder and narrow escapes to make an eight year old abandon an errant older brother in favor of a black and white television.

Now his partner's made for TV masterpiece plays out on just that, in real time on every local channel hurdling not towards Constitution Avenue but instead CNN and the writing on the wall says Green is going down in flames and in the aftermath his own career might well be wiped out like words written in the sand alongside the newest Stephen King novel a synonym for hanging in on the wrong end of an ass left flapping in the breezing by someone else's errors.

And gosh darn it he wasn't going to take it anymore. *I'm not eight and this lazy son of a bitch is as much my brother as I'm black which, if nothing else, should help me blend in and blend I intend cause I sure as hell plan to dig myself out of the hole he's dug for me even if I have to bury him to do it.*

True, he isn't the same bright eyed bush fucking tailed eight-year old who fell asleep in an old trench coat and hat convinced he'd wake up the next Sam Spade but he ain't a fox in a henhouse either. He stands, like his name, gray, and while that might not make him a knight in shining armor he can still look himself in the face at the end of the day...*as soon as I find Mr. Fletcher's body*, which has, contrary to Green's promise, simply gotten up and walked away.

@@@@@

Well dressed gentlemen exit limousines and enter the palace in Qatar flanked by armed guards. Inside, their equally armed compatriots are everywhere, searching everyone and thing that enters.

"What we know but they don't," Rick says, over the silent movie short, "Is that wrap-around bombs disguised as piping were planted in the plumbing when the palace was remodeled."

"How many johns are in this place?" Harry asks looking up from the virus[93] he's nursing.

A parade of opulent potties continues to march across the widescreen.

"Sixty-four," Rick answers, "All ornate and wired for action."

"And who do we owe for such illustrious backwards planning?" Athena queries, unimpressed.

"Rebels, just like us, different agendas common goals," Rick continues, "All one hundred and forty delegates will circulate, sipping champagne and feasting on a myriad of delicacies, all laced with potent all-natural laxatives."

"That's just nasty," Ree-Ree decrees, rising from her chair as the 140 WTO Delegates race for one of the sixty-four ornate toilets outfitted, during renovations, with wrap-around bombs disguised as piping.

"As soon as three of them flush the can at the same time, all sixty four babies explode…"

"Now this is some wild shit," Dr. Dates observes, gazing at his hairy Love who's too busy with his silly little virus to notice.

"You were afraid to toss rocks in South Carolina but you're on board with this?" Athena demands of Dr. Dates.

"These are the same guys who are denying gays life-partner health benefits," Rick defends, betting on a sure pony.

"Vanderbilt offers life partner benefits," Dr. Dates answers softly, causing Harry to look up from his silly little virus long enough to blow him a kiss.

"Change starts at the top you know," Rick continues, "But let us not fail to visualize the alternative," He starts the projector back up.

"You have to give the crazy white fuck credit," Athena concedes, "He comes prepared."

---

[93] as in computer

The screen fills with images of decay, the earth waxing old like a garment while all the while war rages and children starve until bridges explode followed by electrical generators and utilities, plunging entire populations into darkness as forest fires span the hills like vast oceans and air and water evaporate as if licked up by giant balls of hydrogen from the sky giving birth to smoke that rises and expands like burnt clouds parting to reveal piles of bones... all burned beyond recognition as the curtain closes and the lights came up.

"Tea anyone?" Dr. Dates proposes, and he and his love disappear as foxes in a hole.

"So," Camille observes, rising and turning to Rick, "You have extracted your rod, measured, and determined that sixty-four is an acceptable number?"

"Insurance adjusters do it all the time," the Idealist answers, as if they're the magic words. When she says nothing he prepares to pull his next sure bet out of the bag.

"No need," she assures, extending a hand to Athena who takes it in her own, "I'm just a witness not a judge."

"I appreciate your generosity," he returns to the retreating backs abandoning him.

"That was an impressive presentation," Ree-Ree commends, walking over and giving him a long, passionate kiss that rolls over into heated touching then grinding then the frenzied losing of clothing culminating in him eating her as if there is not only no tomorrow but no next month either.

"Baby that was sooo good," Ree-Ree gasps, fifty nine minutes and a magnitude of waves later, "But everyone on God's green earth deserves to take a crap without getting their ass blown off."

Silence answers as he climbs atop her, slipping between her warm, wet walls. He sighs as does she," This is sooo good honey," she moans, unfolding her forest, "But if you blow the cans I'll do the same to your cover."

@@@@@

243

It's good and windy the day Ms. Mary blows back into town from an extended foray to South Africa and she's feeling finer than cash on payday. The trip proved a cultural, sociological, and theological experience that left her, literally, too drained for words. While visiting the more primitive[94] she took a vow of silence only to be stricken by a nasty strain of laryngitis that devolved into a vocal cord malady the likes of which hadn't been seen since the Commodore[95] paid retribution for abandoning the wife of his youth but all is well.

She found, after the first few frightful days, that there was much to be said for silence. It was golden in fact, almost as golden as the collection of coins she discovered in a dark corner in Cape Town, far from the maddening crowd ceaselessly chattering about who knew what.

The point is, in the midst of this madness she found both the coins and her blessing in silence—a place deep within where no one tries to get a hand out or a handle on you. There, deep in the pit of her consciousness, she discovered within the quiet a great weariness born of defined standards of rank, race, wealth, and everything that deprives one of elbowroom even when you *are* the only one in the room.

It was here, in this place of nothingness that she came face to face with the mirror of her soul and swore to strive to simply *be*, at any cost, for freedom, she now knew, must be the birthright for which she rose each morning or she wanted to wake no more and she yearns to wake for now she realizes just how much she has to be thankful for.

She is happy and relatively healthy and owns a wonderful mansion in Belle Meade, the most exclusive neighborhood in but outside of Nashville. She has in her possession a well bred, hard working, if hopelessly hapless, husband who loves her down to her dirty underwear,[96] spoils her shamelessly and knows that she knows that he better make partner and soon.

When one multiplied this equation by the absence of the silly little political aspirations she long ago squashed, its clear their future foretells their living happily ever after like the affluent couple she so long ago insisted they must be. Cruising up the winding drive she

---

[94] See the Mandelas
[95] See the Commodores, Lionel Ritchie, R&B.
[96] Colloquialism meaning "dearly"

opts, on a lark, to stop by the mailbox. *If this doesn't give him his first hint he has a new woman on his hands my name isn't Ms. Mary.*

She opens the Rooster to find the cock packing more mail than a clandestinely striking postman. *If I didn't know better I'd think he hadn't been home in a month*, she thinks, chuckling—only to be shocked, yet again, when no sound emerges. *How soon we forget*, she observes, *when our orbit once again submits to the magnetic energy of the maddening crowd.*

She stops and breathes deeply, traveling further into herself, "Selah," she says silently, out of necessity as well as choice and steps inside where she immediately notices them—"Well, I'll be damned," she hisses silently.

Cobwebs hang in the left corner of her kitchen.

Holy Moses, she continues then remembers to relax, breathing deep then more, searching for then finding her peace at the pit's bottom … *What ever has my fat clumsy mouse been doing while his pussycat was away?*

Her choice of thoughts takes her by surprise, *pussycat?*…leaving her feeling just a little naughty which, surprisingly, feels a wee bit nice. Six weeks in the wild living among the more primitive[97] has rendered her, if she is not mistaken, a tad bit horny. She giggles, silently, like a silly schoolgirl. *Maybe this silence thing somehow triggered an increase in oxygen, estrogen, progesterone or whatever hormone controls how aroused or horny even, for heavens sake, people get.*

Determined to put things in order she heads into the laundry room, collects the dust mop, and silently whistles Dixie while attacking the intricate work that went into Charlotte' web.[98] The phone near the oven rings. She instinctively answers it. "Hello," a woman's voice snaps, impatiently, "Hello… look, I know you're there I can hear you breathing you little pussy—
Ms. Mary drops the phone.
It lands on the receiver with a thud and immediately rings again.

---

[97] See the Mandela's
[98] See W.E. Dubois

"Hello," the voice says when she again answers without speaking, "Listen Cinderella, could you at least pretend to have an ounce of progesterone or estrogen or whatever hormone controls how aroused or horny—

Ms. Mary rips the phone from the wall. The phones in the other rooms begin tolling, *"Ask not for whom the bell tolls,"* she mouths, feeling uncharacteristically spooked. First her voice vanishes and now some pervert calls repeating her thoughts; what kind of madness is that? The phones continue to toll, incessantly, driving her room to room where she repeats the wall ripping ritual before arriving at the mouth of the master suite where a fishy smell stops her dead in her tracks.

So that's what the horny rat has been up to she realizes, entering the bedroom and ripping the comforter from the bed. Empty cans litter the sheets...*how many times have I asked him to put away his toys when he's finished playing with them?* She thinks, finally starting to feel irritated when she finds herself distracted by beige, blue, and then red translucent balloons lying in clusters on the carpet.

Oh my God, she mouths, tracking a trail of rainbow colored circles past the matching overstuffed chairs, the fireplace, and to the newly remodeled marble whirlpool where rests a full bottle of Viagra perched atop a pyramid fashioned from condom wrappers. *How many times have I asked the twins not to play in their father's things? Obviously they're off their Ritalin again. Do they have any idea how hard Viagra can be on an eighteen year old heart?*

She stops and breathes deeply, traveling further into herself, "Selah," she says silently, out of necessity as well as choice. Determined to prolong the peace she discovered deep within herself in silence she rips the last ringing phone from the wall and heads back downstairs where she attacks the mound of mail multiplying like Mexicans renting a house in the suburbs.

*Bill, bill, bill...bill...bill...*a rose embossed envelope blooms amid a sea of white commerce coming home to roost, *come to momma Cinderella,* she mouths plucking the vibrant rose from the weeds and opening its petals...

246

Dear Ms. Mary,

First and foremost I want to thank you for being my life partner for the past two and a half centuries oops, decades. In many ways our strengths and weaknesses were very complimentary and created a life that we can be proud of, maternally and materially. I am sorry for any pain this might cause you but I have to book oops leave in order, I feel, to save my own life. That said, I believe, though not in my heart, that we are both better people for having spent this time together. I thank you for any contribution you have somehow managed to make in my life and I accept your thanks in advance for any I have made in yours.

It is my goal, at this point, to make our parting as painless as possible. I am willing, therefore, to pay for any psychiatric treatment and, or, hospitalization you might need to assist you in coping during this difficult time. In addition, I am willing to allow you full ownership of the mansion and all its contents, to include my clothes, if that will help facilitate the healing process. Beyond this I am willing to continue making the mortgage payment and paying all household expenses for up to six months while you seek some form of gainful employment. Also, I promise to faithfully fulfill my obligation to deposit your current allowance into your checking account each month. Our other assets are listed below and would become our individual property:

	Yours	Mine
Bank Account	$820,000.43	$1, 348, 522.02
Money Market		$435,070.24
SEPP Account	$342,000.00	$331,000.00
Life Insurance	$100,000.00	$3,000,000.00 (term)
Stocks & Bonds		undetermined
Land		undetermined

I propose we sell the land and S&B and split the proceeds 50-50. Let me know what you think ASAP (as soon as possible).

Thank you in advance for your time and attention to this matter.

Respectfully yours,
    (Your soon to be ex) Husband

Keeping the Ball Rolling

One after another nondescript trucks arrive at the clandestinely resurrected Marathon building in the warehouse district. The assembly line stretches from the sidewalk to the sub basement where another wave of young workers, under the tutelage of seasoned men, move like clockwork, transferring boxes of all sizes into their assigned storage spaces.

"About time you dragged your hind parts in," Methuselah muses from a chair in the corner, when Big Dog and Athena crawl in looking like beat and down.

Big Dog lights up like a downed power line, "Man, I'm beat as a bitch who don't know something, but I'm sure happy as shit to see your old ass."

"What'd you do bust out?" Athena asks.
"Come on in here," he instructs, leading them beyond the boxes and into the basement where a secret door housed wall to wall computer terminals manned by heads busy at work.

"We have a backlog of a thousand orders for Viagra," Methuselah informs them, "The Vicodin is going like pancakes at the Pantry and there's enough vitamin H floating around here to keep hell happy."

"And the gangs all here," Camille adds, creeping up on them quiet as a boa with a meal on its mind, "Need me to help knock that pain outta your back?" she inquires of Athena who happens to be stretching the same.

"If you let me knock one out of yours first," Athena answers as Hook limps in looking like the cat that swallowed the canary.

Hook catches sight of Methuselah, "What'd you do, shed your skin and slide out!"
"Did you get the black pot?" The usually Patient Man snaps.
"We did," Hook assures him.
"Then let's celebrate," he says, leading the way upstairs, "We'll drink to Aegri somnia."
"A sick man's dreams," Athena translates, "I like it."
"So they think *you're* crazy?" Hook laughs.

"Which makes him the perfect spokesman," Camille says and bows her thanks.

"Hey dog," Hook barks, over his shoulder, "You owe me five Grovers."

Big Dog stops in his tracks, "Do I owe this green-eyed motherfucker five G's?" He demands of Camille who's standing damn near on top of Athena.

Athena takes a step back, "Is that supposed to be a rhetorical question?" she asks Camille who says nothing.

"Hmm." The Dog barks, following his boys.

"Hmm," Athena says, when they are alone, "You should've told me there was a pot on the table and you were the prize, maybe I could have gotten in on it."

"C'est la guerre[99]" Camille responds, reaching out—.

"Snake," Athena hisses, slapping her hand away.

"Aut vincere aut mori[100]," the Snake answers with a smile and slithers away to join the party.

@@@@@

Sound the bells of Notre Dame Ms. Mary screams silently running through the mansion like a South African Huntress with no chickens and her head cut off. *This is agony, anarchy; Armageddon in fact* she realizes, fighting back tears. *What went wrong?* She wonders, trying this time to read between the lines that lined the page, soldiers at the ceremonial execution of an educated housewife who wore both her air of arrogance and her jewels as a cloak, *Why this is the most shocking thing to happen since suddenly and under mysterious circumstances, the Chaplain turned up missing and theories abounded about what fate befell the unofficial greeter of the Harvard of the South's highly esteemed Divinity program…That was the last thing the program needed— to garner unwelcome attention in a theological arena ripe for Armageddon on the heels of the West uprising at Harvard and the pulpit plagiarism that rocked the Disciples of Christ like Elvis on the Ed Sullivan show…but the Chaplain with the Colgate smile's death, while shocking, had, in the end, been chalked up to the most mundane*

---

[99] This is war.
[100] Either conquer or die

of circumstances: life and death mistakes where answers were nothing more than mysteries waiting to unearthed...

    My present circumstances make that B grade soap opera dissipate in comparison. My husband is planning to leave me! *Whatever or...whoever gave my clumsy mouse the idea he could do such a thing?* She muses; *did he crack the code to the parental lock and watch MTV?* She wonders, frantically searching for the remote control a la deposed South African dictator whose life depends on it.

@@@@@

    Rena is having an Eminem moment. That once in a lifetime opportunity you better get it right moment when you can't blow it when you can turn back time and right wrongs by hitting the big one out of the park in the bottom of the ninth. She knows that much and she isn't even a baseball fan. Her father, the vessel who spawned her from the fruit of his loins then remained silent through seven presidential elections and the death of Arafat, has decided to speak.

    "Rena Mary Steinman," The same father who cursed her with the name of a Catholic virgin who gave birth to not one but several sons whispers, pulling her close, "I don't know if you're this Mary or not and I really don't care but you know and I know there's a good chance you'll neither marry nor get another chance to steal the show during the bridal march so don't fuck this up."

    Then he kisses her good night and heads to bed.

    The fact that her father has spoken his mind is proof positive, pin your money to the seat of your underwear evidence she will never possess another moment's peace on either side of eternity unless she breaks the story perched on her lap like a Chippendale dancer. Thanks to the new manna[101] her box overflows with requests for interviews and job offers from every rag and TV station in town, all whoring like knocked up nannies, looking to scoop whose political St. Peter had gotten caught in the chicken coop.

    Rena, this instant, coins this phenomenon Clinton syndrome. An "outted" entity that wagged when it walked didn't stand a chance in hell in a house of cards supported by folks living to watch you fall

---

. [101] E-mail

from grace—talk about giving an above average economically and artificially enhanced Joe an incentive to dive for cover and cover her ass she will while hedging her bets and towing the line and her gut says this Mary, while obviously the last person you would suspect, is also someone you didn't want to screw around with unless you lived to wake up with a sore ass flapping in the breeze like a Broadway flop on opening night.

Maybe I'm on to something, she thinks, recording the phrase into her phone for posterity. *Maybe...the e-mail has less to do with sour grapes and libido and more to do with free press and ambitious political aspirations...after all, advertising and airtime didn't come cheap and pockets, especially incumbent ones, tended to run deep... a man looking leapfrog would have to have one of two things, a huge bankroll or huge balls.*

If that's not a recipe for wedded bliss I don't know what is, Rena decides, recording that for posterity as well. This story was already writing itself and what a story. A man with passionate political aspirations but finite funding throws propriety and political protocol to the wind by airing his own dirty laundry ahead of his opponents. What could be more brilliant in it's simplicity than casting your skeletons from the closet before the contest ever began?

After all, what has he lost? His hands are still relatively clean by today's standards. He hasn't shamed his office because he hadn't been elected to one yet. He hasn't killed his wife, at least not yet, and odds are running 2 to 1 that he won't kill his love letter writer either. In fact, while it might be lost on the casual reader, the e-mail actually reads more like a promo ad than an attempt to bring someone's political aspirations crashing down.

Case in point (CIP):

"a repeatedly resuscitated St. Peter"
trans: He thinks about more than sex.

"all he could think about/overboard"
trans: honest, shares feelings

"affinity for hardware"
trans: handy, W.O.T.N.E[102]

---

[102] Wide Open To New Experiences

251

"doggy style/mirrors"
trans: animal lover, perfectionist

"calls you Ms. Mary"
trans: polite to a fault

"all that Viagra"
trans: always there for you

"dust mop/man"
trans: versatile

    See what I mean? Nothing about him screams evil or even unelectable, in fact, while you might not want to marry him, on paper he's the poster child for a decent senator, governor, or mayor. He is a rake of a man with a plan and a timeframe, a player, a constant in a sea of variables.

    This Mary was the mystery.   What was the motivating factor behind her letter? Peace?
Please.
Revenge?
Possibly but for what and against who, her lover for having a wife with a tattletale tongue or his wife for changing churches faster than frigid women change underwear and sobbing on the shoulder of anybody wearing a pair? Was it all or none of the above? Mary "T. Messenger" hadn't exactly painted herself into a corner.

    Case in point (CIP)—she never says she doesn't love the guy just that he's a limp wimp who occasionally enjoys being anally penetrated with a panorama of prosthetics. Was that so bad—there's somebody for everybody right? Little Mary Sunshine's epistle is no Song of Solomon but Rena's money, or at least her daddy's, says its writer is as wily as her lover and that the dinner hour bomb was all part of a bold, well orchestrated, pre-political strategy hatched over hardware and pillow talk—these days anything was possible.

@@@@@

    His mom, Loretta, worked hard to get them out of the hood and finally accomplished that goal when Big Dog, whose nickname was Pooch at the time, was thirteen. The wrinkle was that by then the hood

252

was home, and the neighborhood where they moved was as real to his eyes as Disney World on any given Wednesday.

At every opportunity, which was soon everyday, he escaped back to the real ride, an amusement park where people dealt with reality, a camp where not only life but any second could be a bitch of a struggle where the strong survived and a moving target was harder to hit so you better be in a hurry or you were bound for hell.

He acknowledged those who attempted to escape to the suburbs for what they were: punks pretending they weren't prey just like the pofolks they left behind in the hood— colored ostriches with their heads in the sand in Fantasyland and that shit was a fact, as in keeping it real, like Bill, except he wouldn't give the time of day to a fat white chick too trifling to get her clothes dry cleaned.

Bill could have avoided all that drama if he had just followed the golden rule: keep it real, not just in public but in every aspect of life. No illusions, no lies. Anyone who knew him or of him knew he was a drug dealer, a lover to many, a daddy to more, and, on occasion, a cold-blooded killer— not because he was evil but simply because it was the nature of both the beast and the business.

He made money, much of it, married his high school sweetheart, added other women as they tickled his fancy, employed men looking to make a living, killed men who trespassed on his territory, and took no prisoners as it pertained to what rightly belonged to him—reality. No pretending, no faking, no excuses.

His reality was not necessarily the only one he wanted for his kids however, which was why he ultimately gave in to the collective demands of his wife, women, prospects and many progeny to take some time off and take them on vacation so they could enjoy the "quality time" that everyone from Bush to the Baptists were squawking about.

His wife, Marvella, wanted to go to Mexico and see the place where her grandmother was born. Wilhelmina wanted go to Rio and party with the Rastas and Keisha wanted to take a cruise. The prospects got no say in the matter and since he didn't give a damn he decided to go democratic and put the shit to a vote. The kids won, thirteen to three.

Disney World it was.

Now a man who didn't believe in keeping it real might have booked them all separate reservations on different airlines but he knew better. When you're dealing with a woman, much less multiple women anything can be misconstrued leading to ugly, unnecessary bullshit. Separate does not mean equal and everybody would then want their own rental car, their own suite at the hotel, anything and everything that had anything to do with making sure they were getting their fare share and shit.

As a man who believed in keeping it real he could appreciate that— everybody wants his or her fair share. Appreciation did not however automatically equate to catering to though, which is why he decided they would all travel together on the same plane, in first class like one big happy family. It might sound like a beast to some but it is, in reality, a thing of beauty to Big Dog, businessman, daddy, employer, assassin, lover to many, and daddy to more.

@@@@@

Ms. Mary fails to find the remote but has uncovered a cache that includes three bottles of Viagra, a plethora of condoms, foreplay cards, chocolate body paint, and a feathered dildo the size of a bald eagle rotating around the ceiling fan in the sunroom.

She didn't panic. As chairman of the Planning and Convention Commission, her husband was probably responsible for product testing as part of the gully business development project.

The alternative is a possibility too frightful for words in this age of AIDs and the alternative lifestyles that go along with the destabilization of the marital institution among sub Sahara mammals in the western hemisphere…in any case this whole thing apparently has something to do with sex. That much she is convinced of.

What deficiency of nature plagues mice and men? Beasts all, even when Ivy League educated, fail to appreciate that sex isn't everything but instead hardly anything more than un-necessary motion perpetuated by improperly cultured people whose parents never imparted upon them, bless their souls, the willpower to do something more constructive with their time. Like read a book.

There must be a book for this! She thinks, finding herself back in the kitchen where this tragedy began. *Has my clumsy rat been playing the fool, feasting on artificial aids in an attempt to squeeze his spineless St. Peter into some unsuspecting whore's immoral hole?*

Her connection with the Motherland still in tact she stealthily stalks further evidence ultimately discovering it in the form of unopened tubes of desensitizing crème a garden variety synonym for pasteurized embalming fluid—she takes a step back, horror gripping her heart...*the Viagra bottles were full...the cream unopened...used condoms...unopened cream...full Viagra bottle...he erected without artificial aids?! But that was impossible*...he couldn't keep St. Peter up if she nailed it to a cross!

Ripping the linen from the bed she comes face to face with her nastiest nightmare—a mattress cover stained by seminal fluid. She feels in fear of fainting...
Her husband had...com—no. She dare not even think aloud the four letter word that strikes terror in the heart of class conscious women leaving them holding not only their tongues but also their breath while their clumsy, sweaty, lesser halves try to hump their way to happiness on their time.

The cat is out of the bag *and* there are cobwebs in her kitchen. Apparently the mouse got bold, over dosed on MTV, strayed, and forgot the name of the game. It is not charades, though he plays a rat opposite Ruth, Mary Magdalene or some other garden variety daughter of Moab whoring after respectability when what she deserved was a scarlet letter followed by a public flogging.

The game is not red-light, green-light or mother may I or Simon says but what Ms. Mary says and she says, albeit silently, that Mickey will pay and dearly for this mutiny in the making. *Unless he's dead,* she thinks and perks up considerably at the thought, *he has a lot of explaining to do—starting with those cobwebs in my kitchen.*

@@@@@

Interior Secretary Daisy Duke waltzes around her suite at the Opryland Hotel and Convention Center in her favorite white robe, stripping fresh sheets from the bed and replacing them with on her own satin ones to the strains of *Madame Butterfly* spreading her wings in the background. She always traveled with the music, her favorite, having discovered long ago that such touches make all the difference in the world when you're a Gold Level preferred customer far from home with neither friends nor enemies to love or yearn to be left alone.

The Opryland Resort, with waterfalls, indoor atriums, and glass that threatened to touch heaven, stood more visually pleasing and stimulating than most but once you entered the true belly of the beast, you found yourself, by its very nature, encased in just another hotel room and life didn't get much more mundane than that.

It doesn't help that she's an insomniac since age six and yes even then she knew what the word meant. She also knew what hypocrite, Hippocratic oaths and oral copulation was but that was another story altogether. The point is by then she already knew politics would be both her passion and path to glory.

She places her favorite silk roses in the center of the room that is, like everything about her, unremarkable. She is no Janet Reno, mind you but instead more a Jane Hathaway[103] or, in a certain light, Janet Leigh. Daisy had, like all three, worked hard as a kid, fighting to get people to notice the nerdy but otherwise ordinary girl whose name just happened to be Daisy Duke.
"Daisy put up your dukes."
Ignorant little bastards chanted at recess though, needless to say, it was the last thing she'd ever think of doing.

Daisy strolls into the bathroom and places her second favorite basket of silk flowers on the vanity before turning on the shower jets. Steam blankets the room leaving her barely able to make out her face in the brightly lit mirror. *Maybe I'll try some lipstick tonight* she ponders, and then dismisses it as silly. *It's just a dinner meeting for Christ's sake.*

The two of them were getting together to discuss standard practices, policies, and practical ways to head those pesky elves off at the pass....*but*...she remembers now with a smile, *that was what our last meeting was supposed to be about and the sex, all six hours of it, proved more than a little lovely. ..*

The man who, just moments before, personified evil and everything she detested politically dove into her flesh faster than Lector[104] after a fast neither noticing nor nitpicking over her non-

---

[103] See Beverly Hillbillies.
[104] See Silence of the Lambs

existent breasts, flat butt, or even her tiny fin, which he insisted was perfectly fine, which really allowed her to just relax and let go, *I might even be in love,* she decides then scoffs, *I'm not in love, thank God, just in lust and enjoying every second of it.*

This whole fiasco with the elves proved a blessing in disguise. *Sans the shrimp with a dynamite fetish I'd miss being bitten by the Nashville lust bug.* Using the sleeve of her robe she rubs a circle in the mirror and studies her surprisingly fragile face through the fog, "I could be Janet Leigh," she whispers, then giggles before stepping into the shower.

A warm champagne waterfall celebrating a hard won victory greets her eliciting a contented sigh filled with anticipation over this evening's possibilities...*before this night is over* she decides, reaching for her favorite soap but discovering instead a sharp but otherwise unremarkable, ten inch knife slicing through the fog and into her unremarkable frame over and over and over again as *Madame Butterfly* folds her wings and fades in the background.

@@@@@

"Nice little pickle you have us in, don't you think?" The Mayor muses, stepping from the shadows in the office where Opie already sits.

"I'll pull the files," Green offers, trying to remember where he hid them.

"I already did and there isn't shit in them," the Captain Somers answers, stepping from the shadows, "I've already brought everyone up to speed on the deceit involved and while you've given valuable service to the department in the past the hole you've dug is just too deep—

"Everybody fucks up eventually," the Mayor offers empathically.

"You just got greedy," the Captain continues, "You've spent too much time this past year either knee deep in pussy or playing with your own dick while on duty."

Green sits, speechless... stunned... yet proud of the candor displayed by these comedic assholes.

"The kid you 252'd was clean by today's standards," The Mayor educates, holding up a hand as Green prepares to interrupt him, "Now we all know why you did it, and call it karma or the luck of the draw or whatever but we can't afford the heat," The Mayor rises to his feet, "We're gonna have to feed the beast somebody and it wants you," he says, pointing to Green, "And you," he adds, walking to Captain Somers.

"I understand, sir," Captain Somers says, dropping his head and exiting the room.

After the door closes, Green rises leisurely to his feet, "Might I suggest that you stick to feeding the fine citizens of Nashville finger food that slides down like fine wine but steer clear of bristly bastards from way back who'll kick, claw, and snatch your punk ass right down into the belly of that old beast with him."

The Mayor stands with his lower lip lying on the floor. Green steps over it, blows him a kiss, and strolls out the door whistling Dixie. "If these peckerwoods think I'm the hanging kind they've got the wrong asshole," he chuckles, getting back into his car and driving off without Opie or a backwards glance. *None of this is my fault.*

He had never asked to be assigned to homicide; people who committed murder were killers and that shit is not his game. He is neither a murderer nor a groupie trying to get paid under the guise of solving crime, he is just an ex-con turned dirty DC cop on the lam looking to collect an easy paycheck in the next Big Easy until early retirement rolled around.

He didn't invent rule 252, informed of its existence he simply used it to his advantage. Now the scared shitless vote chasers want to offer *him* up as the sacrificial lamb for the remission of their collective sins? Fuck that. No way will he let them strip him of his badge and gun. He'd be scared to death to drive around in East Nashville without them.

@@@@@

As darkness drifts in and out like spirits, Ms. Mary keeps bundles of incense from South Africa burning in the fireplace along with the contraband she discovered earlier. All that lay left to incinerate was the elaborate etching of a nude in repose she uncovered in the guest room and edible underwear lined with cherry flavored testosterone patches.

The magnifying glass resting on her lap bore witness to the awful gut wrenching truth— seminal fluid stains every sleeping, sitting, and sink area in her mansion. Mickey and the whore have defiled her sanctuary and violated the cardinal rule of polite society to boot.[105] "When did *sans semen,* go out of style?" She quips, silently, and cracks up despite herself.

The prized gold coins she discovered in a dark corner in Cape Town, far from the maddening crowd rest at her feet, keeping her company while she waits for her beloved to return home...*For he is my beloved.* She realizes that now. *My reason for living, my reason for—*
Wait.
Is that another cobweb in the corner?

She stops rocking, lifts her breasts from her lap, and sprints to the kitchen where she meticulously inspects each corner, nook, and cranny for signs of Charlotte. Satisfied the pig lover is not at work weaving another plot to separate her from her love, she returns to her post to rock with her incense, gold coins, and silence, all of which she discovered while speechless in South Africa.

There has to be a book addressing this situation, she decides and reaches for the phone only to freeze. She forgot again—she can't talk...she breathes deeply, shaking off the spirits of defeat seeking to slay her and cloaking instead in self assurance which she uses to ascend the spiral staircase leading to her secret closet.

She won't just allow her marriage to go down in flames like so much puritan flesh burning at the stake. As God is her witness she will save this marriage or her name isn't Ms. Mary. She will send out a great call from the mountain. She will rally troops to rival the army of Armageddon: family, friends, ministers, colleagues, classmates, counselors, rabbis, whoever or whatever it takes to keep this, the most sacred of God's institutions, intact.

She logs into her e-mail. Incoming messages flood her account like the Nile during rainy season. Taking advantage of this stitch in time she runs, breasts flapping as sheets in the wind, back to the master

---

[105]never hump in another housewife's home and forget to call a cleaning service

bedroom where she takes a deep breath, rips the semen soaked sheets from the bed, and suspends them from the front windows—the secret signal of the Deflowered and Un-Humped Daughters of the Confederacy.

They, like her husband, would come but ready to lend the communal support she will need to save what pledged to be hers until death did them part. Bursting with exhilaration she runs back to her secret closet well pleased and eager to keep the ball rolling. As she reaches for the mouse Dolly's saggy daughters slap the keyboard, striking the "enter" key.

An animated .jpeg from the Tennessee Performing Arts Center heralding the opening of their new play fills the screen. Its title, *A Great Divide*, unfolds like a scroll opening to curtains parting on center stage to a second e-mail entitled: *A Message from the Mountain*.

Dear Wife of the Man who will be Senator, Governor, or at a minimum, Mayor,

As I send forth salutations Tammy Wynette's *Stand by Your Man* plays softly in the background. *I Will Survive* is closer to my own taste but as we are in Nashville and it is high noon, I bow to southern tradition.

Like Moses before me I bring word down from the mountain that iniquity has befallen your household and your husband is the bandit in gray, blending black and white until it is all that matters or manifests itself to be.

So gird up your loins, breathe Selah from deep within your soul, and call upon your messengers for the weak are many and the wicked are at hand and outside your door like the daughters of Lot, watching, waiting, and listening for the wail of the poor Goofy mutt who will soon find himself locked in your upper room like flowers in the attic.

North of Dixie lust demands abandon or some semblance of sexual satiation but when a whorish but repeatedly resuscitated dick religiously flat lines on the way to the bonfire it's time to douse the flame—not because hope is not alive (my burning bush revives the dead) but because I've arrived at a place in my life where I revere peace for it is priceless.

Since your mutty mega has wandered before (and before) and will wander— *you guessed it*— again, might I offer a few tips on keeping him home (and yourself alive)?

• **Stay away from the water:** All he could think about at his firm's deep sea fishing shindig was shoving you overboard.

• Stop making him call you Ms. Mary— especially during sex.

• Use your mouth for more than gossip, all that Viagra is gonna leave him blinder than a bucket of bats.

• **Invest in good hardware:** Buy a sturdy, heavily hung dildo and a high quality leather harness to handle your business. He lives for doggie style w/mirrors. Add crystal for special occasions.

P.S. – I recommend the Hollywood Hustler on Church Street. The Purple Onion is another option but *eeks* it's on Nolensville Road, the selection is limited, and their harnesses really flimsy— you'll need one with real cowhide behind it to drill him home right.

A bush is calling so that'll just about do it for now. While I do not expect you to lavish me with praise I pray the least you will do, in time, is thank me for transforming your dust mop into the man you are now so desperate to keep. In parting I wish you love, wealth, health, happiness, and, above all, peace.

With Well Wishes,

Mary T. Messinger

Mary T. Messinger
P.S.
Bcc:
facstaff@list.vanderbilt.edu;
divinity_students@list.vanderbilt.edu;
law_students@list.vanderbilt.edu;
med_students@list.vanderbilt.edu,
mba_students@list.vanderbilt.edu;   metroclerk@nashville.gov;
Howard Gentry, Jr. howard.gentry@nashville.gov David Briley
mayor@metro.nashville.org;
RenatheRovingReporter@comcast.net.
senator_thompson@thompson.senate.gov;
senator_frist@frist.senate.gov;   rep.jenkins@mail.house.gov;
jjduncan@mail.house.gov
http://www.house.gov/wamp/citdirect.html;van.hilleary@mail.
house.gov
bob.clement@mail.house.gov;   bart.gordon@mail.house.gov;
john.tanner@mail.house.gov;   gkerr@tennessean.com
david.briley@nashville.govAdam Dread adam.dread@nashville.gov,
sen.th@legislature.state.th.us; sen.jh@legislature.state.tn.us;

sen.dh@legislature.state.tn.us;   rep.tg@legislature.state.tn.us,
rep.mt@legislature.state.tn.us;   rep.rb@legislature.state.tn.us;
rep.js@legislature.state.tn.us;   rep.el@legislature.state.tn.us;
rep.go@legislature.state.tn.us;   rep.bh@legislature.state.tn.us;
rep.tg@legislature.state.tn.us;lipscomb-
community@list.lipscom.edu,;   belmontdiv-
facstaff@list.belmont.edu;   belmontdiv-
facstaff@list.belmont.edu;

Cc:
The Tennessean, Green Hills News, Nfocus Magazine, Belle Meade News, Brentwood Weekly, The Scene, News and Nashville Today, First Baptist Church North Brentwood The Presbyterian Church (PCUSA), Woodmont Christian Church, Ray of Hope Non-Denominational Church, Metropolitan AME, Belle Meade Catholic Church, Baha'I Temple, Brentwood United Methodist Church

News Station(s) WKIX, WRTW, & WFOX,
Radio Stations 106.7 the River, 107.5, 102.5. WFSK, Woody & Jim, Tom Joyner, and Doug Banks in the morning.

Direct all comments and inquiries to RenatheRovingReporter@comcast.net.

The guest sat in the corner, deep in the shadows where white rings of smoke rose, forming a full halo around darkness; who sat in the corner, far in the shadows waiting to be entertained. A task in itself for darkness had seen it all, done it all, thought it all, had conquered all and just kept coming back for more.

One by one, candles mimic dominoes falling in an intricate design flickering then springing to life like snakes swaying in time to the whisper waiting for eternity to dance into view. When it arrives, it is soft, feathery magic mixes with chimes, a siren song of charmers, enchantresses, and seducing spirits sent to hypnotize the heart whilst stealing the soul.

A second spirit appears in the doorway as vapor, a beautiful dream with the aura of an angel and the raiment of a nun, floating in rhythm with light, blowing as reeds in cool breezes, slithering high above, caressing the heavens with hips painting soft circles in the sand; imparting tales of intent and purpose, of passion and purity of embracing and exposing, of pain that is beautiful and beauty that is painful and peace that is painful in it's very beauty—

Love giving rise to what is ripe and raw, full, empty, and abandoned to a dance of desire and desperation, stirring then daring darkness to rise from the shadows, to draw nearer, to lean in and lend itself to lust and to learning, to peace and to passion to beauty that is pain and pain that is beautiful as the chameleon bends, spreads her legs wide, wraps her arms around her ankles…

… And invites darkness in.

@@@@@

Athena was well aware that Monroe's Nashville and Knoxville funeral homes were being searched pillar to post as part of the ongoing investigation into the murdered and still missing Roderick Fletcher, but she is surprised to find cops at the door of their headquarters in Chocolate City.

"We're here to serve a search warrant on behalf of Davidson County in the vicinity of Nashville in the state of Tennessee covering any remains and records you have on the premises," a DC Cop says with a straight face.

"You guys have got to have better things to do," she comments upon checking the verity of their papers.

"It's overtime."

"My taxation without representation dollars at work."

"Take it up with the Mayor," the head of the three man search team says, sending his colleagues in different directions, "He and his hillbilly counterpart attend bow tie conventions together."

"Don't disturb the dead," Athena cautions then fades into the shadows.

This was the craziest thing since the crematory fiasco that still had corpses in the Bible belt shaking in their boots. *Like people don't already have enough issues with death and the industry that serves its inevitability*, Athena thinks, mixing herself a dirty martini before settling deep into her father's well worn wingchair. Sure there was the occasional necrophilia freak and others who might be found guilty of being a less than respectfully nice in the worse of situations but overall it was an honorable profession that didn't deserve to be dragged through the mud like a whorish hussy sleeping with her hostess' husband.

Death, like life, was a work of art that often went unappreciated. To die was to be no longer useful, to be removed to a place where what was no longer useful could be put away, out of sight of those who still had things to do. Those who work with the dead are the middlemen, attending to remnants with compassion while offering the same to the walking dead who remain behind. When handled with professionalism and empathy, it was more than mere work it was beauty.

This Rod Fletcher situation lies diametrically opposed to everything Monroe's represents. Back in Nashville, heads were rolling to rival the French Revolution. The new Chief of Police, Winters, if memory served her right, was the first one axed followed by the Medical Examiner who's hedging his bets by dropping hints that reek of extortion.

The family was offering a $50,000.00 reward for their son's body. News of the manna from heaven had everyone from off duty cops to Country Music hopefuls lining up to search funeral homes, morgues, science labs, and a grave or two in hopes of stumbling across the sought after remains. Starving artists were crafting etchings, renditions, and caricatures of what the deceased might look like some eleven or so months into the decomposition process embalmed or sans, optimal weather or sans, animal consumption or sans…

"This is really sick," Athena concludes and wonders, for a moment, if she should just put an end to the whole miserable thing.

But she can't.

She promised Ms. Clara who appeared to her clear as day that night and whispered, right next to her ear, "Promise me you'll never tell them where he is."

"I won't," she promised and they retreated from the dance so she could answer the ringing phone.

It was Ms. Eula saying someone killed poor Clara and she knew, immediately, that this was what Camille meant earlier that evening but she missed it.

"What's beyond the green door?" A cop asks, huffing as he makes his way back up three steep flights of stairs.
"The sub-basement."
"We'll need to search it."
"Just more storage, it's where we keep the more exotic overstock...are you sure you want to go all the way down there?"

"I'm sure," he insists.
More than once, until she reluctantly gives him the keys.
"Don't worry, we won't disturb the dead," he says over his shoulder, re-descending into the dark.

@@@@@

The man who was Mayor paces the lobby of the Vanderbilt Loews, loathe to go in. The crème de la crème of Nashville society is just inside, partying like it's 1999 except it's way past then, gas prices are through the roof, and he's coming up on an election year to boot. The public is far more fickle than any female quite possibly because man allowed himself to become polluted by them...*stop thinking like that*...he tells himself and does, choosing instead to focus on his issue laden agenda.

First, the election. He has to get re-elected and that's all there is to it. On average, one had to put in at least five years as Mayor in order to move up to the Governors Mansion. Getting beaten before one moved up to one's rightful place was a sure recipe for political death. Who could recover? The best one could hope for was to wait for a

265

favored son to come of age and restore the family honor and in his case that isn't likely to happen.

Life is so much easier for lucky fuckers like Frist, he thinks, taking a seat on the stairs, just off the elevator. Fortune, family, and friends in high places—how could he lose? But ordinary Joes like him, well, they spent their lives working hard, tossing the dice, and praying all the way to the grave.

It had been hard enough trying to keep up with the preppies, the preferred from long patriarchal lines, but now the meppies[106] are knee deep in the act, mother you know whats every one of them, trying to claim, what they claimed was their rightful place in a political pool already ripe with sharks spawned by the very piranha trying to claim male manifest destiny sanctioned electoral offices...*and now a dead, though thankfully, female, cabinet member, to boot*?

It just wasn't fair!

He's no Frist, for the love of Christ; he's a seventh generation Tennessean from a trailer park just outside McMinnville whose family, in true Volunteer fashion, pulled themselves up by their own bootstraps. By the time he was a teen-ager his father managed to move them to Green Hills. It wasn't Belle Meade but it put them on the map.

Between his grades and his ability to run, relatively fast as well as far, he was afforded the opportunity to attend Montgomery Bell Academy, an important stepping-stone if one hoped to spring forward to the Ivy League. And spring he did but was resolute to return to Tennessee, and Vanderbilt, for Law School.

A trail of court victories, committees, meetings, social activism, kissing babies, old ladies, and asses later he was elected a council member then Mayor. But it isn't as if he's in the clear. The public, while opinionated, are equally uninformed so when issues from TennCare to whether dogs should be allowed to crap in Sylvan Park hit the fan it's his balls hanging in the breeze.

Sure the crap stopped at his door but TennCare is both the domain and the imminent death of the man he hopes to soon replace and as far as dogs are concerned he has his own two-legged variety to deal with.

---

[106] those of the matriarchal line, women

A reliable source close to his breast allowed gold coins to fall from his mouth when he couldn't hold his wad—someone close to his breast intends to challenge him for his seat and he's more than insulted. Not because the upstart is not, in the end, a nice enough Joe but because the traitor is plotting a game of leapfrog when politics is a synonym for Simon Says.

@@@@@

"I could be cruising right now," Athena reminds herself again, mixing another martini.

Right now, at this very moment, she should be by lying on somebody's ship somewhere outside these United States. Nothing if not anal she researched her options endlessly only to arrive, in the end, at the only possible option—water was the only true requirement.

"Whatcha' doin'?" Camille asked, coming into the room.

"Watching a webcam of what comes off and goes on aboard the good ship *Anything Goes.*"

"Sounds like fun."

"Maybe a Yoga cruise," she countered.

"Pussy," Camille coos.

"I like the way you say that."

"So shed your inhibitions and run away with me."

"That's what I'm trying to do," The Cat says, reaching for the Snake.

"Not right now," Camille says in such a way as to suggest the subject was closed, "I have to leave town and the hunters arrive soon after so you need to hang out here and tiptoe through the tulips while mommy takes care of business."

"So what if I say I'm willing to hop aboard *Anything Goes* but the ship sails tonight?"

"I'll say for fifty bucks we can hop an all nude version that sails from Orlando, on the hour, seven days a week."

"That sounds nasty."

"It looks nastier but beauty is in the eye of the beholder, right?" Camille asked, giving her a kiss for good measure, "You must be physically on the property when they open the box," she reminded then disappeared like a mirage.

For a search warrant I forsook a cruise to Belize, she realizes. The phone rings.

"I assume your visitors have arrived?"

"A heads up[107] would have been nice."

"I know how you like surprises. Where are they now?"

"In the lower basement, they want to search the sub-basement."

"So let them."

"You know I can't."

"Aide-toi le ciel t'aidera."[108]

"It's not for myself that I fear."

"C'est la guerre."[109]

Athena pauses, "There must be another way…"

"Aut vincere aut mori."[110]

"Are you sure?" Athena finally asks.

"Ad majorem Dei gloriam,[111] always," the Snake whispers.

And the line goes dead.

@@@@@

Who advised Brutus that now was the time to seize and subdue Caesar? The Mayor wonders, *surely not a friend...more likely a woman or worse yet, his wife leading him by the balls to his own demise yet the pathetic pile of testosterone shuffles, smiles, and kisses my ass at every opportunity all the while plotting tyranny...but no matter, he'll kick the shiftless mutt back into place as soon he gets rid of that fat asshole, Green.*

He knew it was a bad idea to climb into bed with the fat bastard but fate left him few options. He suffered the misfortune of running into the rapidly rising ex-DC detective one night during a feverish foray on the sunny side of the street. After that the asshole slowly tightened the noose until he was hanging by his toenails, a tough trick

---

[107] warning
[108] *Help yourself and heaven will help you*
[109] That's' war; it cannot be helped
[110] Either to conquer or to die
[111] *to the greater glory of God*

unless you're a bat and for Christ's sake unchecked how far would the fat bastard go?

First extorting funds from the fruits then losing the body of a well connected young man who, the fat bastard stated, *on camera and for the record*, was a serial killer...*holy fuck, how much of his doublewide ass does the fat bastard think I can cover without getting my own balls beaten against a downtown sidewalk? Well, I'm done* he decides, taking several deep breaths. *I'll confront the fat bastard face to fat face and find out who's packing the bigger balls.*

The most important decision of his next political move made the Mayor strides confidently into the ballroom filled with Tennessee's finest, the crème de la crème of polite society—*not bad for a boy from McMinnville* he thinks, taking in the view from the top. *Life is all quite beautiful really when everything comes together.*

Perfect case in point: for weeks the monster that fueled the community engaged in its annual review process. It is, in a word, war, hell, or some close facsimile thereof during which priorities are debated, theories debunked, and budgets cut faster and finer than Wisconsin gold because, in the end, it's all about the cheese, the money the behemoth gives birth to then feeds back into the community.

It is this, the commonality of their communal goals, that, annually, brings all the infighting and backstabbing to a peaceful resolution sans last hour squabbling between families and behind closed doors so no one is forced to lose face before outsiders. By nightfall wounds were licked and egos and anatomies stroked to such comfort that doctors who, a day before, swore to kill everyone in accounting now court number crunchers over champagne to the strains of *Madame Butterfly*.

Lawyers happily hunt potential clients while the business contingency broker deals disguised as fundraising for the Owen Foundation. The folks from finance bite their fingernails over the fiscal irresponsibility of it all while the Divinity community drink, strip, and espouse arson.

"The roof, the roof, the roof is on fire, we don't need no water let the mother fucker burn," Dean Debbie screams from her post atop the baby grand piano, "Burn motherfucker burn!"

Dr. Dates spreads his rose embroidered fan wide and cools the poor dear who's close to collapsing from over exertion and every day sex and strain.

You can always count on Commie's kids to be the life of the party the Mayor observes, finally relaxing enough to enjoy some champagne. When it all came together—
theory, science, practice, and positive results; it was a thing of beauty... *with one wrinkle, anything less is immediately labeled unacceptable and hung out to dry like yesterday's underwear except people hardly used clotheslines anymore...but no matter, tonight, I am his honor, the belle of the ball and all this beauty calls for a toast.*

He motions the band who cease at the agreed upon signal of tinkling glass.

"Welcome Board Members, Administrators, Faculty, Doctors, Lawyers, Politicians, Pastors, and pals," he begins with raised glass, "Before dinner is served—"

"Sorry pal," Detective Green interrupts, pushing past the Mayor, "I have some papers I need to serve first."

The outrage among the assembled mass registers audible and unmistakable as the aforementioned fat bastard, with his honor standing speechlessly nearby, rains proof of service notices down like manna from heaven on the crème de la crème of Vanderbilt's medical community while champagne flows, Dean Debbie blows, and the Vampires among them salivate over the feast to be had here.

@@@@@

When Detective Green exits the belly of the beast fifteen minutes later he feels finer than three fifths of the stiffs he left behind in the ballroom.
Suckers.
You were already the walking dead when you were rich, white, and willing to let getting served with a lawsuit before soup spoil your five hundred dollar a head fun. Leave it to folks who didn't have anything to lose sleep over to lose the most sleep over it.

Silly suckers, he amends, getting into his car and driving away. The weight of the world nowhere near their shoulders yet there they were, bitching, wailing and moaning over getting sued by some grief stricken lipstick lesbian with blood on her hands and vengeance in her heart…whining about their reputations like he cared… hell he was only there because it was easy money, a legit street hustle until the heat died down.

That trifling Jewish bitch should have captured the look on the hiz Honor's face he thinks, cracking up. This was the second time he had caught the Mayor with his pants down, the first being when he busted him in the can at the Po' White Trash Café getting his pecker drained by a queen named Peggy with the semen capacity of a camel.

Yep, the Mayor became his bitch that night and while Green gave him his proper due in public they both knew who swung the bigger balls in private.

"You're going to have to straighten up and fly right," His bitch begged like a cunt on the phone this morning, "The public is banging my balls against the sidewalk over this missing body…"

"I'll find you a body, just don't mess around and make it your own," he warned the little pussy who, even Green can admit, has a point.

He knows what his honor doesn't, or maybe does since you can never trust a bitch, but someone was trying to royally fuck the biggest fucker of them all. Who did they think they were f— with? He knows he filled out the f— form 252. He knows he's not losing his motherf— mind. He knows he sat his fat, greasy black ass down and wrote out a long mother— ass account of how it was that Rod whatever his f— name was had come to kill those five other f— who were too motherf—scared or just too f— lazy to point him out to their own demise.

And his shit rocked, even if he had to say so himself. He spun a web to make that spider who fell in love with the pig proud and that's how he knows somebody is really trying to screw with his motherfucking mind…*Is Opie trying to stage a mutiny in Mayberry?* Green wonders and cracks up, *That can't be it…that red haired pup is halfway up his own ass in dirty dealing…more likely my recently booted boss* he decides, cruising by Fisk and coming to rest at the corner facing Wings and Things, a chicken joint that served the best biscuits in town.

It had been a long day spent working his detail, the street, an angle on this whole brouhaha, then the piece de resistance, pissing on the far from poor's parade, and plumb near tuckered out doesn't begin to describe the half of how tired he is. Truth be told he finds himself more and more exhausted these days. Time was he could hang out all night in an un-air-conditioned hole in the wall like the one tucked in that alley and dance 'til dawn.

Nowadays he wound down by nine and was out for the count by ten. *It's just about that time now he realizes*, checking his watch with a yawn. *I'm tired tonight, uncommonly so. Maybe I'm losing a step. Maybe it's time to slow down a little and enjoy some of the fruits of ...* "the Fruits," he says aloud and laughs, "I really do enjoy my own ass I must say," he chuckles, checking his watch again.

He'll wait a few more minutes to see if his new score shows then head across the street to Knock Out for a few hot ones, he decides, looking around for this sorry son of a sea biscuit...he figured him for a smart kid but heaven help him if he wasn't here in one second— then a third and fourth pop ring out in the night like bad news that was nobody's business.

And the curtain falls on Detective Samuel "Sammy" Green whose one man show is brought to an abrupt end by four bullets to the back of the head—the calling card of a professional or a close friend.

@@@@@

Francesca steps out onto the candlelit deck of the cruise ship *Breeze,* which is, at this very moment, headed to Belize, a country on the eastern coastline of Central America, where the rainy season nears its end. At least that's what the prognosticators forecast but the sky proclaims mother nature operates on her own schedule but no matter, tonight her daughter was about the business of life, love, and the pursuit of happiness and feeling really good about the possibilities.

She is dressed to the nines, looking fine, and surrounded on all sides by a rainbow of testosterone; Creoles, Mestizos, Mennonites, Garifunas, Mayans, Anglo-Europeans, Middle Easterners, Asians... Any woman who couldn't hook a honey here was high on ether or packing heat like a Honduran hit squad.

Yet hesitations abounded about this trip. The ink said Belize boasts two seasons: rainy and dry. It rained from June to November, which meant there should be smooth sailing but traveling on the cusp was always a tricky proposition in places where transitions between seasons are surprisingly abrupt —especially when you can't swim but step out of the past and into the path of new possibilities anyway.

Francesca's light fades, just a bit. For some strange reason she can't stop reflecting on the Man who would be senator, governor, mayor, or some garden variety mega, tonight. In the end their demise had little to do with his fundamentally inept appendage— a mighty river washes away the old bringing life anew—no, nada, nay, make not mistake, it crumbled under another unuttered yet unrelenting variable, ego, a synonym for the goofy motherfucker had no idea who he was fucking with.

After sex or some garden variety facsimile thereof they often joked, giggled like little girls in fact, about what an undercover mega the mutt was but she never bothered to mention she was an undercover mega too—from a long way back but no matter, all that drama is over... for now. Her sexual harassment suit against his law firm and the Presbyterian Assembly USA are cats she plans to keep in the bag 'til Christmas, it being the season for giving and all.

"In the beginning his dickie really was less than a quickie," Mary the Marionette giggles, joining her on the deck.

"But that's what made it bearable," little Mary Sunshine chimes in, "At least he was never all hard and long winded like daddy."

"And he served a need," Mary adds, quietly, "Who can say what ways the Lord uses to provide?"

"And they *were* quickies...in the beginning at least," Mary the Marionette offers, nervously.

"Quickies," Francesca repeats and laughs despite herself, "As always you, Ms. Papins, are the generous one. No, nada, nay, make no mistake a quickie implies sex, abandon, hell some semblance of fun but when a repeatedly resuscitated dick dies while being worshiped at the alter of everything and nothing what could be worse?"

273

"Acting as canned stand in?" Mary suggests, popping the lid off the same.

They share a laugh and the can, passing it ritualistically around the circle of sisters before Francesca bids them farewell and sends them on their way.

There is, after all, life, love, and the pursuit of happiness to be found this night…she can feel it in her bones. A twinkle of a tingle lurks there, quiet and distinct and she plans to give birth to it and begins now, breathing with arms and heart open wide…it's love, baby; the love she lost but in another form and something tells her life is about to get interesting.

@@@@@

"You are the greatest," the Man who will someday be senator, governor, or at a minimum, mayor, says aloud, strolling around the honeymoon suite of the *Breeze* where he and his bride dress for a dinner engagement at the Captain's table.

Mary, who's been stripped of her salutation, watches with just concealed disgust as he prances in front of the mirror, proud as a prize gamecock, *He's a dog*, she thinks, returning his smile in the mirror. The tables have turned and her lapdog no, nada, nay, her mutt, is now treating her like his bitch.

"You fucking bastard," she screams,[112] blowing him a kiss, *Sex and smiles and smiles and sex on demand all the while knowing if I so much as frown or close my legs he'll be out sniffing around someone's ass or his own if he could reach it*…the thought elicits a wide smile.

Seeing it he walks over and slaps her on the ass, "Don't worry, later" he whispers, then licks her ear and heads to the bathroom.

She detests this shit, endlessly rutting around and around like pigs in slop, their dry bellies clapping together like hands at a revival…his heavy, labored breathing…him forever insisting she try to breathe hard too…the way he makes her watch, not only in mirrors but also everything she says or does or there was hell to pay—cold shoulders, silence, late nights at the office…*in all likelihood slipping off to be*

---

[112] *okay* thinks

274

with someone else or thinking about slipping off, or plotting to divorce her again or push her overboard...

"Don't think like that!" She snaps, breathing heavy and labored.

They had, after all planned this trip together not only for the sake of appearances but also to celebrate the third renewal of their wedding vows. "We can't pretend not to be the couple in the letter and avoid cruises like the plague when I'm planning a run for political office," her husband insisted, repeatedly, when she hesitated.

Trapped in the states since he tried to walk away from her like a messy, half eaten dessert she longed to escape to anonymity where no one ever heard of e-mail let alone one entitled a message from the mountain but now...what had she let him talk her into? *Oh my God,* she thinks, head and heart pounding as one, and *once is never enough when you want to push someone overboard,* she can't breathe, white walls race to meet her *wait... there's a mega of a mutt strolling by...* she reaches out to steady herself...

"Don't worry, later," he whispers, slapping her on the ass and exiting the cabin.

Stepping into the heavenly night air, he inhales deeply. *Affirmation,* he observes, *is a wonderful thing.* It sure felt good to be able to look yourself in the mirror like the man you were and say, "You're a mutt but I love you anyway." It was freedom that's what it was, freedom, and it feels beautiful just as Mary said it would. "Selah," he sighs and heads on his way.

Sure it's been hard— pledging to do the "right" thing and give his marriage to Mary another good 'ole college try. After all Ms. Mary, oops, Mary had been a part of his life for more years than he cared to remember, it shouldn't be easy for him to just turn tail and run for the hills like his life depended on it.

Was he not a man?

Men know there are times and situations where prudence wins out over principles and anyone who practices law knows the world is not black or white but instead gray which means you keep as many variables[113] in play as possible. Besides he loves himself enough to be

---

[113] See loop holes

able to admit it now—he allowed the lawyer in him to take over along with the good son and the Boy Scout and the Lay Minister and the Mouse who just wanted to be loved and win everyone's approval.

He had wanted to be the good guy.

Now was that so bad? He thinks pausing to really appreciate the sweet sea breeze, *certainly not; who didn't want, deep in their heart to be the good guy? No one, after all, crawls out of the crib wanting to be a criminal or a crack head... some big balled bastards are just born wealthier, luckier or better endowed than your garden variety Peter, Paul, or Mary.*

@@@@@

On the west side of the ship Mary hasn't the foggiest idea why she's here. The idea of cruising to Belize never crossed within a million miles of her mind yet, when it happened by, she decided to go with the flow. The beauty of the name, *Belize*, the way it just rolls off your tongue produced clear skies, tiny umbrellas in large glasses, and sunglasses to ward off the glare of a commercialized Garden of Eden.

Geography has, however, never been her strong suit so when a Brazilian informs her, in a heavenly accent, that paradise rests on the eastern coastline of Central America where it borders Mexico and Guatemala and serves as a neighbor to Honduras she can only whisper, "Be still my heart because I can't swim and the shore is long gone."

Her nightmare's saving grace resides on the Eastern, as in Caribbean, portion of the island which, if Mary recalls correctly, no longer practices cannibalism so unless vampires hover at high noon her cocoa butter butt disembarks this banana boat at the first hint of east. A large wave heads their way, reaching then rocking the ship before rolling beneath and barreling down in search of prey.

Grief is a tidal wave that overtakes you, smashes down upon you with an unimaginable force, sweeps you into its darkness where you tumble and crash against indefinable surfaces, only to be thrown out on an unknown beach...bruised... reshaped, and unwittingly better for the wear...Grief will make a new person out of you, if it doesn't kill you in the making.

So who is she? She stands not sure yet a survivor of an eternity of seasons spent absolutely convinced she would never live through this yet here she wavers—*so who am I?* This woman who gorges on running, who dumped her favorite show, ER, because too many patients survived, who slashed Law and Order—get real, crime and punishment? Who was still picking up that paycheck?

Who is this woman who slept, or some facsimile thereof, with her hostess' husband, the only corpse she knew who had been walking around dead longer than she, *this unfaithful lover who accepted a piss poor facsimile of the love I lost after it dumped me for that which loved her more?* A knock on her door breaks the reverie.

Mary cracks it then swings it wide. A bouquet of black roses tied with a blood red ribbon rests at her feet with the wind as its only deliverer. It is a welcome sign and she thanks the Providence before opening the attached card which reads: *amicus us que ad aras.*[114] She glances up. Here with land and lights a thing of the past, pure night steps to center stage to share its beauty with, it seems, only her.

This, the roses, the note, the sky show, is love—her constant companion, just in a different form, "Selah," she says aloud and breathes deeply, *Life is*—she pauses, loathe even to think it.

"There is no turning back now." Barnabus whispers, just above her ear.

"Life is beautiful again," she whispers and closes her eyes, fully expecting Armageddon to descend.

@@@@@

Camille loved Belize. It was a land ripe with mystery and magic, the birth and resting place of the Mayans, an ancient civilization renowned for its mask making, resourcefulness, and occasional cannibalism. It is not the destination but the accommodations that could bear improving.

On her own time she'd far prefer *Anything Goes* whose passengers were contractually required to live up to their ship's name but the *Breeze?*

---

[114] a friend as far as the alters

Please.

The hearts on this dredge couldn't be any heavier if they were loaded with trash and headed out of New York Harbor. *Anything Goes* was boldly, honestly, gray and gray, in the end, usually rules the day but "Cha•cun 'a son gout"[115] she muses, settling in to enjoy the show.

She lived for this, watching from behind the scenes, a silent witness to the comings and goings of players trying to flee a life lived behind masks made by themselves in concert with ancestors of old and societies of new, marionettes all, trying to discern not only what lay beyond the door but also what lay in wait before and behind them when all the sillies would find was a mirror for she was them reflected for all the gathered to see.

This really is the perfect place for this drama to play itself out, she decides, breathing in the tension that was always a welcome, though oft uninvited, undercurrent in these situations. Belize was a most unusual place. Bordered on the north by Mexico, on the west and south by Guatemala, and on the east by the Caribbean Sea, it consists of over 200 islands, most located inside a Reef.

A melting pot it boasts one of the most ethnically diverse populations known to man so neither nepotism nor sure bets will prevail here. This was the secret of Belize and the reason people were drawn here without so much as a clue to why they should find themselves visiting such a place…a maximis ad minima.[116]

---

[115]everyone to his own tastes

[116]from the greatest to the least

Whose Ring is it Anyway?

The Man who now loved himself and his wife immersed themselves in a regimen of intensive marital counseling to make Bill and Hillary proud: workshops on relearning to love each other's bodies in Stinky Creek Tennessee, sensual massage led by his wife's spiritual advisor and a hands-on seminar on how to re-sensitize St. Peter, taught by the National Eunuch Society of Middle Tennessee.

Mary custom ordered new matching wedding bands, their third set, after he agreed to a re-commitment ceremony, their third. They agreed to simply start over. After she promised to worship the ground he walked on. After she promised to do everything but wipe his ass with her tongue. After she promised to open her legs wide and often. After she promised not to do the same with her mouth.

His bride would, upon default, never mention his indiscretions or expect him to make apologies in full or part for anything he engaged in before, during, or after her foray to South Africa. He would, in return, agree to wear yet another symbol of servitude on a ring finger fast taking on the appearance of a totem pole.

Decision made he committed wholeheartedly to salvaging their marriage and to give Ms. Mary her due, so did she. The new bride tried and tried and tried some more, so much in fact that, truth be told she tried a bit too much awakening him to an e-fucking piphany that lay, literally, at his feet like dirty underwear—he was married to a mutt.

Sure she packed lots of bark, some fierce growls, and a bite that still gave him nightmares. True he spent a quarter century scared to death of her. Truer the widow Mary assured him, long ago, while she was yet woozy with wine, that Ms. Mary would not only never leave him but also suck him dry or die trying. And suck she had, albeit ineffectively, while pulling out every stop from Nashville to Nazarenes to keep their holy bonds of matrimony bound.

And him?
He can admit to feeling not only flattered but also shocked as a blonde with her finger in a light socket. You could've nailed St. Peter to a cross and told him it was Christmas when his haughty heap of hell wrapped her beefy arms around his ankles and sobbed sweet nothings while he offered up flagrant confessions of infidelity.

279

But let us not forget his career. One point on which his parents, pastors, and miscellaneous parties agreed was that a messy divorce could bring a screeching halt to his political aspirations. On the other hand his wife whose favorite mantra was once : *I'd sooner leave you than hand out a single flyer with your name on it* is now whistling Dixie all the way to Kinko's and investing in a chicken suit.

On the flip side sits a fat chance, at best, that he can abandon the wife of his youth for a younger woman and win office. *Just give Ms. Mary one more chance* his conscience and everyone else to include his parked in the pasture parents counseled, "Maybe it'll all work out." He didn't buy it for a minute but here they are, three months into their new life together and Mary remains sweet as honey and docile as a lamb.

Being top dog feels mighty fine after decades spent sniffing around her anal opening like a homeless mutt looking for love. These days, behind fabricated smiles and impersonal whispers he knows and she knows and he knows she knows there's a new sheriff in town and he's it...*yep, I have the old nag exactly where I want her: gagged, bent over, and from the back, doggie style.*

She complies, reluctantly, but with a smile, albeit a fabricated one, obviously viewing the act as something far too common, as in peasants, but she accommodates him, grudgingly... just this once—a welcome change and more than good enough for him.

@@@@@

Jackson was Mary's heart and soul and, all at once, everything people expected a Chaplain to be...or not. Well educated, empathetic, affirming wisdom packing an easy smile that immediately put anyone who happened into its midst at ease...unless you were someone who could find fault with the ocean...a razor sharp wit and bristling insight slashing towards hypocrisy...unless you were already a wounded branch in fear of breaking...generous salt peppered hair blended into a gray quite becoming; eyes lighting up like fireflies or blazing with the wrath of hell...unless your preferred destination was a one way trip to heaven...

"...Hath no fury like a woman scorned or born with a silver spoon in her mouth," Jackson enjoyed sharing, "But a beauty born to bear the burden of a beast will join your head to the earth with a tent spike despite the fact that she's a bona fide Christian."

280

The Love of her Life could grill up a steak and veggies like nobody's business, guzzle beer with the best, and tell a ell of a war story while all the while imparting advice, humor, or a new age art deco take on the theological impact of whatever the flavor of the month recommended. Jackson believed you could say anything to anyone as long as you said it with a smile, a staple to be kept not only in stock but also in mind since humor sometimes travels without wisdom 'oft falling off course....a cuddly, bubbly wealth of things worldly, wise, witty, and warm wrapped in a package that made life everything Mary needed it to be.

It was the afro that usually took a patient or blue blood or two aback as did the jeans and sneakers. She was as chocolate as she was sure of herself and she was pretty damn sure except when it came to being a Chaplain.

"Who pray tell did you think was going to need to see the chaplain?" I asked when she came home shaking like marijuana leaves under a ceiling fan after her first shift.

"I don't know, people who want confession or communion or just don't wanna be lonely?"

"Uh huh," I say, handing her a beer.

"I had only been there five minutes when they told me Mr. Johnson was dying and needed to see the chaplain right away," she explains, weary body collapsing into an overstuffed chair, "I walked in and there he was," she pauses to guzzle, "A dirty, old bag of naked bones propped on a bedpan blowing kisses at me."

My giggles flow as oil despite the gravity of the situation, "Well, did you inform the old pervert that you were the new chaplain?"

She takes a more relaxed swig before leisurely releasing a hearty burp, "I did. He told me to come closer so he could see how well I filled out my holy jeans."

I die while she rolls her eyes high above the ceiling, "Then he croaked right there and overflowed the bedpan," she shared, draining the bottle and reaching for another.

Half the time you didn't know whether to believe half of what she said...unless she knew you needed to. Over the years she mostly taught me to simply go on faith, words thrown back at my mouth well fed, hope, and the prayer that, in the end, there is always a plan, we just didn't know it yet...

"As I prayed with his better half and that bedpan was dumped for the last time," she confesses, eyes twinkling, "I couldn't help but hope there's a special place in God's kingdom for a shitty bag of bones with a fetish for holy jeans."

"I hope so," I said, and we joined hands and prayed that Providence would make it so.

Then, just like that, on an otherwise garden variety Wednesday, the Heavens parted and turned against her in the most vicious of manners, without warning or mercy, and Mary couldn't fathom how to wrestle such a beast. So she first tried to flow with pain; to surrender to it like labor engulfing a little a girl transformed too young from peach to pit.

Next, each morn she died anew until she was a corpse most of the time, coming up every so often for air when forced to surface but giving up the ghost religiously, with a vengeance just as the vampires so that, on an otherwise ordinary day, she awoke just another member of the family, destined to take her rightful place among them.

It liberated her, allowing her, a full year later to admit aloud what she knew down to her heart and soul the minute Death came to call on everything she had in all the world—that God was punishing her for the oldest of sins, for loving the Servant more than the Master. But she knows better now, knows that she had loved just as she was meant to—with complete abandon and an overflowing heart, like there was no tomorrow, like her life depended on it, which it had...she just didn't know it then.

@@@@@

"Have you ever tried hanging on to flab for dear life?" The groom sporting a totem pole asks Joe, the bartender, tossing back his third scotch, "Try doggie style with a frigid wife rearing to chew through her belly's twin to get away from the artificially rejuvenated hell on wheels husband of her youth."

"No way," Joe responds, pouring him another.
"Now try staying erect while that fountain of flab overflows,

wedging between your fingers and getting stuck there like play dough
…it ain't easy."

"Can't be," Joe agrees, "Especially not after you've floated down a
foamy white river under a tent where laughter spills out like wine and
lovers languish in waves that pound against each other like confused
thunder."

"You know Francesca?"
"Nope, not like that," Joe assures, pulling his tip back from the
brink of disaster.

"After lightening, sex with the new and improved Ms. Mary is like
an old shoe, dependable and broken in but it'll never set your foot on
fire except there's fungus."

"Hey, you made a funny," Joe says with a chuckle, eager to escape
this newlywed barrel of bliss.

"Already," the Delusional Dude continues, "I have, shall we way,
sampled side dishes to keep me afloat but even that torments me with
real time consciousness of everything I'm missing shackled to my
bride."

"Sometimes," his new best friend, Joe, counsels, "It's best to face
the facts: when you've been to the river and, in the words of Al Green,
washed down—

"And up and over and through and through," The Man who will be
senator, governor, or, at a minimum, mayor interrupts, "Really, really
well…well let's just say bottled water won't do so I'm sure as hell not
settling for tap," he resolves, settling his tab and throwing in a fifty for
good measure.

Divorce, he realized, waiting at the alter, is inevitable *for while
great beauty manifests anew each day in my new found ability to love
myself in spite of, or perhaps even because, I'm a mutt doesn't mean I
have to wake up next to one.* This e-fucking piphany of a beast arrived
as if on the heels of the hounds of hell on holiday, resuscitating his
hope in happy endings even as he said, "I do" thus inspiring him to
follow his heart and Mary Papins to Belize.

That said though he longs to deposit his needy half breed
bloodhound at the nearest kennel, prudence must prevail. He can't just

dump the trice wedded wife of his youth cold— appearances and political strategy demand retribution. No, nada, nay, he must maintain their present regimen of her loving him desperately and him tolerating her in return while he engineers an appropriate damage control package… worse case scenario: six months to kick Lassie to the curb and six to usher the widow Mary down the aisle in an appropriate shade of off white, leaving time to spare before the primary.

Meanwhile his soul cries out, yearning for freedom in the form of a perfect reunion with Francesca. He knows and she knows and he knows that she knows he should have sooner fallen on his own sword than glance back towards Sodom and Gomorrah but sharp things scared him almost as much as change. *They'll be hell to pay…*

At first, he adds, a smile of remembrance creeping across his thin lips, *but, I know her softer side better than most and behind that strong mask lurks a little girl, longing for a dad*—"The ring!" he squeals, suddenly convinced he dislodged it while banging the fountain of flab from behind but no…*thank heavens, it's right here in my hip pocket.*

@@@@@

Little Mary Sunshine, who sprang from the womb ready to love, now realizes that even with all the love she gave she still fell short on a multitude of fronts but such truth matters not anymore. The only fact and factor that remains is that she fell, hard and deep only to have her foundation, and with it her hope, crumble under a tidal wave that washed her world away.

But she thinks she can make out, just in the distance, a shore line not so far away.

A great divide often separates fact from fiction but you don't travel from A to B without seeing a few things through to their natural end even if it kills you in the process. She has been running for, it seems eternity, from vampires and vengeful dolls and dolly's daughters and sons of Adam, Eve, Sophia or whoever originally ate the apple thus dooming us all but still…

But she would kill to have been a fly on the ballroom wall when a sea of legal paper rained down like manna from heaven on the horde of suckers clothed in respectability, celebrating the success of sickness and death. *Having the echelon of the medical community humiliated by an up and coming Asshole from the hood was icing on a cake to make the Commodore proud. They don't call us commie's kids for nothing.*

She remains one and they, a legion, but she travels with love and has learned that drowning anger is a synonym for smothering love, a two-edged sword slicing the very core of existence and she lies utterly drained. *It is not the Lord but losing what one loves most that separates bone, marrow, soul, spirit...it was and is the eternal...*Laughter arrives as tinkling glass, glistening just beyond the green door, "Come, join us," Mary hears, over and again in the wind, inviting as a siren's song.

"What a beautiful idea," she whispers, "Let's rise from our coffin and join them."

@@@@@

The three carats will go far in Francesca's book. He remembered well her tearful tale of intrigue, lust, and a not so little engagement ring the Chaplain gave her.

"She gave it to me on Christmas Eve, wrapped in the prettiest little box I had ever seen..."

Just wait 'til she gets a look this baby, he anticipates, arriving on the South side of the ship. *There she is.* He sighs, says, "Selah," and suddenly feels quite nervous...maybe he's making a mistake.

Perhaps he shouldn't run over, drop to one knee, gaze into her eyes and confess "I wanna be your mutter, I wanna be the only mut-ter that you come run-ning to, I wanna be your mut-ter, I wanna be the only mutt you come for[117]... or some facsimile thereof." Perhaps he should give the ring to Mary Papins and offer Francesca a house in Hound's run...*there's one for sale next door to Dean Debbie...*

...Or he could buy a second ring ...*but I hate shopping...*Mary is an old fashioned girl, Francesca, a materialist...real estate would rule for a girl who had been homeless but would the symbolism of a ring cause the former Little Mary Sunshine to open like a rose blooming amidst the first sunlight of Easter morn?

---

[117] See "I Wanna be your Lover"/Book of Prince

Or…dare I throw all societal inhibition to the wind and declare allegiance to Camille, the big balled babe under investigation for everything from facilitation of terrorist activity to misdemeanor dick fraud?

Which dessert best crowns a decadent course when the best-case scenario has his bride plunging irretrievably overboard and the worst has him wading to shore with her body in tow when he can't even swim?

Anything in the middle, he decides, *will be a win.*

@@@@@

Rena the Roving Reporter abides aboard the *Breeze* neither creating nor chasing a story. The trail on everything from the elves to the mutt to the missing and murdered Rod Fletcher to the case of Ms. Clara and why couldn't Ms. Eula get a phone call are all cold as cases of beer on ice in a morgue. No, nada, nay, make not mistake, she whores behind not a byline aboard this boat but instead, seeks to wed, the tall, dark, slightly beastly man of her dreams.

Having plotted a surefire elopement plan she was none too pleased when the pussycat pounced out of the sack, compliments, she suspects, of her hunk of heaven, who some might believe a bit on the beastly side. His surreptitious hat trick was quite the feat given he's been super-glued to her side since St. Pete plugged in two weeks ago. The bride to be suspects he crept while she was slept; quite the feat when there's something tickling, literally, your funny bone without ceasing…

Anyway she's hiding out on the deck in a shaded corner far from the maddening crowd with her very own hunk of heaven a la above garden variety non-minority class female in a not so little blue dress wishing, hoping, and praying for the ship to sail already. Her very own slice of paradise pulls her nearer, nibbling her funny bone 'til laughter spills out like water set free from a hydrant that evaporates to dust when a yellow banana boat crowned with a tacky, make-shift menorah screeches to a stop in the parking lot.

"Mom," she said, when the Captain defied naval protocol and subverted public decency by allowing passengers to board a ship scheduled to depart port *five minutes ago.*

286

So here they are, all forty-five of them, three days into a journey to Belize and no one has uttered a single unkind syllable about her tall, dark, slightly beastly but otherwise nice Jewish boy. No one in fact dares even glance at him funny lest the Merchant of Venice slice them as venison so close to the Promised Land.

Perched on the window seat in her parent's cabin, Rena watches as Mommy Dearest morphs into Joan Crawford looking to score; proof positive daddy somehow managed to conjure up a dinner invitation at the Captain's table.

"Sure, I've invited myself to a Captain's table or two and challenged them to be less than a gentleman," Joan confides, powdering her nose, "After all didn't I purchase a ticket too?"
"I agree mom."
"Am I not a woman, a lady even?"
"You are mom."
"But to receive an official invitation from the captain, signed and all..."
"Oh mommy, you're tearing up!"
It's a beauty of a mother-daughter moment and the closest Rena has felt to the old hag in a really long time.

She glances at her now, seated next to the Captain, the belle of the ball basking in not only the envy of every woman in the room over fifty but also the love that has finally come to call on her prodigal daughter *and* he's Jewish!

"I can't find my husband," All of a sudden, out of the blue, in the middle of nowhere anyone wants to be, a woman who the Belle is willing to bet lacks a personal dinner invitation, cries, wringing her hands and pushing past Rena, "I've been calling his cell phone for the last hour and I can't get an answer."

"Well, hello and who are you?" Joan asks the Captain who shares her sense of timing.

"Did you hear me?" the Interloper screams, "One hour, ringing nonstop but no answer!"

"Lady, do you know the last time my husband answered me?" Joan inquires, happy to play hostess in this awkward situation, "When was it papa?"

Rena's father neither answers nor looks up.
"See?"

The Captain leans forward slightly and takes another bite of peach custard.

"You don't understand," the Pain in the Ass insists, fighting to be heard above the orchestra.

The well compensated band plays on.

Frantic eyes light on a bullhorn, propped in the corner pretty close to the maddening crowd, "My name is Ms. Mary," she bellows, "And someday my husband is going to be senator, governor, or at a minimum, mayor and he's missing." The room goes silent as the climax to an E.F. Hutton commercial.

The Captain savors his last bite of custard, thanks Joan for a lovely evening, and gives the signal. Bells ring then toll 'til silence reigns once more. The Captain reaches for his cane, rises on shaky legs and salutes.

"Be still my heart," the belle of the ball sighs.

"Drop anchor, notify the Coast Guard, and strip search this love boat like it stole something," Ms. Mary commands, wielding the bullhorn, back in the saddle again.

Epilogue

The Cooperative, as they were now called, was making money hand over fist, which was really tripping them out considering how much of it they were pumping into those damn church programs. Big Dog and Methuselah suspect Athena and the Fisherman scammed them and that the Snake put them up to it.

All Hook knew for sure was that his shit[118] went pure de soft when the lawyer highlighted, in red, the clause in the contract obligating them to tithe not only ten percent of their profits but also ten percent of the profits they collected over and above what they generated this time last year. The famed hook finished shrinking and plain shriveled up when the Snake's sidekick double highlighted his John Hancock on the dotted line.

It took Methuselah ten minutes to calm him down. As soon as he could breathe again the Messenger with the death wish triple highlighted even smaller print:

    With tithing ten percent being defined as not only money
    but also each signer's time, talents, and miscellaneous
    intangibles.

Never trust a lawyer who's also an undertaker, they hang around with dead people, saying prayers over the living and looking for someone to work the night shift.

"Damn," Hook says, stopping short, "Did I get someone to cover that shift?"

Between diversifying his illegal and more illegal business interests and teaching pups how to restore and detail cars, he was working harder than a whore at Christmas which explains why he hasn't had sex in longer than he can remember or at least two weeks, he can't remember.

Not that he doesn't think about sex, hell, he's no eunuch; when he sees a fine piece of real estate Hookie taps him on the leg and begs to come out just long enough to bang that drum slowly or like his life depends on it which it will if he can't get that worrisome bitch to

---

[118] See genitals

289

understand that tithing in the form of teaching these little hood rats how to repair, detail, and restore cars is really tapping into his tap tap tap time.

"You're going to have to learn to multi-task," The worrisome Bitch answers without preamble.

"So you're suggesting I fuck and give kids a lecture on anti-freeze at the same time?"
"Only if you can do it from the back seat but why don't you take a few days, relax, and think about it?"

Which sounds like a plan.

@@@@@

The Coast Guard arrived in short order and divers began searching the suddenly murky waters off the West Coast of Belize. All night, in shifts, the splash of fresh teams can be heard as they dive in doubles like dolphins, searching for the man who would be Senator, Governor, or at a minimum, well, you know.

At dawn divers recover a cell phone and wallet but the body is nowhere to be found. The Coast Guard orders the ship anchored and baby sits it to ensure nothing is disturbed until the proper authorities arrive and the FBI does, right before dinnertime. Agent A and B see themselves to the dining room where they dine at the Captain's table with the bridal party while the bullhorn keeps things moving at the buffet line.

After enjoying cognac and Cubans[119] they retire to the Captain's quarters to review the evidence. The waterlogged cell phone yields no immediate clues so the agents next turn to the wet wallet from which they extract several photos, business and credit cards bearing the name and face of the man who would be, you know, and three one hundred dollar bills with the same message, *you're dead!*, scrawled across Franklin's face in indelible ink.

The bullhorn steps to center stage, "This ship is now a crime scene, everyone and thing on it will remain anchored as an African rear in a puritan church pew…"

---

[119] cigars

290

@@@@@

Big Dog and Methuselah agree that it is, indeed, time for a little f&f[120] and after some discussion they decide to attend a bachelor party in Harlem for a homeboy who has booked a honey of a stripper who performs under the name Beast Master. Their host has been acting as ringmaster all night, going on and on about how he has in store an untamed beauty who slices ice cubes in mid-air with whips she wears as tittie tassels.

And when the honey arrives she does not disappoint. Six foot six in stilettos, the Amazon wears her black leather thong like tooth floss and boasts a trunk that spreads its branches wide to reveal ample breasts from which peek perfect succulent peach shaped nipples from which hang thin, multi-colored, tasseled whips which she uses to pop Big Dog's ass as soon as he offers it to her.

The trifling niggah knows he likes it, Hook thinks, chuckling when the Dog tries to put on a horse and pony show for his ego.

Penny, for he had dropped a dime and gotten the rag on her, was feeling her oats round about now; whacking away at the hiney of their host who was down on all fours, his once pale but now candy apple red ass high in the air; blushing with shame while all the while loving like there's no tomorrow the way those tassels are tearing his ass up.

"What's my name?" the Beauty demands, hitting her rhythm now.
"Beast Master!" the punk screams, for all Harlem to hear.
Then comes.
"Damn," Big Dog says, taking a step back.
"I am the Beast Master," she bellows, kicking the puddle at her feet out of her way to clear space so she can swing her tassels 'til they rotate like a Ferris wheel.

Hookie taps him on thigh.
"Hey Penny," Hook calls from across the playground.
The tassels stop swinging and she's turned before she knows it.
"Crack head Benny says they named you that cause that's how much your momma charged back in the day."

Angry daggers stop just short of his heart.

---

[120] Fun and frolic

The puddle scurries out of his come and across the room before she can reach him.

Hook holds up two Grovers and three Bens "Are you the Beast Master of twenty three positions?"

Penny doesn't answer.
She rips off her floss, flings it in his face and, ponytail and tassels swinging, heads for the bedroom.

Hook and Hookie follow, waving to their fans.
The bachelor party trails, betting all the way.

He'd show Penny, she might be the *beast master* but he was the master of the seven surrender positions: wall grip, ankle grab, split, pied piper; puss in boots and two secret ones he dared not even whisper, *If you can handle more than five administered by a hook, ten inches before it's hard, I'll let you beat my big balls to hell and back,* he swears and laughs at the thought.

"Let the old man handle the pot," Penny directs when they reach the mouth of the master destined to be her undoing.

"Oh so you're a businesswoman, now," Hook taunts, allowing the beast to spring from his pants unassisted.

Those who have heard of the hooked wonder but never had occasion to share a urinal with that which was whispered of, stare in awe before looking quickly away—lest anyone think they're interested in anything other than a National Geographic sort of way.
They steal peeks, reassess bets then shell out, albeit grudgingly, the additional door fee Penny demands before placing their final bets.

Hook and his right hand man stand next to the bed blowing kisses at the *Penny who dreams of being a Beast Master when she's just an ex basketball player with really muscular titties and,* he suspects, *one peach of a pussy un-pierced by man or beast.*

"Hook, that thing is like Medusa except with one head," Methuselah observes, closing the bets.

"Okay Hookie, show the *Beast Master* where to go."

292

Before Hookie can wave west, Penny assumes her position at the wall, where she grips it hard before spreading her legs wide.

"Oh so you ready for a snaking, huh Penny?" Hook chides, pulling out a custom made, double extra large, curved condom, "You probably got some cobwebs in some of those corners but don't be shy, spread that peach wider," he orders, diving deep into her pit only to fall flat outta' the hole.

@@@@@

The Senator from Tennessee always enjoyed a special affinity with his half breed mutt, Brutus, who was indeed the man's best friend. It was beloved Brutus who wagged when he walked, slipped, or dragged himself home in the dead of night after long days spent kicking or kissing the ass of anyone above or below him on the political food chain. He followed the law of Luke's steward[121] to the letter and knows just as king David did that it is far wiser to fall on the sword of God rather than man.

It was Brutus who guarded him so he could slumber, not an easy endeavor for a son of a bitch who bore a world of secrets on his back and didn't plan to get stabbed in it. It was Brutus whose loyal comfort constantly reminded him that the world was not such a cold, desolate place. Truth be told it was the very thought of Brutus that kept him going through torturous committee meetings, inane political actions groups, and garden variety assholes all with their mouths open and their hands out like Christians dishing out grub in crappy soup lines leading straight to hell he needed sleep but there was none to be found this night...

"*Brutus loves me yes I know, for the Bible tells me so,*" he sings in little more than a whisper to his dearly departed comrade.

For murder and its companion, fury, are his bed partners tonight for it was Brutus who consoled and soothed him when all he wanted out of life was to kill, with his own bare, brass-knuckled hands, any motherfucker who fucked up by treating him as less than a trusted friend. It was Brutus who licked first his hands, then his hamstrings and then to his heart's delight until his master curled up, a content

---

[121] St. Luke 16:1-9

fetus in the womb riding waves of joy that always ended in sixty-nine, the number created by the universe for him and his lover alone.

Now his beloved Brutus lays beside him still, silent, and stiff of tongue, poisoned—the calling card of a professional or a close friend. The lips that had so often touched his own are soft no more, further confirmation they could no longer venture low to quench a carnal lust only a well trained canine who was a slave to its nature could satisfy leaving his tortured lover to oft masturbate in anticipation of what lay ahead, *oh to be licked, licked, licked until you can be licked no more of what greater pleasure can the heavens boast*?

Who, besides the chameleon, knew that to kill Brutus would be to slay Caesar himself for his heart feels in fear of failing and his soul cries out for the ghost to carry it away for woe is he who has done this most vile, evil of deeds for indeed they shall soon suffer the wrath of one who possesses neither a conscience nor a comforter.

@@@@@

Hitler, Adolph hail heir, hangs out in the corner of his usual spot in Shem, painting and watching the melee involving MacArthur from the corner of his eye. *Poor guy*, he muses, never missing a stroke, *the Big Mac still didn't get he wasn't the top burger around here*. The delusional American had gone so far as to assemble an army and draw up plans to overthrow St. Peter who encouraged him by providing additional troops on a daily basis.

And him? He just paints—watercolors mostly, consciously seeking flowers and flowing landscapes but endlessly finding storms atop a tossing sea emerging from the canvass yet again...Nebuchadnezzar happens by, "Nice," he says and continues on his way with J. Edgar Hoover or Jed as they call him here, on his heels hounding him to divulge any information he has on Martin Luther King Jr.

The gang is all here: Abraham, Adam, Isaiah...you name the Patriarch, Prophet, or Pope and they are present and accounted for right along with all the other high brow and just plain ordinary Joes.[122] You didn't get to be omnipotent and you didn't get any news from the

---

[122] Christ's Descent into Hell, The Book of Nicodemus, The Other Bible, Ancient Alternative Scriptures

front, except what came from new arrivals and most of them are liars, *wait that didn't sound affirming* he realizes and adjusts his thinking— *newcomers are endowed with an uncanny talent for embellishing events especially those involving themselves, inevitably leading to pathological fibbing brought on by acute ego-tripping.*

You didn't get to sleep but how could you when you didn't know what the hell was going on up there? Everyone longs for news from home, the front, the range, the hood, the farm; anywhere and everywhere some form of resistance was being acted out. Between broadcasts the present company engages in an honored tradition, hanging out, to each his own definition of hanging, and generally just try to get along seeing as how eternity is ever present.

It isn't that bad. Some say because there's neither hide nor hair of a woman around unless you count Camille but who knew *what* she was let alone where she was going to be on any given day. The chameleon came and went as it pleased, usually staying only long enough to broker a few deals, shed, then slither *oops* float off to see dear old Dad.

In the end, Hitler found hell wasn't so much horrid as simply a place where you got to hang out with people with compatible proclivities—kind of like high school but with a family secret as open as the Book of Life:

    Tell the truth, the whole truth, and nothing but the truth.

Follow the rule that doubled as the family secret and you were safe here. Violate it and you learned the hard way that the shortest road to Shem ran through a lie. Of course some learn faster than others, which is what the melee in the corner between Big Mac and some private named Green is all about.

But no matter, he decides, as yet another gray wave rises as thunder from the canvas, *rumor has it a contingency of 64 World Trade Organization Delegates are due any minute...*Bells begin to not ring but toll signaling the gates of Shem swinging wide. The welcoming party, which it is his turn to lead, meets their new arrival, an ordinary Joe not only wet and nervous but also fast shedding his last vestiges of light, Hitler greets him warmly, placing a comforting arm around his shoulder.

"I was a very important man up there," the New Arrival begins, "I was a mayor, then governor, and finally, a senator—

"Of course you were," Hitler assures soothingly, shepherding the new lamb into the fold.

@@@@@

Once upon a time she could have remembered immediately but now it escapes her altogether…

Even as a little girl she had always been a wordsmith. The day she discovered she was a damsel in distress she comforted herself by reading the dictionary, one of the two books in her mother's collection because it was easier to understand. This predilection toward the written word proved yet another act of nature that set her apart from her meat packing brothers.   The bunch of them failed to grasp the excitement contained between two covers stuffed to the gill with every word in the world just waiting to tell you its truth.

It was here that mystery began, in the essence of a word waiting, albeit impatiently, to be unmasked at the ball—like Cinderella, Snow White or some other garden variety woo-woo in distress running down route 66 in the dark in the wrong direction, naked, and shrieking like some destiny filled dilemma on really bad dope.

Where was she?

Oh, six and knee deep in schizophrenics and incest obsessed sociopaths and anticipation as she cracks the cover and releases an ocean from which springs a sea of sounds joined into words waiting to carry her to another universe where the unknown becomes known knowing all the time it contains even more secrets encased in deflowered virgins and pearls obtained easily were often of limited value.

Somehow, amid the insanity, rested a prayer, answered, for each day's mysteries sufficiently gave birth to litters of fresh treasure long buried in utterances, waiting to be dug for with bare hands from the sands of obscurity—signs to be collected along a journey to discover the end, the final mystery that lay immortalized in scrolls buried alive long ago to preserve their secrets in preparation of, perhaps, this very day.

Now that smacks of Shakespeare, she decides, *or Marlow the mad scientist conjuring up spirits who walk around among men remembering trespasses and broken vows written in blood and good intentions intangibly tied together by vice seeking victory once the honeymoon is over and the Diner's Club is due.*

Where the fuck did that come from?

"Don't ever start having sex, because once you start, you can't stop," Jesus Christ warned, threading a needle, "It'll suck the life right outta you just like vampires if you let it; but the good news is, you can't miss what you...never... had and that's a promise."

The men in white arrived with Halcydol before mommy could stitch her legs shut.

Little Mary Sunshine hadn't believed her mommy then and she didn't believe her now. You could decide to stop doing something.
You didn't have to do it again and again.
You could miss something you never had.

Miss it more in fact because it is that thing of which your mind mantras, *with this I would be well pleased*, the quintessence, realization, and manifestation of the imagination braced through bondage; married with children, confined in covenants; constricting and constraining, seeking solace amid alternate worlds where up is never down, right is never wrong, circumstances never collide with proximity *and* it never rains in Sunny California.

Miss it more because it remains an eternal mystery; knowledge known of yet unknown like who shot Kennedy or poisoned Marilyn and it is always the not knowing that draws you back to its arms even upon the death bed. Miss it more because not knowing slithers next to you in the night as a lustful lover, entreating you to allow entrance, willing your spirit to relax into nature where shadows shine like beacons that, while hollow, join light with death fashioning a wrinkle in time, the gateway to fate waiting to be reunited with its consort, eternity.

Indeed you could miss something you never had.
Desperately.

There's probably a book on that, Mary thinks, but since the Chaplain died she didn't read much. She had neither the time nor the inclination discovering, as often as not, that what lay within their skins disappointed; players on a stage, furnishing little of what they implicitly promised by virtue of donning a cover and taking their place on the shelf. *Maybe I should rejoin the living and just write one myself,* she thinks, *but not a fairytale, it must be real, dealing not just with life but also with death and how, when it came to call, it wished to be welcomed, well fed, and held close in its lover's arms... until it was time to wake once more.*

If there were any words of wisdom she could impart now, as someone who survived, lived, thrived, died, walked around dead, stirred from the dead, and lived to talk about it, it would be these:

Those we adore die or whatever it is they do when we no longer count them among the living but what is die or death other than words, unremarkable grains of salt among a sea of apples and zebras, bananas and peaches, Eden and Hell, not holding hands but walking in the same garden were Good and Evil both lay their heads at day's end among tinkling bells and xylophones floating or being buried in ashes two pages over from Wednesday; mere words; garden-variety machinations fashioned out of convenience by men and mice with wings all falling like Love, Manna from Heaven baby

Amen.[123]

---

[123] Selah.

Printed in the United Kingdom
by Lightning Source UK Ltd.
114157UKS00001B/233

9 781846 852503